全新！NEW TOEIC 新多益閱讀題庫解析

All Fresh

新鮮直送
不添加
無效題

別擔心多益考題更新，我翻新、你放心！

Hackers Academia／著

（自己的姓名）______________ 的新多益 Reading 目標分數

______________________________ 分

達成日期：________ 年 ________ 月 ________ 日

目標達成表

	Test 1	Test 2	Test 3	Test 4	Test 5	Test 6	Test 7	Test 8	Test 9	Test 10
495									多益高手！	
450						獲得高分只是時間問題！				
400			對多益有感覺了！							
350	多益新手！									
300										

完成各回的試題後，在上面表格的相應分數上填寫 ●，以便查看自己的分數變化與進步情況。

前言

由於 HACKERS 授權台灣國際學村出版社出版的新多益系列，在出刊以來持續維持於暢銷書榜上，因此匯集長久以來 HACKERS 專屬的解題技巧，出版了這本《全新！NEW TOEIC 新多益閱讀題庫解析》，讓需要做大量問題來提升應答技巧的練習者，能夠有充足的考前準備。

《全新！NEW TOEIC 新多益閱讀題庫解析》是一本「多益閱讀實戰題目集」，完美地分析多益的最新題型及難易度，使考生能夠在短期間內以有效率的方式解出大量問題，能夠在多益考試中獲得意想不到的高分。

本教材為了使多益考生能夠獲得與實際考試相同的考試環境，希望考生能有處於考場的真實感，藉此模擬實際考試時的感覺，因此題型也與多益考試一模一樣。並且為了能夠完美準備考試，也收錄十回與多益最接近的問題內容。而且分成題目本及解答本，能讓考生對於正確理解題目的閱讀能力向上提升。不只如此，更收錄了依據考生水準制定的學習計畫與不同的學習方法，可以讓考生有計畫地進行學習。甚至，考生們也能上線上教育網站：ChampStudy（www.ChampStudy.com）聽名師們依據題型解題的課程。（編註：ChampStudy 的網路線上服務為韓國原書之服務，與本出版社無關。）

而且，提供線上即時討論及分享情報的 HACKERS 網站（www.HACKER.com）中，可以讓學習者針對學習中的困難點與其他學習者討論，若同時利用免費的英語學習資源，學習效果將會加倍。（編註：同上方的 ChampStudy 網站，HACKERS 網站的線上服務亦為韓國原書之服務，與本出版社無關。網站內容皆為韓文，懂韓文的讀者不妨至這兩個網站蒐集資料。）

希望能夠透過《全新！NEW TOEIC 新多益閱讀題庫解析》，讓許多考生能夠達成想要的目標，往遠大的夢想踏出一步。

HACKERS 語言研究中心

目錄

TEST 01

Part 5

Part 6

Part 7

自我檢測表

等等！考前確認事項：

1. 關掉行動裝置電源了嗎？□ 是
2. 答案卷（Answer Sheet）、鉛筆、橡皮擦都準備好了嗎？□ 是
3. 手錶帶了嗎？□ 是

如果都準備齊全了，想想目標分數後即可開始作答。
透過 TEST 01 了解自己的實力後，可以在學習計畫（參看解答本p.16~17）中選擇最適合自己的學習計畫，並有效率的利用本書進行學習。

考試結束時間為現在開始 70 分鐘後的______點______分。

Reading Test

In this section, you must demonstrate your ability to read and comprehend English. You will be given a variety of texts and asked to answer questions about these texts. This section is divided into three parts and will take 75 minutes to complete.

Do not mark the answers in your test book. Use the answer sheet that is separately provided.

PART 5

Directions: In each question, you will be asked to review a statement that is missing a word or phrase. Four answer choices will be provided for each question. Select the best answer and mark the corresponding letter (A), (B), (C), or (D) on the answer sheet.

101. Keynote speaker Melanie Allen will send the draft of ------- speech to the events committee on Thursday.
(A) she (B) hers
(C) her (D) herself

102. Should customers need additional ------- about the features of the company's appliances, they may call our toll-free number to speak to a technician.
(A) inform
(B) informs
(C) information
(D) informed

103. Please fill out the enclosed customer data sheet ------- we can let you know about our latest offerings and promotions.
(A) instead of
(B) as much as
(C) so that
(D) as well as

104. Ms. Darcy is searching ------- office space with a capacity of at least 50 staff members.
(A) at
(B) to
(C) from
(D) for

105. Milkins Corporation will negotiate a two-year employment ------- with the former vice president of BG Holdings.
(A) arrangement
(B) arrangeable
(C) arranged
(D) arranger

106. To apply for a library card, please proceed to the circulation desk ------- the second floor and present valid identification.
(A) against
(B) as
(C) beside
(D) on

107. As part of their ------- routine, the mechanical department conducts maintenance inspections on factory equipment.
(A) normality
(B) normally
(C) normal
(D) normalize

108. Organized by the Confectioners Society, the first Vale Confectionery Trade Fair will be ------- at the Anderson Assembly Hall from November 5 to 9.
(A) grown
(B) held
(C) passed
(D) appeared

109. During the morning session of the program on well-being, a speaker will explain the benefits ------- various teas.
(A) by (B) for
(C) of (D) at

110. Relations between Lune Hospital and Alma Healthcare have become ------- ever since they organized a fundraiser together.
(A) friendlily
(B) friendlier
(C) friendliness
(D) friendliest

111. ------- newly hired technical support representatives are required to undergo a complete physical examination.
(A) All (B) Either
(C) Another (D) Much

112. The company has grown so much that it is running out of ------- and will need to move to a bigger office.
(A) area (B) land
(C) room (D) location

113. Ghyll Precision Industry's service department is known for finishing repairs ------- and in an efficient manner.
(A) noticeably
(B) promptly
(C) indirectly
(D) equally

114. The event staff will need to be at the conference venue an hour ------- everyone else to prepare.
(A) in between (B) provided
(C) until (D) ahead of

115. The inexperienced accountant ------- recorded the CEO's personal trip to London as a company expense.
(A) mistaking
(B) mistaken
(C) mistakenly
(D) to mistake

116. Gift certificates will be given to those ------- complete Oriang Health Spa's service survey by July 18.
(A) who (B) they
(C) what (D) theirs

117. Ms. Sofia Davis, president of Green Habitat Society, led an ------- lecture about the impact of global warming on the world's ecosystems.
(A) instructs
(B) instructionally
(C) instruct
(D) instructive

118. The objective of the Bogota International Forum is to help South American countries ------- better diplomatic ties.
(A) advise (B) develop
(C) happen (D) mention

GO ON TO THE NEXT PAGE

119. Because of Mr. Doyle's busy schedule today, his meeting with the personnel director about organizing employee interviews was -------.

(A) released (B) isolated
(C) canceled (D) expired

120. Only journalists with relevant experience and writing skills will be ------- for the *Jatayu Business Journal*'s associate editor position.

(A) estimated (B) published
(C) promoted (D) considered

121. More than 50 young artists across the state will be participating in a painting ------- sponsored by the National Museum of Contemporary Art.

(A) contestant (B) contesting
(C) contest (D) contested

122. Effective March 3, human resources director Arlene Rochester will ------- Dougal Seton in the role of vice president of Lawson Corporation.

(A) inquire (B) suppose
(C) replace (D) respond

123. The company's mobile phone plans are usually offered at ------- prices to new customers.

(A) equivalent
(B) introductory
(C) proportional
(D) dependent

124. Due to unforeseen circumstances, the organizer of the "1000 Megawatt" concert series suggested that the event ------- until further notice.

(A) postponed
(B) postpones
(C) be postponed
(D) has postponed

125. During the Showroom Expo, more than 30 interior designers presented the ------- furniture pieces that attracted much attention.

(A) redeemable
(B) innovative
(C) proficient
(D) impressed

126. Mentor Technologies' ------- line of computers comes with faster processors and vastly improved storage capacity.

(A) similar
(B) typical
(C) optional
(D) newest

127. Crimson Wellness Center continues to be the most popular fitness facility on the West Coast ------- the establishment of several local gyms in the past years.

(A) meantime
(B) likewise
(C) despite
(D) nevertheless

128. *Health Trails* magazine featured an article last month on how and why staying inside an air-conditioned room for long periods can ------- illness.

(A) produce
(B) producing
(C) to produce
(D) has produced

129. ------- has been made to ensure that participants in this year's music festival will have sufficient parking.

(A) Accomplishment
(B) Amendment
(C) Accommodation
(D) Approval

130. The Bloomfield Science Library in Texas is ------- equipped with security devices, such as surveillance cameras and door alarms, to monitor activities inside the building.
(A) completely
(B) complete
(C) completed
(D) completion

131. One of Vector Historical Foundation's focuses for next year is to put more ------- on establishing close partnerships with other similar institutions.
(A) emphasis
(B) emphasize
(C) emphasized
(D) emphatically

132. Many students at the institute have complained that they find it challenging ------- their tests within the given time limits.
(A) finishing (B) finished
(C) to finish (D) have finished

133. The factory supervisor ------- instructed the workers to clean the plant and make certain that all equipment was in good working order before the inspector's visit.
(A) arguably
(B) invisibly
(C) forgetfully
(D) explicitly

134. Because of the high cost of rent in the downtown area, Nelia Deluca is ------- as to whether or not she should open a copy center outlet in the city.
(A) incorrect (B) relative
(C) arguable (D) uncertain

135. The secretary informed Mr. Wallaby that the Merlin Restaurant ------- to provide a dining room that seats 100. people.
(A) to contract
(B) contracting
(C) contracts
(D) has been contracted

136. Chekwa Community Center often promotes free courses or activities to its long-term members in appreciation of their -------.
(A) performance
(B) loyalty
(C) application
(D) intention

137. Winners of this year's literary contest will be announced ------- in both the print and online versions of the publication *Literatura*.
(A) persuasively (B) officially
(C) truthfully (D) exceedingly

138. A Web developer ------- the social networking site 10 years ago to help people stay in touch with friends online.
(A) began (B) begins
(C) was begun (D) would begin

139. Tourists who purchase a travel pass have ------- to ride any bus or subway within the city limits for a period of 24 hours.
(A) compliance (B) authorization
(C) determination (D) allocation

140. The salon's supplier asked for payment of the hair products in full, ------- they cannot be shipped until next week.
(A) even though (B) apart from
(C) as soon as (D) due to

READING TEST 1 2 3 4 5 6 7 8 9 10

GO ON TO THE NEXT PAGE

PART 6

Directions: In this part, you will be asked to read an English text. Some sentences are incomplete. Select the word or phrase that correctly completes each sentence and mark the corresponding letter (A), (B), (C), or (D) on the answer sheet.

Questions 141-143 refer to the following announcement.

COME TO THE FIRST EVER DIOP TRADE SHOW!

More than 200 Algerian manufacturers are scheduled to ------- their products at Maktub

141. (A) deliver
(B) order
(C) reserve
(D) showcase

Convention Center in November. A variety of Algerian-made merchandise will be featured at the trade show.

Trade and Industry Minister Samir Klouchi ------- the exhibition on November 5.

142. (A) opened
(B) will open
(C) was opening
(D) has opened

The month-long event aims to support local businesses and to promote national pride among citizens.

It ------- on November 30 with a 15-minute fireworks display. For more information,

143. (A) concludes
(B) results
(C) stops
(D) fulfills

please send an e-mail to diopshow@maktubevents.net.

Questions 144-146 refer to the following letter.

February 2

Ingrid Helgarson
43 Thompson Avenue
Lansing, MI 48920

Dear Ms. Helgarson,

Our records indicate that you have been a regular visitor to Aberdeen Grocers for the past four years. We appreciate your -------.

144. (A) feedback
(B) business
(C) donation
(D) understanding

To help us enhance our products and services, we would like to request input from customers such as you.

Thus, we would like you to answer a ------- on our Web site, at www.aberdeengrocers.com,

145. (A) questionnaire
(B) questionable
(C) questions
(D) questioning

about your most recent visit to the Aberdeen branch nearest you.

We assure our customers that any personal information collected during the survey will be kept confidential. The answers will be used ------- for monitoring our performance and

146. (A) openly
(B) externally
(C) solely
(D) roughly

identifying areas in need of improvement.

Thank you in advance for your cooperation.

Yours truly,

Aberdeen Grocers Customer Service Team

GO ON TO THE NEXT PAGE

Questions 147-149 refer to the following e-mail.

From: Larry Keith <l.keith@str.com>
To: Norma Jennings <n_jennings@unitedmail.com>
Date: January 5
Subject: Truck Rental

Dear Ms. Jennings,

Thank you for choosing Simons Truck Rental. The moving truck you requested for -------

147. (A) my
(B) our
(C) your
(D) their

upcoming relocation to Los Angeles may be picked up for use.

If you are unable to retrieve the truck yourself, you may send a representative who must present a valid identification card and a letter ------- that you permit him or her to claim

148. (A) indicates
(B) indicating
(C) indication
(D) indicated

the vehicle on your behalf.

Should you need additional assistance with your transfer, please let us know. We provide services to help you unload and arrange your belongings quickly upon -------.

149. (A) occupancy
(B) partnership
(C) purchase
(D) operation

Feel free to contact us if you are interested.

Truly yours,

Larry Keith
Simons Truck Rental

Questions 150-152 refer to the following announcement.

Maincore Diving Center
Au Cap, Seychelles

Dear Students,

Congratulations on ------- the three-day open water scuba diving course at Maincore

150. (A) joining
(B) completing
(C) developing
(D) scoring

Diving Center.

As a final requirement for certification, you will perform your first deepwater dive tomorrow. Please be sure to follow the safety precautions you have learned from your instructors. This will help guarantee a ------- diving experience.

151. (A) secure
(B) moderate
(C) partial
(D) lengthy

In addition, check whether your gear is in working order before getting on the boat. It is highly recommended that you wear gloves to shield your hands from sharp coral. The staff at the center ------- you in selecting and assembling your equipment.

152. (A) assisted
(B) is assisting
(C) has assisted
(D) will assist

We hope you found this course to be a pleasant experience. Should you have any problem with our services, do not hesitate to send an inquiry to our office so that we can deal with your concern immediately.

Thank you.

Maincore Diving Center

GO ON TO THE NEXT PAGE

PART 7

Directions: In this part, you will be asked to read several texts, such as advertisements, articles or examples of business correspondence. Each text is followed by several questions. Select the best answer and mark the corresponding letter (A), (B), (C), or (D) on your answer sheet.

Questions 153-154 refer to the following announcement.

Green Valley High School

You are entering a school zone. Please observe the following guidelines to maintain orderly traffic inside the campus:

- Keep a speed limit of 15 miles per hour.
- Give way to pedestrians.
- Avoid honking vehicle horns during class hours.
- Do not park in front of school building entrances.
- Display a parking pass on the windshield.

Thank you and enjoy your visit.

Green Valley High School Security

153. Why was the notice written?
(A) To notify students about class schedules
(B) To inform motorists of traffic rules
(C) To remind employees of new campus policies
(D) To announce the temporary closure of a parking lot

154. What are visitors asked to do?
(A) Register at the security office
(B) Sign up for a parking permit
(C) Drive slowly inside the campus
(D) Show an identification card

GO ON TO THE NEXT PAGE

Questions 155-156 refer to the following letter.

Hernandez Construction Supplies
Guernsey Street
Dallas, TX 75209

December 1

Clifford Sparks
Credit Manager
Aero Door Handles
Evengrade Towers, Houston, TX 75101

Dear Mr. Sparks,

It was a pleasure meeting you at the construction supplies fair last month. After learning about your wide range of door handles and comparing it with other manufacturers', we have decided to carry your line in our hardware stores in Dallas. I was very impressed with both your products and presentation and feel that such an agreement could be mutually beneficial.

Therefore, we would like to apply for consignment, preferably with a charge account ranging from $3,000 to $4,000 in value. As this is a rather large consignment, I was hoping you could offer us a higher rate of commission than the 18 percent you mentioned at the fair. May I suggest a commission of 20 percent? If that is agreeable to you, please let me know as soon as possible.

Enclosed is a copy of our company profile, business license, and the credit references you requested.

Thank you, and we look forward to a successful business relationship with you and your company.

Truly yours,

Bryan Sims
Operations Manager
Hernandez Construction Supplies

155. Why did Mr. Sims write to Mr. Sparks?
(A) To ask for a revision to an agreement
(B) To propose a business partnership
(C) To request information about construction supplies
(D) To invite a supplier to an event

156. What is mentioned about Mr. Sparks?
(A) He only works on consignment.
(B) He already filled out an order form.
(C) He was sent a product catalog.
(D) He met Mr. Sims at a trade fair.

Questions 157-159 refer to the following information.

The ALL NEW Dockland Split Type Air Conditioner (BA501)

Committed to producing energy-efficient products, Dockland Electronics has created the BA501, a new split type air conditioner with features designed to conserve power without compromising efficiency.

Speed Cooling
This function allows the unit to reach preset temperatures in a short time.

Temperature Equalizer
This function enables the unit to cool areas evenly by using dual-direction air vent technology.

Sleep Mode
This function decreases the cooling temperature after the unit's first two hours of operation and maintains the room temperature for the next five hours before it automatically shuts off the unit.

The BA501 is equipped with a patented refrigerant and has a Seasonal Energy Efficiency Ratio (SEER) rating of 14. SEER measures the energy efficiency of air conditioners.

157. What is mentioned about the Dockland Electronics product?
(A) It is powered by alternative energy.
(B) It obtains high market sales.
(C) It is made of durable materials.
(D) It consumes less electricity.

158. What is NOT a feature of the air conditioner?
(A) Equalization of temperatures
(B) Remote control
(C) Automatic shutdown
(D) Fast cooling

159. What is stated about the SEER rating system?
(A) It is used by countries with limited fuel supplies.
(B) It was set by an international organization.
(C) It measures the durability of appliances.
(D) It calculates the energy performance of machines.

GO ON TO THE NEXT PAGE

Questions 160-161 refer to the following catalog page.

iConstruct

www.iconstruct.com

Find exactly the color you are looking with iConstruct for your next painting project!

Painting your home is a major task, and deciding on which colors to use can be very tricky. To help you create a unique theme for your living space, check out the hundreds of colors from various manufacturers listed in this catalog.

In addition to our extensive collection of hues and shades, this catalog includes photos showing different combinations that you may use for your bedrooms, living room, and dining area. You will be amazed at how many combinations you can make with our selection of paint.

The colors in the catalog may vary slightly from the actual shades, so we give customers free paint samples, which they may test on their walls. If you wish to get some samples, all you need to do is choose colors from our catalog and give us a call. Our customer service representatives will be happy to process your request. You may also order in person at our outlets.

iConstruct

160. What is NOT suggested about iConstruct?

(A) It sells products made by other companies.

(B) It guarantees the accuracy of paint colors in its catalog.

(C) It provides customers with design ideas.

(D) It offers to process orders over the phone.

161. How can customers receive product samples?

(A) By calling an interior decorator

(B) By making an online request

(C) By visiting an establishment

(D) By coordinating with a manufacturer

Questions 162-164 refer to the following advertisement.

Rundin-Summers

Business solutions for the modern world!

Chart your career and make your dreams a reality at Rundin-Summers!

If you have talent and want to become part of a team determined to succeed at the highest level, then we need you.

Work at Rundin-Summers and take advantage of the career opportunities we have in store for you. As a world leader in business solutions, Rundin-Summers provides exceptional human resource services for more than 500 companies internationally. Our numerous clients require us to employ people from various industries. That is why our company is actively seeking qualified people from the healthcare, personnel management, finance, and publishing fields.

In addition to ensuring our employees' career growth, we offer competitive salary and compensation packages as well as travel opportunities.

Join our team now. To learn more about job openings at Rundin-Summers, please visit www.rundinsummers.com.

162. Why was the advertisement written?
(A) To introduce a service
(B) To describe expansion plans
(C) To promote a newly established company
(D) To attract job applicants

163. What is indicated about Rundin-Summers?
(A) It is a global company.
(B) It plans to operate additional branches.
(C) It is involved with stock investment.
(D) It publishes medical material.

164. Who most likely would NOT be considered for a position at Rundin-Summers?
(A) Engineers
(B) Personnel officers
(C) Accountants
(D) Editors

GO ON TO THE NEXT PAGE

Questions 165-167 refer to the following announcement.

The Discovery Center's Special Events

The most-visited interactive science museum in Asia is celebrating its 20th birthday! Join us in commemorating the Discovery Center's two decades of educating the world about great scientific breakthroughs in fun and exciting ways.

During the entire month of June, we will conduct special exhibits related to technology, space exploration, environment, and biology. The schedule of events is as follows:

June 1-8: Robots and Mechanical Devices
June 9-14: Exploring Outer Space
June 15-21: Ecosystems and Habitats
June 22-30: Plants and animals

Entrance to the exhibits is included in the museum's regular admission fee. Take your family and friends to the Discovery Center and enjoy a new learning experience. For inquiries, call 555-8406.

DISCOVERY CENTER
Canine Road, Great Heights
www.discoverycenter.com

165. What is the announcement about?
(A) An establishment's anniversary
(B) An upcoming lecture series
(C) Changes to operation hours
(D) New admission rates

166. What will the event on June 20 most likely be about?
(A) Technology
(B) Astronomy
(C) Environment
(D) Biology

167. What is mentioned about the exhibits?
(A) They are exclusively for students.
(B) They will be conducted in two months.
(C) They will feature the work of local inventors.
(D) They are covered by the admission fee.

Questions 168-171 refer to the following letter.

Letters to the Editor

The article written by Vicky Mendel that appeared in last month's issue of *Metro Chic* was fascinating. It featured various types of safe and fast weight-loss treatments. I work long hours and have no time to go to the gym, so learning about convenient ways to reduce weight really interests me.

Convinced by the article, I tried the radio frequency treatment. It is a non-surgical technology that breaks down fat cells by using a machine that emits radio waves deep into the layers of a person's skin. At the same time, it reduces the appearance of cellulite and makes the skin look smoother. According to Ms. Mendel, she had the procedure done on her abdominal area and lost four inches around her waist after just one session.

Last week, I had my appointment to receive radio frequency treatment at the same clinic Ms. Mendel visited. The procedure was painless and took approximately 30 minutes, but after measuring the results, I was disappointed to learn I had only lost one inch.

The physician at the clinic then told me that results can vary greatly and depend on the number of times a person goes in for treatment. Also, in order to maintain my desired figure, I would need to return for additional sessions on a regular basis. With each session costing $175, I find this treatment just isn't worth the money. Other readers may have a different point of view.

Marilyn Patterson
Chicago, IL

168. What is the main purpose of the letter?
(A) To correct information in an article
(B) To congratulate the writer of a magazine
(C) To provide an opinion about a treatment
(D) To make a suggestion to an editor

169. What is mentioned about Ms. Patterson?
(A) She contributes stories to *Metro Chic*.
(B) She is trying to publish a new book.
(C) She conducted an interview with Vicky Mendel.
(D) She cannot exercise due to a busy work schedule.

170. What does Ms. Patterson say about her experience at the clinic?
(A) It was not worth spending a lot of money on.
(B) Results became visible after one week.
(C) The procedure caused some pain.
(D) The clinical staff was not very professional.

171. What is NOT stated about radio frequency treatment?
(A) It lasts for about half an hour.
(B) It may require several sessions.
(C) It improves the appearance of a person's skin.
(D) It involves regular visits to a local gym.

GO ON TO THE NEXT PAGE

Questions 172-175 refer to the following letter.

Percussion Unlimited

1214 Robson Street, Vancouver, BC V5Y-1V4

April 6

Dear Mr. Howard,

Thank you for inquiring about our sound equipment. We have been in the business for more than twenty years and have been providing music for weddings, business events, and music festivals. We would be happy to make arrangements for your company's upcoming anniversary party with a 1970s theme. In fact, we did something similar for Gentech Corporation just last month, which was attended by more than 500 guests. We can offer you a complete sound system package with a digital mixing console, amplifiers, loudspeakers, vocal microphones with stands, and disco lights. We also have hundreds of 1970s tracks to keep your guests partying throughout the night. In addition, our seasoned disc jockeys and technicians will ensure that our equipment provides high sound quality.

We have a base rate for delivery to locations in the Vancouver area, including Victoria, Burnaby, and Surrey, but do charge more for events held in other locations within the province. For more information on our rental and delivery rates, see the enclosed brochure. If you are interested, please call me at 555-0606 so that we may reserve equipment for your event.

Respectfully yours,

Tanya Byers
Manager
Percussion Unlimited

172. Why was the letter written?
(A) To promote a new line of sound equipment
(B) To answer a question about services
(C) To inquire about a technical repair
(D) To decline a business offer

173. What type of event was Percussion Unlimited previously involved in?
(A) A musical concert
(B) A trade show
(C) A company celebration
(D) A product launch

174. What does Ms. Byers NOT suggest about Percussion Unlimited?
(A) It has a staff of technicians.
(B) It has several branches.
(C) It guarantees high sound quality.
(D) It provides musical recordings.

175. What does Ms. Byers indicate?
(A) The company offers services to locations throughout the province.
(B) She met Mr. Howard at another event.
(C) Discounts are offered in Vancouver.
(D) She is unable to meet all of Mr. Howard's requirements.

Questions 176-180 refer to the following article.

Furniture Maker Debuts on Morrow Stock Exchange

Jerome Furnishings made history yesterday by becoming the first-ever publicly listed furniture company on the Morrow Stock Exchange. The firm floated 500,000 shares of stock at $20 apiece and collected $10 million equity capital in its initial public offering (IPO).

The capital obtained from the IPO is expected to allow the company to create new products and expand its range of services. Jerome Furnishings hopes to venture into customizing furniture for corporate centers, hotels, and recreational areas, in addition to creating new models of household furniture.

Theodore Campbell, Jerome Furnishings' managing director for East Asia, said the company is currently in talks with Ohana Bay Hotel over a proposal to renovate the establishment's rooms and facilities.

Founded in 1985, the company has been famous for its stylish products and innovative interior design solutions. Since its initial launch, the company has seen many successful expansions, becoming one of the largest home furniture and décor manufacturers and retailers in the world with more than 30 branches all over Asia, Europe, and North America.

Nevertheless, Jerome Furnishings was acquired by real estate developer Meredith Construction seven years ago when the furniture giant shut down some outlets due to alleged mismanagement of funds.

The successful stock auction, however, proves that Jerome Furnishings has regained its strength. "The event confirmed the public's confidence in the company and gave hope for the fulfillment of its future plans," Campbell said.

176. Where would this article most likely appear?
(A) In a furniture brochure
(B) In a company's press release
(C) In an architecture magazine
(D) In a business newspaper

177. According to the article, why are Jerome Furnishings' products popular?
(A) They are custom-made.
(B) They last a long time.
(C) They are fashionable.
(D) They are inexpensive.

178. Why did Jerome Furnishings raise capital?
(A) It has to repay its loans.
(B) It needs to open new outlets.
(C) It wants to broaden its offerings.
(D) It plans to renovate its office building.

179. The word "alleged" in paragraph 5, line 2 is closest in meaning to
(A) supposed
(B) written
(C) doubtful
(D) warranted

180. What is implied about Meredith Construction?
(A) It has several offices around the world.
(B) It will construct a hotel.
(C) It is seeking new investors.
(D) It operates Jerome Furnishings.

GO ON TO THE NEXT PAGE

Questions 181-185 refer to the following advertisement and e-mail.

Cuddly Rascals' Fall Fever!

This fall, we are offering our pet care services at reduced prices! Check out our discounted rates below:

Service	NORMAL RATE	DISCOUNTED RATE
Pet sitting	$25	$16/hour (daytime)
Pet boarding	$40	$35/24 hours
Pet grooming	$53	$45
Dog walking	$24	$18/30 minutes
Prices are on a per-pet basis. Pets staying overnight are given three daily meals and regular walks. Grooming consists of bathing, drying, brushing, and nail trimming.		

Take advantage of these low prices by booking a service for this fall. Customers who book in August will receive a voucher for our fall prices. Don't delay, as this promotion is valid only until the end of October. And if you are a first time customer, check out our excellent range of pet services.

Stop worrying about where to leave your dog or cat while you're busy at work or away on vacation. At Cuddly Rascals, we guarantee the best services for your pet - or you'll get your money back!

Please give us a call at 555-9312 for more information.

To: Arthur Grady <arthurgrady@tymail.com>
From: appointments@cuddlyrascals.net
Date: August 25
Subject: Re: About Services

Dear Mr. Grady,

This is regarding your service request form that we received yesterday. Thanks for considering Cuddly Rascals for your pet care needs. We appreciate your interest in our services.

You asked for two appointments on your form, one for this week and another for next week. Unfortunately, all our staff members are fully booked for this week and will not be able to provide you with the grooming service you requested. However, the pet sitting and dog walking services are available for next week. If you would like, we can schedule all three services together and perform the grooming service in your home. Feel free to contact us at your earliest convenience once you make a decision regarding our services. Also, if you do decide to use our services, we need some information about your dog to help us prepare for the appointments, such as its name, breed, and age. So please have this information on hand when you contact us.

Should there be other services that you would like to request for your dog, let us know so we can prepare for them right away.

Best regards,

Eloise Tyler
Cuddly Rascals Staff

181. What is being advertised?
(A) Services for domestic animals
(B) A job at a pet store
(C) Seasonal fashions
(D) The opening of an establishment

182. What is indicated about Cuddly Rascals' promotional offer?
(A) It is exclusively for current customers.
(B) It is available on weekdays.
(C) It is limited to a particular branch.
(D) It is a seasonal offer.

183. What is suggested about Cuddly Rascals?
(A) It includes food with its pet sitting service.
(B) It requires customers to fill out a form.
(C) It takes in animals that have been abandoned.
(D) It offers coupons to those booking several services.

184. What is indicated about Mr. Grady?
(A) He qualifies for a special promotion.
(B) He is a frequent customer of Cuddly Rascals.
(C) He has met Ms. Tyler in the past.
(D) He wants to work in the pet care industry.

185. What is NOT included in the services Mr. Grady requested?
(A) Brushing
(B) Walking
(C) Feeding
(D) Bathing

GO ON TO THE NEXT PAGE

Questions 186-190 refer to the following e-mail and schedule.

To	Genevieve Javier <genevievejavier@shinodauniversity.edu>
From	Michael Eisenberg <michaeleisenberg@shinodauniversity.edu>
Date	May 20
Subject	Commencement Exercises
Attachment	1 file

Hello Genevieve,

I received a call this morning from Damien Sullivan's secretary, Kristy Cook. She said that Mr. Sullivan will be arriving later than expected from a business conference in Kentucky at around 10 o'clock on June 3. That will leave him with just enough time to get here before his scheduled speech at the graduation ceremony. She apologized for the inconvenience, but I told her we could make changes to the program prior to his speech so he can take time to prepare before he goes onstage. We also decided to include an activity right before the introduction of the guest speaker. I have already e-mailed her a copy of the program schedule, and she said she would forward it to Mr. Sullivan right away.

As with previous commencement exercises, you will be assigned to accompany our guest of honor. Make sure to be at the campus an hour before the program starts. Once Mr. Sullivan arrives, take him to the conference room in the faculty office, so he can rest a bit or prepare before his speech. I'll let you know when he can come onstage, since I'll be in charge of introducing him.

I have attached the revised schedule for your reference. If you have any questions, do not hesitate to call me at 555-9963.

Thank you.

Michael Eisenberg
Vice president, Shinoda University

35TH COMMENCEMENT EXERCISES

SHINODA UNIVERSITY

Winchester Quadrangle ▪ Friday, June 3 ▪ 8 A.M. – 2:30 P.M.

TIME	ACTIVITY
8:00 – 8:30 A.M.	Processional
8:30 – 9:00 A.M.	Pledge to the Flag/National Anthem
9:30 – 9:50 A.M.	Opening Remarks (Constantino Tejero, President)
9:50 – 10:00 A.M.	Introduction of Student Speaker
10:00 – 10:30 A.M.	Student Association President's Address (Alyssa Caronongan)
10:30 – 10:45 A.M.	Intermission (Armstrong Choir performance)
10:45 – 11:00 A.M.	Introduction of Guest Speaker
11:00 – 11:30 A.M.	Address (Damien Sullivan, Attorney, CEO, Sullivan and Associates)
11:30 A.M. –12:00 P.M.	Presentation of Special Awards
12:00 – 1:30 P.M.	Awarding of Diplomas
1:30 – 1:45 P.M.	Class Song
1:45 – 2:00 P.M.	Closing Remarks (Michael Eisenberg, Vice president)
2:00 – 2:30 P.M.	Recessional

186. Why did Ms. Cook apologize to Mr. Eisenberg?
(A) A flight will be delayed.
(B) A meeting had to be postponed.
(C) An event venue has not been prepared.
(D) A schedule needed to be altered.

187. What is mentioned about Damien Sullivan?
(A) He is delivering a speech to a group of business professionals.
(B) He graduated from Shinoda University with top honors.
(C) He is planning to donate some money to a school.
(D) He will receive a program schedule from his secretary.

188. What is suggested about Genevieve Javier?
(A) She has assisted important visitors at graduation ceremonies before.
(B) She will receive an award for her outstanding service.
(C) She is responsible for reviewing Mr. Sullivan's speech.
(D) She will introduce the guest speaker this year.

189. What is indicated about the program?
(A) Lunch will be served after the awarding of diplomas.
(B) The principal will be absent from the ceremonies.
(C) A musical group will perform before a guest is introduced.
(D) The closing remarks will be moved to a later time.

190. Who is Alyssa Caronongan?
(A) A speech writer for an executive
(B) The leader of a student group
(C) A secretary from a law firm
(D) The president of an academic institution

GO ON TO THE NEXT PAGE

Questions 191-195 refer to the following advertisement and letter.

Haven for Animals Clinic

Application period: November 1 – December 16

Job Opening for Veterinarians

Haven for Animals is a veterinary clinic accredited by the American Animal Hospital Organization and dedicated to providing quality healthcare to domesticated animals. Since our establishment in San Diego 15 years ago, we have expanded into other cities such as Los Angeles and San Francisco. We are opening another facility in Sacramento and need five experienced veterinarians to join our team. We offer new doctors a high starting salary and comprehensive compensation package, including retirement savings plans, professional liability packages, medical and dental health insurance, and continuing education allowance.

Qualifications:

- A doctor of veterinary medicine degree
- A license to practice veterinary medicine
- At least five years of work experience in a veterinary clinic or hospital
- Outstanding interpersonal skills and a positive, friendly attitude
- Ability to work alone or in a team

Responsibilities:

- Conduct physical examinations as well as medical, dental, and surgical procedures
- Explain examination results to clients and recommend treatments for illnesses as well as supplements for preventive healthcare
- Maintain records of animal patients
- Represent Haven for Animals Clinic at conventions and seminars

Interested applicants are advised to send their résumés and reference letters to our human resources department in San Diego. The deadline for submission of requirements is on December 16. Shortlisted candidates will be notified by phone or e-mail.

November 3

Robert Rodriguez
Human resources director
Haven for Animals Clinic

Dear Sir or Madam,

I am writing in response to your job advertisement for veterinarians that appeared in *The Daily News* on November 1. I am a licensed veterinarian in California and am currently employed at St. Bernard Animal Hospital in Oakland. I have been with the hospital since I finished my doctor of veterinary medicine degree at Riverbank University in San Diego two-and-a-half years ago.

I would like to apply for a position as I wish to continue to practice my profession when I move to Sacramento next January. Although I have been in practice for only a short time, I have been highly trained in veterinary surgery and dentistry. Because of this, I am confident that my skills and professional experience will allow me to provide significant contributions to the development of your new clinic.

Enclosed are my résumé and reference letters. If you need more information about my credentials, please contact me at your convenience.

Thank you for your consideration.

Respectfully yours,

Natalie Marquez

191. What is indicated about the Haven For Animals Clinic?
(A) It first opened in Los Angeles.
(B) It has several different locations.
(C) It is looking to hire veterinary assistants.
(D) It plans to renovate a facility.

192. What benefit is NOT included in the compensation package?
(A) A retirement plan
(B) Financial aid for future studies
(C) A housing allowance
(D) Medical insurance coverage

193. In the letter, the word "confident" in paragraph 2, line 4 is closest in meaning to
(A) secretive
(B) certain
(C) satisfactory
(D) communicative

194. Why might Dr. Marquez not be selected as a candidate for the job?
(A) She has insufficient experience.
(B) She does not perform surgical procedures.
(C) She does not have a professional license.
(D) She is unwilling to travel for work.

195. What is mentioned about Dr. Marquez?
(A) She has applied for a promotion.
(B) She currently manages an animal clinic.
(C) She is enrolled at a university in Sacramento.
(D) She plans to relocate to another city.

GO ON TO THE NEXT PAGE

Questions 195-200 refer to the following e-mails.

To: Mathilda Bauwens <owner@wizobakeshop.be>
From: custserv@robbinsbakerysupplies.be
Date: September 7
Subject: Order No. 81692-07

Dear Ms. Bauwens,

Robbins Bakery Supplies has been the preferred supplier of bakery shop owners all over Europe for nearly 50 years. With our extensive product knowledge and years of experience, you can be assured that we sell only the best baking ingredients and equipment.

We received your order on September 6 for the following products and are now preparing them for shipment. Please note that items may ship separately based on their availability.

PRODUCT NO.	DESCRIPTION	UNIT PRICE	QTY.	AMOUNT
EFS520	20-gal electronic flour sifter	€755.18	2	€1,510.36
RCP433	14" round cheesecake pan	€22.74	5	€113.70
SDC871	150-ml square dessert cup (set of 50)	€434.95	1	€434.95
EDC106	6-wheel expandable dough cutter	€98.60	2	€197.20

Domestic deliveries are free of charge and will take one to two business days, depending on location. Your credit card will not reflect the payment for the costs of your order until the items are sent to the address you specified.

You can follow up at any time by visiting our Web site at www.robbinsbakerysupplies.be. Just enter your order number in the appropriate box to see your purchase history. Once again, thank you and we hope for your continued business.

All the best,

Robbins Bakery Supplies
Customer Service

To: custserv@robbinsbakerysupplies.be
From: Mathilda Bauwens <owner@wizobakeshop.be>
Date: September 19
Subject: Re: Order No. 81692-07

To whom it may concern,

I received all the products I ordered, but instead of 14" cheesecake pans, I got 10" ones. Unfortunately, I needed pans of the correct size to complete a job for a loyal and important client. In order to make the deadline, I was forced to take time away from my busy schedule, and pay substantially higher, to get the pans from another store. Needless to say, I am very disappointed, especially after I'd heard so many good things about you from my business partner. Since I have no use for 10" pans, I am sending them back to you this week in exchange for a full refund. In addition, I feel it is right to ask that you also reimburse me for the difference in price that I had to pay for the 14" ones. I hope to hear from you soon about this matter.

Mathilda Bauwens
Owner
Wizo Bakeshop

196. What is NOT mentioned about Robbins Bakery Supplies?
(A) It allows clients to view prior orders on a Web site.
(B) It has locations in several European cities.
(C) It has been in the supply business for several decades.
(D) It makes local deliveries at no extra charge.

197. In the first e-mail, the word "reflect" in paragraph 3, line 2 is closest in meaning to
(A) show
(B) copy
(C) appear
(D) think

198. What is suggested about Ms. Bauwens?
(A) She wants to increase the quantity of her order.
(B) She received separate shipments.
(C) She missed a deadline for promotional offers.
(D) She was referred to Robbins by a colleague.

199. Which product is Ms. Bauwens referring to in her e-mail?
(A) SDC871
(B) EDC106
(C) RCP433
(D) EFS520

200. What does Ms. Bauwens ask Robbins Bakery Supplies to do?
(A) Compensate her for her purchase
(B) Mail her an updated catalog
(C) Recommend her to some clients
(D) Consider a business venture

This is the end of the test. You may review Part 5, 6, and 7 if you finish the test early.

簡答 p.286 / 分數換算表 p.289 / 題目解析 p.19（解答本）

▮ 請翻到次頁「自我檢測表」檢視自己解答問題的方法與態度。
▮ 利用 p.289 分數換算表換算完分數後，請翻至解答本 p.16～p.17 查看適合自己的學習計畫，並請確實實踐。

自我檢測表

TEST 01 順利的完成了嗎？

現在要開始透過以下的自我檢測表檢視自己在考試中的表現了嗎？

我的目標分數為：　　　　　　　這次測試的成績為：

1. 70 分鐘內，我完全集中精神在測試內容上。

   □是　□不是

   如果回答不是，理由是什麼呢？

2. 70 分鐘內，連答案卷的劃記都完成了。

   □是　□不是

   如果回答不是，理由是什麼呢？

3. 70 分鐘內，100 題都解完了。

   □是　□不是

   如果回答不是，理由是什麼呢？

4. Part 5 和 Part 6 在 25 分鐘以內全都寫完了。

   □是　□不是

   如果回答不是，理由是什麼呢？

5. 寫 Part 7 的時候，沒有一題花超過五分鐘。

   □是　□不是

   如果回答不是，理由是什麼呢？

6. 請寫下你需要改善的地方以及給自己的忠告。

*回到本書第二頁，確認自己的目標分數並加強對於達成分數的意志。
對於要改善的部分一定要在下一次測試中實踐。這點是最重要的，也要這樣才能有進步。

TEST 02

Part 5

Part 6

Part 7

自我檢測表

等等！考前確認事項：

1. 關掉行動裝置電源了嗎？□ 是
2. 答案卷（Answer Sheet）、鉛筆、橡皮擦都準備好了嗎？□ 是
3. 手錶帶了嗎？□ 是

如果都準備齊全了，想想目標分數後即可開始作答。

考試結束時間為現在開始 70 分鐘後的______點______分。

Reading Test

In this section, you must demonstrate your ability to read and comprehend English. You will be given a variety of texts and asked to answer questions about these texts. This section is divided into three parts and will take 75 minutes to complete.

Do not mark the answers in your test book. Use the answer sheet that is separately provided.

PART 5

Directions: In each question, you will be asked to review a statement that is missing a word or phrase. Four answer choices will be provided for each question. Select the best answer and mark the corresponding letter (A), (B), (C), or (D) on the answer sheet.

101. The accountant ------- the expense reports of those who attended the Seville Conference by next Monday morning.
(A) will obtain
(B) has obtained
(C) obtaining
(D) obtainable

102. Shunju Airways passengers may purchase their tickets online ------- make a phone reservation, and seats should be paid in full at the time of the booking.
(A) yet
(B) both
(C) because
(D) or

103. The marketing strategies ------- want to use for our client's new product line were explained in detail in the document sent last week.
(A) we (B) our
(C) ours (D) us

104. Both the tenant and the owner share the responsibility of ------- the safety and cleanliness of the apartment.
(A) assure
(B) assuring
(C) assured
(D) assures

105. Marcia Winters proved that she was the most ------- member of the staff when she secured the company several new clients.
(A) products
(B) productively
(C) producing
(D) productive

106. Based on the information collected in the survey, many office employees are ------- with a flexible schedule than one that is fixed.
(A) busied
(B) busier
(C) busying
(D) busily

107. Due to a problem with production, the ------- of orders to clients will be delayed for up to two days.

(A) delivers (B) deliverable
(C) delivery (D) deliver

108. Pinnacle Company's digital camera is more expensive than other brands, but it produces high-quality pictures -------.

(A) less effective
(B) least effective
(C) most effectively
(D) more effective

109. The new art center on Brentville Avenue, which was inaugurated on Friday, is ------- exhibiting the works of several local artists.

(A) presented (B) present
(C) presents (D) presently

110. Alessandro Fox ------- goes to the driving range at least three times a week to practice his golf swing.

(A) always (B) softly
(C) forever (D) sharply

111. The third-level parking area is ------- to all residents at Arjuna Condominiums.

(A) qualified (B) understandable
(C) provable (D) accessible

112. After concluding the negotiations, the CEOs from the two electronics manufacturers are expected to ------- their partnership at a press conference.

(A) inspire (B) categorize
(C) require (D) confirm

113. The memo reminds supervisors to ------- implement the new office dress code beginning next month.

(A) rigor (B) rigorously
(C) rigorous (D) rigorousness

114. Urban Textiles will not refund down payments to Ms. Smith ------- she cancel her order after the products have been shipped.

(A) should
(B) otherwise
(C) although
(D) instead

115. The Stymphal Library Web site provides detailed ------- on how interested individuals can apply for membership online.

(A) directed
(B) directing
(C) directions
(D) directly

116. To promote seasonal vegetables, the sales staff ------- displays them at the main entrance of the supermarket.

(A) intends
(B) intentional
(C) intentionally
(D) intention

117. Sean Lucas was ------- by the International Symphony Society as one of the best composers of today for the stunning musical scores he has created for ballets.

(A) compensated
(B) discharged
(C) recognized
(D) enforced

118. Because the human resources director was on leave, Ms. Hong was asked to interview candidates for the managerial position ------- herself.

(A) to
(B) by
(C) from
(D) near

GO ON TO THE NEXT PAGE

119. Elspeth Fanshaw is in charge of contacting all major banks ------- main headquarters are located in Northern Europe.

(A) when (B) whom
(C) whose (D) which

120. Successful overseas workers not only support their families, but also bring ------- to their countries.

(A) level (B) pride
(C) population (D) division

121. As indicated in the schedule, crisis management consultant Mimi Kim will conduct the ------- on labor disputes.

(A) information
(B) incident
(C) agenda
(D) discussion

122. ------- Baklase Pharmaceuticals shut down two factories last month, it still managed to meet its production target this year.

(A) Although
(B) Since
(C) So
(D) However

123. Due to the supplier's failure to deliver key ingredients, some pasta meals ------- in the menu are unavailable today.

(A) pictured
(B) guided
(C) demonstrated
(D) imitated

124. Alizarin Electronics began its foreign operations ------- the opening of a new factory in Seoul this year.

(A) in (B) against
(C) between (D) with

125. A property developer was dispatched to the ------- to determine whether it was feasible for a residential building project.

(A) scale (B) layer
(C) extent (D) area

126. For its fifth anniversary, Youngsters Sports released a new line of bicycles designed ------- for children aged five to seven.

(A) closely (B) swiftly
(C) marginally (D) exclusively

127. The organizers were ------- in their choice of the Quillen Hotel ballroom as the venue for the Advertising Awards event.

(A) total (B) entire
(C) gathered (D) unanimous

128. ------- make articles as concise and clear as possible, most writers recommend using short and simple sentences.

(A) As if
(B) In reference to
(C) In order to
(D) Owing to

129. Customer service representatives are trained to speak to shoppers ------- and work out the best solutions to a complaint or problem.

(A) generously
(B) undeniably
(C) arguably
(D) politely

130. Coles Press is in need of professional ------- to oversee the publication of a news magazine.

(A) editions (B) editorials
(C) editors (D) edits

131. With the latest security devices installed throughout the museum, the curator is prepared for virtually any -------.

(A) availability
(B) prohibition
(C) position
(D) contingency

132. Visitors to the special exhibition are asked to leave their bags at the counter ------- to protect the displays as to ensure a pleasant experience for all.

(A) as well as
(B) as much
(C) so long
(D) only if

133. Anna Vertugi's accomplishments as a landscaper have been largely ------- on her unique abilities in design and innovation.

(A) basis
(B) based
(C) basing
(D) baseness

134. To increase rice output in agricultural areas, the local government ------- additional funds for the acquisition of farming tools and equipment.

(A) anticipated
(B) allocated
(C) contained
(D) surpassed

135. Since the concert hall renovations are still not finished, Kevin Ockham's upcoming concert ------- to next month.

(A) being postponed
(B) was postponing
(C) to postpone
(D) will be postponed

136. Despite having warned motorists about the speed limits, the Transport Department ------- a high number of traffic violations on Honglin Boulevard this year.

(A) performed
(B) offered
(C) recorded
(D) infused

137. The city council will be accepting bid proposals for the Welby Library restoration project ------- the end of next month.

(A) onto
(B) between
(C) until
(D) where

138. All members of the Baja basketball team are required to commit to a high-protein and carbohydrate diet ------- training for the national games.

(A) when (B) that
(C) by (D) at

139. Kurd Corporation's 40 percent production rate improvement is an achievement that many ------- to the factory's streamlined assembly methods.

(A) attribute (B) state
(C) claim (D) pass

140. In order to extend a commercial license in the district, business owners are required to present their old ------- and pay a renewal fee of $1,000 to the Business Authorization Agency.

(A) consent
(B) patent
(C) treaty
(D) permit

GO ON TO THE NEXT PAGE

PART 6

Directions: In this part, you will be asked to read an English text. Some sentences are incomplete. Select the word or phrase that correctly completes each sentence and mark the corresponding letter (A), (B), (C), or (D) on the answer sheet.

Questions 141-143 refer to the following memo.

To: Staff
Re: Attendance Policy
Date: December 5

As discussed in the meeting, management will implement a stricter policy on -------.

141. (A) tardiness
(B) confidentiality
(C) security
(D) breaks

This is scheduled to go into effect on January 1 and applies to all office staff, except those who engage in field work. In this regard, employees who arrive late more than two times a month will be obligated to serve one day's suspension, ------- will be recorded in

142. (A) it
(B) what
(C) this
(D) which

their employee evaluation.

However, there are exceptions to this rule, ------- late arrivals due to emergencies or bad

143. (A) so that
(B) but also
(C) such as
(D) in addition

weather conditions. For questions and concerns regarding the new policy, please get in touch with the personnel department. Thank you.

Questions 144-146 refer to the following letter.

August 10

Jordan McLeod
451 N Garnet Drive
Nashville, TN 37209

Dear Mr. McLeod,

Thank you for your interest in ------- JointHands Foundation. We will have to match your

144. (A) expanding
(B) incorporating
(C) assisting
(D) celebrating

time commitment and skills with our organization's needs. Please fill out the enclosed volunteer application form and return it to us no later than August 31.

Qualified applicants will be contacted for interviews. If you are accepted, you will go through an orientation session ------- starting your volunteer work.

145. (A) except
(B) prior to
(C) even though
(D) whereas

At JointHands, volunteers are directly involved in the ------- phases of our outreach

146. (A) organizing
(B) organizer
(C) organizes
(D) organize

projects.

If you have any further questions or concerns, please do not hesitate to call our office at 555-3719.

Best regards,

Vonda Barlow
Coordinator
JointHands Foundation

GO ON TO THE NEXT PAGE

Questions 147-149 refer to the following e-mail.

To: Letticia Lopez <letty_lopez@mailstream.com>
From: Norah Bailey <n.bailey@centennialhospital.org>
Subject: Seminar Speakers
Date: June 8

Dear Letticia,

We were informed of your intention to invite James Cortez to be a guest speaker at your ------- seminar in July.

147. (A) nutrition
(B) health
(C) finance
(D) literature

I'm sorry to say this, but he ------- unavailable during that month. He is scheduled to

148. (A) was
(B) has been
(C) will be
(D) had been

attend a medical conference from July 12 to 15 and will conduct clinical research after the event. If you have ------- other neurologists in mind, give me their names, and I will

149. (A) every
(B) any
(C) all
(D) no

personally request one of them to speak at the seminar. In fact, most of our neurologists at the hospital are colleagues of James Cortez in the Neuro Society, so I am confident that any one of them can provide an informative talk.

I will wait for your reply.

Sincerely,

Norah Bailey
Director of public relations

Questions 150-152 refer to the following article.

Creative Director Announced for Limelight Studios

Burbank - William York will become Limelight Studio's creative director starting next month, the company announced yesterday in a press release. The ------- of York comes

150. (A) resignation
(B) investigation
(C) promotion
(D) authorization

as no surprise to industry insiders, who predicted that York would take over the position, as current creative director Liza Michaels retires in May. Since Michaels announced her retirement, she has been ------- training York for his new role at the studio.

151. (A) doubtfully
(B) formerly
(C) infrequently
(D) actively

In his new position, York will supervise the production of the studio's television series and films, as well as develop new ideas for future projects.

York has been a producer and director for Limelight Studios since 2003. Michaels comments that "------- knowledge of this company makes William York the perfect

152. (A) Her
(B) His
(C) Our
(D) Their

candidate for the job."

GO ON TO THE NEXT PAGE

PART 7

Directions: In this part, you will be asked to read several texts, such as advertisements, articles or examples of business correspondence. Each text is followed by several questions. Select the best answer and mark the corresponding letter (A), (B), (C), or (D) on your answer sheet.

Questions 153-154 refer to the following advertisement.

Brighten up your celebrations with Sky Sparks!

Wuxi Sky Sparks produces a wide selection of safe and high quality fireworks that have earned us the Shoppers' Choice Award and the Global Excellence in Product Manufacturing Award. Our company has been recognized by the Asian Pyrotechnics Association as the number one fireworks brand in the region.

We are also an official fireworks provider for world class sports events, Independence Day celebrations in the United States, and other occasions that are held in amusement parks all over the world.

Present this advertisement from December 16 to 28 at any of our outlets in Sydney and get 25 percent off when you buy fireworks from our aerial display line worth at least $100.

Don't settle for an ordinary brand when you can have the best. Celebrate the New Year with a loud bang and light up the night with Wuxi Sky Sparks, a trusted name in fireworks.

153. What is NOT stated about Wuxi Sky Sparks?
- (A) It is a recipient of different kinds of awards.
- (B) It is a sponsor of sports competitions.
- (C) It is a brand used at prominent events.
- (D) It is a recognized maker of quality products.

154. What will happen after December 28?
- (A) A type of merchandise will be discontinued.
- (B) A fireworks display will be held in Sydney.
- (C) A business will open stores in different locations.
- (D) A promotional offer will no longer be valid.

GO ON TO THE NEXT PAGE

Questions 155-156 refer to the following e-mail.

From: Now Mail <info@nowmail.com>
To: Eloise Pendleton <eloise.pendleton@nowmail.com>
Subject: Welcome!
Date: December 18

Dear Ms. Pendleton,

Thank you for signing up for a Now Mail Plus account. Stay connected with your friends and family with the useful features of this e-mail account. With Now Mail Plus, you can see what e-mails you have received at a glance and decide which ones to read. This allows you to delete e-mails without having to click on them. You can save a lot of time with this feature. We have also upgraded Now Mail Plus's attachment capacity! You can send up to 25 megabytes, which is twice as much as comparable services.

Please use the following user ID and password every time you sign in to your account.
User ID: eloise.pendleton
Password: eloise501

We recommend that you change your password monthly for security reasons. To get started and learn about the features of your e-mail account, click here. If you have any questions please feel free to e-mail us at cuserve@nowmail.com.

Best Regards,

Now Mail Team

155. What is the main purpose of the e-mail?
(A) To inform a client that an account has been renewed
(B) To offer free online data storage
(C) To provide information on a service's features
(D) To clarify privacy terms and conditions

156. What can Ms. Pendleton do with Now Mail Plus?
(A) Transfer a large amount of information
(B) Sign in without typing a password
(C) Store up to 25 megabytes of e-mails
(D) Upload pictures in seconds

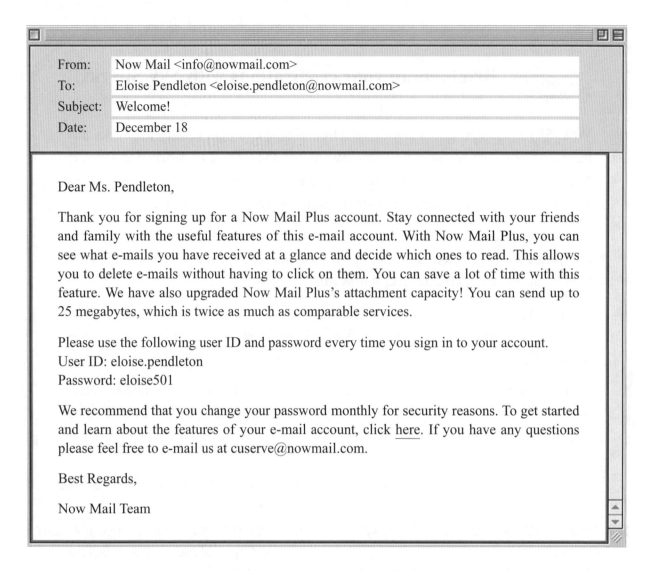

Questions 157-159 refer to the following article.

A Niche for the Classic and Beautiful

By Hanna Crowell

PARIS, June 5 – After seeing the beautiful collection of home furnishings and decorative items at The Nostalgia Corner in Place d'Aligre, visitors agree that it is a necessary stop for anyone interested in antiques.

Established two years ago by Parisian antique collectors Jeremy Almary and Sandra Baude, the shop features European pieces dating back to the 17th century. What is fascinating about this shop is the effort it puts into displays. Items are arranged according to which part of the world they come from. Each vintage piece is also tagged with information about its composition, style, and the period in which it was made, thus allowing customers to appreciate the item even more.

"We would like people who visit our shop to be delighted by the beauty and artistic worth of our collection," Baude said. Because of this, The Nostalgia Corner has become not only a store, but also a must-see attraction for travelers to Paris.

With the business doing well, the proprietors plan to expand their collection by offering antique pieces from East Asian countries. "Within the next 10 years, we hope to provide our customers with a larger selection of antiques by including items from China and South Korea," Baude added.

157. Why was the article written?
(A) To introduce a new trend in interior decoration
(B) To explain the history of antique collecting
(C) To guide consumers in appraising items
(D) To describe a successful business venture

158. What does the article suggest about The Nostalgia Corner?
(A) It recently sold a famous piece of artwork.
(B) It regularly conducts sales on furniture.
(C) It was inherited from one of the owners' relatives.
(D) It carefully plans the presentation of its merchandise.

159. What do the proprietors want to do within a decade?
(A) Seek additional investors
(B) Offer pieces from other global regions
(C) Establish a branch in another European country
(D) Build a warehouse for fragile collections

GO ON TO THE NEXT PAGE

Questions 160-161 refer to the following memo.

MEMORANDUM

To: Food safety inspectors
From: Director Raymond Jensen, Rockford Food Department
Date: March 3
Re: Training

The Bureau of Food and Drugs and the Health Department will hold a state-wide training seminar on food safety inspection at the Health Department conference hall in Springfield on March 15. The seminar has been arranged to ensure proper evaluation of food handling procedures in restaurants and fast-food outlets. The Bureau will also introduce new inspection guidelines during the event. These will include new policies from the bureau that must be implemented by the end of this year. Therefore, all Rockford Food safety officers are required to attend. Theresa Lloyd, our new administrative assistant, is responsible for reserving seats at the seminar and making transportation arrangements. All attendees will also be booked to stay at the Printemps Hotel. Please contact her to confirm your attendance before the end of the week so that she can make all the necessary bookings and reservations.

160. What is the memo mainly about?
(A) Inspection instructions
(B) Employee responsibilities
(C) Scheduling corrections
(D) Event information

161. What is suggested about Ms. Lloyd?
(A) She is Mr. Jensen's personal assistant.
(B) She will compile an attendance list for an event.
(C) She is organizing an upcoming seminar.
(D) She was recently transferred to the Health Department.

Questions 162-164 refer to the following brochure.

The Garden Fields

Where dreams do come true!

Celebrate life's special moments at The Garden Fields. With our enchanting gardens and Spanish-inspired courtyards, you can plan an occasion that will definitely be a unique experience for your clients and their guests. If you want to organize a formal garden wedding or birthday party, we can help you. The Garden Fields has different reception venues for anniversaries, corporate events, and other functions. In addition, we have affiliated catering companies ready to arrange extravagant meals for different occasions. We provide tables, seating, serving dishes, and floral arrangements. If you have any other requirements or additional requests for decorations, our expert event planners will do their best to accommodate you. Contact us today and let us help you create the celebration of a lifetime!

The Garden Fields

20 Cluny Drive
Singapore

To make a booking or for further information, please contact The Garden Fields office at 555-4144 Or visit www.thegardenfields.com.

162. For whom is the brochure most likely intended?
(A) Wedding photographers
(B) Event planners
(C) Landscape architects
(D) Flower shop owners

163. What feature of The Garden Fields is mentioned?
(A) It has a variety of event facilities.
(B) It offers vegetarian menu options.
(C) It has on-site kitchen facilities.
(D) It is famous for its collection of exotic plants.

164. What should clients do to learn more about The Garden Fields?
(A) Visit the venue
(B) Send an e-mail
(C) View a Web site
(D) Call an affiliated hotel

GO ON TO THE NEXT PAGE

Questions 165-167 refer to the following notice.

Mangrove Resort

Special Packages

Bask in clear beach waters at Mangrove Resort and enjoy five-star treatment in our luxurious rooms, restaurants, and sports facilities! Everyone can find something to take part in with Mangrove's variety of tours, diving excursions, and recreational activities. Mangrove Resort is the perfect place for a vacation with your friends and families. And as a special promotion, from July 20 to August 20, we will offer vacation packages at 15 percent off peak rates. Take advantage of this chance for incredible savings and enjoy the beach with your loved ones.

Day Tour Package
Adult: $40 Children: $30

Includes:

- Buffet lunch
- Airport transfers by land and sea
- Speed boat trips to snorkeling sites
- Use of water sports equipment, including kayaks and full snorkeling gear
- Use of resort facilities, basketball courts, beach volleyball courts, and music room

Overnight Package
Bay Cottages and Beach Villas

Single: $130 per person, per night Double: $110 per person, per night

Includes:

- Airport transfers by land and sea
- Speed boat trips to snorkeling sites
- Room-service breakfast, lunch, and dinner buffet
- Lunch on Alligator Island*
- A choice of an introductory scuba diving course* or free spa services
- Use of water sports equipment, including kayaks and full diving gear
- Use of resort facilities, basketball courts, beach volleyball courts, and music room

*Only available to guests staying more than two nights.

All packages include service charges and applicable government tax.

165. What will most likely take place after August 20?
(A) New recreational activities will be offered.
(B) Regular prices will apply.
(C) Travel package options will be changed.
(D) Tax will be excluded from the package.

166. What is NOT included in the day tour travel package?
(A) Snorkeling equipment usage
(B) Boat tours to nearby locations
(C) Use of sports facilities
(D) Beginner diving classes

167. What is offered exclusively to guests staying two nights or more?
(A) Tickets to sporting events
(B) A meal at a special site
(C) Scuba diving excursions
(D) A room upgrade

Questions 168-171 refer to the following letter.

Trade Explorer Magazine
1030 Newbury Street, Philadelphia, PA

March 12

Lance Hughes
Marketing Manager
E-book Station

Dear Mr. Hughes,

Our records show that you haven't published an advertisement with *Trade Explorer Magazine* for the past six months. We sincerely value the business of customers like yourself and would like to offer you a special promotion. In the past, you have taken out several full-page advertisements in our monthly publication. We would like to offer you the chance to post a full-page advertisement at half the standard rate for our next four issues. If you accept our proposal, we will also provide you with a free button advertisement on our Web site.

To place an advertisement, please fill out the enclosed form and mail it back to us. Should you need any assistance with the layout or design of your advertisement, we are also willing to accommodate you in that regard. You may contact our business representative, Juliet Abbot, at 555-0306 for additional information.

We hope you will find our offer beneficial and cost-effective.

Sincerely yours,

Liza Huntington
Managing Editor
Trade Explorer Magazine

168. Why was the letter written?
(A) To update a subscription
(B) To revise a mailing list
(C) To offer services to a client
(D) To advertise a local business

169. What is suggested about Lance Hughes?
(A) He owns a business journal.
(B) He works for an advertising agency.
(C) He requires assistance with layout.
(D) He is a former client of the magazine.

170. How long will the promotion be available?
(A) Two months
(B) Four months
(C) Six months
(D) Seven months

171. How can Mr. Hughes receive a reduced rate?
(A) By renewing a membership
(B) By placing a large order
(C) By sending a completed form
(D) By extending his subscription

GO ON TO THE NEXT PAGE

Questions 172-175 refer to the following memo.

MEMO

To: All staff members

From: Matilde Montagna, Chairperson, Turini Film Festival

Date: October 5

Subject: Film Festival Schedule

I have finalized the timetable of activities for the film festival. Since we are currently understaffed, I want you to start on the necessary preparations as soon as possible to ensure that the schedule is strictly followed. Below is the timetable for the event:

Date	Activity	Venue(s)	Time
Friday, February 16	Film Festival Launch	Giovanni Boccaccio Theatre	7 P.M. - 8 P.M.
Saturday, February 17	Feature Films	Arthur Place Cinemas 1-7	9 A.M. - 12 P.M.
Sunday, February 18	Short Films	Arthur Place Cinemas 1-5	9 A.M. - 9 P.M.
Monday, February 19	Documentaries	Arthur Place Cinemas 1-5	9 A.M. - 5 P.M.
Tuesday, February 20	Awards Presentation	Tasso Dome	8 P.M. - onwards

As discussed at the meeting, the film and the documentary committees are responsible for arranging show times for all entries. The list containing each entry's screening time should be finalized by October 20 to give enough time for the preparation of invitations, advertisements, and press releases for the festival.

Moreover, I want to inform you that a dinner party will be held following the awards presentation. Ms. Belle is currently looking for restaurants and bars that might be interested in providing food and beverages. If you want to recommend a business, please coordinate with her.

172. What is the purpose of the memo?
(A) To report recent management changes
(B) To confirm the opening of an establishment
(C) To gather suggestions for a print advertisement
(D) To provide additional information on event preparations

173. What will happen on the last day of the festival?
(A) Food will be served.
(B) Film production will begin.
(C) The committee meeting will be held.
(D) Short movies will be shown.

174. What needs to be submitted on October 20?
(A) Responses to invitations
(B) A list of screening times
(C) Press releases
(D) Drafts of advertisements

175. What is Ms. Belle responsible for?
(A) Adjusting event schedules
(B) Catering service arrangements
(C) Invitation distribution
(D) Organizing the awards ceremony

Questions 176-180 refer to the following e-mail.

From: Josie Roberts <j.roberts@brentontradehall.com>
To: Kurt Bowman <k_bowman@expressmail.com>
Date: July 24
Subject: Re: Booth Reservation
Attachment: Services and Facilities

Dear Mr. Bowman,

I received your e-mail this morning regarding the Great Homes Fair at Benton Trade Hall from August 20 to 22. I appreciate your interest, and I hope my reply will provide you with sufficient information.

The facility is located in downtown Seattle. As the largest real estate fair in the Northwest, the event attracts more than 300 property developers, broker firms, and financial companies every year. Real estate firms will sell various properties, ranging from residential apartments and office spaces to industrial facilities. Last year more than 12,000 people attended the event, and a grand total of 720 buildings, homes, and properties were sold.

We highly recommend that your company arrange for a booth at the fair, as the vast majority of companies that do so report successful sales. Arrangements can be made to accommodate your staff, and a variety of types and sizes of booths are available. We also suggest that you and your sales agents attend the free real estate seminar on the last day of the event. Summerset Development Corporation vice president Anita Cooper will deliver a talk on client relations, which we are certain that brokers like you will benefit from.

Attached to this message is a list of services and facilities offered by Benton Trade Hall. This includes detailed descriptions of booths and a list of fees. To view images of our event halls, booths, and facilities, visit our Web site at www.bentontradehall.com.

Josie Roberts, Events Coordinator, Brenton Trade Hall

176. Why did Ms. Roberts send the e-mail to Mr. Bowman?
(A) To promote a new property development
(B) To reply to an inquiry about an event
(C) To request attendance at a meeting
(D) To answer a question about a product

177. What does Ms. Roberts recommend Mr. Bowman do?
(A) Attend a lecture given by Anita Cooper
(B) Take advantage of a promotional offer
(C) Reserve an exhibition hall for a fair
(D) Submit the forms as soon as possible

178. What is NOT mentioned about the Great Homes Fair?
(A) It attracts a large number of attendees.
(B) It is the most advertised real estate fair in the country.
(C) It yields a significant amount of sales.
(D) It is held on an annual basis.

179. What is indicated about Mr. Bowman?
(A) He is in charge of setting up trade shows.
(B) He previously rented a booth at an event.
(C) He registered for the fair already.
(D) He works as a real estate broker.

180. According to the e-mail, what can Mr. Bowman do on the company's Web site?
(A) Register for an event
(B) Review facility rental fees
(C) See pictures of Benton Trade Hall
(D) Make arrangements for a booth

GO ON TO THE NEXT PAGE

Questions 181-185 refer to the following Web page and e-mail.

Robertson's

Your Neighbourhood Superstore

Sign in | Register | Search all departments

OTHER DEPARTMENTS ▼

You are shopping in > Indoor Appliances > Vacuum Cleaners

Shop by Category

Upright Vacuums
Canister Vacuums
Sticks & Handhelds
Robotic Vacuums
Parts & Accessories

Shop by Brand

Baronial
Irona
Jiffy
Lutschen
Macdougal
Samuelson

Related sections

Warranties
Return policy
Repairs

SPECIAL OFFER

Register for an account before September 1 to enjoy single-click transactions, free shipping on orders worth $100 or more, and discounts on select online purchases. Terms and conditions apply.

Click for details.

Need more assistance?

Click here to contact a live operator, 24 hours a day, 7 days a week, or call 555-0101.

VACUUM CLEANERS

Click on the links below to view models from each category.

Robertson's carries all the leading brands at the best prices. In fact, if you find one of our products advertised for less on other retailers' Web sites, send us a link to their page and we will match their price—guaranteed!*

UPRIGHT VACUUM CLEANERS

Ideal for cleaning carpets, upright vacuum cleaners provide a wide cleaning swath to remove dirt buried deep within floor coverings. They include a variety of attachments and special features. This month only, all Baronial upright vacuums come with an extended two-year manufacturer's warranty.**

CANISTER VACUUM CLEANERS

Canister vacuum cleaners are convenient to use and easy to operate. They are recommended for cleaning bare floors, upholstery, stairs, and difficult-to-reach places. Get a 5 percent rebate when you buy a Lutschen TK50.

STICK & HANDHELD VACUUM CLEANERS

Stick and handheld vacuum cleaners are perfect for cleaning up spills and getting in between tight spaces. They come in both corded and cordless varieties. Take advantage of a buy-one-get-one-free offer on Jiffy handheld car vacuums (select models only).

ROBOTIC VACUUMS

Robotic vacuums are becoming one of our best-sellers, as they take all the work out of cleaning floors. Simply charge the robot, input a few settings, and the machine takes care of the rest. Best for maintaining the overall cleanliness of floors in common areas. Buy an Irona and get a free set of replacement batteries.

* Does not apply to items sold second-hand

** Valid only when you send a scanned copy of the completed manufacturer's warranty card to customerservice@robertsons.com

About Us | Contact Us | Privacy Policy | Terms and Conditions | Site Map

To:	customerservice@robertsons.com
From:	Francis Tordesillas <francistordesillas@happymail.net>
Date:	September 7
Subject:	Some Concerns
Attachment:	Warranty Card

To whom it may concern,

I ordered a vacuum cleaner from your online store last week and it was just delivered this morning. As per the instructions on your Web site, I have attached a scanned copy of the manufacturer's product warranty card. I trust that I still qualify for the extended two-year warranty since I completed my purchase in August.

In addition, I am enclosing a link to the Web site of an appliance retailer in Florida. According to their advertisement, they are selling the Goldline compact refrigerator for just $156, versus $172 on your Web site. I would prefer to order the appliance from you since I have already registered for an account, but I'd like to confirm that you are able to match this competitor's price.

Here is the link: http://www.plotkinappliance.com/refrigeration/goldline.html

Best regards,

Francis Tordesillas

181. What is NOT indicated about Robertson's?
(A) It sells second-hand items for less than its competitors.
(B) It provides services any time of the day.
(C) It does not manufacture its own line of products.
(D) It offers customers information about repairs.

182. According to the Web page, which category of vacuum cleaners is in high demand?
(A) Stick
(B) Canister
(C) Upright
(D) Robotic

183. In the e-mail, the word "trust" in paragraph 1, line 3 is closest in meaning to
(A) acknowledge
(B) rely
(C) expect
(D) commit

184. Which brand of vacuum cleaner did Mr. Tordesillas most likely buy?
(A) Jiffy
(B) Lutschen
(C) Baronial
(D) Irona

185. What is suggested about Mr. Tordesillas?
(A) He resides in the state of Florida.
(B) He missed the deadline for a promotion.
(C) He wants a refund for a recent purchase.
(D) He will get free shipping for his next order.

GO ON TO THE NEXT PAGE

Questions 186-190 refer to the following letter and schedule.

April 2

To our new accountants,

Welcome to Yagit Consulting! We are delighted that you are joining our team and look forward to a long and mutually rewarding work relationship with you. I am sure you will all have a lot of questions about the company's systems, structure and organization, so please don't hesitate to ask. You can reach me by e-mail at amno@yagit.org or give me a call at extension #402.

However, I hope many of your questions will be answered during your new employee orientation. To help you all make smooth transitions into your new roles, an orientation will be held on your first day of work. You will see in the enclosed schedule that the orientation begins with a speech from Yagit's vice president of finance. Then talks from some of our senior-level executives will follow. They will include a presentation about our company and its goals, and one more from the accounting director before lunch. After my closing remarks, there will be a reception on the second floor of our office building to provide you with an opportunity to meet your new coworkers.

Finally, I would like to remind all of you to submit the results of your medical examinations on or before April 10. Please e-mail them or bring them in person to the human resources department on the fifth floor. Thank you.

Best regards,

Amber Norris
Human Resources Director
Yagit Consulting

YAGIT CONSULTING
Accounting Orientation
April 18, 7:30 A.M. - 5:30 P.M.

SCHEDULE OF EVENTS		
7:30 A.M.	Welcome Remarks	Roger Pate
8:00 A.M.	Introduction to Yagit and its Mission and Vision	Brenda Clements
10:00 A.M.	Presentation: The Yagit Style to Creative Financial Planning	Todd Whitley
12:00 P.M.	LUNCH	
1:00 P.M.	Creating and Analyzing Budgets	Kelly Irwin
3:00 P.M.	Financial Modeling and Forecasting	Danny O'Hara
5:00 P.M.	Closing Speech	Amber Norris
5:30 P.M.	COCKTAIL PARTY	

186. What is indicated about the new accountants at Yagit?
(A) They recently completed a series of orientation sessions.
(B) They will have flexible work hours after the training period.
(C) They must have a health check-up on April 10.
(D) They will have a chance to socialize immediately after Ms. Norris' speech.

187. When are the new accountants expected to report to the office?
(A) On April 2
(B) On April 10
(C) On April 18
(D) On April 26

188. Who is the vice president of finance for Yagit Consulting?
(A) Brenda Clements
(B) Danny O'Hara
(C) Kelly Irwin
(D) Roger Pate

189. Which talk will be given by Yagit's head of accounting?
(A) Financial Modeling and Forecasting
(B) The Yagit Style to Creative Financial Planning
(C) Creating and Analyzing Budgets
(D) Introduction to Yagit and its Mission and Vision

190. What time will the new accountants learn about estimating expenses?
(A) At 8 A.M.
(B) At 10 A.M.
(C) At 1 P.M.
(D) At 3 P.M.

GO ON TO THE NEXT PAGE

Questions 191-195 refer to the following e-mails.

To: Lauren Crawford <Lcraw@double.net>
From: Anthony Dixon <dixony@leeland.com>
Date: October 14
Subject: A favor

Hi Lauren,

How are things going in Madagascar? I expect you are very busy working on the Faritany project, and hope everything is coming along smoothly. Actually, the reason why I'm writing to you is because I need your expert guidance with a project I am currently planning. I'll be going to Belize next year, not as a member of the archaeological crew but as its project administrator. Since I've never held a position like this before, I'd really appreciate it if you could assist me regarding the preparations that my staff and I have to make before the excavation in January. I know you have led many such expeditions, and I am hoping you may be able to provide some insight concerning the planning stages of my project.

I'm attaching a tentative schedule for the project and a brief outline of our goals and what we hope to accomplish during the given time. Please have a look at them and let me know if you think we've scheduled enough time to meet our goals. Any suggestions you could give me would be very welcome. Also, I am interested in knowing what particular supplies we will need to bring, especially in regard to equipment.

Thanks in advance, and I'll be waiting for your reply.

Anthony

To: Anthony Dixon <dixony@leeland.com>
From: Lauren Crawford <Lcraw@double.net>
Date: October 16
Subject: Re: A favor

Hello Anthony,

So far, everything's been going smoothly here in Madagascar and we're ahead of schedule with the Faritany project. It's a lot of hard work, but the results we've seen so far are promising.

Anyway, I'm sure you'll do a great job as a project administrator. It can be challenging at first, but I think your knowledge of archaeological sites will really help you with the project. But before you begin your excavation in Belize, make sure you have all the required permits from the local government. I've had some difficulties with this before, so make certain that all your documents are in order before you proceed with anything.

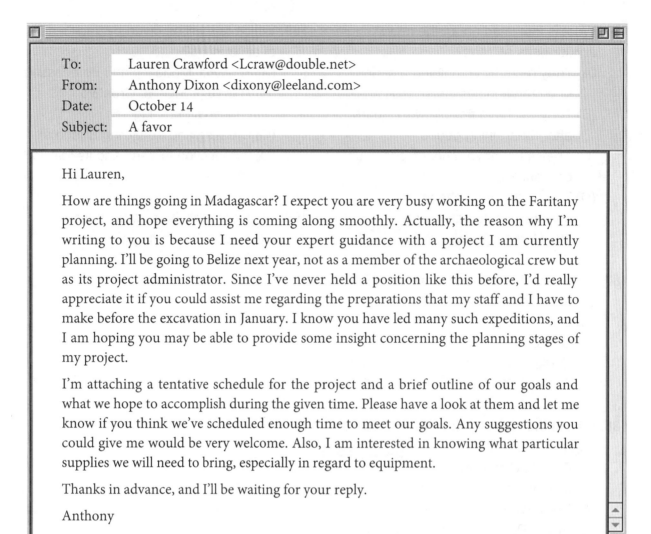

Also, you and your staff will need on-site access to both shelter and toilet facilities for convenience purposes. It will definitely make your work on the site more comfortable, and I would make arrangements for those facilities before leaving for Belize. You will need Internet access, but don't expect 24-hour service as the connections aren't very reliable. And make sure to bring a couple of small power generators for recharging mobile phones, computers, and other equipment. Of course you will also need to develop safe working procedures for your team to reduce the risk of accidents and injuries.

I had a look at the schedule and outline you sent me, and it seems like you've allotted the perfect amount of time to finish the project.

Good luck and keep me updated on your project.

Lauren

191. Why did Mr. Dixon write the e-mail?
(A) To provide information on an archaeological discovery
(B) To give suggestions about a research proposal
(C) To ask for recommendations about an upcoming project
(D) To invite participants to an international conference

192. What is attached to Mr. Dixon's e-mail?
(A) A map of his destination
(B) A flight schedule
(C) An archeological report
(D) A list of objectives

193. What is indicated about Mr. Dixon?
(A) He wants to work with Ms. Crawford.
(B) He is currently in Belize for business.
(C) He has never led a team before.
(D) He is having difficulty with his current project.

194. In the second e-mail, the phrase "in order" in paragraph 2, line 5 is closest in meaning to
(A) aligned
(B) prepared
(C) shipped
(D) packed

195. What is NOT a suggestion given by Ms. Crawford to Mr. Dixon?
(A) Implement safety measures
(B) Gather essential documents for field operations
(C) Ensure ready access to sanitation facilities
(D) Minimize the use of electrical devices

GO ON TO THE NEXT PAGE

Questions 196-200 refer to the following job advertisement and e-mail.

Jamadevi: Job openings

Jamadevi has provided excellent service in Thailand's tourism industry for the past 15 years. We've developed a strong reputation among visitors to Thailand and are proud to have a lot of repeat business. Due to popular demand for our tours and charters, we at Jamadevi have immediate job openings for experienced tour guides.

Applicants must possess a certificate from a reputable tour guide training academy and should be energetic, reliable, and adventurous. In addition, they must possess a valid driver's license as it will be necessary to operate a vehicle from time to time. Proficiency in other languages besides Thai and English is an advantage, as well as an extensive knowledge of local geography and history.

Interested individuals are encouraged to call +66-23-555-7119 and ask for Chariya Kasem for application instructions. Ms. Kasem can be reached from Tuesday to Sunday between the hours of 8:00 A.M. and 7:00 P.M.

To: ckasem@jamadevi.th
From: sujit_khongmalai@lamphunmail.th
Date: March 25
Subject: Tour Guide Application

Dear Ms. Kasem,

Based on your instructions for applying for the tour guide position, I am sending you my qualifications and employment history. Unfortunately, I was not able to attach a copy of my driver's license as I am still in the process of obtaining one.

Name	Sujit Khongmalai
Address	3541 Chao Street, Pomprab, Bangkok 101008
Contact Number	(00662) 555-6280
Goal	To work as a tour guide for an established firm that will help enhance my skills and experience in this field
Experience	Tour Guide, Nakorn Travel (Present) • Lead tour groups, give talks about the culture, language, and history of Thailand, and make tour itineraries Promotions Officer, Mahayana Tours (3 years) • Oversaw the creation, promotion, delivery, monitoring, and evaluation of day tours Travel Agent, Banchee Vacations (2 years) • Processed ticketing transactions and coordinated the details of travel packages
Education	Bachelor's degree in sociology, Bangkok National University
Skills and Certifications	• Tourism Licensure Certificate, Thai Academy of Licensed Tour Guides • Competent in all computer programs, especially word processing, spreadsheets, and image and video editing software • Proficient in Thai, English, and Chinese
References available upon request.	

Thank you for your time and consideration. I look forward to hearing from you soon.

Sincerely,

Sujit Khongmalai

196. What is mentioned about Jamadevi?
(A) It has been operating for over a decade.
(B) It advertises its services overseas.
(C) It offers tours throughout Southeast Asia.
(D) It was recognized with an award.

197. What is a requirement for the advertised position?
(A) A history degree
(B) Knowledge of local geography
(C) A professional certificate
(D) Travel agency experience

198. Why might Mr. Khongmalai not be considered for the position?
(A) He cannot speak Chinese.
(B) He has an expired passport.
(C) He has no driver's license.
(D) He is not a Thai resident.

199. At which company is Mr. Khongmalai employed?
(A) Banchee Vacations
(B) Nakorn Travel
(C) Mahayana Tours
(D) Thai Academy

200. What is NOT indicated about Mr. Khongmalai?
(A) He speaks three languages.
(B) He organizes tour schedules.
(C) He is knowledgeable in computers.
(D) He manages a travel agency.

This is the end of the test. You may review Part 5, 6, and 7 if you finish the test early.

解答 p.286 / 分數換算表 p.289 / 題目解析 p.67（解答本）

▮ 請翻到次頁「自我檢測表」檢視自己解答問題的方法與態度。

自我檢測表

TEST 02 順利的完成了嗎？

現在要開始透過以下的自我檢測表檢視自己在考試中的表現了嗎？

我的目標分數為：　　　　　　　這次測試的成績為：

1. 70 分鐘內，我完全集中精神在測試內容上。

   □是　□不是

   如果回答不是，理由是什麼呢？

2. 70 分鐘內，連答案卷的劃記都完成了。

   □是　□不是

   如果回答不是，理由是什麼呢？

3. 70 分鐘內，100 題都解完了。

   □是　□不是

   如果回答不是，理由是什麼呢？

4. Part 5 和 Part 6 在 25 分鐘以內全都寫完了。

   □是　□不是

   如果回答不是，理由是什麼呢？

5. 寫 Part 7 的時候，沒有一題花超過五分鐘。

   □是　□不是

   如果回答不是，理由是什麼呢？

6. 請寫下你需要改善的地方以及給自己的忠告。

*回到本書第二頁，確認自己的目標分數並加強對於達成分數的意志。
對於要改善的部分一定要在下一次測試中實踐。這點是最重要的，也要這樣才能有進步。

TEST 03

Part 5 ① 超过1分

Part 6 ⑤ 对61

Part 7 23 300.

自我檢測表

等等！考前確認事項：

1. 關掉行動裝置電源了嗎？□ 是
2. 答案卷（Answer Sheet）、鉛筆、橡皮擦都準備
 好了嗎？□ 是
3. 手錶帶了嗎？□ 是

如果都準備齊全了，想想目標分數後即可開始作答。

考試結束時間為現在開始 **70** 分鐘後的_____點_____分。

Reading Test

In this section, you must demonstrate your ability to read and comprehend English. You will be given a variety of texts and asked to answer questions about these texts. This section is divided into three parts and will take 75 minutes to complete.

Do not mark the answers in your test book. Use the answer sheet that is separately provided.

PART 5

Directions: In each question, you will be asked to review a statement that is missing a word or phrase. Four answer choices will be provided for each question. Select the best answer and mark the corresponding letter (A), (B), (C), or (D) on the answer sheet.

101. All visitors to the Kentworth Plant are asked to sign in at the security office ------- pick up a guest pass.
(A) and (B) yet
(C) in (D) which

102. Lara Karowski's chances of winning last year's badminton finals ------- when she sustained a major knee injury.
(A) diminish (B) diminished
(C) diminishingly (D) diminutive

103. Marina practiced some ballet steps by ------- while waiting for the instructor to show up and class to begin.
(A) she (B) her
(C) herself (D) hers

104. We suggest you look around the computer store for a while, and one of our staff will attend to you -------.
(A) moment
(B) momentum
(C) momentarily
(D) momentary

105. Drivers leaving their vehicles unattended in front of the terminal may have to pay a fine or risk the ------- of their car by a towing service.
(A) removal
(B) communication
(C) damage
(D) transit

106. Neither the restaurant manager ------- the supervisor was notified about the fire safety inspection scheduled for tomorrow.
(A) of (B) both
(C) while (D) nor

107. Because Eye Specialists will move to a new location, management has decided to ------- the hospital's operations for a week.
(A) provide
(B) advertise
(C) distribute
(D) suspend

108. If you have questions or problems with your security equipment, please call our 24-hour customer service hotline to receive prompt -------.
(A) attend (B) attention
(C) attendance (D) attentive

109. Grant applications submitted after the ------- of October 1 will not be considered for this year's funding.
(A) rule (B) deadline
(C) limit (D) grade

110. The supervisor was ------- with the performance of most of the trainees and recommended that all but one be given permanent employment.
(A) satisfying
(B) satisfied
(C) satisfies
(D) satisfy

111. Thank-you letters will be sent to ------- the benefactors to express the community's appreciation for their donations.
(A) all (B) much
(C) whose (D) what

112. Some inconsistencies in the report convinced the accounting manager to go back and double-check the ------- records.
(A) future (B) narrow
(C) leading (D) previous

113. Sales of luxury vehicles fell ------- during the fourth quarter of last year due to the reduction in consumer spending.
(A) signifying
(B) signifies
(C) significant
(D) significantly

114. It is crucial ------- all employees comply with the dress code to create a unified, professional image for the company.
(A) among (B) why
(C) that (D) with

115. The opinions given by Mr. Tolentino differed from ------- of the accounting department's other staff.
(A) those (B) they
(C) this (D) them

116. Customers who already own a licensed software are automatically ------- to upgrade to the latest one for free.
(A) qualify
(B) qualifies
(C) qualification
(D) qualified

117. Mr. Roberts was named ------- the new head of IVN Bank following the former CEO's resignation.
(A) at (B) as
(C) along (D) around

118. Briseis Bakery in downtown Manhattan is known for using only ingredients of the freshest ------- in its baked goods.
(A) property (B) quality
(C) feature (D) manner

119. The tour guide ------- prepared to give the guests a tour of the island resort after they check in.
(A) was being
(B) have been
(C) would have
(D) will be

120. Because of the high demand, office spaces in the city's financial district ------- cost more than anywhere else.
(A) type (B) typing
(C) typically (D) typical

GO ON TO THE NEXT PAGE

121. Some of the attendees at the technology convention were charged a ------- fee, as they were able to register as a group.
(A) final
(B) total
(C) reduced
(D) costly

122. Charity foundations and educational institutions are ------- from paying income tax to the government as they are considered nonprofit organizations.
(A) contented
(B) guaranteed
(C) exempt
(D) isolated

123. Those who are attending the economic forum should pay the registration fee in full ------- a week of signing up for the event.
(A) within
(B) besides
(C) over
(D) behind

124. Use of the penthouse and conference rooms for special occasions requires the ------- of the building administrator.
(A) permissive
(B) permitted
(C) permission
(D) permissible

125. Benoic Bikes encourages its first-time customers to buy helmets with their bicycle purchase, but it is completely -------.
(A) wide
(B) solitary
(C) optional
(D) reachable

126. All short-term rental apartments at Thompson Suites are equipped with stoves, refrigerators, and other necessary household -------.
(A) materials
(B) appliances
(C) belongings
(D) souvenirs

127. The members of the tour group decided that they would rather visit the city's shopping district ------- the history museum as planned.
(A) up to
(B) instead of
(C) apart from
(D) farther than

128. Government officials attending the trade summit hope to increase ------- within the region's sizable business community.
(A) collaboration
(B) collaborative
(C) collaborator
(D) collaborate

129. By the end of the writing workshop, participants will have gained a thorough ------- of the rules of grammar.
(A) understand
(B) understanding
(C) understandably
(D) understands

130. Drivers waiting in the loading zone must switch off the engines of their delivery vans and avoid leaving them -------.
(A) idle
(B) valid
(C) blank
(D) empty

131. Starting in September, use of the parking spaces located at the back of Winklevoss Tower will be ------- to tenants from the first to fifth floors of the building only.
(A) automatic
(B) matched
(C) precise
(D) limited

132. Business entrepreneur Todd Mallory is known not only for his various ------- ventures, but also for his generous contributions to charity.
(A) profited
(B) profitable
(C) profitably
(D) profiteer

133. All expenses incurred during the company outing have been ------- for in a report submitted by the branch supervisor to the head office in Jakarta.
(A) account
(B) accountant
(C) accounting
(D) accounted

134. It is widely recognized that adults who engage in sports ------- social activities experience less stress.
(A) within
(B) as well as
(C) as long as
(D) ever

135. Owner Sylvia Aspen decided to hire more servers for her café ------- the increasing number of customers.
(A) whereas
(B) if only
(C) due to
(D) besides

136. ------- the expansion plan was not authorized by the board, the company will no longer be accepting bids from construction firms.
(A) Apart from
(B) Given that
(C) As if
(D) Which

137. To mark Lukering Technologies' 50th -------, the company will launch its first-ever charity foundation benefiting science scholars.
(A) intention
(B) initiation
(C) anniversary
(D) command

138. ------- a ship maker canceled its contract with Asia Steelworks, the value of the steel manufacturer's shares on the stock market dropped.
(A) Yet
(B) Unless
(C) Along
(D) Since

139. Fast Mail returns packages and documents to senders ------- it fails to deliver the items to their intended recipients.
(A) still
(B) where
(C) or
(D) when

140. The factory's production ------- has been relatively low this month because of recurring problems with the equipment.
(A) study
(B) output
(C) designation
(D) establishment

GO ON TO THE NEXT PAGE

PART 6

Directions: In this part, you will be asked to read an English text. Some sentences are incomplete. Select the word or phrase that correctly completes each sentence and mark the corresponding letter (A), (B), (C), or (D) on the answer sheet.

Questions 141-143 refer to the following letter.

December 9

Winston Wheeler
Manager
ATA Electronics

Dear Mr. Wheeler,

This is in response to the letter you sent me regarding the information about the overhead projectors I requested on behalf of Northshire University. I appreciate your taking the time to recommend some of the brands ------- in your shop. However, the ones

141. (A) avails
(B) availability
(C) availably
(D) available

suggested are too expensive. In addition, I have found a different ------- that can provide

142. (A) courier
(B) vendor
(C) developer
(D) advisor

the university with what it needs. Nevertheless, I would like to know more about the speaker system you suggested for the university's multimedia classrooms. ------- you

143. (A) Do
(B) Could
(C) Why will
(D) How should

present a demonstration in my office on Monday? Please let me know if you are free on that day as soon as possible. Thank you.

Matt Nicholson
IT Department Head
Northshire University

Questions 144-146 refer to the following information.

Replacing printer ink cartridges is expensive. Moreover, disposing of them is ------- to the

144. (A) beneficial
(B) harmful
(C) trivial
(D) wasteful

environment. Most cartridges still work after their first use. Recycling them is better than throwing them away because it not only saves money but also reduces pollution.

If you do not know how to ------- your cartridges, Office Center is here to help. Illinois'

145. (A) reuse
(B) exchange
(C) clean
(D) resell

largest office supplies store has ink-refilling stations in its outlets. All you need to do is drop them off at a service counter and have them -------. Once we find that the cartridges

146. (A) tested
(B) to test
(C) testing
(D) tests

are still in good condition, we will refill them with ink at half the price of a brand new cartridge. You can save money and assist in conserving nature.

Log on to www.officecenter.com now to learn more about this service.

Note: Office Center supports the government's Clean and Save campaign by selling brands of biodegradable office materials.

GO ON TO THE NEXT PAGE

Questions 147-149 refer to the following letter.

Dear Ms. Sunders,

Edildburgh Technologies has been in the media lately for ------- reasons. It is now being

147. (A) commercial
(B) good
(C) social
(D) misunderstood

reported that we are the fastest-growing technology company in the region. Without the support of shareholders, we would not have become one of the top ------- companies in

148. (A) finance
(B) electronics
(C) insurance
(D) furnishing

Western Europe that we are today. In this regard, we would like to show our appreciation of your valuable support of Edildburgh Technologies at a dinner party that ------- the

149. (A) will commemorate
(B) commemorating
(C) commemorated
(D) commemorative

company's achievements over the past two and a half decades.

Enclosed is an invitation to the event. To confirm your attendance, please contact our public relations department and ask for Ruth Mendez. Thank you.

Respectfully yours,

Jasper Diaz
President
Edildburgh Technologies

Questions 150-152 refer to the following memo.

To: Security guards
From: Michael Reni, Building Security Head
Subject: Security Inspections

There have been several instances when staff members working overtime have forgotten to lock their offices, leaving the building vulnerable to burglary. ------- this, management

150. (A) Apart from
(B) On account of
(C) In addition to
(D) In spite of

wants guards on the night shift to conduct their security checks immediately after all office workers have left the building.

Conference rooms and offices on every floor -------. Moreover, please make sure all

151. (A) must be inspected
(B) were inspected
(C) had inspected
(D) could be inspected

fluorescent lights are switched off, except in the hallways and stairwells. Air conditioning units and other office equipment should also be turned off.

This new ------- takes effect tonight. Feel free to contact me if you have questions.

152. (A) routine
(B) proposal
(C) recommendation
(D) appointment

GO ON TO THE NEXT PAGE

PART 7

Directions: In this part, you will be asked to read several texts, such as advertisements, articles or examples of business correspondence. Each text is followed by several questions. Select the best answer and mark the corresponding letter (A), (B), (C), or (D) on your answer sheet.

Questions 153-154 refer to the following announcement.

Broughester University Drama Guild and *The Scholar*
present

Anita

Join us for this season's production of the English musical *Anita* from June 2 to 4 at the Valdez Auditorium. The show features award-winning actress Bernadette Summers and actor George Fair, star of the popular TV series *Best Friends*. The rest of the cast is made up of members of the drama guild.

Show times:

June 2, Friday - 5 P.M.
June 3, Saturday - 8 P.M.
June 4, Sunday - 6 P.M.

Tickets are available at *The Scholar* press office.

153. What is being announced?
(A) An awards ceremony
(B) A movie premiere
(C) A theatrical performance
(D) A news conference

154. Where would the announcement most likely be found?
(A) At a science museum
(B) On a school campus
(C) At a country club
(D) In a research center

GO ON TO THE NEXT PAGE

Questions 155-156 refer to the following e-mail.

To: ADT Bank finance managers <managersgroup@adt.com>
From: Peter Honorat <p.honorat@adt.com>
Subject: Annual Budget Proposal
Date: December 1

Hello everyone,

The finance department is completing a budget proposal for next year. The proposal will be discussed at ADT Bank's yearly planning meeting in January. In connection with this, we request that you submit the budget estimates for your respective branches within the week.

In particular, we need your recommended salary adjustments as well as your estimated expenses for supplies and equipment. As agreed in the last meeting, your budget proposals should meet the standards provided by the finance department. Please turn in the documents no later than December 8.

Sincerely,

Peter Honorat
Administrative Assistant
Finance Department

155. What is the e-mail mainly about?
(A) A proposed project
(B) A submission deadline
(C) The schedule of conference activities
(D) The promotion of an employee

156. According to the e-mail, what is the finance department's role in budget planning?
(A) Assigning accounting consultants to branches
(B) Updating the shareholders on company income
(C) Soliciting price quotations from suppliers
(D) Setting guidelines for estimating expenses

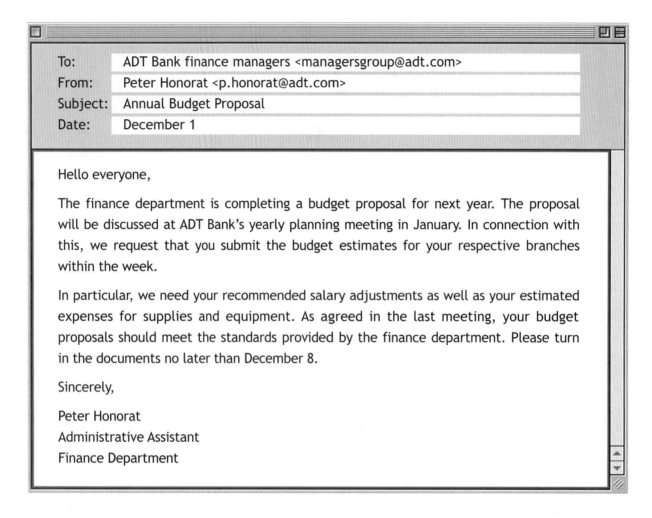

Questions 157-159 refer to the following information.

Savor a good cup of brewed coffee the easy way!

The Coffee Bits French Press

Try our recommended method of brewing with the Coffee Bits French Press and enjoy quality coffee in your own home.

Suggested mix:

10 grams or 2 tablespoons of ground Coffee Bits coffee = 180 milliliters of water*

*Use hot filtered water.

Brewing instructions:

Remove the plunger, add ground coffee, and pour in hot water based on the recommended proportion. If you find the suggested mix too strong, fill the French Press with water up to about 1.25 centimeters below the rim. Then stir the mixture and put the plunger on top of the container. Allow the coffee to steep for about three minutes. Press the plunger and pour the coffee into a cup. Enjoy.

157. What is NOT stated in the information?
(A) The method of adjusting coffee strength
(B) The steeping process duration
(C) The steps for cleaning the press
(D) The way to operate the equipment

158. What is mentioned as a characteristic of the French Press?
(A) It comes in a variety of sizes.
(B) It is simple to store.
(C) It is made of strong materials.
(D) It consists of several components.

159. What should users do after pouring water into the French Press?
(A) Stir the mixture
(B) Add hot milk
(C) Filter the ground coffee
(D) Put some sugar

GO ON TO THE NEXT PAGE

Questions 160-163 refer to the following article.

Decoding the Happiness Formula

Happiness is not only found but also created. This is the message of celebrated psychiatrist Jonathan Hammond in his new book, *The Happiness Formula*, which unravels the secrets of leading a happy and contented life.

According to Hammond, happy people are healthier, have better relationships with their families and friends, and are more productive at work. Although it is true that much of people's happiness is influenced by their genes and other factors such as income and socioeconomic status, happiness is also heavily influenced by the activities people do in their everyday lives. Based on this, Hammond studied how people find joy in life. He found out that those who are active and positive experience lasting contentment, compared with people who live more passively and have a more negative outlook on life.

He said people can motivate themselves to be happy by engaging in sports and participating in activities that help them find meaning in life. Doing simple things, such as dancing, singing, smiling, or laughing out loud also stimulates positive energy. Hammond stressed that the key to long-lived happiness is making the decision to stay optimistic.

Hammond, who is also a respected professor at Southcane University, has authored different books about personality enhancement and developmental psychology. *The Happiness Formula* was launched two weeks ago by Leehorn Publishing House and is currently number one on the *Fortnightly Informant*'s best-seller list.

160. What is the article mainly about?
(A) Ideas featured in a publication
(B) Secrets of successful people
(C) Tips on time management
(D) Stories reviewed in a journal

161. What does the article mention about happy people?
(A) They are more popular.
(B) They have more money.
(C) They are healthier.
(D) They have more friends.

162. What is stated about Dr. Hammond?
(A) He publishes his own work.
(B) He has written previous publications.
(C) He is a career adviser.
(D) He heads a university department.

163. According to Dr. Hammond, how can a person stay happy?
(A) By being more physically active
(B) By having a stable job
(C) By being independent
(D) By setting reasonable goals

Questions 164-165 refer to the following flyer.

Don't let another year go by!

Get in shape today at Phoenix Fitness

Come to the Phoenix Fitness gym and see all of our improvements for yourself! Visit us on Ballard Street in Elmwood, between Pita Wraps and Gilbert's Cycles to see our enlarged exercise facilities and newly renovated locker rooms and lobby! To celebrate the completion of renovations, present this flyer to get a 50 percent discount on a one-year membership! In addition, all new members get a trial session with one of our professional trainers.

This promotion is valid until February 15 at the Elmwood branch exclusively.

Phoenix Fitness
18 Ballard Street, Elmwood
Tel. 555-3243

164. What is suggested about Phoenix Fitness?
(A) It sells athletic equipment.
(B) It plans to renovate its lobby.
(C) It has several locations.
(D) It is looking to hire trainers.

165. What will NOT be offered to customers?
(A) A 12 month membership
(B) Discounts on bicycles
(C) A free training session
(D) Usage of a locker room facility

GO ON TO THE NEXT PAGE

Questions 166-168 refer to the following memo.

TO: Taxi Drivers
FROM: Mike Holt, Transpoway Chief Operator
SUBJECT: Some Things to Keep in Mind

It has come to my attention that many passengers have complained about the rude behavior of some Transpoway taxi drivers. Please remember that many of our passengers are tourists, and transportation is a significant part of their experience. As such, it is our duty to give them the utmost respect and our best service. Here are some basic guidelines on treating passengers properly.

(A) Be polite. Always smile and let passengers feel that you are happy to serve them. Don't forget to say "please" and "thank you" whenever necessary.

(B) Be honest. If passengers do not know how to get to a destination, take the fastest route. Do not take advantage of passengers by taking long routes to keep your meter running.

(C) Do not be choosy about passengers. Many people have said Transpoway drivers refused to take them to locations outside the city. Except for security reasons, no driver is allowed to reject passengers.

These are simple points that, if remembered and put into action, will allow us to win back the loyalty of our clients. Please note that the company will continue to solicit comments and suggestions from passengers through its hotline.

166. What is the memo mainly about?
(A) Traffic regulations
(B) Customer relations guidelines
(C) License renewal
(D) Revised company policies

167. What did Mr. Holt mention about the passengers?
(A) They are particular about taxis.
(B) They often lose their valuables.
(C) Some feel that the rates are too expensive.
(D) Some have complained about drivers.

168. What are drivers expected to do?
(A) Find alternative routes
(B) Give directions to tourists
(C) Practice defensive driving
(D) Treat passengers with respect

Questions 169-172 refer to the following brochure.

Nashville Eagles Bowling League
"We Produce Champions!"

We are Southern Tennessee's oldest surviving bowling club, with hundreds of members from every age group and skill level.

Club meetings are held every Thursday, from 4 P.M. to 6 P.M., at Global Bowl in downtown Nashville.

League Tournaments Wednesdays and Saturdays
Open Tournaments Second and third Sunday of the month
Juniors Saturday mornings only
Seniors Tuesday and Friday afternoons

The Nashville Eagles thanks its sponsor, Global Bowl: Supporting Fair Play and Family Fun for All!

Global Bowl is located at
98 Hamlet Avenue, Nashville, TN
Tel. 555-2382

Lane Hours

Monday to Thursday	10 A.M. to 10 P.M.
Friday	10 A.M. to 12 A.M.
Saturday	8 A.M. to 2 A.M.
Sunday	9 A.M. to 7 P.M.

(Closed every other Wednesday)

Office Hours
Weekdays
10 A.M. to 4 P.M.

Extensions
104 Lane Reservations
105 Brownie's Café
106 League Administrator
107 League Updates

Teams may register for league play by calling or visiting the administrator anytime during office hours.

Global Bowl is wheelchair-friendly.
No pets allowed!

169. Where would this brochure most likely be found?
(A) At a recreational facility
(B) At a community library
(C) At a sports arena
(D) At a university clubhouse

170. Which number should people dial to arrange for league play?
(A) 104
(B) 105
(C) 106
(D) 107

171. What is stated about Global Bowl?
(A) It doesn't operate after midnight.
(B) It is the venue for a national competition.
(C) Pets are allowed inside the premises.
(D) Lanes are closed on some Wednesdays.

172. What is NOT indicated about the bowling league?
(A) It holds weekly meetings.
(B) Children can play for free on weekends.
(C) It is sponsored by Global Bowl.
(D) Regular tournaments are held.

GO ON TO THE NEXT PAGE

Questions 173-175 refer to the following announcement.

East Scholastic Institute

East Scholastic Institute is inviting its graduates to the Grand Alumni Homecoming on Saturday, February 4, at 7 P.M., at the Marina Bay Hotel. The event will mark the anniversary of the founding of East Scholastic Institute and the establishment of East Scholastic Foundation.

Reunite with your classmates, friends, and professors while remembering old times. This is also the perfect opportunity to renew your commitment to your alma mater. Support the plan to increase the institute's annual scholarship grants. East Scholastic Foundation will be sponsoring the education of at least 15 students every year through the help of the alumni association and other benefactors.

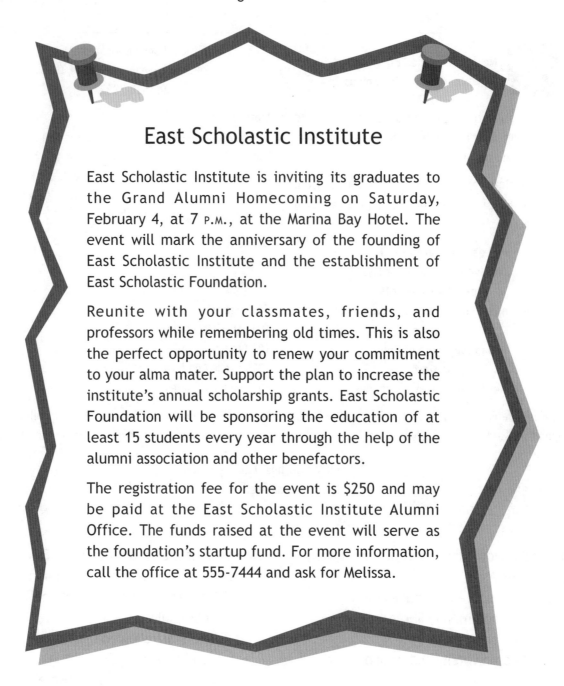

The registration fee for the event is $250 and may be paid at the East Scholastic Institute Alumni Office. The funds raised at the event will serve as the foundation's startup fund. For more information, call the office at 555-7444 and ask for Melissa.

173. For whom is the announcement intended?
(A) Faculty members
(B) Former students
(C) Administrative employees
(D) Previous donors

174. What is the goal of the foundation?
(A) To award scholarships
(B) To train professors
(C) To keep alumni connected
(D) To fund the institute's operations

175. How can readers register for the event?
(A) By sending a check payment
(B) By contacting the alumni office
(C) By coming by the institute
(D) By writing to Melissa

Questions 176-180 refer to the following letter.

Antoinette Ricks, Manager, Fiesta Catering
78 Park Avenue, Detroit, MI 48206

Dear Ms. Ricks,

I am sending this letter to contest the billing charges for the catering service you provided for Zaider Corporation last Saturday night. During the occasion, my staff noticed that the buffet menu differed from the one included in the package we had selected. In particular, the entrées were dishes included in Package B and not Package A, which is the more expensive menu. In spite of the error, your staff charged us the full price for Package A.

In addition, my guests were served only one round of soft drinks, even though our contract states that drinks would be unlimited at no extra charge. If my memory serves me right, you even told me that the upgrade was complimentary for regular clients, such as Zaider Corporation. I mentioned this to your head waiter, but he indicated that he was not told to provide bottomless drinks. As a result, the additional soft drinks consumed that night were charged to my running total.

I am seriously disappointed with what happened. I request that you personally look into the matter, as I will not submit my payment until the excess costs of the entrées and extra charges for the drinks have been deducted from the total. A copy of our contract is enclosed for your reference.

I look forward to your immediate action on the matter.

Katherine Bailey, Sales Manager, Zaider Corporation

176. What does Ms. Bailey say about the services she was provided?
(A) The charges are excessive.
(B) The food selection was limited.
(C) The catering staff was rude.
(D) The guests were served late.

177. What is indicated about Zaider Corporation?
(A) It violated the terms of its contract.
(B) It will hold its next event at a restaurant.
(C) It has hired Fiesta Catering before.
(D) It chose few main courses for the party.

178. According to Ms. Bailey, what did Ms. Ricks mention about the drinks?
(A) They would be served in small quantities.
(B) They are not included in the package.
(C) They are limited to juices and other non-alcoholic beverages.
(D) They would be available throughout the event at no extra cost.

179. Why did the waiter refuse to recognize the agreement between Ms. Ricks and Ms. Bailey?
(A) The catering service does not normally serve complimentary drinks.
(B) He was not given specific instructions to do so.
(C) He failed to contact Ms. Ricks and verify the contract.
(D) There was an inadequate supply of beverages.

180. What does Ms. Bailey plan to do?
(A) Meet Ms. Ricks
(B) Withhold payment
(C) Demand an apology
(D) Submit a legal complaint

GO ON TO THE NEXT PAGE

Questions 181-185 refer to the following article and e-mail.

Cuelebre Business Journal Page 12

PERCHTA APPOINTS NEW CHIEF OPERATING OFFICER

VIENNA, February 4 - Perchta Incorporated, one of Austria's largest department store chains, recently named former vice president for operations Leonie Gruber as its new chief operating officer. Ms. Gruber replaced Johann Müller, who retired on January 28 after 35 years of service to the company.

In her new post, Ms. Gruber will be responsible for all of Perchta's day-to-day sales, marketing, and service operations. She will also play a key role in developing strategic retailer-supplier relationships, which will ensure Perchta's flexibility in the constantly changing marketplace.

Ms. Gruber has more than 20 years of experience in operations management and strategic communications. Since she joined Perchta as a marketing supervisor 12 years ago, she has been instrumental in securing the company's position as an industry leader.

"I believe Perchta has the potential to become one of Europe's premier retail chains." Ms. Gruber said during a telephone interview. "As we open our first overseas branch in Argentina in June, I look forward to contributing to our company's continued success."

Reported by Franz Heideck

To: Franz Heideck <heideck@cuelebrebizjourn.at>
From: Esther Schwarz <esther158@bibelotphotography.at>
Date: February 5
Subject: Leonie Gruber article

Hi Franz,

As you know, I've been organizing a portrait photo exhibit of some of the country's most successful business executives. I read your article yesterday about Leonie Gruber's recent promotion at Perchta Incorporated, and I was wondering if you could give me her phone number and e-mail address. I'm interested in featuring her as a subject in my exhibit, which will be launched in the same month that Perchta's Argentine branch opens.

Thanks, and I hope you can accommodate my request.

Esther Schwarz

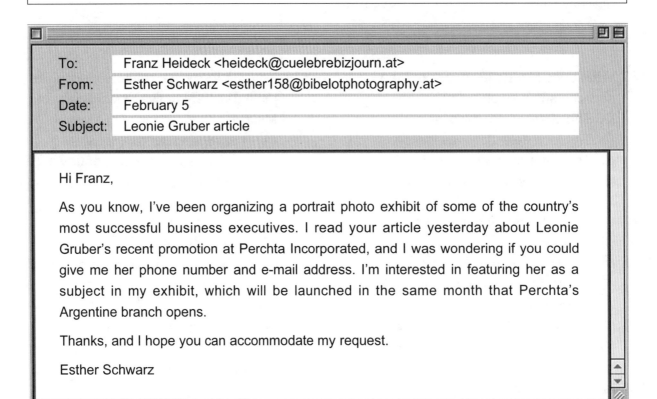

181. What is suggested about Mr. Heideck?
(A) He works for a daily newspaper.
(B) He interviewed Ms. Gruber for an article.
(C) He has met Ms. Schwarz before.
(D) He is unable to provide some contact information.

182. What is mentioned about Perchta Incorporated?
(A) It plans to open a new store abroad.
(B) It is renovating its headquarters.
(C) It will offer more product lines in all its stores.
(D) It has temporarily stopped hiring new personnel.

183. What is stated about Ms. Gruber?
(A) She organized a retirement party for Mr. Müller.
(B) She will be stationed at a branch in Argentina.
(C) She first held a marketing position at Perchta.
(D) She has agreed to meet with Ms. Schwarz.

184. When will Ms. Schwarz launch her photo exhibit?
(A) In January
(B) In February
(C) In May
(D) In June

185. What does Ms. Schwarz request from Mr. Heideck?
(A) Perchta's mailing address
(B) Ms. Gruber's contact information
(C) A copy of his article
(D) Details on the Argentine branch

GO ON TO THE NEXT PAGE

Questions 186-190 refer to the following itinerary and e-mail.

PRAHA EXPRESS

Your No. 1 Express Train Across Czech Republic!

Customer Name: Jakob Ginsberg
Reservation No.: 20385446
Type of Ticket: Round-trip
Date of Booking: July 21

ITINERARY (as of July 31)						
Train No.	Departure			Arrival		
	Station	Date	Time	Station	Date	Time
JW8121	Prague	August 16	5:50 A.M.	Ekaterinburg	August 17	8:10 A.M.
Stopover Time: 1 hour						
JW0993	Ekaterinburg	August 17	9:10 A.M.	Kiev	August 17	7:40 P.M.
JW1476	Kiev	August 23	4:30 P.M.	Ekaterinburg	August 24	3:00 A.M.
Stopover Time: 1 hour						
JW5074	Ekaterinburg	August 24	4:00 A.M.	Prague	August 25	6:20 A.M.

Please present a copy of this document to the ticketing desk at the station. Customers are advised to check in at least 40 minutes prior to their scheduled departure. Should you wish to make a change to your itinerary, please contact our customer service department no later than 10 days before your departure date. A fee of €45 must be paid for changes or cancellations.

Starting September 1, Praha Express' free luggage allowance for each passenger will change from three to two bags. A flat rate of €25 per bag will be applied to any additional luggage.

To: Jakob Ginsberg <jakobg@checkmail.com>
From: Barbora Kodetova <b.kodetova@prahaex.cz>
Date: August 3
Subject: Itinerary Update

Dear Mr. Ginsberg,

We would like to let you know that your train to Kiev will arrive at its destination an hour early on August 17. This is because there will no longer be a stopover at the Ekaterinburg station contrary to what was shown in your original itinerary. So, the train departing from Prague will travel nonstop to Kiev. The schedule for your return trip to Prague, on the other hand, will remain the same.

Please respond to this e-mail to confirm receipt of this information. Once we hear back from you, we will send you another e-mail with your finalized itinerary. Thanks for your cooperation.

Barbora Kodetova
Customer Service
Praha Express

186. What is NOT indicated about the itinerary?
(A) It must be shown to an agent when checking in.
(B) It contains details for a two-way journey.
(C) It includes an overnight stopover.
(D) It may be changed up to ten days before departure.

187. What is indicated about Praha Express?
(A) It allows passengers to make changes for free.
(B) It will reduce its free luggage allowance.
(C) It plans to expand its list of destinations.
(D) It sells tickets on a Web site.

188. Why did Ms. Kodetova write to Mr. Ginsberg?
(A) To recommend a travel agency
(B) To verify his flight information
(C) To inform him of a modification
(D) To notify him of new ticket prices

189. When will Mr. Ginsberg arrive in Kiev?
(A) At 4:30 P.M.
(B) At 6:40 P.M.
(C) At 7:40 P.M.
(D) At 8:10 P.M.

190. What will Mr. Ginsberg most likely do?
(A) Make a phone call
(B) Contact the Kiev station
(C) Post an office notice
(D) Reply to an e-mail

GO ON TO THE NEXT PAGE

Questions 191-195 refer to the following e-mails.

To: evan.bearden@avesmail.com
From: sales@raptorconstructionsupplies.com
Date: August 8
Subject: Purchase Confirmation No. 10039

Dear Mr. Bearden,

Thank you for using Raptor Construction Supplies' online order form. Below is the list of items you ordered on August 7.

PRODUCT NO.	DETAILS	UNIT PRICE	QTY.	AMOUNT
CT6311	Condor all-weather clay tile	$3.10/sq. ft.	2,000	$6,200.00
BG4570	Falcon black utility pipe (16")	$54.75/piece	4	$219.00
RN1907	Eagle stainless steel roofing nails (5-lb box)	$35.49/box	5	$177.45
GM7496	Vulture extra-strength stain remover	$73.99/gallon	2	$147.98
SP3884	Osprey aluminum siding attachments (box of 8)	$6.82/box	10	$68.20
		Sub-total		$6,812.63
		Tax		$681.26
		Shipping and Handling		$340.63
		TOTAL		**$7,834.52**

Based on our records, you paid 30 percent of the total amount with your credit card. Please be reminded that your outstanding balance must be paid in full before we can ship your order. Deliveries will arrive 3 to 5 days after payment has been received. In addition to credit cards, other acceptable payment methods are cash, check, money order, and bank transfer.

Please do not hesitate to call our customer service hotline if you have any questions or concerns. Once again, thank you for your purchase.

To: sales@raptorconstructionsupplies.com
From: evan.bearden@avesmail.com
Date: August 9
Subject: Re: Purchase Confirmation No. 10039

Thank you for sending me the purchase confirmation. All the details are accurate, but I would like to request three more boxes of product number RN1907. In addition, I want to inquire whether your shipment of the Hawk fiber cement siding cutters has already arrived. The cutters were sold out on the day I made the order online for the other items, so I called your customer service department and was informed that the shipment was scheduled for today. If it has been received, please include two of the cutters in my order and send me a revised invoice. That way, I can pay the balance by bank transfer as soon as possible.

Evan Bearden

191. Why was the first e-mail written?
(A) To provide feedback on a report
(B) To verify changes to an account
(C) To confirm an online purchase
(D) To give service recommendations

192. What is indicated about Raptor Construction Supplies?
(A) It manufactures its own products.
(B) It charges extra for shipping fees.
(C) It has several branches around the state.
(D) It provides discounts for large orders.

193. In the first e-mail, the word "outstanding" in paragraph 2, line 2 is closest in meaning to
(A) unpaid
(B) incredible
(C) complete
(D) separated

194. Which item does Mr. Bearden want to increase the quantity of?
(A) Clay tiles
(B) Aluminum siding
(C) Roofing nails
(D) Utility pipe

195. What is suggested about Mr. Bearden?
(A) He wants the items delivered at an earlier time.
(B) He was unable to buy some items on August 7.
(C) He is asking for a discount on his total purchase.
(D) He paid the full amount by credit card.

GO ON TO THE NEXT PAGE

Questions 196-200 refer to the following advertisement and e-mail.

Explore the Scottish Highlands with Baketbah Travel and Tours!

If you're looking for a fun and educational tour of Scotland for your history students, Baketbah has just the right tour package for your class! Our affordable three-day, two-night Highland Tour Package is ideal for a group of 30 travelers.* The package includes hotel accommodations with breakfast and lunch buffets. On board our spacious minivans, our expert local guides will engage you and your students with their animated storytelling as you go along each point of your itinerary.

For price quotes and other inquiries, please e-mail Audrey Boggs at aboggs@baketbah.com.

*Discount rates available for groups of 30 or more

To: Erwin McGhee <ermc@emailing.com>
From: Audrey Boggs <aboggs@baketbah.com>
Date: February 8
Subject: Highland Package

Dear Mr. McGhee,

Thanks for contacting us about our Highland Tour Package. The regular rate per person is £290, but because of our special group rate, you will only have to pay £220 per person. In addition, if you pay on or before February 20, your class will be entitled to a further 10 percent discount as part of our ongoing promotion.

Regarding your question about the payment methods, we cannot accept bank transfer transactions at the moment. I am sorry for the inconvenience. However, you can still pay by cash, check, or money order. You also asked whether or not we can arrange for round-trip flights to Scotland for your group. For that, you can directly call our booking agent, Gladys Kessler, at 555-4144. Ms. Kessler will be more than happy to contact our affiliate airline companies on your behalf and reserve tickets for you.

I have attached the itinerary of the Highland Tour Package and some pictures of the local scenery. If there is anything else I can help you with, please do not hesitate to contact me. Once again, thank you for your business and we look forward to serving you again in the future.

Yours truly,

Audrey Boggs
Customer service manager
Baketbah Travel and Tours

196. Where would the advertisement most likely be found?
(A) In a hotel brochure
(B) In a teachers journal
(C) In a business publication
(D) In an airline magazine

197. What is NOT included in the Highland Tour Package?
(A) Food
(B) Lodgings
(C) Tourist guidebooks
(D) Ground transportation

198. What is suggested about Mr. McGhee?
(A) He teaches a geography class in secondary school.
(B) He has been to Scotland more than once.
(C) He has experience doing business with Ms. Boggs.
(D) He wanted to pay through bank transfer.

199. What is indicated about the students in Mr. McGhee's class?
(A) They are studying in Scotland.
(B) They cannot pay the fees by February 20.
(C) They total more than 30 in number.
(D) They want to reschedule the tour to an earlier date.

200. What will Mr. McGhee probably request Ms. Kessler to do?
(A) Make changes in an itinerary
(B) Take photographs of the tour
(C) Deliver a message to a colleague
(D) Book plane tickets to Scotland

This is the end of the test. You may review Part 5, 6, and 7 if you finish the test early.

解答 p.286 / 分數換算表 p.289 / 題目解析 p.119（解答本）

請翻到次頁「自我檢測表」檢視自己解答問題的方法與態度。

自我檢測表

TEST 03 順利的完成了嗎？

現在要開始透過以下的自我檢測表檢視自己在考試中的表現了嗎？

我的目標分數為：　　　　　　這次測試的成績為：

1. 70 分鐘內，我完全集中精神在測試內容上。

   □是　□不是

   如果回答不是，理由是什麼呢？

2. 70 分鐘內，連答案卷的劃記都完成了。

   □是　□不是

   如果回答不是，理由是什麼呢？

3. 70 分鐘內，100 題都解完了。

   □是　□不是

   如果回答不是，理由是什麼呢？

4. Part 5 和 Part 6 在 25 分鐘以內全都寫完了。

   □是　□不是

   如果回答不是，理由是什麼呢？

5. 寫 Part 7 的時候，沒有一題花超過五分鐘。

   □是　□不是

   如果回答不是，理由是什麼呢？

6. 請寫下你需要改善的地方以及給自己的忠告。

*回到本書第二頁，確認自己的目標分數並加強對於達成分數的意志。
對於要改善的部分一定要在下一次測試中實踐。這點是最重要的，也要這樣才能有進步。

TEST 04

Part 5

Part 6

Part 7

自我檢測表

等等！考前確認事項：

1. 關掉行動裝置電源了嗎？□ 是
2. 答案卷（Answer Sheet）、鉛筆、橡皮擦都準備好了嗎？□ 是
3. 手錶帶了嗎？□ 是

如果都準備齊全了，想想目標分數後即可開始作答。

考試結束時間為現在開始 70 分鐘後的______點______分。

Reading Test

In this section, you must demonstrate your ability to read and comprehend English. You will be given a variety of texts and asked to answer questions about these texts. This section is divided into three parts and will take 75 minutes to complete.

Do not mark the answers in your test book. Use the answer sheet that is separately provided.

PART 5

Directions: In each question, you will be asked to review a statement that is missing a word or phrase. Four answer choices will be provided for each question. Select the best answer and mark the corresponding letter (A), (B), (C), or (D) on the answer sheet.

101. To indicate that Mr. Drake had been refunded for the broken items, the invoice was ------- by the accountant.
(A) modifies (B) modified
(C) modifying (D) modificatory

102. Ms. Lee saw the delivery person ------- through the window, and went to the front doors.
(A) arrived (B) arriving
(C) has arrived (D) to arrive

103. The tourists were very ------- to learn that the Palm Hotel was as beautiful in real life as it was in the advertisement.
(A) pleases (B) pleasing
(C) pleased (D) pleasingly

104. A chemist from the Science Bureau was given extra funding for ------- study on herbal medicines and its effects on blood pressure.
(A) she
(B) herself
(C) hers
(D) her

105. Spec Glass ------- with Iron Spark and is now able to sell glass windows in both local and international markets.
(A) will merge (B) merging
(C) has merged (D) to merge

106. Kerb Holdings is ------- conducting negotiations with some private investors regarding the company's expansion plans in Asia.
(A) currently (B) hardly
(C) anyhow (D) far

107. The Vernon Medical Center administration is considering adjusting the ------- it charges for laboratory tests and outpatient treatments.
(A) amounts (B) duties
(C) taxes (D) damages

108. Since its establishment 10 years ago, Klapius Foundation has been ------- college scholarships to deserving students.
(A) moving (B) deciding
(C) providing (D) asking

109. The marketing team had to ------- study all the information gathered during the recently conducted consumer surveys.
(A) comprehend
(B) comprehensively
(C) comprehension
(D) comprehending

110. Louise Simms wants workshop participants to be in the art room ------- she begins her lecture so as to avoid any interruptions.
(A) before (B) off
(C) except (D) on

111. Building administrators must carry out ------- maintenance checks on electrical wiring to reduce the risk of fire.
(A) contrary
(B) routine
(C) absent
(D) former

112. Peter Delara said that he would like ------- a different venue for the annual stockholders meeting scheduled for next month.
(A) suggests
(B) suggested
(C) to suggest
(D) is suggested

113. Keeping with its expansion plans, United Oil established a new fuel processing plant ------- Indonesia early this year.
(A) in (B) over
(C) by (D) out

114. The plant species that Dr. Kinghorn discovered in Puerto Rico proved to be ------- to his medical research.
(A) joint
(B) useful
(C) precise
(D) competent

115. The increasing demand for Rubber Barter's merchandise enabled the company to grow faster than ------- projected.
(A) finally
(B) accidentally
(C) previously
(D) physically

116. Gastown Corporation will give discounts on ------- automobile parts at the trade show this week.
(A) much
(B) little
(C) all
(D) every

117. The editorial board of *Business and Industry* magazine apologized for a factual error in last month's cover story in an ------- released to the press.
(A) announce
(B) announcing
(C) announces
(D) announcement

118. Please be reminded that the finance department only ------- expense reports that have been signed by an immediate supervisor.
(A) obtains
(B) accepts
(C) limits
(D) sponsors

119. To ensure that its customers' complaints are processed -------, Haula Shipping upgraded its Web site to include an online feedback form.
(A) directly
(B) directed
(C) directing
(D) directness

GO ON TO THE NEXT PAGE

120. It takes only five minutes for vehicles to pass _______ the tunnel that was built on the highway leading to the country's largest province.
(A) over
(B) onto
(C) down
(D) through

121. For exceptionally difficult cases, Mr. Hallis makes it a habit to _______ his associates in the firm to make certain he takes the correct approach.
(A) appeal
(B) consult
(C) support
(D) assure

122. _______ poor weather conditions resulting from a coming hurricane, all Cailleach Airway flights have been postponed until further notice.
(A) Regardless of
(B) But that
(C) As though
(D) Because of

123. The _______ of the surveys on laundry soaps reveal that Jobert is still the most popular brand on the market.
(A) impacts
(B) methods
(C) results
(D) effects

124. For your convenience, a list of authorized repair centers in all major cities is _______ on Cornelius Appliances' Web site.
(A) capable
(B) suitable
(C) possible
(D) available

125. A tour of showroom houses _______ at Sunrise Court, the newest residential property in the state.
(A) is holding
(B) held
(C) is being held
(D) holds

126. At the psychology forum, Dr. Dukes explained what can lead to _______ in a child's speech and language development.
(A) reversely
(B) reversed
(C) reversals
(D) reversible

127. Software manufacturers expressed concerns about the _______ development of a current programming language that developers consider very complicated.
(A) puzzled
(B) ongoing
(C) rotating
(D) silenced

128. Not once did the supervisor _______ during the staff dispute, hoping the employees involved would find a solution for themselves.
(A) intervene
(B) to intervene
(C) intervening
(D) intervened

129. A _______ of the local government in the region is providing residents with efficient, speedy, and adequate public transportation.
(A) magnitude
(B) contract
(C) profession
(D) responsibility

130. After the leadership training, the organizing committee will meet ------- to discuss the event.
(A) lately
(B) oppositely
(C) reliably
(D) briefly

131. As he was not aware that the shirt was on sale, the cashier ------- charged Ms. Adams the full cost of the item.
(A) wronged
(B) wronging
(C) wrongs
(D) wrongly

132. The attorneys of Lawfield Associates are adept at ------- professional lectures for lawyers and state prosecutors.
(A) organizing
(B) organized
(C) organizes
(D) organizations

133. Award-winning director Marion Poole's new film drew ------- acclaim from viewers who attended the special screening.
(A) inventive
(B) enthusiastic
(C) purposeful
(D) anxious

134. The feasibility research ------- that the corner lot on Siam Avenue is a strategic location for the supermarket.
(A) centers
(B) changes
(C) indicates
(D) measures

135. The Habana General Hospital is in need of doctors willing to deliver healthcare ------- to the residents of rural communities.
(A) services (B) worries
(C) prospects (D) collections

136. The city council requires blueprints of the old buildings so that the original designs can be ------- before the owners begin restoration work.
(A) monitored
(B) summarized
(C) preserved
(D) resisted

137. Mr. Stevens ordered full-color brochures ------- the black-and-white ones he previously handed out at the trade fair.
(A) instead of
(B) even if
(C) as of
(D) owing to

138. Management has decided to shut down the factory in Pennsylvania on account of ------- malfunctioning equipment, which raised the company's overhead expenses last quarter.
(A) its (B) his
(C) any (D) whose

139. Had the publishing firm sent the manuscript to the printer earlier, the advertising team ------- to issue an announcement on a change of date in the book's release.
(A) did not need
(B) could not have needed
(C) would not have needed
(D) is not needing

140. It was declared that Carla Meyers would temporarily take over as Pennington Bank's chief financial officer after Joshua Greenberg ------- submitted his resignation.
(A) reasonably
(B) primarily
(C) impossibly
(D) unexpectedly

GO ON TO THE NEXT PAGE

PART 6

Directions: In this part, you will be asked to read an English text. Some sentences are incomplete. Select the word or phrase that correctly completes each sentence and mark the corresponding letter (A), (B), (C), or (D) on the answer sheet.

Questions 141-143 refer to the following letter.

Dear Editor,

I read an editorial regarding the influx of foreign language schools in the country. I could not have agreed more when you mentioned that most of them are highly business-driven and offer poor-quality courses. -------, I beg to differ with your comments on the quality of

141. (A) With this in mind
(B) However
(C) Therefore
(D) As such

education given by Lingua Universal.

I took an advanced Spanish course at the school. I can say that its instructors are experts in teaching foreign languages to nonnative speakers, providing clear translations, and directly ------- to inquiries about grammar and word usage. After studying at Lingua

142. (A) discussing
(B) rejecting
(C) transporting
(D) responding

Universal, I was able to acquire a full-time job as an interpreter in a Spanish-owned corporation.

Because of this experience, I would have no reservations about endorsing Lingua Universal for professionals who seek career ------- in the field of foreign languages.

143. (A) search
(B) extension
(C) aspiration
(D) growth

Thank you for taking the time to read my letter.

Best regards,

Janice Ong

Questions 144-146 refer to the following letter.

Carmen Francisco
President
Francisco Skin and Body Clinic

Dear Dr. Francisco,

I am writing in response to your proposal to ------- me as an associate at your clinic.

144. (A) promote
(B) interview
(C) petition
(D) employ

I looked through the details of your offer and found it very interesting, but ------- a

145. (A) after
(B) into
(C) although
(D) while

thorough reflection on the advantages and disadvantages of accepting the position, I have decided to pass up the opportunity. Accepting the job would require my family and me to move to Manhattan. It is the middle of the school year now, and my children would definitely have a hard time adjusting to a new school if we were -------.

146. (A) relocating
(B) to relocate
(C) relocate
(D) relocation

I am optimistic that we will find the chance to collaborate in the future. Thank you for considering me for the position.

Sincerely,

Greta Castro

GO ON TO THE NEXT PAGE

Questions 147-149 refer to the following e-mail.

From: Tristan Beach <t_beach@breadcrumbs.com>
To: Brian Craft <b.craft@jetway.com>
Subject: Bread and cupcake orders
Date: April 1

Dear Mr. Craft,

We have received the follow-up letter about your orders for next week. I sent an e-mail to our main branch to inform them about the _______ you made. They will supply you with all

147. (A) policies
(B) requests
(C) improvements
(D) presentations

the baked items you require for your business. The main branch verified your orders on Sunday and notified us that they _______ them on Monday morning.

148. (A) delivered
(B) has delivered
(C) will deliver
(D) was delivering

We are confident _______ your customers will be more than satisfied once they sample our

149. (A) what
(B) which
(C) them
(D) that

products.

We look forward to continuing to serve you.

Sincerely,

Tristan Beach

Questions 150-152 refer to the following notice.

NOTICE TO VALUEMART SHOPPERS

Valuemart management would like to announce that the city has ------- a request to

150. (A) denied
(B) submitted
(C) encouraged
(D) approved

convert the empty lot adjacent to the store into a parking space.

The lot has to be paved and fenced off and undergo other light construction. However, this has already been arranged and work ------- to commence very soon.

151. (A) expects
(B) is expecting
(C) is expected
(D) expectancy

The parking lot should be usable before the end of the month. During this time, we ask that customers avoid parking in front of the lot in order to allow the passage of construction personnel and equipment. -------, additional spaces are available at a

152. (A) Instead
(B) Nonetheless
(C) In short
(D) Provided that

parking facility on Boer Road, one block west of the store.

Please bear with us as we work toward making your Valuemart shopping experience a more convenient and enjoyable one. Thank you.

Petra Magno
Branch Manager
Valuemart Retail

GO ON TO THE NEXT PAGE

PART 7

Directions: In this part, you will be asked to read several texts, such as advertisements, articles or examples of business correspondence. Each text is followed by several questions. Select the best answer and mark the corresponding letter (A), (B), (C), or (D) on your answer sheet.

Questions 153-154 refer to the following notice.

Jones Gas Company

Account Name	Christy Winston	Date	July 1
Account Number	000521-141-011	Amount Overdue	$156.25
Service Address	5555 West 6th Street, Los Angeles, CA 90036	Final Payment Date	July 31

Notice of Disconnection

Our records show that as of July 1, your account has exceeded the credit limit. To avoid service disconnection, please pay the amount overdue in full at any of our branch offices before July 31.

If it becomes necessary to suspend the service, reactivation will require a fee of $50. However, the standard $70 installation charge applies when a reconnection request is made more than 10 days after the final payment date.

For questions and concerns regarding this notice, please call our customer service hotline at 555-2368. Thank you.

153. What is suggested about Ms. Winston?

(A) She has missed a deadline for a payment.

(B) She made a service deactivation request.

(C) She charged an installation fee to her credit card.

(D) She complained about incorrect account details.

154. What should Ms. Winston do to avoid paying reactivation fee?

(A) Submit a request form to a department

(B) Confirm some of her personal information

(C) Settle an account before the end of the month

(D) Schedule an installation within the next ten days

GO ON TO THE NEXT PAGE

Questions 155-157 refer to the following form.

Cooper Memorial High School

September 10

Dear Families,

As part of our curriculum, we are taking our students on an educational trip to Meadows Farm in Bodmin, Cornwall, on October 15. The purpose of this tour is to expose students to practical activities for science learning and introduce the concept of countryside conservation.

If you wish for your children to attend, please note the following information about the trip:

Date: October 15
Time: 8 A.M. – Departure time from school
7 P.M. – Expected time of arrival from the trip
What to bring: Packed lunch and refreshments
What to wear: Comfortable and casual clothing and athletic shoes

Students are required to be at school at least 30 minutes before departure. To notify the school about your decision, please complete the permission slip below and return it to us no later than September 25. Thank you.

Sincerely,

Russel Hibbard
Year 4 level coordinator

Student's name: Cassandra Fuentes   Date: September 20

__X__ Yes, my child will join the school trip.

____ No, my child will not join the school trip.

Signature of parent or guardian over printed name: *Ronaldo Fuentes*
Ronaldo Fuentes

155. What time should students arrive at school for the trip?
(A) 7:00 A.M.
(B) 7:30 A.M.
(C) 8:00 A.M.
(D) 8:30 A.M.

156. Why did Mr. Fuentes fill out the slip?
(A) To express support for an environmental project
(B) To approve of an institution's dress code policy
(C) To provide formal consent for an activity
(D) To confirm attendance to a parents meeting

157. What is suggested about Cassandra Fuentes?
(A) She will be visiting a farm with her classmates.
(B) She needs to pay extra for an educational tour.
(C) She has to purchase a new set of uniforms soon.
(D) She will be taking a science exam in advance.

Questions 158-159 refer to the following article.

October 25 *The Informant* Page 10

Hotel Giant Halts Jumeirah Project

DUBAI - France's largest hospitality chain, Arnaud Hotels, has decided to postpone the construction of a one-billion-dollar hotel complex in Palm Jumeirah due to recent global economic problems. "The decision was made in an effort to secure the company's funds since the crisis has been adversely affecting Dubai's tourism industry," Arnaud Hotels spokesperson Sebastian Lefebvre said. Tourism in the Arab city has suffered heavy losses after several companies slashed jobs and real estate prices tumbled. Lefebvre said Arnaud Hotels will resume the construction once Dubai's economic condition becomes stable. The spokesman, however, dismissed rumors about the suspension of ongoing renovation projects in London, Rome, and Madrid.

158. What is NOT indicated about Arnaud Hotels?
(A) It experienced great financial losses.
(B) It has branches in several global cities.
(C) It will resume a project in the future.
(D) It is the largest chain in a country.

159. Why did Arnaud Hotels delay the construction plans?
(A) It could not find a suitable location.
(B) It wants to conserve capital.
(C) It is reducing its overseas workforce.
(D) It was unable to get a building permit.

READING TEST 1 2 3 4 5 6 7 8 9 10

GO ON TO THE NEXT PAGE

Questions 160-161 refer to the following e-mail.

From:	Suzanne Gilmore <sgilmore@united-steel.com>
To:	Matthew Nelson <mnelson@beaverton-builders.com>
Date:	January 22
Subject:	Meeting

Dear Mr. Nelson,

I am sorry to inform you that I will not be able to meet with you on Tuesday, January 27. I know that we planned to discuss the materials we will be supplying for your upcoming building project then, but I have mixed up the dates on my calendar. My director asked me to attend a trade fair in New York at the last minute, and my return flight does not arrive until late Tuesday evening. Therefore, I would like to request that we move the date to Wednesday, the 28th instead, at around 1 P.M. Please let me know if this time is OK with you by calling me at 555-3812 anytime during office hours.

Thank you very much.

Sincerely,

Suzanne Gilmore
Sales representative
United Steel Corporation

160. What does Ms. Gilmore want Mr. Nelson to do?
(A) Modify a flight itinerary
(B) Participate in a convention
(C) Delay the start of a project
(D) Reschedule a meeting

161. What is suggested about United Steel?
(A) Its offices are open every day.
(B) It distributes building materials.
(C) Its management will fund a project.
(D) It will merge with another company.

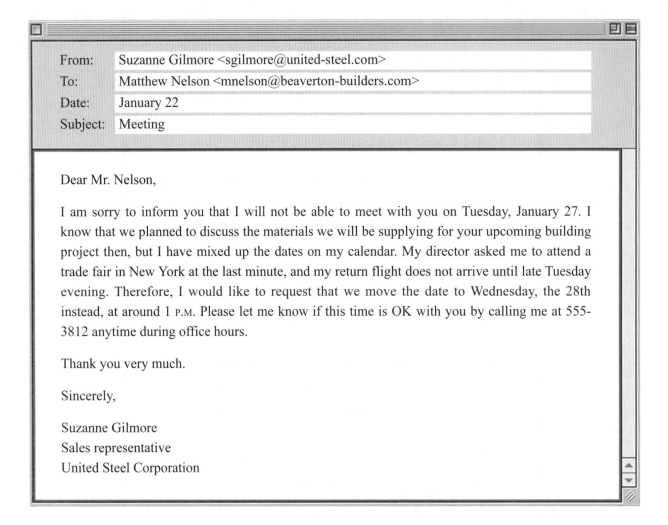

Questions 162-164 refer to the following advertisement.

Pacific Boltmaster

345 Richwell Drive
Daly City, CA 94017
www.pacificboltmaster.com

Have you ever locked yourself outside your house or office and just couldn't figure out what to do? The next time it happens, don't delay and call Pacific Boltmaster!

With 15 years of professional experience in the field, Pacific Boltmaster provides emergency services for residential and commercial clients 24 hours a day, seven days a week. We offer key duplication, broken key removal, provision of master keys, and the installation of knob locks and deadbolt locks, which can also be purchased at our shop.

Locked out of your car? Not a problem! We provide emergency vehicle lockout services as well. Our services are available to customers in the counties of San Mateo, Santa Clara, and San Francisco only. For inquiries or service requests, you may call 555-8080.

162. What is the advertisement mainly about?
(A) A package delivery company
(B) A variety of lock services
(C) A surveillance equipment supplier
(D) A residential security system

163. What is NOT offered by Pacific Boltmaster?
(A) Distribution of door knobs
(B) Consultation over the phone
(C) The replication of different kinds of keys
(D) The shipping of items to multiple locations

164. What is suggested about Pacific Boltmaster?
(A) It responds promptly to customers.
(B) It transferred its headquarters to San Francisco.
(C) It produces a range of surveillance devices.
(D) It has partnered with a vehicle manufacturer.

GO ON TO THE NEXT PAGE

Questions 165-167 refer to the following notice.

NOTICE: Tenants of Rosenmore Place

FIRE DRILL

Monday, August 15,

8 A.M.

In accordance with state laws, Rosenmore Place will hold a fire drill on Monday next week. All tenants are required to participate. The exercise is meant to familiarize residents with the building's alarm system and emergency exit points. It also aims to educate them on how to evacuate the building safely in case of a fire.

A complete set of instructions on the drill has been distributed to all units. Tenants are advised to read the exit procedure thoroughly to avoid accidents during the exercise. It will start with the ringing of the alarm, which will signal everyone to leave the building and proceed to the open parking area. After that, security personnel will inspect all floors to make sure that the building is vacant. Please note that no one will be allowed to return to their units until the alarm has been shut off.

The drill is expected to last for about 15 minutes provided that everyone vacates the building as instructed. Management looks forward to tenants' full cooperation and hopes that this exercise will make them more knowledgeable about fire safety procedures.

165. What is the notice mainly about?
(A) Emergency tips
(B) New apartment units
(C) A procedural change
(D) A safety exercise

166. According to the notice, what should residents do upon hearing the alarm?
(A) Proceed to a designated location
(B) Look for a security guard
(C) Read the drill instructions
(D) Contact the building management

167. What is suggested about Rosenmore Place?
(A) It acquired new equipment.
(B) It has many fire hazards.
(C) It adheres to government policies.
(D) It has hidden exit points.

Questions 168-171 refer to the following e-mail.

From: Brent Watson <bwatson@dixon-solutions.com>
To: Marketing Staff <marketingstaff@dixon-solutions.com>
Date: October 12
Subject: New Office

To all staff members,

You may have observed that the demand for our department's services has increased substantially over the last two quarters. As a result, we have had to double our workforce. Unfortunately, the addition of staff has not produced the expected increase in productivity. After studying the problem, I have found the cause to be a lack of adequate facilities.

I raised the issue with upper management and am happy to announce that during last week's meeting, the board approved a proposal to move our offices to a larger space on the eighth floor of the building. The new office will come with fully equipped workstations for everyone, as well as several rooms for holding meetings and training seminars.

Renovations on the eighth floor are expected to begin at the end of this month and last through November. In the meantime, some of us will begin working out of a temporary office space on the third floor.

I appreciate your understanding. Please let me know if you have any questions.

Sincerely,

Brent Watson
Marketing director

168. What problem does Mr. Watson mention?
(A) Employees do not have a suitable work environment.
(B) The company cannot increase wages as planned.
(C) Customers have been complaining about the staff.
(D) Management is unhappy with the quality of its products.

169. What is suggested about the marketing department?
(A) It has moved to another location.
(B) It plans to hire more staff members.
(C) It is located at the company's headquarters.
(D) It experienced a period of growth.

170. According to Mr. Watson, what happened last week?
(A) A training seminar was held.
(B) An order of furniture arrived.
(C) An organizational meeting took place.
(D) A board member was introduced.

171. What is NOT stated about the proposal?
(A) It was approved only recently.
(B) It will be included in next year's budget.
(C) It contained a provision for new equipment.
(D) It will go into effect at the end of October.

GO ON TO THE NEXT PAGE

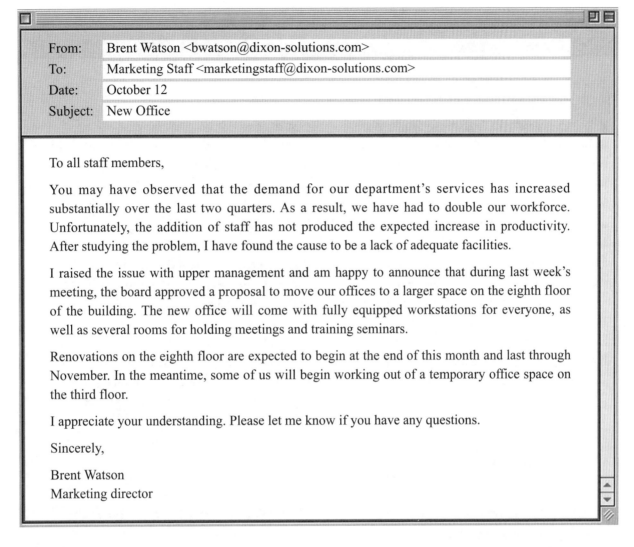

Questions 172-175 refer to the following article.

Business Today

In the spotlight: Heyworth Industries

A known producer of high performance protective equipment, Heyworth Industries ensures the safety of workers in the chemical, healthcare, and automotive industries, as well as other sectors that involve the handling of hazardous materials. Founded 30 years ago in Syracuse, New York, it began by designing and manufacturing a broad array of protective garments such as fireproof clothing, chemical resistant clothing, and limited-use and disposable clothing. Over the years, these products became widely known and used by companies not only within the United States but all over the world. As a result, Heyworth Industries developed from a small local business into a multinational corporation.

To meet rising client demand, Heyworth Industries established its first overseas headquarters in Toronto, Canada. Two years after that, it opened a factory in Guadalajara, Mexico, to increase its production capacity. Last year, another facility began operations in Shanghai, China, which helped in the manufacturing process while at the same time lowering costs. Heyworth Industries also boosted its logistics system by building a warehouse in Birmingham, Alabama. Finally, a shipping and distribution center was opened in Chicago, Illinois, to handle the shipment of products to various locations in the United States.

In addition to the continuous improvement of its facilities, Heyworth Industries has made the placement of orders easier for customers. Orders are now received through its toll-free hotline at 1-800-555-2948, by fax at (315) 555-2950, and through its Web site at www.heyworth.com.

172. Why was the article written?
(A) To highlight the development of a company
(B) To outline the achievements of an individual
(C) To discuss the uses of protective equipment
(D) To introduce a new line of merchandise

173. Where did Heyworth Industries open its first foreign headquarters?
(A) In Shanghai
(B) In Chicago
(C) In Syracuse
(D) In Toronto

174. What is stated about Heyworth Industries?
(A) It will relocate its logistics division to Asia.
(B) It plans to establish more facilities overseas.
(C) It has been operating for three decades.
(D) It needs to improve its sales performance.

175. What is suggested about Heyworth Industries' ordering system?
(A) It presents a selection of different shipping services.
(B) It allows clients to make requests through various methods.
(C) It was designed to help the company save on operational costs.
(D) It requires that all payments be made through a Web site.

Questions 176-180 refer to the following memo.

Delta Technologies

To: Sales department employees
From: Pete Springer, director
Alice Lee, assistant director
Date: February 15
Subject: Wholesale Operations

The board is pleased with the sales department's performance last year. By forming agreements with distributors across the country, Delta Technologies increased retail sales of desktop and laptop computers by 20 percent. This year, the board wants us to intensify wholesale operations by bidding for supply contracts with public and private companies.

In connection with this, we have decided to create a standard procedure for preparing bids:

* **Research your client.** Find out the nature of the client's business to identify its equipment needs.
* **Define the client's bid evaluation criteria.** Read quotation requests thoroughly to learn the client's decision-making process and preferences for selecting equipment.
* **Identify price trends.** To make a competitive offer, learn the standard wholesale packages, discounts, and special services provided by competitors.
* **Create a strategy for product endorsement and pricing.** Once you have identified the client's needs and the most probable offers from competitors, determine the best bid you can give without compromising the transaction's profitability.
* **Prepare a bid presentation.** Create a presentation discussing your offer. Highlight product features and their benefits to the client's operations.

If you have questions or comments regarding the procedure, please contact us.

176. Why was the memo written?
(A) To outline a project plan
(B) To schedule a meeting
(C) To detail an office policy
(D) To explain a set of procedures

177. Why are members of the board pleased?
(A) Production rates rose.
(B) Brand awareness improved.
(C) Sales levels increased.
(D) New clients have been found.

178. What is mentioned about Delta Technologies?
(A) It has several outlets around the world.
(B) It sells items in large quantities.
(C) It is owned by public investors.
(D) It has elected a new board member.

179. What do employees need to know about prospective clients to prepare bids?
(A) Their shipping and handling preferences
(B) The budget for their advertising campaigns
(C) Their equipment purchasing habits
(D) The status of their current assets

180. What is indicated about Delta Technologies' bidding strategy?
(A) It will guarantee large profits from transactions.
(B) It was designed by a consultant.
(C) It compares prices to those of competitors.
(D) It is primarily for private clients.

GO ON TO THE NEXT PAGE

Questions 181-185 refer to the following memo and e-mail.

Asgardheim Incorporated
Where Your Dreams Reign Supreme
Giallanghorn 89, SE-102 29 Stockholm, Sweden

To: Customer Service team
From: Georgina Lindberg, Customer Service Director
Date: March 15
Subject: New Assignments

Finally, our new offices in Reykjavik, Oslo, and Helsinki will open next month. As our business expands into other European countries for the first time, we expect a significant increase in the number of client inquiries. That is why the management has decided to rearrange our client service system. Starting April 1, the following people will be in charge of addressing all questions and concerns that fall under their respective fields of responsibility:

Britta Ostergard	Membership changes and terminations
David Gronholm	Membership upgrades and renewals
Eva Andersen	Membership suspensions and transfers
Hans Birkeland	General inquiries about Asgardheim insurance plans

We trust that everyone will continue their outstanding performance in the new assignments. If you have any questions, you may contact me directly at extension number 188.

To: cs@asgardheimincorporated.co
From: Astrid Jakobsson <astrid.jakobsson@odinsmail.com>
Date: April 8
Subject: Membership

To whom it may concern,

I moved here from Copenhagen last March 31 and heard from one of my new colleagues that your company provides excellent homeowners' insurance plans. I am currently living in a one-bedroom apartment unit in Helsinki at Freyja Towers, and I would like to have my personal property insured, particularly those items that are not covered by the building association's policy.

I would really appreciate it if you could get back to me with information about your available insurance plans. Thank you for your time.

Astrid Jakobsson

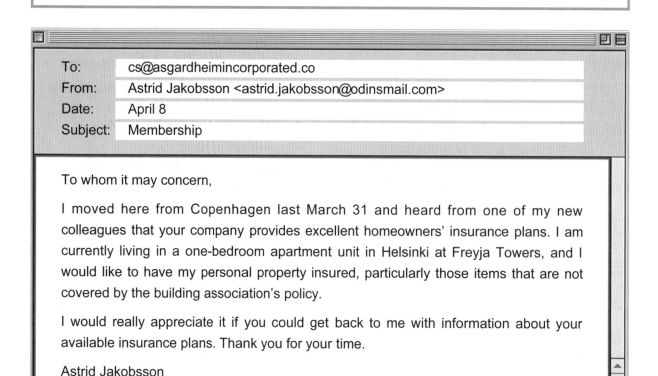

181. What is most likely Asgardheim Incorporated?
(A) A travel agency
(B) A marketing firm
(C) An insurance company
(D) A shipping corporation

182. What is suggested in the memo about Asgardheim Incorporated?
(A) It already has offices in Europe.
(B) It plans to launch a service in April.
(C) It needs to downsize its workforce.
(D) It will reorganize its management structure.

183. In the memo, the word "addressing" in paragraph 1, line 4 is closest in meaning to
(A) revising
(B) forwarding
(C) answering
(D) directing

184. Who will probably attend to Ms. Jakobsson's inquiry?
(A) Britta Ostergard
(B) Hans Birkeland
(C) Eva Andersen
(D) David Gronholm

185. What is mentioned about Ms. Jakobsson?
(A) She was recently offered a promotion.
(B) She will move into an apartment soon.
(C) She wants to cancel a policy.
(D) She previously lived in Copenhagen.

GO ON TO THE NEXT PAGE

Questions 186-190 refer to the following application and e-mail.

City of Paphos
Cyprus

Permit No.: 849410
Date: August 20

SIGN PERMIT REQUEST FORM

Type of Sign: _ Industrial _ Residential
X Temporary (includes promotional materials for events, such as banners, posters, etc.)

Organization / Company Name	:	Victrix Travel Agency
Contact Person	:	Ophelia Persakis
Phone No. / E-mail Address	:	(+35726) 555-2189 / ophie23@victrixtravels.com
Event Title	:	Pygmalion Travel Festival
Event Location	:	Galatea Heritage Park
Event Date(s) / Time(s)	:	September 22 to 25 / 10 A.M. to 10 P.M.
Setup / Cleanup Dates	:	September 21 / September 26

Completed permit applications should be submitted directly to the City Planning and Development Office (CPD). Please note that promotional materials must first be inspected by a CPD official at least three weeks prior to the event. Requests for inspection may be sent to cpd_argyros@paphos.gov. Applicants whose signs do not meet the ordinance requirements will be notified within two working days following the inspection.

To: Basil Argyros <cpd_argyros@paphos.gov>
From: Ophelia Persakis <ophie23@victrixtravels.com>
Date: August 23
Subject: Sign Permit Application

Dear Mr. Argyros,

I am writing on behalf of my company, Victrix Travel Agency, about the sign permit application that we submitted to your office on August 20. We are planning to have a booth at the Pygmalion Travel Festival to promote some of our new package tours. The two banners that we intend to use at the festival have just been delivered to our office from the printer. Could you please dispatch one of your representatives to our agency to inspect the material as soon as possible? I would bring them to your offices myself, but they are too large to transport easily. We need the banners to be approved by the city's deadline on September 1. Please call me directly at the number indicated in our application to let me know when someone will be available. Thank you for your assistance in this matter.

Sincerely,

Ophelia Persakis

186. For whom is the form most likely intended?
(A) Residents wanting a business license
(B) Businesses hoping to host events
(C) People wishing to post signs
(D) Organizations applying for sponsorship

187. What is NOT indicated about the event?
(A) It will begin on September 22.
(B) It will involve tourism and travel.
(C) It will be free to the public.
(D) It will be held in a park.

188. What does Ms. Persakis ask Mr. Argyros to do?
(A) Follow up on a report
(B) Send an inspector
(C) Provide an update on a project
(D) Pick up an event application

189. Who most likely is Mr. Argyros?
(A) A travel agent
(B) A city official
(C) An event organizer
(D) An advertising executive

190. Where are Victrix Travel Agency's banners now?
(A) At a travel agency
(B) At a printing shop
(C) At an event venue
(D) At a city office

GO ON TO THE NEXT PAGE

Questions 191-195 refer to the following advertisement and e-mail.

Volledig Incorporated: For those with a sweet tooth!

Special New Year Offer!

For more than 50 years, Volledig Incorporated has been one of the leading providers of chocolates, caramels, toffees, and other confectionery products in Europe. Whether your company is looking for top quality finished products or ingredients to manufacture your own sweets, Volledig Incorporated has the perfect items to suit your needs. Based in Antwerp, Belgium, our business is built on providing individualized attention to customers and manufacturers alike. Our product diversity and numerous locations make us capable of catering to businesses of all sizes, from small candy stores to large chocolate corporations.

Starting January 1, our new clients can take advantage of a 20 percent discount on their domestic and international shipment totaling a weight of 10 tons or more. Additional information on this offer are available on our Web site at www.vollediginc.com. You can also contact our sales director, Hendrik Bushnell, at henbush@vollediginc.com should you have any questions.

To: Hendrik Bushnell <henbush@vollediginc.com>
From: Liesbeth Weidman <weidlies@zoet.net>
Date: February 8
Subject: Promotional Offer

Dear Mr. Bushnell,

I am the sales manager of Zoet Bonbon Company, a chocolate manufacturer specializing in hand-finished chocolates and other cocoa-based products like chocolate drinks, brownies, and cookies. You can find our products sold in malls and supermarkets in Belgium, France, the UK, and the Netherlands.

We are pleased to say that this year we are expanding our operations into the Asian market, starting in Japan and South Korea. However, we are concerned that our current supplier, Ganesvoort Distributors, does not offer a large enough variety of items. That was why we were pleased to find out that your company has such a huge selection. We also know that you offer a special promotion to new clients. While Zoet Bonbon only requires 9 tons of products for this year, we are hoping that you will provide us a 20 percent discount if we sign a five-year contract. Let me know if this is possible.

I would appreciate it very much if you could provide us with more information about your services. Please contact me directly at (+32) 555-8169 as soon as possible. Thank you.

Liesbeth Weidman

191. What is being advertised?
(A) A manufacturing plant
(B) A department store chain
(C) A shipping service
(D) A product supplier

192. What is NOT indicated about Volledig Incorporated?
(A) It has won many prestigious awards.
(B) It will start a special promotion from the first day of the year.
(C) It deals with overseas orders.
(D) It provides customized service to its clients.

193. What is implied about Zoet Bonbon Company's products?
(A) They will be offered in regional hotels.
(B) They are manufactured in Belgium.
(C) They will be sold in Korea this year.
(D) They are made with imported ingredients.

194. What is suggested about Ganesvoort Distributors?
(A) It is a subsidiary of Zoet Bonbon Company.
(B) It will relocate to an office in Antwerp.
(C) It will stop its business operations next year.
(D) It has a limited selection of products.

195. Why might Zoet Bonbon be ineligible for the special discount?
(A) It will not order enough to qualify.
(B) It cannot sign a long-term contract.
(C) It is not a first-time customer.
(D) It will not ship the items within Europe.

GO ON TO THE NEXT PAGE

Questions 196-200 refer to the following e-mails.

To: Bertram Kiersted <bertkiersted@laufeypoolcleaners.dk>
From: Adriana Handsel <handsel@forsetibandb.dk>
Date: March 16
Subject: Price Inquiry

Dear Mr. Kiersted,

My name is Adriana Handsel and I am the owner of Forseti Bed-and-Breakfast, located at 8261 Jostein Road. Your business was recommended to me by my associate, Damian Jantzen, who runs a small inn close to your office in Roskilde. He vouched for your reasonable prices and competent staff.

I would appreciate it if you could send me a quote for the weekly cleaning of the 50-meter pool at my establishment. Is it possible for the first cleaning to be scheduled next week, specifically on March 25? I would like to personally meet the crew in charge and introduce them to my assistant, who will be overseeing their work in April while I am away on a business trip.

Thank you, and I hope to receive a response soon.

Adriana Handsel

To: Adriana Handsel <handsel@forsetibandb.dk>
From: Bertram Kiersted <bertkiersted@laufeypoolcleaners.dk>
Date: March 17
Subject: Re: Price Inquiry
Attachment: Brochure

Dear Ms. Handsel,

We appreciate your choosing Laufey Pool Cleaners! We have been the leading pool cleaning service provider in the city for more than seven years, thanks to a steadily growing client base and hardworking staff. We pride ourselves on using only the most advanced equipment to ensure that we can provide results of the highest quality. I also encourage you to look through the attached brochure for additional details on our services.

My staff is free on the day you requested. Just let me know what time you want the cleaning done so the crew can prepare ahead of time. Please note that there is a €60 surcharge for establishments that are outside of the city limits, so we will have to charge you for that. The full service cleaning of your pool will cost €170 and will take three to four hours to complete.

Please respond to this e-mail if you find the quote acceptable so I can confirm the schedule. Once again, thank you, and I look forward to doing business with you.

Yours truly,

Bertram Kiersted
Manager
Laufey Pool Cleaners

196. What does Ms. Handsel NOT mention in her e-mail?
(A) The name of her assistant
(B) The location of her business
(C) The size of her swimming pool
(D) The type of establishment she owns

197. What is indicated about Forseti Bed-and-Breakfast?
(A) It is currently undergoing some renovations.
(B) It will come under new management in April.
(C) It is located outside the city limits of Roskilde.
(D) It will hire more personnel to accommodate its expansion plans.

198. In the second e-mail, the word "encourage" in paragraph 1, line 4 is closest in meaning to
(A) support
(B) recommend
(C) assist
(D) relieve

199. What information is included in the attachment?
(A) A list of branch locations
(B) A complete work schedule
(C) Information on pool cleaning services
(D) Fees for home repairs

200. When will Mr. Kiersted's staff most likely clean Ms. Handsel's pool?
(A) On March 16
(B) On March 17
(C) On March 24
(D) On March 25

This is the end of the test. You may review Part 5, 6, and 7 if you finish the test early.

解答 p.286 / 分數換算表 p.289 / 題目解析 p.167（解答本）

▮ 請翻到次頁「自我檢測表」檢視自己解答問題的方法與態度。

自我檢測表

TEST 04 順利的完成了嗎？

現在要開始透過以下的自我檢測表檢視自己在考試中的表現了嗎？

我的目標分數為：　　　　　　　這次測試的成績為：

1. 70 分鐘內，我完全集中精神在測試內容上。

   □是　□不是

   如果回答不是，理由是什麼呢？

2. 70 分鐘內，連答案卷的劃記都完成了。

   □是　□不是

   如果回答不是，理由是什麼呢？

3. 70 分鐘內，100 題都解完了。

   □是　□不是

   如果回答不是，理由是什麼呢？

4. Part 5 和 Part 6 在 25 分鐘以內全都寫完了。

   □是　□不是

   如果回答不是，理由是什麼呢？

5. 寫 Part 7 的時候，沒有一題花超過五分鐘。

   □是　□不是

   如果回答不是，理由是什麼呢？

6. 請寫下你需要改善的地方以及給自己的忠告。

*回到本書第二頁，確認自己的目標分數並加強對於達成分數的意志。
對於要改善的部分一定要在下一次測試中實踐。這點是最重要的，也要這樣才能有進步。

TEST 05

Part 5

Part 6

Part 7

自我檢測表

等等！考前確認事項：

1. 關掉行動裝置電源了嗎？☐ 是
2. 答案卷（Answer Sheet）、鉛筆、橡皮擦都準備好了嗎？☐ 是
3. 手錶帶了嗎？☐ 是

如果都準備齊全了，想想目標分數後即可開始作答。

考試結束時間為現在開始 70 分鐘後的______點______分。

Reading Test

In this section, you must demonstrate your ability to read and comprehend English. You will be given a variety of texts and asked to answer questions about these texts. This section is divided into three parts and will take 75 minutes to complete.

Do not mark the answers in your test book. Use the answer sheet that is separately provided.

PART 5

Directions: In each question, you will be asked to review a statement that is missing a word or phrase. Four answer choices will be provided for each question. Select the best answer and mark the corresponding letter (A), (B), (C), or (D) on the answer sheet.

101. After the members of the volleyball team attended the awards ceremony, all of ------- went to Daphne's Grill to celebrate the victory.
(A) they (B) them
(C) their (D) theirs

102. Coeval Museum of History recently opened a new ------- as part of its summer calendar of events.
(A) exhibitory (B) exhibitor
(C) exhibit (D) exhibited

103. The workers ------- about the modified work schedule, as notices were put up on bulletin boards yesterday.
(A) know
(B) are knowing
(C) will have known
(D) knows

104. A representative called to notify the manager that the office's fire insurance policy ------- on May 30.
(A) expires (B) extracts
(C) transfers (D) leaves

105. The Easy-Update system ------- Heritage cardholders to change their personal information on the company's Web site.
(A) permission (B) permissible
(C) permitting (D) permits

106. Ella Santiago had to overcome a variety of ------- when she decided to open her own travel agency a few years ago.
(A) difficulty (B) difficulties
(C) difficult (D) most difficult

107. Neglecting to clean the filter of the air conditioner regularly will cause the unit to work less -------.
(A) effective (B) effectiveness
(C) effectively (D) effect

108. The well-known saxophone player Thomas Winthrop is currently busy rehearsing for his ------- concert in Guam at the end of the month.
(A) upcoming (B) late
(C) rising (D) replayed

109. Clover Cosmetics decided to modify its advertising campaign ------- suffering a significant decline in sales last year.
(A) next
(B) after
(C) yet
(D) except

110. According to a recent census, suburban residents today have become ------- more diverse in cultural background than they were in the 1960s.
(A) remarkable
(B) remarkably
(C) remarks
(D) remarked

111. Due to some problems with the lease, Mr. Jackson has postponed his ------- move to the new apartment by two weeks.
(A) anticipate
(B) anticipates
(C) anticipated
(D) anticipating

112. With the new contract, the monthly rate of Agate Corporate Tower's office rental space now ------- all utility charges except electricity costs.
(A) reveals
(B) covers
(C) finishes
(D) reaches

113. The company director announced that Coleen Reyes will be overseeing the branch ------- a couple of months while our manager is away on vacation.
(A) to
(B) for
(C) with
(D) along

114. The supervisor wants to know Mr. Brown's e-mail address so that she can inform ------- about changes in work assignments.
(A) he (B) him
(C) himself (D) his

115. With some advance -------, Pamela will surely save a lot of time and money on her trip to Asia in December.
(A) plan
(B) planners
(C) planned
(D) planning

116. Article drafts should ------- be reviewed thoroughly to ensure that they follow the rules in the style manual.
(A) quite
(B) almost
(C) always
(D) hardly

117. Attendants on the train treated all the passengers ------- and made sure they were comfortable during the trip.
(A) courted
(B) courteous
(C) courteously
(D) courting

118. Mr. Mitchell had to ------- his car alarm after it accidentally went off, to avoid disturbing his neighbors.
(A) silent (B) silence
(C) silently (D) silenced

119. One of the highlights of the seminar was Mr. Choi's talk on how to deal with ------- difficult tasks.
(A) firmly
(B) particularly
(C) carefully
(D) quickly

GO ON TO THE NEXT PAGE

120. Provided that the laboratory results arrive on time, Ms. Yap is ------- that she will finish the analysis of the drug sample by Tuesday.

(A) rapid (B) useful
(C) confident (D) evident

121. The submission deadline for financial aid ------- for international students at Ostlere University has been put off until June 28.

(A) methods
(B) contestants
(C) notices
(D) applications

122. Arab Energies ------- to announce its merger with petroleum supplier Kuwait Petrochemical at a joint press conference.

(A) would like
(B) is liking
(C) is liked
(D) was liked

123. It is ------- for all construction workers to wear protective gear when they are at the project site.

(A) mandator
(B) mandate
(C) mandatorily
(D) mandatory

124. Ms. Hilburn will teach the accounting course for new employees ------- the financial manager attends the conference.

(A) in (B) while
(C) due to (D) without

125. Because of all the conventions and special events taking place in the city, not a ------- hotel room is available this weekend.

(A) solitary (B) remote
(C) reserved (D) hidden

126. A Veldspar Phone Service representative can help you determine ------- calling plan is perfect for your budget.

(A) when
(B) whom
(C) which
(D) who

127. In preparation for her new position at the Montreal branch, Ms. Thatcher chose to ------- for an intensive French course to improve her language skills.

(A) register
(B) access
(C) attend
(D) submit

128. One of Maxwell Distributor's ------- as a supplier of raw materials for industrial plants is to deliver needed goods in a timely and efficient manner.

(A) obligatory
(B) obligation
(C) obligations
(D) obligator

129. ------- Dulce Country Club is already fully booked for May, suggestions on a suitable venue for the sports festival are urgently needed.

(A) Because
(B) Whereas
(C) During
(D) Nevertheless

130. The wait staff has gotten used to the rotating shift system designed by the manager, and the executive chef has found that the setup is -------.

(A) reflective
(B) resistant
(C) productive
(D) decreasing

131. Defective ------- should be returned to the store together with the official receipt within seven days from the date of purchase.
(A) option
(B) wholesaler
(C) merchandise
(D) reimbursement

132. Global Patent Association is ------- to supporting the production of vehicles fueled by renewable energy.
(A) dedicate
(B) dedicated
(C) dedicatory
(D) dedication

133. Upon checkout, hotel guests can drop their feedback forms in the brown box located ------- the reception desk.
(A) through
(B) among
(C) beside
(D) into

134. According to a news bulletin, Dido Megatrade Hall was ------- with job seekers during the career fair last weekend.
(A) pack
(B) packs
(C) packed
(D) packing

135. Following lengthy discussions, the board agreed to ------- the workers' dispute by offering them a modest increase in pay.
(A) achieve
(B) implement
(C) resolve
(D) determine

136. Students ------- careers in journalism are recommended to apply for internships at publishing companies for which they would actually want to work.
(A) describing (B) revising
(C) pursuing (D) attracting

137. Like other dining establishments in the city, Shadow Restaurant uses tableware made of recycled material ------- environmental conservation efforts.
(A) to support
(B) as supporting
(C) in support
(D) for the supported

138. Participants at yesterday's meeting were convinced by Benjamin York, who spoke ------- on expanding the range of Bateman Firm's charitable sponsorships.
(A) seemingly
(B) consequently
(C) eloquently
(D) mutually

139. Fionnad Telecom's recently launched broadband service promises to be faster and more ------- compared to those of the company's competitors.
(A) relies
(B) reliable
(C) reliability
(D) relying

140. According to analysts, the steady decline in Oregon's unemployment rate over the last three years is a positive ------- of the state's economic growth.
(A) indicator
(B) collector
(C) regulator
(D) messenger

GO ON TO THE NEXT PAGE

PART 6

Directions: In this part, you will be asked to read an English text. Some sentences are incomplete. Select the word or phrase that correctly completes each sentence and mark the corresponding letter (A), (B), (C), or (D) on the answer sheet.

Questions 141-143 refer to the following notice.

Exodus Manpower Services

Wanted: Cashiers

The Mandarin Sports Club is ------- need of two cashiers for its new restaurant.

141. (A) on
(B) in
(C) within
(D) by

Candidates should have at least a year of experience working in a restaurant, resort, or retail environment.

------- university degrees are not required for this position, priority will be given to

142. (A) Only if
(B) Furthermore
(C) Even though
(D) Whichever

applicants who have some applicable education.

To apply, please e-mail your résumé and references to req@mandarinpersonnel.com on or before May 6. Those who qualify will receive a reply containing the date of their -------

143. (A) entry
(B) cooperation
(C) interview
(D) admission

with the manager of the sports club.

Questions 144-146 refer to the following letter.

November 31

Dear Mr. Terence Collins,

Thank you for choosing to ------- the services of Bali Transport! As you requested, the

144. (A) use
(B) improve
(C) expand
(D) fund

payment for this service has been charged to your credit card. You may drive our Rivelette Beam 512 (plate number: DK 1025) ------- tomorrow, December 1, until Sunday,

145. (A) starts
(B) started
(C) starter
(D) starting

December 7.

Enclosed are your receipt and a copy of the car's registration certificate. Please remember to take these documents and your driver's license with you when driving. In case of mechanical problems, do not hesitate to contact us for assistance.

We hope that ------- one of Bali Transport's vehicles will make your travels more

146. (A) purchasing
(B) renting
(C) testing
(D) personalizing

comfortable.

Respectfully yours,

Bali Transport

GO ON TO THE NEXT PAGE

Questions 147-149 refer to the following information.

All newly hired tour guides ------- the first part of their hospitality management training

147. (A) will begin
(B) have begun
(C) will have begun
(D) were beginning

with a seminar on customer service and public relations. Attendance is required, as it is part of your orientation for the position.

On June 5, instructors from the East Tourism Institute in Singapore, which has produced top travel administrators, will deliver ------- lectures at Charten Cruise Lines' main office

148. (A) weekly
(B) recorded
(C) public
(D) separate

from 2 P.M. to 4 P.M. in the conference room on the second floor. Class materials will be handed out on the days each lecture is held.

Note that the ------- will consist of a one-hour talk on a given topic followed by a

149. (A) researches
(B) sessions
(C) tests
(D) trials

40-minute group activity. The group activities will provide participants with the opportunity to test their learning in a fun and social environment. The final 20 minutes will be used to recap discussions and allow participants to ask the speaker questions.

For inquiries, please contact the personnel department at 555-8963.

Questions 150-152 refer to the following e-mail.

From: Harold Merritt <h.merritt@eventsmaster.com>
To: Beatriz Lester <b.lester@eventsmaster.com>
Date: June 2
Re: Museum Event

Dear Beatriz,

I'm sorry for the delayed response to your e-mail. I've been busy all day making arrangements for the inauguration of the Natural Science Museum.

The guest list for the event -------. I took care of that this morning and also sent invitations

150. (A) will be revised
(B) has been revised
(C) had been revised
(D) is being revised

to major broadcasting companies and newspapers to ensure full media coverage of our event. Although we are done with the guest list, there are still some changes ------- in the

151. (A) to be making
(B) have been made
(C) to be made
(D) are being made

program.

I spoke with the museum's chief curator this morning to finalize the details of the performances, and she asked that we make a shorter line-up for the ------- ceremony so

152. (A) awards
(B) graduation
(C) opening
(D) signing

that the guests will have more time to enjoy the sights at the museum. In addition, she wants us to purchase some small souvenir items that can be given away to those in attendance.

Perhaps we should meet with the team to revise the program and discuss the souvenir items. Please reply to this e-mail as soon as possible so that we can post an announcement for the staff tomorrow. Thanks.

Best regards,

Harold

GO ON TO THE NEXT PAGE

PART 7

Directions: In this part, you will be asked to read several texts, such as advertisements, articles or examples of business correspondence. Each text is followed by several questions. Select the best answer and mark the corresponding letter (A), (B), (C), or (D) on your answer sheet.

Questions 153-154 refer to the following memo.

MEMO

To: Joseph Pruitt, Marketing Manager
From: Carl Scallot, Marketing Director
Date: January 12
Re: Proposal

I reviewed your proposal this morning. Overall, you have some excellent ideas, but you will need to confirm your financial projections with Katherine. In addition, I have made some other recommendations, which you will find in an e-mail I have sent you.

After you have revised your proposal, please contact me on my mobile phone at 555-1324. I will be out of the office until 2:30 P.M., but we can meet sometime later in the afternoon.

Thanks.

Carl

153. Why was the memo written?
(A) To discuss a product
(B) To provide feedback
(C) To introduce a client
(D) To schedule a seminar

154. What does Mr. Scallot ask Mr. Pruitt to do?
(A) Call him on the telephone
(B) Meet him at a restaurant
(C) Prepare a video presentation
(D) Collect money from a customer

GO ON TO THE NEXT PAGE

Questions 155-156 refer to the following letter.

TRANSATLANTIC IMPORTS INCORPORATED

Demos Nikolaidis
Jolly Greek Grocer
82 Armistice Avenue, Glendale, CA

July 15

Dear sir,

This is a second reminder that your account with us is past due (please see the enclosed copy of the invoice). A payment of $320 was due two months ago on May 15. Please settle your account before August 1. Otherwise, we will have to turn the matter over to a collection agency. Should you wish to explore other payment options, you may call our accounts department at 555-0392. Our office is open from Monday to Friday, 9 A.M. to 5 P.M., and on Saturday from 9 A.M. to 12 P.M. Please ignore this letter if payment has already been sent.

Thank you.

Susan Crane
Chief Accountant
Transatlantic Imports

155. What is the purpose of the letter?
(A) To ask for a billing statement
(B) To apologize for overcharging
(C) To request a payment
(D) To place an order

156. What is indicated in the letter?
(A) Transatlantic Imports is open seven days a week.
(B) Mr. Nikolaidis has already mailed in his payment.
(C) Transatlantic Imports operates a collection agency.
(D) Mr. Nikolaidis has been previously contacted.

Questions 157-159 refer to the following announcement.

Pacific Shots

March 5 and 6
From 9 A.M. to 5 P.M.
Location: The Landien Tower Exhibit Center

The Omega Scuba Club invites you to a two-day photo exhibit featuring the Pacific Ocean's natural wonders at the Landien Tower exhibit center. Explore the rich marine life of the world's largest ocean through the lenses of our very own underwater photographers. The show will also feature the works of more than 20 renowned photographers, and is an event not to be missed!

Omega chairperson and *Wild Voyager* photographer Allen Crowley will open the event with a short presentation on underwater photography. This will be followed by a guided tour of the exhibition area. Many of the photographers will be on hand to discuss their photographs and answer your questions. Admission is free and open to the public. For more information, please visit Omega Scuba Club's Web site at www.omegadive.com.

157. What is the announcement mainly about?
(A) A diving lesson
(B) A photography display
(C) A leadership seminar
(D) A sea exploration

158. What is mentioned about Allen Crowley?
(A) He will conduct a guided tour.
(B) He is the owner of a magazine.
(C) He is the leader of an organization.
(D) He will give a series of lectures.

159. What is stated about the event?
(A) It is open to everyone.
(B) It is held once every year.
(C) It is organized by a travel agency.
(D) It is sponsored by *Wild Voyager*.

GO ON TO THE NEXT PAGE

Questions 160-161 refer to the following article.

The Bond Street Journal folds, to Reemerge Online

Hornbull Corporation has announced it will cease publication of *The Bond Street Journal*, effective January 1, ending the newspaper's 60-year run as the nation's leading source of financial news. On the company's Web site, CEO Jack Diamond explains that the newspaper will continue to exist, but only in cyberspace. "With the excessively high cost of printing daily, the board of directors wisely decided to pursue an Internet-only strategy first proposed two years ago," he said. It was further revealed that *The Bond Street Journal*'s 200,000 subscribers would automatically receive free subscriptions to the online version of *The Bond Street Journal*.

Hornbull will still publish its most popular monthly titles, *Observer*, *Magnate*, and *Livret*, which continue to enjoy significant newsstand sales. Among the remaining industry players, Deep Blue's *Oracle* is expected to emerge as *The Bond Street Journal*'s successor, although most observers believe it is only a matter of time before all print publications make the transition online.

160. Why did Hornbull Corporation decide to stop printing *The Bond Street Journal*?
(A) Readership had gone down.
(B) Consumers found it uninteresting.
(C) The owner chose to retire.
(D) Publishing it was too expensive.

161. What is NOT indicated in the article?
(A) Free memberships to a site will be given.
(B) Hornbull will continue to publish other titles.
(C) Competitors are experiencing rising sales.
(D) Experts believe printed materials will become obsolete.

Questions 162-165 refer to the following schedule.

Sportswear Manufacturers Association of America (SMAA)
SIXTH ANNUAL TRADERS CONVENTION
Plebeian Center, 39 Larkspur Way,
Jericho Springs, IL
Thursday, June 4 - Sunday, June 7

EVENT HIGHLIGHTS

DAY ONE	
9 A.M. to 1 P.M.	Introductory remarks and press conference with SMAA by outgoing president Dean Caldwell (Dorset Hotel)
1 P.M. to 4 P.M.	Networking event (Dorset Hotel) Trade show opens (Main Hall)
DAY TWO	
9 A.M. to 7 P.M.	Closed-door exhibit for industry professionals (Main Hall)
DAY THREE	
9 A.M. to 12 P.M.	Trade show opens to the public Special appearance by hockey hall-of-fame inductee Greg Hellman (Main Hall)
12 P.M. to 4 P.M.	Free basketball youth clinic hosted by legendary Iowa coach Tim Waterson (Activity Center)
4 P.M. to 8 P.M.	Raffle draw for all trade show participants and guests; prizes include autographed sports memorabilia, athletic wear, instructional videos, and more (Main Hall)
DAY FOUR	
10 A.M. to 2 P.M.	Autograph signing sessions and photo opportunities with visiting gold medalists (Activity Center)
2 P.M. to 5 P.M.	Final remarks, cocktail party and farewell banquet (Dorset Hotel)

162. What is suggested about the event?
(A) Some activities are limited to sportswear manufacturers.
(B) There will be a farewell party for the president.
(C) It is organized for sports athletes.
(D) It will offer products at reduced prices to the public.

163. Why would hockey fans probably be interested in attending the event?
(A) To obtain product samples
(B) To bid on auctioned memorabilia
(C) To see Mr. Hellman in person
(D) To get Mr. Waterson's autograph

164. What will take place in the activity center?
(A) A product demonstration
(B) Sports classes
(C) Career seminars
(D) Team trials

165. What will NOT be held at the hotel?
(A) A speech by the association's president
(B) A social gathering for attendees
(C) A meeting with press members
(D) Announcement of prize winners

GO ON TO THE NEXT PAGE

Questions 166-168 refer to the following e-mail.

To:	mildred.barrie@hostmost.com
From:	anthony.steadman@spotplan.com
Re:	Last Weekend
Date:	May 20

Dear Ms. Barrie,

On behalf of our CEO, Mr. Jenkins, and everyone else at SpotPlan, thank you for putting together such a stunning event for us last weekend in Redmond. We received many compliments from visitors who were visibly impressed with our booth exhibit. You really made our products stand out and your colorful displays attracted a lot of attendees. We had a 12 percent increase in orders, which we believe was partially thanks to your company's incredible work.

Due to our success, I'd like to offer your company the chance to assemble another exhibit for us at our next event in Atlanta this July. It will once again be for a trade fair, and although the venue will be smaller than the one in Redmond, we consider the event to be no less important. We will need you to make a few changes to the exhibits you did before, as we have some additional products to show. I will be flying up to New York in the next two weeks to attend a conference. Could I stop by your office to discuss the event with you? I hope to hear from you soon.

Sincerely,

Anthony Steadman
Marketing Director
SpotPlan

166. Why was the e-mail written?
(A) To find a sponsor for a trade show
(B) To schedule a product presentation
(C) To thank a client for attending an event
(D) To offer additional business

167. What does Mr. Steadman thank Ms. Barrie for?
(A) Organizing a trade fair
(B) Creating a product display
(C) Speaking at an event
(D) Assembling some equipment

168. What is suggested about Ms. Barrie?
(A) She has a busy schedule.
(B) She is unable to attend the fair.
(C) She was recommended by an associate.
(D) She works in New York.

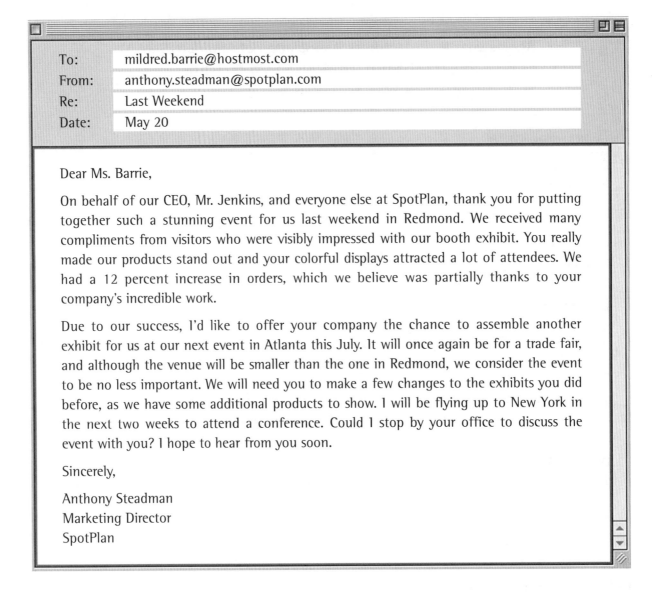

Questions 169-171 refer to the following flyer.

Noah's Full Service Carwash in Geyserville

Welcomes you to the neighborhood!

For over 20 years, Noah's has established itself as the leading chain of full-service car wash facilities in Pasadena County. We use state-of-the-art equipment, nonabrasive cleaners, and environmentally conscious methods.

We do hope you will try us for your vehicle maintenance needs! To welcome you to the area, we are attaching a coupon for a markdown on any one of the following car wash packages, which you will need to present upon receiving the services:

BASIC
Regular Price: $29.99
Special Introductory Price: $19.99
Foam wash, Hand dry, Glass cleaner, Tire polish

PREMIUM
Regular Price: $39.99
Special Introductory Price: $29.99
Same as basic plus: Interior vacuum, Blow dry, Air-freshener

ULTIMATE
Regular price: $49.99
Special Introductory Price: $34.99
Same as premium plus: Rainbow wash, Interior shampoo, Exterior wax

We take all forms of payment with the exception of personal checks.

169. What is mentioned about Noah's?
(A) It has just opened in Geyserville.
(B) It does not accept credit cards.
(C) It offers basic car repair services.
(D) It has several branches in Pasadena.

170. What is NOT a part of the premium service?
(A) Rainbow wash
(B) Air-freshener
(C) Tire polish
(D) Blow dry

171. How can customers receive the special introductory price?
(A) By paying in cash
(B) By submitting a coupon
(C) By purchasing a package offer
(D) By trying out a new service

GO ON TO THE NEXT PAGE

Questions 172-175 refer to the following article.

Arthur to Boost Asia Presence

Arthur Holdings has just revealed that it will be building three new shopping malls in Thailand, Vietnam, and Cambodia this year. The largest shopping mall developer in Southeast Asia has reserved $4 billion in capital for the project.

During a press conference for the company's upcoming stock offering, Arthur Holdings president Francis Brewster said the new malls are part of the firm's two-year development plans. Last year, the firm opened malls in Myanmar and Taiwan despite the gloomy economy.

Each of the three shopping malls will have an approximate area of 20,000 square meters. The malls to be established in Thailand and Vietnam will have convention halls and activity centers equipped with conference rooms, gymnasiums, bowling alleys, and movie theaters.

According to Brewster, funding will be derived from recently sold bonds amounting to $3 billion, foreign loans, and proceeds of the upcoming stock offering.

The president believes that Arthur's notable achievements in the past year will help the company collect more capital when it auctions off new shares on Monday.

According to financial figures released by Arthur Holdings last year, revenues from its Singapore operations grew 15 percent, to $250 million. Moreover, profits went up 20 percent, to $175 million.

"Arthur Holdings has proven itself to be a strong company in Asia. Because of this, we are expecting more people to invest in our rapidly growing business," Brewster said.

172. What is mentioned about Arthur Holdings?
(A) It owns a chain of shopping centers.
(B) It is in need of foreign capital.
(C) It is seeking investment opportunities.
(D) It operates corporate buildings.

173. What will NOT be included in Arthur's Vietnam facility?
(A) Conference areas
(B) Museums
(C) Theaters
(D) Sports venues

174. The word "derived" in paragraph 4, line 1 is closest in meaning to
(A) originated
(B) generated
(C) destined
(D) departed

175. What does the company expect on Monday?
(A) A loan approval
(B) Additional funds
(C) A growth in profits
(D) Business proposals

Questions 176-180 refer to the following memo.

TO: Events Staff
FROM: Marinella Garnet, Project Manager
SUBJECT: Upcoming Seminar
DATE: September 23

As announced at the recent meeting, our company is organizing a three-day business seminar on e-commerce. The seminar, to be held six months from now, will be attended by small and medium business owners wishing to learn how to sell their products and services on the Internet.

In line with this, I have posted a list of seminar committees and their members on the bulletin board. The committees are as follows:

Speakers Committee, Venue Committee, Food Committee,
Marketing Committee, Registration Committee

You will notice that, except for the marketing committee, all committees are composed of new members. The marketing committee must coordinate with Mr. Donaldson, our marketing director, so that they will be familiar with the company's new sponsorship packages. Since the seminar is free, I would like the marketing committee to look for many sponsors so that majority of the seminar's costs may be assumed by income from advertisers. Make sure that sponsors are aware of the benefits they will receive in return for their assistance, including the use of their logos in promotional materials for the seminar.

Furthermore, I also want the speakers committee to present a list of potential guest speakers. If possible, invite executives from online books, arts and crafts, computers, and clothing retailers.

176. What is the topic of the seminar?
(A) Employee management
(B) Brand development
(C) Online marketing
(D) Event planning

177. What is mentioned about the committees?
(A) They have yet to select team leaders.
(B) They are composed of temporary employees.
(C) They have been given different assignments.
(D) They have limited budgets.

178. What are members of the marketing committee asked to do?
(A) Consult a colleague
(B) Send solicitation letters
(C) Create client directories
(D) Hire catering companies

179. What is suggested about the seminar?
(A) It will cost less than previous events.
(B) It will take place over six days.
(C) It will be sponsored by businesses.
(D) It will be held at a marketing firm.

180. What will the speakers committee most likely do?
(A) Contact resource personnel
(B) Survey online stores
(C) Interview businessmen
(D) Invite industry professionals

GO ON TO THE NEXT PAGE

Questions 181-185 refer to the following invoice and e-mail.

The Glass House

880 Cottage Grove Road, Bloomfield, CT 06002

INVOICE	
Issue Date	Reference Number
May 3	200-367777

Client	Address	Date Shipped	Payment Method
Abigail Hoffman	Studio Bar and Restaurant 752 Post Road East Westport, CT 06880	May 5	Check

Item #	Description	Unit Price	Quantity	Amount
BC507	Lily sherry glass (3 ¾ oz)	$79.50	1 case (36 pieces)	$79.50
OT289	Rosetta champagne glass (6 ½ oz)	$38.00	4 cases (12 pieces)	$152.00
BP203	Thunder hi-ball glass (10 oz)	$86.90	1 case (35 pieces)	$86.90
PL033	Alexandria all-purpose water goblet (11 ½ oz)	$146.99	3 cases (24 pieces)	$440.97
WT230	Anchor Collins glass (10 oz)	$57.25	2 cases (24 pieces)	$114.50
*All prices are inclusive of sales tax. From May 1 to 31, customers will be given a 10 percent discount on total purchases.			**Subtotal**	$873.87
			Discount	- $87.39
			Shipping	$25.00
			Total*	$811.48

Please make all checks payable to The Glass House.
To report any problem, contact the sales representative who took your order by e-mail or by calling 555-9773.

Thank you for your business!

To:	Robert Smith <r.smith@theglasshouse.com>
From:	Abigail Hoffman <a.hoffman@studio.com>
Date:	May 6
Subject:	Order
Attachment(s):	Glass order e-mail

Dear Mr. Smith,

I would like to report an error in my latest glassware order with the reference number 200-367777. I specifically requested three cases of Rosetta champagne glasses in the previous e-mail I sent you. However, when my delivery arrived at the restaurant yesterday, I noticed that you gave me four cases, which was also incorrectly specified on the invoice that came with the delivery. In addition, when I opened the other boxes, I found that a couple of sherry glasses had broken stems.

I will be returning the extra case, along with the sherry glasses, and expect that you will cover the cost of shipping. In addition, I ask that you replace the damaged items as soon as possible. My assistant manager, Catherine Simmons, will call you this afternoon to make any necessary arrangements.

I have attached a copy of my last e-mail for your reference. I hope you will address my concerns immediately and take measures to prevent this from happening again.

Sincerely,

Abigail Hoffman
Proprietor, Studio Bar and Restaurant

181. What is indicated about the glasses ordered by Ms. Hoffman?
(A) They are sold exclusive of taxes.
(B) They were ordered within a promotional period.
(C) They are popular brands on the market.
(D) They were shipped to the client for free.

182. What is the e-mail mainly about?
(A) An additional order
(B) An inquiry about payment
(C) Problems with a delivery
(D) Price details of products

183. What does Ms. Hoffman mention about her order?
(A) She asked a sales agent for a discount.
(B) She sent photographs of some glassware she requested.
(C) She was specific about the quantity of products she wanted.
(D) She gave special instructions regarding the packaging of merchandise.

184. What is Mr. Smith being asked to do?
(A) Make further arrangements with Ms. Simmons
(B) Deliver an extra case of sherry glasses
(C) Request a full refund from the restaurant
(D) Contact The Glass House's warehouse

185. How much should be subtracted from Ms. Hoffman's bill?
(A) $87.39
(B) $86.90
(C) $57.25
(D) $38.00

GO ON TO THE NEXT PAGE

Questions 186-190 refer to the following advertisement and e-mail.

Vitruvian Gym

As part of our 10th anniversary celebration, we are giving new members the chance to try out any of our fitness classes for free. If you sign up for membership anytime between June 1 and June 15, you will be eligible for one free session of the class of your choice. You will also receive a voucher that entitles you to a full body massage at our affiliate establishment, Triquetra Health Spa. Lastly, new members will get to choose a free gym bag from the two designs available.

Below is the schedule of our classes:

CLASS	DAY	TIME	FEE
Aerobics	Monday	5:30-6:30 P.M.	Member: $15/session Non-member: $18/session Special rates are available for those registering for three sessions or more.
	Wednesday	3:00-4:00 P.M.	
Yoga	Tuesday	7:00-8:00 P.M.	
	Thursday	6:15-7:15 P.M.	
Kickboxing	Wednesday	4:30-5:30 P.M.	
	Friday	6:00-7:00 P.M.	
Dance	Saturday	3:45-4:45 P.M.	

HURRY! Take advantage of this opportunity and become a Vitruvian Gym member today!

To: custserv@vitruviangym.com
From: Sarah Leone <sarah@jocondemail.com>
Date: June 25
Subject: Special Rates

I went to my complimentary class last Tuesday, June 20 and found the exercises to be enjoyable and extremely relaxing. Your instructor Melinda Yale was also very professional and accommodating. Given my positive experience, I would like to continue attending the class. Your advertisement indicated that special rates are available for those who register for a certain number of sessions. I am interested in registering for four. Can you please let me know what the rates are?

Also, I brought my free gym bag to work the other day and received some compliments for it from my colleagues. As we were talking, I told them about signing up at your gym and some of them are now interested in joining. I understand your promotion has ended, but they would like to know whether there is some other enticement they could be offered to become a member. One of them was curious about the possibility of a group discount. Could you let me know whether such a thing is being offered at your gym?

Thanks for your help, and I look forward to my classes at your facility.

Sarah Leone

186. What is mentioned about Vitruvian Gym?
(A) It is partnered with a spa.
(B) It is launching a new branch in June.
(C) It is celebrating 20 years of business.
(D) It is open seven days a week.

187. What is NOT a benefit for new members?
(A) A sports bag
(B) A free massage
(C) A yoga mat
(D) A trial class

188. What class did Ms. Leone most likely try out?
(A) Yoga
(B) Dance
(C) Aerobics
(D) Kickboxing

189. What is indicated about Ms. Leone in the e-mail?
(A) She lives close to the sports facility.
(B) She has been a member for a long time.
(C) She may qualify for a special rate.
(D) She cannot attend a scheduled session.

190. What does Ms. Leone inquire about?
(A) Where to buy a gym bag for a friend
(B) Whether rates are reduced for groups
(C) How to refer new members to the gym
(D) When the next promotion event will be held

GO ON TO THE NEXT PAGE

Questions 191-195 refer to the following letter and e-mail.

VOLARE GIFT SHOP
343 Hedge Street, Hickory Hills, IL 60457
www.volaregifts.com

March 28

Francesca Balaguer
3376 Bruce Avenue
Maryland Heights, MO 63141

Dear Ms. Balaguer,

It was great meeting you at the trade fair in Belgrade last week. As we discussed, I'm interested in purchasing some of your souvenir products for my gift shop in Rockford, Illinois.

We haven't been very pleased lately with the quality of merchandise from our current supplier. In fact, many of our customers have complained about the substandard items. I think that this is one of the reasons why our sales have recently declined.

Viewing your exhibit at the trade fair, I was impressed not only with the quality of the materials that you use, but also with the intricate detail in each design.

Enclosed with this letter is an order form that I downloaded from your Web site. Please let me know if you can produce the requested items for us. We are thinking of introducing your merchandise in time for the summer tourist season, when we get twice as many visitors to our location. If successful, we would be interested in developing a long-term business relationship with you.

If you have any questions, do not hesitate to send me an e-mail at octavio.guzman@volaregifts.com. Thank you and we look forward to hearing from you soon.

Sincerely yours,

Octavio Guzman
Co-owner
Volare Gift Shop

To:	Octavio Guzman <octavio.guzman@volaregifts.com>
From:	Francesca Balaguer <f.balaguer@terrestrialcrafts.com>
Date:	April 15
Subject:	Order
Attachment(s):	Sales invoice Contract

Dear Mr. Guzman,

I appreciate your interest in Terrestrial Crafts. I'm very grateful for your order considering that I started this business just a few months ago. My exhibit at the trade fair was a success, and I received proposals from several companies during the event.

Since you ordered more than 50 different types of items from our catalog, it may take me longer than usual to finish making all of the items. However, I've recently hired five assistants to help me out with production, so I am confident we can send the items to you at the start of your busy season.

Attached is a scanned copy of the signed contract, as well as the invoice for your order. For any inquiries, please give me a call at 555-0099. You may also check out our Web site for information on new products at www.terrestrialcrafts.com for any future orders. Thank you very much.

Yours,

Francesca Balaguer

191. What is the main purpose of the letter?
- (A) To register for a trade fair
- (B) To ask about an upcoming tour
- (C) To change a product purchase
- (D) To inquire about ordering merchandise

192. Why is Mr. Guzman interested in Ms. Balaguer's items?
- (A) They are being sold at reasonable prices.
- (B) They have been featured in a renowned magazine.
- (C) They have particularly detailed designs.
- (D) They have been recommended by his colleagues.

193. In the letter, the word "substandard" in paragraph 2, line 2 is closest in meaning to
- (A) inexpensive
- (B) satisfactory
- (C) average
- (D) inferior

194. What will most likely happen in the summer?
- (A) Some items will be delivered to a store.
- (B) Terrestrial Crafts will open a new branch in Illinois.
- (C) Volare Gift Shop will celebrate its first anniversary.
- (D) Some staff members will be given an orientation.

195. What is NOT suggested about Terrestrial Crafts?
- (A) It is a small family-run business.
- (B) It is a relatively new company.
- (C) It has a list of its merchandise for sale on a Web site.
- (D) It displayed its products at a recent event.

GO ON TO THE NEXT PAGE

Questions 196-200 refer to the following letter and form.

VYPERIAS COMPUTERS
254 Leviath Drive, Green Point, NSW 2251
(+612) 555-9634

Dear Ms. Dempsey,

On behalf of Vyperias Computers, thank you for your business! We hope that you are completely satisfied with your purchase and that you will rely on us for all your computer needs. At Vyperias, we take steps to provide only the highest quality products and services, which is why we have had so many repeat customers over the last 15 years.

We understand that our success relies upon our commitment to our customers, so we are always happy to hear your comments and suggestions on areas you feel need improvement. We would greatly appreciate it if you could take the time to fill out the enclosed feedback form and let us know about your experience using our products and services. One of our supervisors will get in touch with you regarding any concerns you might have:

Sales	Glenn Sinclair
Advertising	Crystal Werner
Customer Service	Marcela Galvan
Technical Support	Oliver Kimball

Once again, thank you, and we are looking forward to hearing from you.

Best regards,
Jimmy Cuevas
Director, Research and Development

VYPERIAS COMPUTERS
Customer Feedback Form

Name	Bethany Dempsey
Address	14-C Hobbes Apartments, 573 Whaler Street, Green Point NSW 2251
Telephone Number	555-6032
Business Purpose	Bought a Zylogo F1000H Laptop

Your responses will be used to enhance our capacity to better address your future requests and concerns.

Please evaluate us on a scale of 1 to 4, with 1 being excellent and 4 being poor:	1	2	3	4
Professionalism and courtesy	X			
Thoroughness and attention to detail		X		
Knowledge and expertise	X			
Punctuality of service		X		
Pricing of products			X	
Overall satisfaction with Vyperias Computers		X		

Comments: I was very impressed with the service I received from your staff. The store representative who attended to me was friendly and patient when I was asking about the features of each laptop. His knowledge of computers really helped me in choosing a unit that is perfect for my lifestyle. However, I think your prices are a little more expensive than others. I was walking around the mall last weekend and learned that some stores are selling the laptop I bought from you at 10 percent less than what I paid for mine. Although I have no complaints about your services, your company might want to look into this matter more closely.

How did you hear about us? I saw your advertisement in a newspaper.

Could a Vyperias supervisor get in touch with you regarding your response?
Sure, that is not a problem.

196. Why was the letter written?
(A) To give details about a transaction
(B) To verify the cancellation of an order
(C) To solicit information from a client
(D) To announce the promotion of an employee

197. In the letter, the word "regarding" in paragraph 2, line 5 is closest in meaning to
(A) accepting
(B) observing
(C) applying
(D) concerning

198. What is NOT included in the survey Ms. Dempsey answered?
(A) What she paid for her purchase
(B) Her personal information
(C) Her opinions about a store
(D) How she learned about Vyperias

199. What did Ms. Dempsey complain about?
(A) The staff's communication skills
(B) The speed of delivery
(C) The manager's lack of expertise
(D) The pricing of products

200. Which supervisor will most likely contact Ms. Dempsey?
(A) Oliver Kimball
(B) Marcela Galvan
(C) Glenn Sinclair
(D) Crystal Werner

This is the end of the test. You may review Part 5, 6, and 7 if you finish the test early.

解答 p.287 / 分數換算表 p.289 / 題目解析 p.217（解答本）

▮ 請翻到次頁「自我檢測表」檢視自己解答問題的方法與態度。

自我檢測表

TEST 05 順利的完成了嗎？

現在要開始透過以下的自我檢測表檢視自己在考試中的表現了嗎？

我的目標分數為：　　　　　　這次測試的成績為：

1. 70 分鐘內，我完全集中精神在測試內容上。

   □是　□不是

   如果回答不是，理由是什麼呢？

2. 70 分鐘內，連答案卷的劃記都完成了。

   □是　□不是

   如果回答不是，理由是什麼呢？

3. 70 分鐘內，100 題都解完了。

   □是　□不是

   如果回答不是，理由是什麼呢？

4. Part 5 和 Part 6 在 25 分鐘以內全都寫完了。

   □是　□不是

   如果回答不是，理由是什麼呢？

5. 寫 Part 7 的時候，沒有一題花超過五分鐘。

   □是　□不是

   如果回答不是，理由是什麼呢？

6. 請寫下你需要改善的地方以及給自己的忠告。

*回到本書第二頁，確認自己的目標分數並加強對於達成分數的意志。
對於要改善的部分一定要在下一次測試中實踐。這點是最重要的，也要這樣才能有進步。

TEST 06

Part 5

Part 6

Part 7

自我檢測表

等等！考前確認事項：

1. 關掉行動裝置電源了嗎？□ 是
2. 答案卷（Answer Sheet）、鉛筆、橡皮擦都準備好了嗎？□ 是
3. 手錶帶了嗎？□ 是

如果都準備齊全了，想想目標分數後即可開始作答。

考試結束時間為現在開始 70 分鐘後的______點______分。

Reading Test

In this section, you must demonstrate your ability to read and comprehend English. You will be given a variety of texts and asked to answer questions about these texts. This section is divided into three parts and will take 75 minutes to complete.

Do not mark the answers in your test book. Use the answer sheet that is separately provided.

PART 5

Directions: In each question, you will be asked to review a statement that is missing a word or phrase. Four answer choices will be provided for each question. Select the best answer and mark the corresponding letter (A), (B), (C), or (D) on the answer sheet.

101. Due to the region's low levels of rainfall, Arizona maintains the lowest ------- of plant and animal life in the country.
(A) affiliation
(B) concentration
(C) alteration
(D) formation

102. Every morning, Levi makes sure to replenish the selection of daily newspapers ------- the coffee table in the staff's lounge area.
(A) between
(B) on
(C) toward
(D) within

103. With the higher grade requirements for admission, it has become ------- more difficult for high school students to be accepted to Madison University.
(A) progress
(B) progressively
(C) progresses
(D) progressed

104. The ticketing clerk reminded the passengers of how ------- it is for them to arrive at the train station at least two hours before their scheduled departure time.
(A) important
(B) importance
(C) importantly
(D) import

105. The ticket prices of Penfold Airlines are ------- to change without prior notice depending on the season and fuel prices.
(A) satisfied
(B) located
(C) invaluable
(D) subject

106. All audio-visual presentations have already been prepared by the staff ------- the seminar, including the video advertisements.
(A) by (B) as
(C) to (D) for

107. Out of all her charitable projects, the ------- of the town library is what Fatima McCoy is best known for.
(A) establishes (B) established
(C) establishment (D) establisher

108. Despite the economic crisis, Blixen Finance ------- generates a return on its investments well above analysts' expectations.
(A) far (B) still
(C) then (D) however

109. After the musical performance yesterday evening, the cast came out from backstage and ------- audience members.
(A) greet (B) greeted
(C) will greet (D) are greeting

110. Subsidiary companies are advised to ------- for the trade show by January 12 to receive a 15 percent discount on fees.
(A) take off (B) show through
(C) put away (D) sign up

111. The company president talked to Mr. Blant about his request and asked him to consider ------- carefully.
(A) he (B) it
(C) himself (D) itself

112. Ms. Grabowski was assigned to ------- the conference speakers from the entrance to the convention hall.
(A) maintain (B) circulate
(C) expedite (D) escort

113. Ms. Glass asked each of the ------- about their previous work experience in the advertising and Internet publishing industries.
(A) applicants (B) applicable
(C) applying (D) applications

114. Customers can download a ------- of Mithras Cosmetics' latest catalog from its Web site.
(A) copy
(B) reminder
(C) schedule
(D) record

115. During the investment seminar, participants were urged to provide examples of their own experiences in ------- stock.
(A) lifting (B) placing
(C) delegating (D) trading

116. The first-place winner at the Annual Geo-Science Fair built a machine to demonstrate ------- earthquakes are caused.
(A) about (B) how
(C) which (D) over

117. If the elevator -------, press this button and someone from the maintenance department will respond to the emergency as soon as possible.
(A) breaks down
(B) stays in
(C) turns out
(D) calls up

118. Your order of printer paper has already been shipped from our warehouse ------- will most likely arrive late due to poor weather conditions.
(A) but (B) until
(C) even (D) since

119. For a minimal fee, customers of Umbria Travels can personally ------- their itineraries online or add options to their bookings.
(A) differ (B) board
(C) change (D) look

GO ON TO THE NEXT PAGE

120. Most outsourcing companies operate on ------- shift schedules to adequately accommodate their clients' needs.
(A) alternation
(B) alternates
(C) alternate
(D) alternately

121. Session Television is planning to broadcast a primetime comedy series for a mature ------- this upcoming season.
(A) portion
(B) audience
(C) fraction
(D) selection

122. Dr. Lillian Stern is trying to ------- which area of the city would best suit the needs of the clinic she plans to open next year.
(A) maintain
(B) develop
(C) launch
(D) decide

123. Merov Technologies, one of Russia's ------- providers of telecommunication services, will launch more affordable broadband packages in June.
(A) more largely
(B) largeness
(C) largest
(D) largely

124. Anson Furnishings supplied all the furniture in the new office ------- for the bookshelves, which were customized by Woodworks International.
(A) as
(B) near
(C) except
(D) apart

125. Victoria paid the enrollment fee by bank transfer this afternoon, ------- her seat for the three-day actors' workshop in July.
(A) secure (B) security
(C) securest (D) securing

126. The scientists are ------- analyzing the results of their experiment to make sure the data in the concluding report is accurate.
(A) extremely
(B) cautiously
(C) vainly
(D) firmly

127. The coupon entitles the holder to a free drink or fries and is ------- until February 28.
(A) valid (B) validating
(C) validation (D) validate

128. After receiving two major clothing orders in a single month, Zeus Couture's manager decided to invest in several sewing machines to increase its -------.
(A) affordability
(B) productivity
(C) subjectivity
(D) attainability

129. As part of its promotion, Pandora Express Train offers discounts to passengers who book their tickets ------- time.
(A) beside (B) through
(C) ahead of (D) due to

130. Andrea Gonzaga chose to work fewer hours per day for the weekly magazine, ------- herself more time to write her first book.
(A) permits (B) permitting
(C) permissible (D) permission

131. Even before the ------- had begun, Chiba Electronics employees expressed their opposition to the merger with Tsukino Industries.
(A) structures
(B) assortments
(C) occupations
(D) negotiations

132. Local and international news reported on the success of the archaeological excavation in Nuremberg, which ------- by Mr. Drescher, the project manager.
(A) will supervise
(B) is supervising
(C) has supervised
(D) was supervised

133. People who travel ------- will benefit from the Platinum Miles credit card as it lets them earn airline points that may be redeemed for plane tickets.
(A) regular
(B) regularly
(C) regularity
(D) regularities

134. Numerous recreational activities are offered at Jade Panglao Resort, making it the perfect place in ------- to spend the holidays with family and friends.
(A) that
(B) when
(C) which
(D) where

135. Ozzo Appliances will begin an advertising campaign for its newest line of kitchen equipment ------- the license from the patent office is released.
(A) once
(B) from
(C) in spite of
(D) along with

136. It is ------- that interior designers keep up with the latest trends in order to come up with new and interesting concepts for their clients.
(A) vital
(B) heavy
(C) punctual
(D) prohibited

137. Tip-Toe's shoes are quite expensive, but ------- other brands, they last for a long time and come with a 12-month warranty.
(A) after
(B) therefore
(C) unlike
(D) upon

138. The advisory from the Ministry of Health listed various ------- measures that could help minimize the risk of heat-related illnesses during the summer months.
(A) protects
(B) protected
(C) protective
(D) protectively

139. As an advocate ------- forest preservation, Steve Riddick has organized many awareness campaigns against illegal logging and farming practices.
(A) of (B) at
(C) by (D) into

140. To save time during her presentation, Ms. Madden decided to give a brief overview of each of Transpacific Translation's offerings ------- a detailed description.
(A) in case
(B) in the event
(C) rather than
(D) whether or not

GO ON TO THE NEXT PAGE

PART 6

Directions: In this part, you will be asked to read an English text. Some sentences are incomplete. Select the word or phrase that correctly completes each sentence and mark the corresponding letter (A), (B), (C), or (D) on the answer sheet.

Questions 141-143 refer to the following letter.

Darlene Amalo
Unit 320, Alto Apartment
St. Peter's Street, St. Albans
Hertfordshire

Dear Ms. Amalo,

We are pleased to inform you that you have passed the final interview for the ------- guide

141. (A) museum
(B) leadership
(C) travel
(D) career

position in Rhodes, Greece. In this regard, we would like you to visit our London office on Friday, February 5, at 9 A.M. to discuss details about your contract.

As we already discussed during your recent interview, the successful applicant ------- in

142. (A) will be
(B) has been
(C) was being
(D) will have been

charge of organizing and facilitating island tours for guests. We believe your superb -------

143. (A) commandable
(B) commander
(C) command
(D) commanded

of European languages and broad knowledge of Greek culture make you the right person for the position.

Please respond to this letter as soon as possible so that we can finalize the appointment and draft a contract. Congratulations, and I look forward to working with you!

Sincerely,

Catherine Flotillas
Manager

Questions 144-146 refer to the following article.

HIALEAH - Bolt's World will be ------- rides on its Thunder Roller Coaster during the

144. (A) offering
(B) scheduling
(C) suspending
(D) managing

anniversary celebration this weekend. "The theme park will have to close the world-class attraction due to a mechanical malfunction discovered by maintenance workers today," Bolt's World facilities manager Nathan Johnston said.

While workers were conducting a safety check on the ride, they noticed that the train stopped running after making a left turn on a sharp curve. The workers determined -------

145. (A) that
(B) where
(C) what
(D) when

the problem was a result of the guide wheels, which need replacing.

"We regret that we cannot offer roller coaster rides. Nevertheless, we are thankful that the breakdown was spotted before the event and nobody was hurt," Johnston said. To ensure guests' safety, Bolt's World will make major mechanical improvements to the ride. An ------- Thunder Roller Coaster will be operational again next month.

146. (A) extended
(B) overworked
(C) upgraded
(D) agreeable

GO ON TO THE NEXT PAGE

Questions 147-149 refer to the following memo.

To: University of Canterblane department secretaries
From: Jefferson Lance, IT Office director
RE: Staff Training

For the entire month of November, the IT Office will hold training seminars to acquaint professors and administrative employees with the university's improved computer system. Attendance is ------- for all teaching staff members. Since new features were

147. (A) required
(B) optional
(C) unlimited
(D) helpful

added, it is necessary for our faculty to learn about these changes.

The IT Office will conduct daily sessions Mondays through Saturdays. ------- professors

148. (A) If
(B) After
(C) All
(D) Although

may attend the training anytime within the month, every department is strongly advised to arrange an exclusive session for its staff. This will allow trainers to give detailed lectures on specific functions ------- to each department.

149. (A) appropriately
(B) appropriate
(C) appropriateness
(D) appropriation

For more information regarding training, please contact the IT Office at extension # 521 and ask for Oscar. We look forward to your full cooperation and hope that the recent modifications to the university's computer system will be helpful for everyone. Thank you.

Questions 150-152 refer to the following letter.

April 1

Dear Valued Client,

We would like to express our gratitude to you for renewing your Internet connection subscription with Magna Link. Your continued ------- is very important to us. To serve you

150. (A) patience
(B) success
(C) observation
(D) patronage

better, we would appreciate your answering a one-page questionnaire dealing with the quality of our network. Please answer the questions and write down any problems you may have encountered with your connection. -------, send us back the form using the

151. (A) Then
(B) However
(C) Meanwhile
(D) Otherwise

enclosed pre-paid envelope.

Rest assured that your answers will remain confidential and be used exclusively for the company's research. ------- your willingness to complete this survey, you will be entitled

152. (A) In charge of
(B) On behalf of
(C) By means of
(D) In appreciation of

to a chance to win a new desktop computer. The lucky winner will be announced on May 25 and contacted in writing.

We look forward to receiving your feedback. Thank you.

Sincerely,

Magna Link

GO ON TO THE NEXT PAGE

PART 7

Directions: In this part, you will be asked to read several texts, such as advertisements, articles or examples of business correspondence. Each text is followed by several questions. Select the best answer and mark the corresponding letter (A), (B), (C), or (D) on your answer sheet.

Questions 153-154 refer to the following invitation.

Margaux Mall Invites you to

THE SPRING FASHION SHOW

On Friday, May 6, 6 P.M. to 8 P.M.

At the Margaux Mall Convention Center

More than thirty designers will showcase their collections at the grandest fashion event of the season

Sponsored by:
The French Fashion Association
and
The Closet Channel

153. What will take place on May 6?
(A) A yearly mall sale
(B) A convention for designers
(C) A fashion presentation
(D) A modeling seminar

154. What is indicated about the event?
(A) It will be hosted by a French designer.
(B) It will be held at a clothing store.
(C) It will be followed by a celebratory party.
(D) It will be sponsored by other organizations.

GO ON TO THE NEXT PAGE

Questions 155-156 refer to the following letter.

Red Block Department Store

923 Westland Avenue, New York City, NY

December 1

Dear Shoppers,

Red Block department store will be briefly closed on Monday, December 15, for its annual inventory. This will permit management to update its accounts and arrange its stockrooms.

The supermarket and signature boutiques within the shopping center, however, will be open during the day. For more details, please log on to www.redblock.com.

Thank you for your continued support.

Sincerely,

Management

155. Why was the letter written?

(A) To promote new products available in the supermarket
(B) To seek feedback from customers
(C) To invite shoppers to an event
(D) To inform patrons of a temporary closure

156. What is mentioned about the supermarket?

(A) It plans to clear out its stock.
(B) It needs to renovate its facilities.
(C) It is being transferred to a new building.
(D) It is located in a shopping mall.

Questions 157-159 refer to the following advertisement.

Metro Sports Club

188 Longview Road, Hamilton City

"Your path to wellness"

Conveniently situated near Highway 10 in scenic Hamilton City, Metro Sports Club provides health and wellness programs for people of all ages. We have state-of-the-art facilities and a staff of competent fitness trainers, sports coaches, and professional nutritionists. We also offer programs encouraging members to get into the greatest shape of their lives.

Body Shape Up

Get fit the right way with the help of a personal trainer. Body Shape Up is highly recommended for members who would like to lose weight. Enroll in this program and we will create a workout routine suitable for your needs and body type.

Sports and Fitness Classes

Enhance your athletic skills and relieve stress by taking sports and fitness classes. We currently offer badminton and swimming lessons three times a week. We also hold aerobics and yoga classes on weekends.

Present this advertisement at our customer service desk to get 30 percent off one-year memberships. For more information, please contact us at 555-6984. You may also e-mail your inquiries to inq@msc.com.

157. What is mentioned as the goal of the Metro Sports Club?
(A) Providing facilities for sporting events
(B) Helping people get in shape
(C) Increasing public knowledge of physical fitness
(D) Getting young people to be more active

158. What is NOT a service offered by the club?
(A) Aerobics classes
(B) Sports training
(C) Weight-loss programs
(D) Tennis lessons

159. How can customers receive a membership discount?
(A) By enrolling in a program
(B) By submitting an advertisement
(C) By calling a number
(D) By sending an e-mail

GO ON TO THE NEXT PAGE

Questions 160-161 refer to the following e-mail.

To: Jamal Swift <j.swift@lordmail.com>
From: Vidur Chander <v_chander@hamadamotors.com>
Subject: Car Seat Covers
Date: February 9

Dear Mr. Swift,

I hope you are enjoying the new Hamada Minivan you purchased recently. If you have any problems with the vehicle, please don't hesitate to contact us. In addition, don't forget to bring your van to our automotive center every six months for a free inspection and oil change under the terms of your five-year guarantee.

I want to apologize for the delayed delivery of the free seat covers that come with the vehicle. I was informed that the seat covers were delivered to your house earlier today. Our supplier, Geisler Auto Interiors, was unable to ship them to our showroom on time due to the recent holiday. They also send their apologies to you for the inconvenience.

To compensate for the trouble, we hope you will accept the attached coupon issued by Geisler Auto Interiors. Simply print it out and present it at any of their businesses anytime within the year to receive two complimentary car mats. As we also have a consignment agreement with Geisler, you may claim the mats here at Hamada Motors.

Once again, I am very sorry for the trouble this has caused you.

Respectfully yours,

Vidur Chander
Sales representative
Hamada Motors

160. What caused the delay in delivery?
(A) Products needed to be altered.
(B) A supplier was delayed because of a holiday.
(C) Machines were malfunctioning.
(D) An order was changed.

161. What is indicated about Geisler Auto Interiors?
(A) It is holding a promotional offer.
(B) It offers free delivery service.
(C) It has more than one branch.
(D) It provides full refunds.

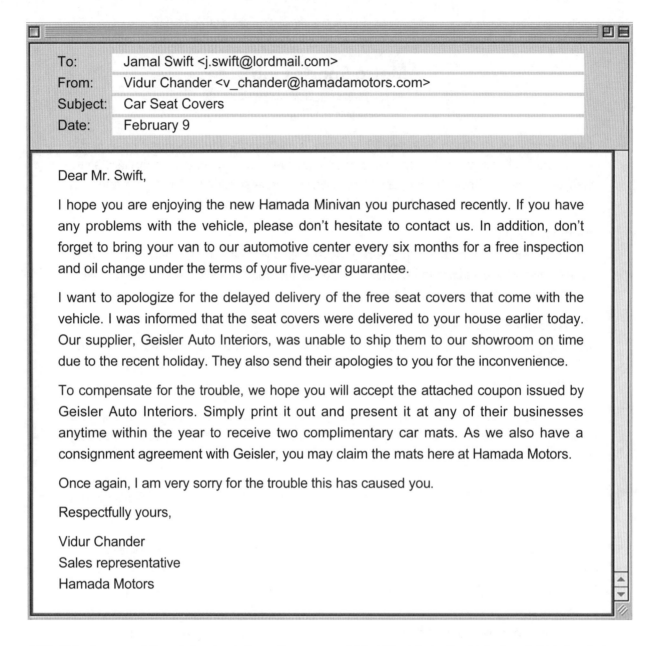

Questions 162-164 refer to the following memo.

MEMO

TO: Staff
FROM: Margaret Vonnegut, administrative assistant
DATE: January 14
SUBJECT: Employee Benefits

Management has decided to upgrade the medical insurance coverage of all employees. Beginning this year, each permanent employee may declare two family members, who will also be entitled to full medical and hospitalization benefits. Probationary employees, on the other hand, will receive an additional $100 in coverage for two dependents. Details of the new coverage have been posted on the Web board for your convenience.

A representative from Healthpath will come by tomorrow morning at 10 A.M. to gather the information necessary to modify your insurance plans. They will also answer any questions you may have about the new policies. If you are unable to attend, please contact the personnel department so that they can collect the necessary information and forward it to Healthpath. We appreciate your cooperation in this matter.

Thank you.

162. Why was the memo written?
(A) To report a salary increase
(B) To explain the staff policies
(C) To provide a list of job opportunities
(D) To request family health histories

163. What are permanent employees entitled to receive?
(A) Free consultations
(B) Lower fees
(C) Personalized care
(D) Extended coverage

164. According to the memo, what will happen tomorrow?
(A) All staff will fill out application forms.
(B) New contracts will go into effect.
(C) A visitor will collect information.
(D) Employment interviews will be conducted.

GO ON TO THE NEXT PAGE

Questions 165-168 refer to the following notice.

Armstrong Town Council

Armstrong will celebrate the 30th anniversary of its foundation on July 5. The council has arranged for numerous activities to mark this special occasion. As always, volunteers are appreciated. Please contact Carol Rhea at (604) 555-9334 if you would be willing to help out. Citizens are invited to take part in this important moment in the town's history by participating in the following activities:

Schedule of Town Festival Activities		
Time	**Activities**	**Venue**
9 A.M.	Opening Ceremony	City Hall Grounds
10 A.M.	Town Parade	Starts at the City Hall Grounds
11 A.M.	Inauguration of Wallace Public Library	Wallace Library Lobby
2 P.M.	Youth Sports Fest	Hilton Complex
8 P.M.	Grand Fireworks Display	Moonlight Bay

Additional Information

Traffic Reminder:
Wilson Boulevard will be shut down to traffic an hour before the town festival activities begin. Motorists are advised to take Morgan Avenue to enter and exit the town. The roadblock will be removed the following day.

Youth Sports Fest Registration:
Children and teenagers are encouraged to join the sports fest. Participants who register at the Community Affairs office will receive a free pass to Wild Water Fun Park.

Wallace Library Membership:
Get a complimentary library membership card when you attend Wallace Public Library's inaugural ceremony. The card gives members free access to the library's books, journals, and media files.

165. What is the purpose of the notice?
(A) To announce the opening of a public building
(B) To provide a schedule to volunteers
(C) To notify the community about some roadwork
(D) To invite townspeople to an event

166. What is suggested about Morgan Avenue?
(A) It is located near Moonlight Bay.
(B) It will be opened after the festival.
(C) It is an alternate route to Armstrong.
(D) It has parking for visitors.

167. What is NOT included in the activities?
(A) A fireworks display
(B) A fundraising event
(C) A celebratory parade
(D) An athletic event

168. What will people who attend the event at 2 P.M. receive?
(A) Customized T-shirts
(B) Free meals from a restaurant
(C) Membership cards
(D) Tickets to a water park

Questions 169-172 refer to the following article.

Wasorkorf Moves Ahead of Squatrust in Aircraft Industry

Russian plane manufacturer Wasorkorf had a whopping 30 percent increase in sales in October through December, according to company records. The Moscow-based company took 450 orders of airplanes this quarter. It has now replaced their German-based rival Squatrust as the world's top aircraft manufacturer. Production rates also climbed nearly 10 percent to 150 units in the same period.

Wasorkorf president Leticia Ivanov relates the jump in sales to the growing popularity of budget airlines. "The rising number of people traveling around the world on cheaper airlines consequently boosted demand for more aircraft," Ivanov said. Wasorkorf has been the leading supplier of passenger aircraft in Southeast Asia for more than ten years. Among its customers are carriers from Singapore, Malaysia, Indonesia, and the Philippines, which have been gradually expanding their fleets.

"The figure indicates that Wasorkorf and the entire airline industry are gradually bouncing back from the economic downturn," Ivanov said. The worldwide recession, which lasted for nearly three years, severely affected the tourism industry and suppressed demand for aircraft.

169. What is the article mainly about?
(A) Travel destinations
(B) Popularity of budget airlines
(C) Increased sales of a company
(D) Marketing strategies

170. What is indicated about Squatrust?
(A) It has lowered its fees in response to rising competition.
(B) It is the world's second-largest aircraft manufacturer.
(C) It is a popular budget airline in Southeast Asia.
(D) It developed a successful advertising campaign.

171. What country does Wasorkorf NOT export aircraft to?
(A) Indonesia
(B) Malaysia
(C) Singapore
(D) Germany

172. What did the article mention about the global recession?
(A) It reduced the number of airplane orders.
(B) It halted the operations of some airlines.
(C) It caused air carriers to lower fares.
(D) It forced Wasorkorf to merge with another company.

GO ON TO THE NEXT PAGE

Questions 173-175 refer to the following information.

Experience the Thrill of the Sea by Joining the

Chesapeake Yacht Club!

Members of the Chesapeake Yacht Club are entitled to numerous privileges throughout the year, including:

* Use of all docks and mooring facilities (for those with their own boats)
* 15 percent off on all items in our sail shop and clubhouse gift shop
* Use of clubhouse facilities including showers, changing rooms, lounge, bar, and restaurant
* Invitations to all CYC functions, including the Annual Grand Gala

Those registering for membership before April 1 will also receive free Chesapeake Yacht Club polo shirts!

Drop by the administrative office to pick up your registration form. If you would like further information on club fees, please feel free to call Mitzi Van Boer at 555-3030.

173. Why was the information written?
(A) To publicize the building of a new facility
(B) To give directions to a tourist area
(C) To provide details about a sporting event
(D) To encourage people to apply for membership

174. What is true about the Chesapeake Yacht Club?
(A) It provides docking areas for members.
(B) It has a high number of applicants.
(C) It has an online registration form.
(D) It is only open during the summer.

175. What is NOT mentioned as a benefit for members?
(A) Lower prices on retail items
(B) Complimentary meals at a restaurant
(C) Invitations to the Grand Gala
(D) Access to clubhouse showers

Questions 176-180 refer to the following letter.

August 25

Dwight Simmons
General Manager
Victoria Cruise Line

Dear Mr. Simmons,

I want you to know that I had a wonderful time during a recent Southeast Asian cruise. I was greatly impressed by Victoria Cruise Line's accommodating and caring staff. In particular, I can never forget Andrew Hudson, one of your tour guides, who helped me locate my purse when I lost it on the second day of the trip.

After a late afternoon stroll on the ship, I went to Flavors Bistro for dinner. As I was about to leave, I noticed that my purse was missing. I searched the table where I was seated, the restaurant, and other places I had gone, to no avail. Mr. Hudson saw me looking for something, so he came up to me and offered his assistance. He talked to waiters and asked some people from housekeeping if they had seen my purse. He also accompanied me to the security department to report my problem. The purse was not found that night, but Mr. Hudson called me in my room the next day to say that a housekeeper had retrieved my purse inside one of the ship's restrooms.

If not for Mr. Hudson's persistence, I think I would never have recovered my purse. He is really an asset to your company. I hope you will appreciate his dedication to his job and reward him accordingly. It is because of employees and service like this that I have often used your cruise line, and will continue to do so. Thank you.

Respectfully yours,

Candymae Suarez

176. Why was the letter written?
(A) To book a travel package
(B) To discuss a security problem
(C) To acknowledge a crew member
(D) To report a complaint about housekeeping

177. What is indicated about Ms. Suarez?
(A) She would like compensation for her lost item.
(B) She travels frequently on business trips.
(C) She was not satisfied with the housekeeping staff.
(D) She has been on trips with Victoria Cruise Line before.

178. What is NOT a measure that Mr. Hudson took to help retrieve Ms. Suarez's property?
(A) Contacting housekeepers
(B) Notifying the security department
(C) Searching restrooms
(D) Asking waiters

179. Who found Ms. Suarez's property?
(A) A waiter from a restaurant
(B) A security guard
(C) A member of the housekeeping
(D) A ship engineer

180. The word "accommodating" in paragraph 1, line 2 is closest in meaning to
(A) comfortable (B) customary
(C) memorable (D) hospitable

GO ON TO THE NEXT PAGE

Questions 181-185 refer to the following e-mails.

To: Leonard Ellis <l_ellis@soulfultravels.com>
From: Donna Hayes <donna369@pathosmail.com>
Date: February 9
Subject: Egyptian Odyssey

Dear Mr. Ellis,

I looked over the brochure you sent me last week, and I must say that I was quite impressed with the wide variety of tour packages that your travel agency offers.

I became particularly interested in the Red Sea Escape, but since one of my traveling companions has already been to the Red Sea, I opted for the Egyptian Odyssey, instead. However, when I looked it up on your Web site to find out more, I became somewhat confused since your Web site contains information that is different from what is in the brochure. The online advertisements stated that the visit to the Valley of the Kings and the Hatshepsut Temple takes place on the third day of the tour, not on the fifth day, as was indicated in your brochure. Can you let me know which is correct? The schedule will influence whether or not my friends and I will book the tour.

Meanwhile, I would greatly appreciate it if you could provide me with a quotation for the Egyptian Odyssey tour for six people by tomorrow afternoon. Since we are planning to travel early next month, we would like to get all of the arrangements sorted out as soon as possible. Furthermore, I would also like to ask what the weather will be like in that area around the time of our trip. We would like to make sure to bring the right kind of clothing.

Thank you, and I hope to hear from you soon.

Donna Hayes

To: Donna Hayes <donna369@pathosmail.com>
From: Leonard Ellis <l_ellis@soulfultravels.com>
Date: February 10
Subject: Re: Egyptian Odyssey

Dear Ms. Hayes,

The tour schedules on the brochure are correct. The other schedules you saw were the result of an error made by our marketing staff. We sincerely apologize for the discrepancy.

I have prepared a quotation for six people for the tour you requested, but a network problem has been preventing me from attaching the file to this e-mail. If you are able to read this by noon today, please reply with your fax number. That way, I can send you the file this afternoon, as you asked. You can also just call me directly at 555-9617.

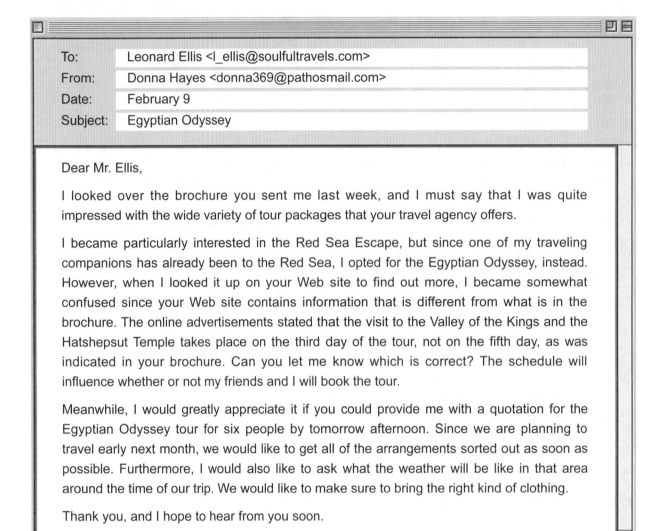

As for your other concerns, you could not have picked a better time to travel to Egypt as the weather is quite ideal for sightseeing. Bringing along some cool, light clothing should suffice, unless you plan to dine out at one of the city's finer restaurants. For that purpose, one set of smart casual clothing will do.

Thank you.

Sincerely,

Leonard Ellis

181. What is the purpose of the first e-mail?
(A) To change a flight schedule
(B) To request a new brochure
(C) To ask about a tour package
(D) To cancel travel plans

182. What is NOT indicated about Ms. Hayes?
(A) She is traveling with a group.
(B) She will contact Mr. Ellis again.
(C) She has not set a firm travel date.
(D) She has been to the Red Sea before.

183. What does Ms. Hayes request?
(A) A price quote
(B) A gift certificate
(C) A calendar of events
(D) A reservation form

184. On which day of the tour does the visit to the Valley of the Kings take place?
(A) On the second day
(B) On the third day
(C) On the fourth day
(D) On the fifth day

185. What does Mr. Ellis recommend Ms. Hayes do?
(A) Reserve flight tickets by this afternoon
(B) Dress appropriately for warm weather
(C) Book a table at a fine dining restaurant
(D) Pack a light suitcase for her trip

GO ON TO THE NEXT PAGE

Questions 186-190 refer to the following Web page and form.

WALDORF SCHOOL FOR CULINARY ARTS

Home | About Us | Courses | News and Events | FAQ

SPECIAL COURSES

Would you like to have a fun and productive summer? Then join us and learn how to cook new dishes. Enroll in any of our weekend classes and become an expert in Asian cuisine!

It's A Thai!
July 14 – September 1
Wisit Chadhury

Discover what makes Thai dishes special through a series of informative lectures and hands-on cooking demonstrations conducted by renowned Bangkok Diner owner, Wisit Chadhury. Learn how to mix sour, sweet, salty, and spicy ingredients to make amazing Thai dishes!

A Taste of Japan
July 22 – August 26
Yukio Kakutani

Ever wondered how sushi, sashimi, udon, donburi, and other traditional Japanese foods are prepared? Award-winning chef Yukio Kakutani will not only teach you how to make delectable dishes, but also introduce you to some regional specialties not often served in local Japanese restaurants.

A Weekend in India
August 11 – August 12
Amir Muhammad

Take a gastronomic journey to one of Asia's most culturally diverse countries. Amir Muhammad leads an intensive two-day course exploring the flavorful vegetarian dishes of India, such as biryani and malai kofta.

Viva Vietnam!
August 18 – September 8
Anh Poc Long

Known for its use of fresh and scrumptious ingredients, Vietnamese cuisine is relatively unknown on this side of the planet. Let Chef Anh Poc Long guide you through the diverse culinary tradition of Vietnam, from making simple meals like dumplings, pancakes, and soups to cooking mouth-watering seafood, meat, and curry dishes.

Interested applicants may download the form below. Just be sure to e-mail it to us at info@waldorfschool.com no later than one week before the start of the selected course. All courses are limited to 20 participants.

Application form

WALDORF SCHOOL FOR CULINARY ARTS

Where cooking is a journey!

944 Fairfield Road, West Alley, AZ 58709
www.waldorfculinary.com

Name: CATHERINE PEÑAFLOR	Age: 22	Sex: Female
Address: 122 Riverside Village, Tucson, AZ 58705		
Telephone Number.: 555-0099	E-mail Address: c_pena@ion.com	
Course: Viva Vietnam!		
Payment Details: __X__ Cash ______ Check ______ Credit Card		
Card Name:	Card No.:	Expiry:
Total Amount: $120	Signature: *C. Peñaflor*	
Do you have any food allergies? Yes, I am allergic to most types of nuts (peanuts. almonds, walnuts...)		
Would you like to subscribe to our mailing list? Sure.		
For inquiries, please call 555-6356 and ask for Janet LeBlanc.		

186. Which lecturer owns a dining establishment?
(A) Wisit Chadhury
(B) Yukio Kakutani
(C) Amir Muhammad
(D) Anh Poc Long

187. According to the Web page, how can applicants sign up for a class?
(A) By making a telephone call
(B) By dropping by the head office
(C) By e-mailing a document
(D) By sending a fax message

188. What is NOT mentioned about A Taste of Japan?
(A) It will be conducted on weekends.
(B) It is the shortest program at the learning center.
(C) It includes lessons in cooking rare dishes.
(D) It is facilitated by a prizewinning instructor.

189. What is true about the Waldorf School for Culinary Arts?
(A) It accepts students of all ages.
(B) It has recently updated its Web site.
(C) It has several openings for instructors.
(D) It requires information about food allergens.

190. What is indicated about Ms. Peñaflor?
(A) She missed the first few sessions of her preferred course.
(B) She joined a class that is scheduled to last until September.
(C) She has prior experience in preparing Vietnamese food.
(D) She specified her credit card information on a payment form.

GO ON TO THE NEXT PAGE

Questions 191-195 refer to the following letter and e-mail.

September 13

Deborah Garret
Circulation Manager
Beryl Publishing Company
5236 Guevara Avenue
Albuquerque, NM 87120

Dear Ms. Garret,

I have been a subscriber of *The Clarion Monthly* for the last two years, and my subscription was not supposed to end until December of this year. However, I have not received a single issue since last July, which prompted me to call your company's customer service hotline yesterday to relay my concern. I spoke with Mr. Ross Lawrence, who informed me that *The Clarion Monthly* is no longer in print, and that the last issue was released three months ago.

Mr. Lawrence also informed me that subscribers were sent a notice via e-mail. I never received this notice, however. Since I have received only six issues of the journal this year, I would like to request a 50 percent refund of the $430 annual fee that I paid.

I am hoping that you will address my concern as soon as possible. Thank you.

Yours truly,

Arthur Clayton

To: Arthur Clayton <clayart@masterson.com>
From: Deborah Garret <dgar@beryl.co.us>
Date: September 15
Subject: Subscription

I am deeply sorry for the inconvenience you experienced with your subscription to *The Clarion Monthly.* Although we notified our subscribers in April that the magazine would cease publication after June, it appears that there was a computer error and a few of our readers did not receive the notification. We hope that you will accept our apology.

We have verified that there are six months remaining in your subscription, and will issue you a refund for the unfilled portion of the agreement. The amount will be transferred to your account unless you prefer a check, which we can mail to your home or office. In addition, we are sending you a 30 percent discount voucher, which you can use to subscribe to any of our other publications.

Thank you, and again, my sincerest apologies.

Best regards,

Deborah Garret

191. Why did Mr. Clayton send the letter to Ms. Garret?
(A) To request a membership extension
(B) To inquire about an unpaid balance
(C) To make a complaint about a subscription
(D) To arrange an interview for a magazine article

192. What is NOT indicated about Mr. Clayton?
(A) He contacted a customer service representative on September 12.
(B) He called Mr. Lawrence to inquire about a subscription extension.
(C) He has received *The Clarion Monthly* for more than two years.
(D) He will be offered a reduced rate for a publication.

193. What does Ms. Garret say Beryl Publishing did in April?
(A) Offered discount vouchers to customers
(B) Printed several revised editions
(C) Informed customers of a discontinuation
(D) Announced an upcoming magazine

194. What is suggested in the second e-mail?
(A) Issues of *The Clarion Monthly* will be unavailable temporarily.
(B) Mr. Clayton's subscription was terminated by mistake.
(C) Ms. Garret would prefer to send a check.
(D) Mr. Clayton will need to provide his payment preference.

195. How much does Ms. Garret agree to send to Mr. Clayton?
(A) $50
(B) $215
(C) $430
(D) $860

READING TEST 1 2 3 4 5 6 7 8 9 10

GO ON TO THE NEXT PAGE

Questions 196-200 refer to the following advertisement and e-mail.

Job Positions Available:

Intima Restaurant, 18 East Second Avenue, New York, NY 10003

Intima Restaurant, *Al Dente Magazine's* Choice Restaurant of the Year, is constantly looking for hardworking individuals to join its elite team of food service professionals. Intima recognizes that people are its most valuable asset, and this summer, it is seeking qualified individuals to fill the following positions:

Line Cook - The ideal candidate should have a basic knowledge of food preparation. The hired applicant will not only prepare food items as directed by the executive chef, but also follow recipes, portion controls, and presentation specifications set by the restaurant. This position requires 20 hours per week, Mondays through Thursdays.

Food Server - The successful applicant will take and serve the guests' orders, make sure that they are satisfied with their food, and efficiently handle any of their requests and concerns. There are shifts available on Mondays, Tuesdays, and Wednesdays from 11 a.m. to 3 p.m.

Host - This is the ideal position for someone with excellent communication skills and a courteous and outgoing personality. The successful candidate will manage all restaurant bookings, meet, greet, and seat guests, and ensure that the front desk area is clean and presentable at all times. This is an evening shift position on Fridays and Saturdays.

Cashier - The selected applicant will handle payment transactions, issue receipts, verify the accuracy of all items on guest checks, and be responsible for calculating the business's revenue at the end of each night. This position is from 6 p.m. to 10 p.m. Tuesdays, Wednesdays, and Thursdays.

Intima offers competitive hourly rates. Overtime pay of 20 percent per hour is given to staff members who work longer than their actual shift times. Staff members also receive a 50 percent discount on all menu items. Only full-time workers are eligible for the company's medical plan. Training will be given to new employees if necessary. Interested parties should contact the assistant restaurant manager, Anita Marks, at asst.manager@intima.com no later than June 10.

To: Anita Marks <asst.manager@intima.com>
From: April Galloway <aprilgall@contact.org>
Date: June 2
Subject: Advertisement

Dear Ms. Marks,

I am writing in response to your establishment's job advertisement and am interested in applying for either the food server or host position. I have had relevant experience with both jobs and I am certain I could make a valuable contribution to the restaurant. I have attached my résumé for your consideration.

In case it might impact your decision, I'd like to add that I am presently attending classes on Monday and Wednesday afternoons, but I am otherwise free to dedicate my time to the restaurant. In addition, I was wondering if the hourly pay for both positions is the same. Thank you for your time and I eagerly await your response.

Sincerely,

April Galloway

196. What can be inferred about the advertised jobs?
(A) They provide fixed wages.
(B) They are part-time positions.
(C) They require relevant experience.
(D) They involve only kitchen duties.

197. What is a requirement for line cooks?
(A) A presentable appearance
(B) Willingness to work nights
(C) Ability to follow direction
(D) A degree in culinary arts

198. According to the advertisement, what benefit is offered to successful candidates?
(A) Medical insurance coverage
(B) Higher hourly wages for extra work
(C) Free meals during shifts
(D) Paid vacation days

199. What position matches April Galloway's schedule?
(A) Cashier
(B) Line Cook
(C) Food Server
(D) Host

200. What does Ms. Galloway ask Ms. Marks?
(A) What hours the restaurant is open
(B) Which days are usually the busiest
(C) How much training will be provided
(D) If the salary is identical for two jobs

This is the end of the test. You may review Part 5, 6, and 7 if you finish the test early.

解答 p.287 / 分數換算表 p.289 / 題目解析 p.269（解答本）

▮ 請翻到次頁「自我檢測表」檢視自己解答問題的方法與態度。

自我檢測表

TEST 06 順利的完成了嗎？

現在要開始透過以下的自我檢測表檢視自己在考試中的表現了嗎？

我的目標分數為：　　　　　　這次測試的成績為：

1. 70 分鐘內，我完全集中精神在測試內容上。

   □是　□不是

   如果回答不是，理由是什麼呢？

2. 70 分鐘內，連答案卷的劃記都完成了。

   □是　□不是

   如果回答不是，理由是什麼呢？

3. 70 分鐘內，100 題都解完了。

   □是　□不是

   如果回答不是，理由是什麼呢？

4. Part 5 和 Part 6 在 25 分鐘以內全都寫完了。

   □是　□不是

   如果回答不是，理由是什麼呢？

5. 寫 Part 7 的時候，沒有一題花超過五分鐘。

   □是　□不是

   如果回答不是，理由是什麼呢？

6. 請寫下你需要改善的地方以及給自己的忠告。

*回到本書第二頁，確認自己的目標分數並加強對於達成分數的意志。
對於要改善的部分一定要在下一次測試中實踐。這點是最重要的，也要這樣才能有進步。

TEST 07

Part 5

Part 6

Part 7

自我檢測表

等等！考前確認事項：

1. 關掉行動裝置電源了嗎？□ 是
2. 答案卷（Answer Sheet）、鉛筆、橡皮擦都準備好了嗎？□ 是
3. 手錶帶了嗎？□ 是

如果都準備齊全了，想想目標分數後即可開始作答。

考試結束時間為現在開始 **70** 分鐘後的______點______分。

Reading Test

In this section, you must demonstrate your ability to read and comprehend English. You will be given a variety of texts and asked to answer questions about these texts. This section is divided into three parts and will take 75 minutes to complete.

Do not mark the answers in your test book. Use the answer sheet that is separately provided.

PART 5

Directions: In each question, you will be asked to review a statement that is missing a word or phrase. Four answer choices will be provided for each question. Select the best answer and mark the corresponding letter (A), (B), (C), or (D) on the answer sheet.

101. It was Governor Richards ------- who took charge of relief efforts last week in the hurricane-affected area near the coast.
(A) himself (B) him
(C) his (D) he

102. Some people who leave their homeland ------- overseas may end up living permanently outside of their native countries.
(A) work (B) works
(C) worked (D) to work

103. The new shop on Maple Street specializes in imported art ------- from China and Thailand.
(A) supplier (B) to supply
(C) supplies (D) supplying

104. Cairo-based Astarte Language School offers high-quality translation services for multinational firms ------- very reasonable prices.
(A) in (B) at
(C) over (D) from

105. Harizze Condominiums' building administrator ------- circulated a memorandum on proper garbage disposal.
(A) while (B) very
(C) before (D) recently

106. As executive chef, Jennifer Windings is ------- to not just the owner of Lucina Ristorante, but also its customers.
(A) accountable (B) accounted
(C) account (D) accountably

107. The board will have a meeting next week to discuss the possibility for ------- with the expansion of the firm's operations in Europe.
(A) rise (B) boost
(C) growth (D) climb

108. By the time Paola Conti became head designer for Fiori Fashions, she ------- more than 15 collections for the company's line of sportswear.
(A) had developed (B) will develop
(C) has developed (D) develops

109. Dupont Air requires that travel agencies ------- passport numbers prior to issuing travel itineraries to customers.

(A) obtain (B) contact
(C) fulfill (D) preside

110. The computer began processing data much more ------- after several large files were deleted from the hard drive.

(A) quick
(B) quickly
(C) quickness
(D) quicker

111. For a $25 fee, Silverbell Florist will extend its delivery ------- to cities as far north as Santa Barbara.

(A) serving
(B) service
(C) is serving
(D) has served

112. Applicants ------- pass the first test will be contacted for a panel interview, which will be conducted by the company's executives.

(A) whoever
(B) whenever
(C) who
(D) where

113. For an additional -------, Doyle Convention Center can provide refreshments at the upcoming corporate event.

(A) value (B) worth
(C) charge (D) bill

114. Since its establishment, Kalywa Textiles has strived to maintain a superior ------- of quality in making its products.

(A) proportion
(B) standard
(C) period
(D) estimate

115. ------- Mr. Harris has been a committed employee of the hotel for ten years, the supervisor recommended him for promotion.

(A) As
(B) Previously
(C) But
(D) Therefore

116. Mr. McLeish and his colleagues ------- need to make any changes to the draft blueprint because the client thought it was excellent.

(A) hardness
(B) harder
(C) hardly
(D) hard

117. Adam Bower and his team of property developers are ------- to start working on the shopping center project, as they only have one year to finish it.

(A) gradual
(B) uniform
(C) absolute
(D) eager

118. ------- attending the workshops, Emily Chassell hopes to improve her interior decorating skills and stay up-to-date on the latest industry trends.

(A) Except
(B) Whether
(C) Into
(D) By

119. Pevensey Cosmetics doubled its production capacity after ------- its goal to upgrade all of its factory equipment.

(A) consuming
(B) practicing
(C) achieving
(D) deciding

GO ON TO THE NEXT PAGE

120. Next week's conference will discuss ------- aspiring entrepreneurs can open their own profitable businesses.

(A) unless (B) during

(C) much (D) how

121. ------- Ms. Willows was delivering her presentation to the board, her secretary was taking minutes of the meeting.

(A) So (B) While

(C) Even (D) As if

122. Columns published in *Weekday Quill* do not ------- reflect the views and opinions of the newspaper company.

(A) temporarily

(B) visually

(C) necessarily

(D) primitively

123. The bridge ------- the fishing village and the town underwent extensive repair work after it collapsed in last week's storm.

(A) commuting

(B) traveling

(C) connecting

(D) transferring

124. Cepeda Food has successfully gained a solid client base on the East Coast after only two years of -------.

(A) operator

(B) operative

(C) operation

(D) operates

125. Although the dance contest is only one month away, participating performers have ------- to schedule a rehearsal.

(A) soon

(B) again

(C) later

(D) yet

126. ------- Kelly Denson possesses the necessary educational qualifications for the accountant position, she doesn't meet the job's work experience requirements.

(A) Provided that

(B) Although

(C) In spite of

(D) Already

127. The historical courthouse contains an ------- selection of thousands of legal documents dating back to the establishment of the city in 1840.

(A) impermissible

(B) ineligible

(C) extensive

(D) urgent

128. When submitting their reports to the Revenue Bureau, property appraisers must attach ------- documentation to support their assessments.

(A) satisfied

(B) relevant

(C) attentive

(D) adhesive

129. According to the National Weather Service's forecast, rainfall will be ------- distributed throughout western Scotland this year.

(A) even

(B) evenly

(C) evening

(D) evener

130. After only two years as advertising manager for Yan Beverages, Mr. Lu has already proven ------- to be a valuable asset to the company.

(A) he

(B) his

(C) him

(D) himself

131. Travelers are required to be at the platform ------- than 15 minutes before the departure time, or they may be prohibited from boarding the train.
(A) no earlier
(B) no more
(C) no later
(D) no longer

132. Jazz singer Elizabeth Stanley confirmed at yesterday's press conference that she had signed an ------- five-year contract with Noril Records.
(A) indifferent
(B) abstract
(C) exclusive
(D) inconclusive

133. The board members of EON Incorporated will ------- review the credentials of the top three candidates for the regional director position at least two weeks before making a selection.
(A) lucratively
(B) memorably
(C) meticulously
(D) overwhelmingly

134. A new ------- procedure has been proposed by the company's financial consultant in order to minimize the potential for fraud.
(A) auditory
(B) auditing
(C) will audit
(D) has audited

135. Chilean-owned firm Uriale Consulting is known for providing outstanding legal services to ------- large corporations and medium-sized enterprises.
(A) each
(B) both
(C) though
(D) whereas

136. Organizers for the Logia Museum's Annual Gala ------- a higher turnout this year, as the fundraiser will be held in a larger venue.
(A) expect
(B) contain
(C) recover
(D) compel

137. Choco Haven was able to launch a new store in Montpellier last month ------- the rising demand for its chocolate products.
(A) in case
(B) due to
(C) except for
(D) so that

138. Ms. Reeds is waiting to hear from the supermarket ------- whether or not they can deliver the meat products to her restaurant by Wednesday.
(A) but for
(B) as to
(C) from which
(D) along with

139. Chris Thomson, CEO of Remar Company Limited, said at a press conference yesterday that he is considering Tisto Corporation's proposal to ------- at least 20 percent of Remar's outstanding shares.
(A) reproduce
(B) acquire
(C) institute
(D) confirm

140. In honor of its second anniversary, Neticroix Gym gave its members ------- gift certificates for a two-hour group training session with one of its fitness specialists.
(A) durable (B) probable
(C) elapsed (D) complimentary

GO ON TO THE NEXT PAGE

PART 6

Directions: In this part, you will be asked to read an English text. Some sentences are incomplete. Select the word or phrase that correctly completes each sentence and mark the corresponding letter (A), (B), (C), or (D) on the answer sheet.

Questions 141-143 refer to the following letter.

Matthew Wang
National Culture Institute

Dear Mr. Wang,

I would like to apply for the position of part-time _______ assistant as advertised in

141. (A) accounting
(B) research
(C) sales
(D) administrative

The Yuan Times. I am currently employed as a writer at Caimen Museum's cultural properties division, which conducts studies on heritage structures in the mainland. As an emplyee at the museum, I have written articles about the preservation of numerous historical sites in China. This experience has given me skills that I think will be useful in completing your report on the evolution of Chinese architecture. _______, I was one of the

142. (A) In addition
(B) Instead
(C) Nevertheless
(D) However

people who documented the restoration work at the Mausoleum of the First Qin Emperor.

I am very _______ in collecting and analyzing data for your project, as I believe doing so will

143. (A) accurate
(B) critical
(C) relaxed
(D) interested

provide me with a greater appreciation of the country's historical sites.

Enclosed are a copy of my résumé and a few samples of my work. Should you find that I am qualified for the position, please contact me at your most convenient time. Thank you.

Sincerely,

Thompson Lee

Questions 144-146 refer to the following letter.

Dear Mr. Miller,

We received your letter requesting help to ------- your access code so that you can gain

144. (A) change
(B) recover
(C) create
(D) remove

admittance to *Chenez's* online magazine. We tried to retrieve your lost code yesterday, but unfortunately a system error is preventing us from accessing many of our users' personal information.

Our technicians are now trying to fix the problem. We plan to register new usernames and access codes for our subscribers once the repair is finished, as we ------- that others

145. (A) debate
(B) negotiate
(C) suspect
(D) doubt

have also been lost. We will provide you with a new access code within two days. If you do not receive this information by Friday, please send us an e-mail again, and we will do our best to resolve the matter.

To compensate you for the inconvenience, we will give you a free two-month subscription to *Chenez*. This will take effect immediately after your current subscription ends and will allow you to continue ------- our stories. This means your membership will be valid until

146. (A) enjoy
(B) enjoyable
(C) enjoys
(D) enjoying

January of next year.

We sincerely apologize for the trouble.

Respectfully yours,

Alice Efron
Chenez Magazine
Account Manager

GO ON TO THE NEXT PAGE

Questions 147-149 refer to the following announcement.

The Tourism Department ------- a cultural exhibit at the Kosan Hall as part of Bhutan's

147. (A) held
(B) should hold
(C) will hold
(D) has held

Cultural Month celebration. The exhibit, which will showcase the country's Tibetan and Indian roots, will be open for viewing from July 2 to 5. It will be an exciting learning experience for everyone who attends.

Opening ceremonies will be ------- by tourism director Jigme Chong on July 2 at 8 A.M.

148. (A) situated
(B) combined
(C) evaluated
(D) conducted

Various public officials and artists are expected to be at the event. The exhibits will showcase a variety of traditional costumes, artifacts, and handicrafts. In addition, the ------- of a limited photography publication about Bhutanese culture will also occur on the

149. (A) binding
(B) release
(C) independence
(D) revision

opening night.

For more details about the exhibit or venue, please visit www.bhutantour.com or call the Tourism Department hotline at 555-3247.

Questions 150-152 refer to the following article.

People from across the country and around the world gathered at Ponda Bay last night to witness the FlyFlicks Festival. The annual ------- attracted nearly 15-thousand

150. (A) screening
(B) competition
(C) reunion
(D) convention

spectators, mostly from the United States and Central America.

The fireworks contest featured entries from 20 countries and was judged by fireworks experts who are well established within the industry. Among ------- were Dragon Gate

151. (A) yourselves
(B) us
(C) them
(D) you

founders Tsien Long and Kenneth Kang. The event began with a vibrant display by the US team. Following that, several European squads displayed their shows before the evening concluded with a set by the Taiwanese team that was accompanied by music. Winners will be awarded tomorrow. Although all the participants delivered unique presentations, observers expect ------- Greece will take home this year's title for its

152. (A) that
(B) thus
(C) and
(D) on

groundbreaking display.

GO ON TO THE NEXT PAGE

PART 7

Directions: In this part, you will be asked to read several texts, such as advertisements, articles or examples of business correspondence. Each text is followed by several questions. Select the best answer and mark the corresponding letter (A), (B), (C), or (D) on your answer sheet.

Questions 153-154 refer to the following registration details.

Venus Swimming School

Enrollment Information
(Summer)

Courses	Fee
Basic Course Will teach water safety drills and basic swimming skills, including submerging, floating, moving forward, and breathing exercises	$140
Advanced Course 1 Will focus on freestyle, backstroke, and basic diving	$120
Advanced Course 2 Will focus on breaststroke, butterfly, and competitive freestyle	$150
Refresher Will review basic swimming skills and strokes	$130

The deadline for enrollment is on April 1. Please visit the school's official Web site at www.venus.com for class schedules.

153. What will NOT be taught in Advanced Course 1?
(A) Freestyle
(B) Butterfly
(C) Diving
(D) Backstroke

154. How much is the fee for a swimming review course?
(A) $120
(B) $150
(C) $140
(D) $130

GO ON TO THE NEXT PAGE

Questions 155-156 refer to the following invitation.

Please join us
for cocktails to celebrate the publication of

Chef Melinda Waterston's
Recipes for Rainy Days: A Cookbook

Myrtle Publishing is proud to present
Chef Melinda Waterston's latest collection of recipes,
gathered over the years from friends, family, and loved ones.
This Seattle native has warmed the local residents' hearts
and bellies as the owner and operator of Waterston's,
a landmark restaurant in downtown Seattle
for the past 15 years.

On Sunday, August 25
at 8 P.M.

Eastside Clubhouse
7 Clarinet Street, Melody Gardens
Clifford Hill, Seattle, Washington

Light refreshments will be served.

Please confirm your attendance by calling
Lance Fox at 555-6910 or 555-5632.

155. What event will be held on August 25?
(A) A company celebration
(B) A family reunion
(C) A book launch
(D) A restaurant opening

156. What is stated about the event?
(A) Directions may be found on a Web site.
(B) Attendees must contact Mr. Fox.
(C) Formal attire is required.
(D) A buffet dinner will be served.

Questions 157-159 refer to the following advertisement.

Derma House

Do you spend thousands of dollars on over-the-counter medications that fail to solve your skin problems? If you want to have that clear and youthful-looking glow, come to Derma House. We specialize in customized skin treatments that match your skin type. Our dermatologists use state-of-the-art equipment and solutions based on natural ingredients for acne, skin whitening, and anti-aging treatments.

Discover what Derma House can do for you. Visit any of our clinics from May 6 to May 10 to get a free consultation and 20 percent off on any regular facial treatment.

Derma House is an affiliate of Skin Medical Center.
www.dermahouse.com
Dial 555-8471

157. What type of business is being advertised?
(A) A fitness facility
(B) A dermatology clinic
(C) A health food store
(D) A hair salon

158. What is NOT mentioned about the Derma House?
(A) It utilizes natural ingredients.
(B) It offers a personalized service.
(C) It provides affordable cosmetic surgery.
(D) It has a number of different locations.

159. What does Derma House offer to do?
(A) Distribute free samples
(B) Hold makeup demonstrations
(C) Extend operation hours
(D) Provide skin consultations

GO ON TO THE NEXT PAGE

Questions 160-161 refer to the following letter.

Scaper Phones

January 15

Diana Price
252 77th Street
Aurora, IL 60504

Dear Ms. Price,

The mobile phone that you shipped to us for replacement arrived this morning. The unit has been forwarded to the technical support department for a diagnostic test, and the results will be released in three days.

Our warranty guarantees replacement of mobile phones returned to us within three weeks of purchase. Should we find the product you purchased defective, we will immediately send you a new unit of the same model.

Thank you for your patience.

Respectfully yours,

Ted Patel
Customer service representative
Scaper Phones

160. Why did Scaper Phones write to Ms. Price?
(A) To introduce a new service to a client
(B) To acknowledge receipt of an item
(C) To request a replacement
(D) To advertise a special offer

161. What will Scaper Phones do if a product is defective?
(A) Forward it to a repair center
(B) Refund the customer's money
(C) Deliver a new one of the same kind
(D) Provide credit for future purchases

Questions 162-164 refer to the following e-mail.

From: Annette Hoskins <ahoskins@zollinger-insurance.com>
To: Raymond Lewis <rlewis@makeityours.com>
Date: October 15
Subject: Products

Dear Mr. Lewis,

I was referred to you by a former colleague, Alfred Newton, who now works at Reflex Media. He told me you could supply us with customized office merchandise and that you give special rates for large corporate orders. I was hoping you could answer some questions.

First, I am planning to buy 225 planners, 250 t-shirts, and 200 coffee mugs, which we intend to give out as mementos to our clients beginning in December. How long will it take for these items to be made? We'd prefer to have them by the end of next month. Next, the items will need to have our company logo printed on them. How do I send you an image of it? Last but not least, would an order of the size we want qualify us for the discount Mr. Newton mentioned?

Please inform me as soon as possible by replying to this message. If you'd like, I can meet with you sometime this week to discuss the matter further. You may also call me at my office number, 555-9312.

Thank you.

Annette Hoskins
Marketing director, Zollinger Insurance

162. What does Ms. Hoskins inquire about?
(A) Whether Mr. Newton is suited for a position
(B) Where to find a company's closest branch
(C) What it will cost to print in different colors
(D) Whether she is eligible to receive a special rate

163. When does Ms. Hoskins want the order delivered?
(A) In September
(B) In October
(C) In November
(D) In December

164. What is suggested about Ms. Hoskins?
(A) She wants to purchase gifts for her staff.
(B) She owns an insurance corporation.
(C) She plans to organize an event in December.
(D) She is in charge of promotional items.

GO ON TO THE NEXT PAGE

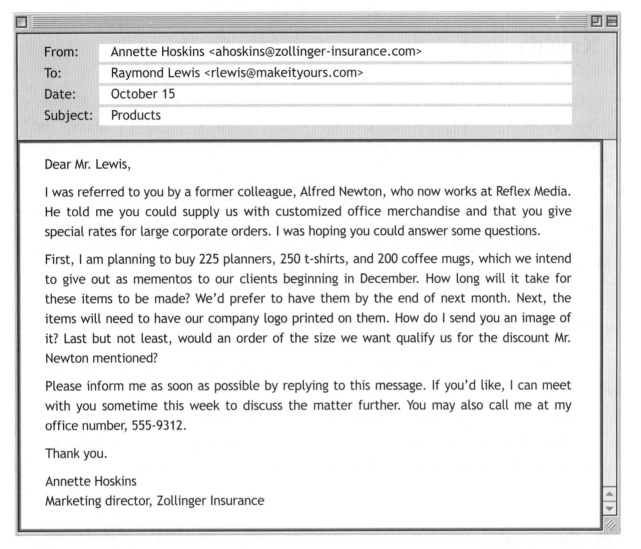

Questions 165-168 refer to the following article.

Kaleidoscope

by Emma Graham

After a stressful week at work, it is always nice to drop by the spa to relax and recharge. For more than three years now, spa treatments have helped me fight fatigue. All the while, I thought I had been enjoying the greatest spa services in the area, but that notion changed when I visited the Red Sea Spa.

The newest spa in the metropolitan area offers a variety of hydrotherapy massages. The Red Sea Spa resembles a water theme park with ten swimming pools, providing soft, moderate, and hard massages using only water pressure. Among my favorite spots in the premises is the hydro-acupuncture pool. It squirts warm water that gives a pricking sensation similar to what is experienced during real acupuncture treatment. The pool works well to soothe sore muscles.

The water spa is also equipped with basic amenities, such as saunas and facial rooms. It also has pools for children, as well as dining facilities serving American and Italian dishes. Regarding the service, the spa employs a pleasant and accommodating staff to ensure that guests enjoy their visit.

If you want a different relaxation experience with your family and friends, then the Red Sea Spa is the place to go. And from June 1 through the end of August, the spa is giving away free gym towels with the cost of admission. The Red Sea Spa is open daily from 8 A.M. to 11 P.M.

165. What is suggested about Emma Graham?
(A) She writes dining reviews for a publication.
(B) She frequently seeks out spa services.
(C) She has visited the Red Sea Spa before.
(D) She was disappointed with the Red Sea Spa.

166. What is mentioned about the hydro-acupuncture pool?
(A) It is inadvisable for children.
(B) It is a popular feature of the spa.
(C) It relieves muscle pain.
(D) It uses soft water pressure.

167. What is NOT a facility at the Red Sea Spa?
(A) Swimming pools
(B) Saunas
(C) Childcare center
(D) Restaurants

168. What is indicated about the Red Sea Spa?
(A) It is offering a special incentive to customers.
(B) It serves a variety of healthy cuisines.
(C) It trains acupuncture practitioners.
(D) It closes later on the weekends.

Questions 169-171 refer to the following memo.

MEMORANDUM

TO: Producers
FROM: Lawrence Bash, *Kitchen Hub* executive producer
SUBJECT: Partial Viewers Survey Report

Below are the preliminary findings from the viewers' survey carried out by the researchers of the show in April. A total of 2,000 local respondents participated in the online survey. It has only been a week since the research team concluded data collection, so we still need to wait another month for the complete findings. In the meantime, take note of the viewers' responses as they might yield some useful insights:

Question number 1: How often do you watch *Kitchen Hub*?

Every week	20 percent
Once a month	50 percent
Twice a month	20 percent
Three times a month	10 percent

Question number 2: How would you rate *Kitchen Hub*?

Excellent	10 percent
Good	20 percent
Satisfactory	20 percent
Needs improvement	50 percent

Question number 3: Please rate the difficulty of *Kitchen Hub recipes*.

Appetizers:	Easy	80 percent
	Moderate	15 percent
	Difficult	5 percent
Main courses:	Easy	30 percent
	Moderate	10 percent
	Difficult	60 percent
Desserts :	Easy	80 percent
	Moderate	17 percent
	Difficult	3 percent

Note: Most of respondents said that many of the main courses were difficult to cook because they required the use of unconventional cooking tools and equipment.

We will have a meeting tomorrow at 9 A.M. to discuss these findings.

169. Why was the survey most likely conducted?
(A) To find out about product usage
(B) To compile a list of new recipes
(C) To research cooking methods
(D) To get opinions on a TV program

170. What do the survey results suggest about *Kitchen Hub*?
(A) It is popular in other countries.
(B) It is broadcast once a week.
(C) It is highly rated by viewers.
(D) It is replayed at the end of each month.

171. According to the memo, why do viewers find featured main courses difficult to make?
(A) Their ingredients are rarely available at supermarkets.
(B) They have long preparation times.
(C) They are prepared with uncommon cooking utensils.
(D) Their recipe instructions require professional skills.

GO ON TO THE NEXT PAGE

Questions 172-175 refer to the following notice.

National Mail Service

Money Orders

The National Mail Service has recently discovered several counterfeit money orders. These money orders are suspected to have come from other countries and have been used for purchasing goods online. A number of local online businesses have been victimized by this fraud.

Please note that US money orders can be purchased from the National Mail Service only. No other institution is allowed to produce US money orders. Therefore, it is more likely that money orders from abroad are forged.

Money orders presented at post offices and banks are subject to validation and clearance before payment. To ensure payment for purchased goods, the National Mail Service advises online businesses to check the authenticity of the money orders they receive before shipping merchandise.

The US Federal Police and the mail service have been investigating the matter.

Information regarding the US money order service may be viewed by logging on to www.nationalmailservice.gov. Those who would like to verify money orders or report counterfeit payments may call (405) 555-3204.

172. Why was the notice written?
(A) To introduce a form of payment
(B) To notify the public about a problem
(C) To inform customers about a new service
(D) To provide details on shipping fees

173. What is indicated about the money orders?
(A) They are rarely accepted by banks.
(B) They are difficult to authenticate.
(C) They are necessary for online transactions.
(D) They are only available from the mail service.

174. How are online companies advised to protect their businesses?
(A) By installing credit card security applications
(B) By discouraging the use of money orders
(C) By verifying payment before sending products
(D) By asking for identification documents before dispatching goods

175. How can people learn more about money order payments?
(A) By writing a letter
(B) By visiting a Web site
(C) By calling a number
(D) By going to a post office

Questions 176-180 refer to the following letter.

May 25

Setsuko Uchiyama, Boksun Fashions
Takaoka Road, Nagoya

Dear Ms. Uchiyama,

Fabric Warehouse is moving!

We are pleased to announce that we are opening a new store in June on Tenmacho Street in Atsuta Ward. We have expanded our silk, cotton, wool, linen, and polyester sections to provide you with a wider selection of materials for clothing and home decoration. In addition, we have set up design assistance counters where you may seek professional advice on choosing the appropriate materials for your projects. Apart from introducing the new service, we guarantee to give you greater shopping convenience with the store's spacious underground car park and nearby food vendors. For directions to our new address, please see the map printed in the enclosed catalogue.

As a devoted client, you are invited to our grand opening on June 5. On that day, all designer textiles will be marked down by 15 percent. We will also hold a raffle where you will have the chance to win a Konoya 525 portable sewing machine.

Thank you for your patronage, and we will see you soon!

Kuneho Tanaka
General Manager, Fabric Warehouse

176. Why was the letter written?
(A) To provide an update on a store's operations
(B) To advertise innovations in tailoring equipment
(C) To let Ms. Uchiyama know about new products
(D) To report the highlights from a design workshop

177. What is NOT a feature of the new store?
(A) Large parking area
(B) Wider varieties of textiles
(C) Snack bars
(D) Fashion exhibits

178. Why did the store add assistance counters?
(A) To conduct membership registrations
(B) To deal with customer complaints
(C) To demonstrate the latest sewing materials and equipment
(D) To recommend the most suitable fabric to clients

179. What is suggested about Setsuko Uchiyama?
(A) She is a newly hired employee at Boksun Fashions.
(B) She needs training in interior design.
(C) She is a regular customer of Fabric Warehouse.
(D) She makes all of her own clothing.

180. What will take place on June 5?
(A) New designs will be presented to the public.
(B) Some fabrics will be sold at a reduced price.
(C) The store will close for a holiday.
(D) A new catalog will be launched.

GO ON TO THE NEXT PAGE

Questions 181-185 refer to the following advertisement and e-mail.

Great Job Opportunities Await You at EMRE!

Recognized as a leading manufacturer of high-quality dairy products, EMRE PASTEURS has enjoyed profitable growth since its establishment 14 years ago. It is constantly seeking out talented and motivated professionals who can help it achieve its global expansion goals.

EMRE currently has openings in the following areas:

Sales Representative – This job primarily entails day-to-day operational support for sales executives, driving brand awareness, and increasing market share. Superb communication and presentation skills are necessary, as is the ability to quickly build rapport with clients.

Quality Controller – The selected candidate will report directly to the operations director on a weekly basis. The applicant should have knowledge of general standards of hygiene, quality, and food safety and must hold a degree in food service management or its equivalent.

Financial Analyst – Facilitation of financial reports in compliance with established accounting practices is the key role of this position. The ideal candidate must know how to use applicable software programs for financial and management reporting and business analysis. Four years of relevant experience is needed.

Distribution Manager – The hired applicant will manage the warehouse and ensure the smooth distribution of finished products. The chosen candidate will oversee the quality, cost, and efficiency of the movement and storage of goods while also managing the departmental budget. Previous experience in a similar role is an advantage.

Interested individuals may send their résumé, together with two letters of reference, to davis@emrepasteurs.co. The deadline for all applications is September 30.

To: Evelyn Davis <davis@emrepasteurs.co>
From: Mehmet Korkmaz <mehmetkorkmaz@anatoliamail.com>
Date: September 25
Subject: Job Advertisement

Dear Ms. Davis,

I saw your company's posting on an online job site, and I would like to apply for the financial analyst position. I can assure you that my academic and professional background, as outlined in detail in the attached résumé, make me an excellent candidate for the job. EMRE PASTEURS has always had a notable reputation in the industry, and I would be grateful for the opportunity to work at your company.

Please feel free to let me know if you need any further information. You can contact me directly on my mobile phone at 555-9082 if you would like to arrange an interview. Your time and consideration is much appreciated.

Yours truly,

Mehmet Korkmaz

181. What is indicated about EMRE PASTEURS?
(A) It requires applicants to send several documents.
(B) It is currently constructing a manufacturing plant.
(C) It is looking to fill executive positions in sales.
(D) It has reduced its workforce in recent years.

182. In the advertisement, the word "oversee" in paragraph 5, line 2 is closest in meaning to
(A) survey
(B) examine
(C) monitor
(D) guide

183. What is NOT stated as a responsibility of the sales representative?
(A) Providing assistance to the sales manager
(B) Increasing brand recognition to consumers
(C) Establishing immediate ties with customers
(D) Searching for additional clients

184. What is suggested about Mr. Korkmaz?
(A) He studied food service management in college.
(B) He held a job in finance for the last four years.
(C) He has supervised the performance of a whole team.
(D) He previously applied for a position at EMRE PASTEURS.

185. What does Mr. Korkmaz want Ms. Davis to do?
(A) Schedule a testing date
(B) Offer him a salary raise
(C) Send him an application form
(D) Make arrangements to meet him

GO ON TO THE NEXT PAGE

Questions 186-190 refer to the following e-mail and schedule.

To	Lauren Wulff <l.wulff@jetsetgo.com>
From	Steven Mansfield <s.mansfield@jetsetgo.com>
Date	February 15
Subject	Flight Schedules
Attachment(s)	Skywing schedule

Dear Ms. Wulff,

I hope that everything in Washington is proceeding as you had hoped. As instructed, I have confirmed your return flight to Paris on Friday. In addition, I am finalizing your travel arrangements for the three-day seminar you will be attending in Spain next month. I tried reserving tickets with Bonjour Airlines, but unfortunately, their flights are already fully booked. It looks like Skywing Airlines is your next best option, though I'd like to consult you about the flight schedule before making a decision.

Please note that the seminar will begin on Tuesday, March 24 at 1 P.M. and end on Thursday, March 26 at 5 P.M. Since your hotel is a 25-minute drive from the airport, it would be good to arrive in Barcelona at least an hour before the event. Also, we might need to reconsider your return flight schedule. I received a call from Martha Tate, an On Foot magazine correspondent, and she told me that her publication is planning to feature our company's new line of luggage and travel accessories. She would like to know if she can conduct an interview with you in Paris on Friday, March 27 at 11 A.M. If you agree to the interview, you can take the second flight to Paris on that day to get back in time for the appointment.

Please let me know what you think about the matters I've discussed, so that I may immediately respond to Ms. Tate's inquiry and book your flights. Thank you.

Steven

Skywing Airlines

Flight Schedules CDG-BCN

Paris, France (CDG) to Barcelona, Spain (BCN)

Departure	Arrival	Flight	Stopover	Frequency	Meals
7:40 A.M.	9:20 A.M.	8699AF	0	3	B
9:35 A.M.	11:15 A.M.	8392AF	0	2,3,5	S
10:55 A.M.	12:40 P.M.	8393AF	0	1,2,6	S
12:55 P.M.	2:35 P.M.	8704AF	0	Except 7	L

Barcelona, Spain (BCN) to Paris, France (CDG)

Departure	Arrival	Flight	Stopover	Frequency	Meals
4:40 A.M.	6:30 A.M.	8700AF	0	1,5	B
6:50 A.M.	8:45 A.M.	8445AF	0	Except 7	B
7:35 A.M.	9:30 A.M.	8377AF	0	7	B
10:25 A.M.	12:20 P.M.	8670AF	0	Except 4,7	S

Certain flights may not be offered on holidays. Please contact a Skywing office in your area for more information.

Frequency Codes:
Flights are offered daily unless otherwise designated.

1-Monday	2-Tuesday	3-Wednesday	4-Thursday
5-Friday	6-Saturday	7-Sunday	

Meal Codes:

B-Breakfast	L-Lunch	D-Dinner	S-Snack

Reservations and Seat Assignments:
Reservations may be made online, by phone, or by visiting any of our ticketing centers and affiliate travel agencies. Flight bookings and seat assignments may be forfeited if passengers are not present at the designated check-in counter or boarding gate as scheduled.

186. What is suggested about Jet Set Go?
(A) It has manufacturing facilities in several locations.
(B) It sponsors events for entrepreneurs.
(C) It creates products for travelers.
(D) It has recently established sales centers abroad.

187. What most likely is Mr. Mansfield's job?
(A) A business executive secretary
(B) A corporate event organizer
(C) A customer representative
(D) A ticketing agent

188. What does Mr. Mansfield recommend Ms. Wulff do?
(A) Allow time to prepare for a workshop
(B) Reconsider her return flight options
(C) Avoid missing a connecting trip in the afternoon
(D) Submit a client contract as scheduled

189. Which flight should Ms. Wulff take to arrive at the seminar on time?
(A) 8704AF
(B) 8393AF
(C) 8699AF
(D) 8392AF

190. What information is NOT included in the schedule?
(A) The types of meals served to passengers
(B) A policy on seat assignments
(C) A set of guidelines for checked baggage
(D) The number of times a flight is offered in a week

GO ON TO THE NEXT PAGE

Questions 191-195 refer to the following letter and e-mail.

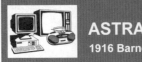

ASTRAL HOME CENTER
1916 Barnes Avenue, Cincinnati, OH 45214

"The Quality You Trust"
Since 1975

September 18

Alessandro Kapranos
798 Duffy Street
South Bend, IN 46601

Dear Mr. Kapranos,

We appreciate your business and hope you enjoy the appliance you purchased from Astral Home Center. As one of the country's most trusted electronic centers, we pride ourselves in distributing the finest appliances to suit our patrons' everyday needs and providing the most efficient customer service.

Your item is under warranty for 12 months starting from the date of purchase. During this period, you are entitled to free maintenance checkup and repair depending on the cause of the damage. In the event that your item needs to be repaired after the warranty period, you can still bring it to one of our service centers and our technicians will be happy to assist you.

APPLIANCE TYPE	OUT OF WARRANTY REPAIR COST (STANDARD FEES)
Air-conditioner	$150
Washing machine	$200
Television	$100
DVD player	$50
Laptop and tablet computers	$250

Please take note that you might need to pay an additional fee for the cost of replacement parts. The out-of-warranty repair cost includes all brands and units that fall under the appliance type.

For complete guidelines on our repair services, please refer to the booklet enclosed with this letter. It also includes a list of service centers located across the country.

Should you have any questions, you may call our 24-hour hotline at 555-9987 or e-mail us at custserv@astralhc.com.

Sincerely,

Blake Boer

Operations manager

Astral Home Center

To	Blake Boer <custserv@astralhc.com>
From	Alessandro Kapranos <alessandro.kapranos@rocketmail.com>
Date	January 25
Subject	Service Center in Alabama

Dear Mr. Boer,

Two years ago, I bought an Automaton LED Plasma TV from your store in Cincinnati. My wife and I were pleased with its excellent picture quality and ability to access the Internet. However, during a recent move to our current residence in Alabama, the TV was damaged while in transit.

Since I no longer have the booklet that was included with my purchase, I was wondering if you could refer me to the nearest service center in our area. We'd like to take our unit in for repair as soon as possible, so I'd appreciate it if you called my office number at 555-5837.

I'm looking forward to your swift response. Thank you.

Sincerely,

Alessandro Kapranos

191. What was included in the letter?
(A) Directions to a nearby repair center
(B) Details regarding a store policy
(C) A list of prices for some new appliances
(D) Information on an upcoming warehouse sale

192. What is suggested about Astral Home Center?
(A) It conducts online transactions.
(B) It ships merchandise internationally.
(C) It has several outlets nationwide.
(D) It organizes promotional offers every month.

193. In the letter, the phrase "fall under" in paragraph 3, line 2 is closest in meaning to
(A) lower
(B) comprise
(C) drop
(D) deteriorate

194. What is indicated about Mr. Kapranos?
(A) He must pay $100 for a repair.
(B) He formerly resided in Ohio.
(C) He recently placed a bulk order.
(D) He maintains a home office.

195. Why did Mr. Kapranos contact Mr. Boer?
(A) To reschedule an appointment with a repairperson
(B) To ask for replacement of a defective electronic product
(C) To inquire about the services offered by a moving company
(D) To request information about a specific establishment

GO ON TO THE NEXT PAGE

Questions 196-200 refer to the following e-mail and schedule.

To:	Curtis Freeman <cfreeman@hyperionskills.com>
From:	Jodi Grant <jodi_grant@theiaristorante.net>
Date:	May 30
Subject:	Excellent Course

I am responding to your request for comments and feedback on Hyperion's classes this month. I saw the advertisement on the Internet and signed up for the class that began on May 5. I thought it would be very useful for me, as I work in the hospitality industry and am planning to open a new restaurant this coming fall. I have to say that I was not disappointed at all with the class. I learned a lot after completing the last session a few days ago. I found the lessons taught in each session to be informative and helpful. I gained a lot of insight and ideas that I will use for my upcoming business venture. The instructor, Mr. Alex Hernandez, was very patient and innovative in his teaching approach. Also, I heard great things about the class on storage space taught by Laura Palmer. I was wondering if you will be offering this class again. If so, please let me know as I am very interested in attending.

Thanks again, and you can be assured that I will refer your center to my colleagues.

Sincerely,
Jodi Grant

Hyperion Skills Development Center

Programs for May

STARTING DATE	CLASS	DESCRIPTION
May 3, 9:30 A.M.	FPC780	Emphasizes the fundamental principles and methods of equipment use in food preparation and proper food cleaning
May 4, 8:00 A.M.	FBP415	Deals with methods for estimating bulk storage space and the quantity of food and beverages needed for running a restaurant
May 5, 10:00 A.M.	MMR823	Teaches the creation of profitable and affordable prices for menu items, as well as the supervision and execution of marketing campaigns
May 6, 7:30 A.M.	ESS609	Outlines the essential safety measures and sanitation methods kitchen staff members need to know

Each course consists of four weekly two-hour sessions and is taught by different instructors.

For inquiries about the registration process and fees,
you may send an e-mail to our registrar, Alicia Paguin at reg@hyperionskills.com.

196. Why was the e-mail written?
(A) To inquire about payment methods
(B) To provide comments on a class
(C) To request instructional materials
(D) To ask for a program brochure

197. What is indicated about Ms. Grant in the e-mail?
(A) She saw Hyperion's advertisement in a newspaper.
(B) She has registered for additional courses.
(C) She has taken several classes at Hyperion.
(D) She plans to open a new business.

198. Who most likely taught a class on pricing?
(A) Curtis Freeman
(B) Alicia Paguin
(C) Laura Palmer
(D) Alex Hernandez

199. What is mentioned about the class on safety and sanitation?
(A) It is intended for kitchen staff.
(B) It has been moved to a later date.
(C) It is conducted by two instructors.
(D) It takes place every Wednesday.

200. What time does the course on equipment use start?
(A) At 7:30 A.M.
(B) At 8:00 A.M.
(C) At 9:30 A.M.
(D) At 10:00 A.M.

This is the end of the test. You may review Part 5, 6, and 7 if you finish the test early.

解答 p.287 / 分數換算表 p.289 / 題目解析 p.319（解答本）

▮ 請翻到次頁「自我檢測表」檢視自己解答問題的方法與態度。

自我檢測表

TEST 07 順利的完成了嗎？

現在要開始透過以下的自我檢測表檢視自己在考試中的表現了嗎？

我的目標分數為：　　　　　　　這次測試的成績為：

1. 70 分鐘內，我完全集中精神在測試內容上。

   □是　□不是

   如果回答不是，理由是什麼呢？

2. 70 分鐘內，連答案卷的劃記都完成了。

   □是　□不是

   如果回答不是，理由是什麼呢？

3. 70 分鐘內，100 題都解完了。

   □是　□不是

   如果回答不是，理由是什麼呢？

4. Part 5 和 Part 6 在 25 分鐘以內全都寫完了。

   □是　□不是

   如果回答不是，理由是什麼呢？

5. 寫 Part 7 的時候，沒有一題花超過五分鐘。

   □是　□不是

   如果回答不是，理由是什麼呢？

6. 請寫下你需要改善的地方以及給自己的忠告。

*回到本書第二頁，確認自己的目標分數並加強對於達成分數的意志。
對於要改善的部分一定要在下一次測試中實踐。這點是最重要的，也要這樣才能有進步。

TEST 08

Part 5

Part 6

Part 7

自我檢測表

等等！考前確認事項：

1. 關掉行動裝置電源了嗎？□ 是
2. 答案卷（Answer Sheet）、鉛筆、橡皮擦都準備好了嗎？□ 是
3. 手錶帶了嗎？□ 是

如果都準備齊全了，想想目標分數後即可開始作答。

考試結束時間為現在開始 70 分鐘後的＿＿＿點＿＿＿分。

Reading Test

In this section, you must demonstrate your ability to read and comprehend English. You will be given a variety of texts and asked to answer questions about these texts. This section is divided into three parts and will take 75 minutes to complete.

Do not mark the answers in your test book. Use the answer sheet that is separately provided.

PART 5

Directions: In each question, you will be asked to review a statement that is missing a word or phrase. Four answer choices will be provided for each question. Select the best answer and mark the corresponding letter (A), (B), (C), or (D) on the answer sheet.

101. Garrison Peters will be the fashion _______ for Tate Clothiers' new line of sportswear for both men and women.
(A) designer (B) will design
(C) designed (D) designers

102. During the staff meeting, Ms. Crabbe emphasized the importance of observing office dress codes at _______ times.
(A) all (B) only
(C) entire (D) whole

103. It is the responsibility of agents at the airline's check-in counters to have baggage tags on hand for travelers who _______ them.
(A) requesting (B) request
(C) requests (D) to request

104. Although she _______ difficulty in the beginning, Marla Ambers learned to cope with the fast-paced work environment at Gordem Entertainment Studios.
(A) will have had (B) is having
(C) was having (D) to have

105. The annual performance _______ allows management to determine whether employees are doing what they are supposed to.
(A) resolution (B) interpretation
(C) evaluation (D) estimation

106. Popular with locals and tourists _______, Gaiman's jewelry store has been a treasured landmark on First Street for many years.
(A) alike (B) all
(C) every (D) same

107. Darius Spencer is the most _______ candidate to replace the retiring senior accountant because of his experience and educational background.
(A) legible (B) legal
(C) partial (D) likely

108. Construction companies should _______ run maintenance checks on all their equipment to ensure optimal performance.
(A) modestly (B) usefully
(C) regularly (D) formerly

109. At last week's meeting, the research team presented the ------- of next quarter's revenues to the company president.
(A) estimates
(B) circulations
(C) engagements
(D) appointments

110. According to the Department of Transportation, the additional street lights and road signs have led to ------- safety conditions on the highway.
(A) improve (B) improves
(C) improvement (D) improved

111. Classrooms are kept at a comfortable temperature to provide an environment that is ------- to learning.
(A) enviable
(B) proficient
(C) profitable
(D) conducive

112. ------- lessen the risk of accidents while on the project site, Theobald Developments created new work safety policies.
(A) Moreover
(B) In addition to
(C) As though
(D) In order to

113. The La Familia residential condominium ------- opened for occupancy following six years of construction.
(A) equally (B) occasionally
(C) finally (D) previously

114. The blueprints for the renovation had to be revised because the apartment's living room was ------- measured.
(A) incorrect
(B) incorrectness
(C) more incorrect
(D) incorrectly

115. Once ------- MacDougal Boulevard, the street is undergoing repairs and will be called Cosa Boulevard after the construction is completed.
(A) name
(B) to name
(C) named
(D) naming

116. The board members of Portia Coffee Company have ------- some administrative changes to accommodate the requests of the workers union.
(A) alternated
(B) refrained
(C) reminded
(D) instituted

117. ------- the Invierna Electronics compound, visitors will find a large production plant, workers' dormitories, and a modern warehouse.
(A) Within
(B) Between
(C) Over
(D) Onto

118. The marketing director arranged ------- with advertising and promotion advisors to obtain feedback on her newly designed advertisement campaign.
(A) proposals
(B) consultations
(C) layouts
(D) deliveries

119. Tennyson Banks' ------- of kindness, in the form of a large monetary donation, has made it possible for the city museum to proceed with the improvements of its exhibit rooms.
(A) entry (B) act
(C) idea (D) option

GO ON TO THE NEXT PAGE

120. On the online order form, Ms. Jung requested that she be notified ------- the packages are shipped from the manufacturing plant.
(A) furthermore
(B) despite
(C) rather than
(D) as soon as

121. Most of the employees said that the new software program has been ------- useful in speeding up the database search process.
(A) consideration
(B) considering
(C) considerable
(D) considerably

122. Viewers may watch the all-new season of *Dining Haven* for ------- recipes specially created by celebrity cook Steven Brant.
(A) prompted (B) described
(C) scarce (D) healthy

123. Even though Ms. Regina had been in transit for 24 hours, she still managed to give an ------- lecture at the university.
(A) energizer (B) energetically
(C) energetic (D) energize

124. ------- changing your mobile phone plan, please present valid identification at the customer service counter.
(A) When (B) As if
(C) Therefore (D) In regards

125. At Mr. Kincaid's retirement party, the staff conveyed their ------- of his 20 years of committed service to the company.
(A) appreciatively
(B) appreciated
(C) appreciative
(D) appreciation

126. Due to a change in tomorrow's work schedule, the refined oil will need to be ------- into the tankers before the end of the day.
(A) expanded
(B) loaded
(C) translated
(D) engaged

127. Andromeda, which ------- Rosy Trinkets' most in-demand jewelry collection for the last six months, will soon become available in Asia.
(A) to be
(B) will be
(C) has been
(D) is being

128. ------- is on duty tonight must check that all the entrances are locked and the security alarm is set before leaving the building.
(A) That
(B) Whoever
(C) Someone
(D) Whenever

129. In accordance with the new company policy, all Fuschia Travels clients will be billed for flights ------- from accommodation costs.
(A) separately
(B) commonly
(C) positively
(D) personally

130. Asaha Telecommunications does not require staff to participate in its community outreach programs, but many employees ------- do so.
(A) voluntarily
(B) memorably
(C) divisively
(D) infrequently

131. The local newspaper reported that the damaged electrical lines were the ------- cause of the four-hour power outage yesterday evening.
(A) clear
(B) clears
(C) clearly
(D) clearness

132. Aqua Mouthwash repackaged its dental care products and launched an information campaign to ------- a favorable reputation.
(A) pass
(B) regain
(C) leave
(D) attach

133. Du Vin Restaurant does not provide delivery service for orders under $50, ------- does it offer catering for groups of fewer than 20 guests.
(A) also
(B) so
(C) either
(D) nor

134. ------- the fierce competition in the shipping industry, Kingfisher Express remains the most successful cargo company in the region.
(A) Frequently
(B) In spite of
(C) As far as
(D) Otherwise

135. Customers patronize the Evergreen Pharmacy because of its ------- to providing the community with high-quality, affordable medicines.
(A) commits
(B) committed
(C) commitment
(D) committable

136. Because of his ------- superb sales presentations, Mr. Lim is always selected to represent the home appliance company at trade fairs.
(A) approximately
(B) variably
(C) impartially
(D) consistently

137. Elven Hotel has three ------- banquet halls that are large enough to hold corporate events and social functions of any kind.
(A) spacious
(B) coherent
(C) fulfilled
(D) insatiable

138. A building located in the financial ------- was sold to a property developer who had offered the owner an amount that was higher than the current market price.
(A) resource (B) industry
(C) system (D) district

139. Out of the 36 applicants, Wally Brennan was ------- the research funding from Indigo Foundation for his well-defined project proposal on the study of alternative fuel sources.
(A) granted
(B) assisted
(C) encouraged
(D) maintained

140. Hermaine Electronics' newly-released photo printer is ------- in price and functionality to those of the company's market rivals.
(A) comparable
(B) momentous
(C) operative
(D) practical

GO ON TO THE NEXT PAGE

PART 6

Directions: In this part, you will be asked to read an English text. Some sentences are incomplete. Select the word or phrase that correctly completes each sentence and mark the corresponding letter (A), (B), (C), or (D) on the answer sheet.

Questions 141-143 refer to the following letter.

December 18

Human Resources
Flavors Group
28 Wood Street, Pittston, PA 18640

Dear Madam or Sir,

I am writing to apply for the franchise supervisor position advertised on your company's Web site on December 15. I believe that I possess the needed expertise for the job, and that my future in your company could be a ------- one.

141. (A) promising
(B) distant
(C) shared
(D) predictable

I have been an account supervisor in Blast Foods Corporation's franchising department for the last four years. As a supervisor, I am in charge of the account executives who sell the corporation's franchise permits. The job has enhanced my marketing skills and -------

142. (A) enabling
(B) enabled
(C) to enable
(D) will be enabled

me to learn how a franchise is operated.

I have included with this letter my résumé and three references. Should you need to know more about my credentials, please call me at 555-6323.

Your ------- is greatly appreciated.

143. (A) donation
(B) recommendation
(C) invitation
(D) consideration

Sincerely,

Ewan Walken

Questions 144-146 refer to the following e-mail.

TO: Victoria Morgan <v.morgan@towerdevt.com>
FROM: Kate Lee <kate.lee@burnmail.com>
DATE: July 14
SUBJECT: Meeting

Dear Ms. Morgan,

We appreciate getting the information packet from you, but we would like to request that our business appointment for Thursday be rescheduled. We need some extra time to consider different ------- before meeting with you.

144. (A) properties
(B) furniture
(C) technology
(D) instructions

My husband and I found Summersville to be a nice vacation place for the family. However, we are as yet ------- about the farm estate you showed us. This is because we

145. (A) uninformed
(B) enlightened
(C) undecided
(D) outspoken

are currently considering beachside properties recommended by other developers. Some of them are willing to provide a 20 percent discount on beachfront lots. That said, your offers are also attractive, particularly the quotations you gave us that ------- a 25

146. (A) specifying
(B) specifies
(C) specification
(D) specify

percent discount on properties of 400 square meters and above. I hope you can give us at least two weeks to review all the proposals. We will let you know of our decision shortly. Thank you.

Best regards,

Kate Lee

GO ON TO THE NEXT PAGE

Questions 147-149 refer to the following article.

Actor Alfred Monaco has been cast in a starring role for a television show ------- this fall.

147. (A) reviewing
(B) premiering
(C) hosting
(D) subscribing

In the comedy series *The Stage*, Alfred will play the role of Donald Williams, an aspiring singer who does ------- it takes to land a career at Park Studios, a company at the center

148. (A) whenever
(B) whatever
(C) most
(D) such

of the country's entertainment industry. In an interview with News Time, the actor said the show ------- a different side of him to the public. "This will be my first time performing on

149. (A) will expose
(B) exposed
(C) had exposed
(D) has exposed

television," Alfred said. "I'm very excited about the project because the script is really engaging."

The season's first episode will be broadcast on November 6 at 9 P.M.

Questions 150-152 refer to the following memo.

TO: Staff
FROM: Dennis Buckmaster, HRD head
SUBJECT: Job Advertisements

DATE: August 5

Since Solano Marketing was established, the human resources department has counted on newspapers to advertise job openings in the company. However, we have observed that ------- to printed advertisements have dropped since the onset of online employment

150. (A) responses
(B) responded
(C) responding
(D) respondent

agencies. To reach out to more applicants, we will use the services of Workhunter.com starting in July.

The ------- agency will post our advertisements on their Web site. And they will match the

151. (A) security
(B) recruitment
(C) transportation
(D) housing

company with job seekers who might qualify for the positions.

Workhunter requests that the advertisements be submitted next week. -------, each

152. (A) Instead
(B) Otherwise
(C) At last
(D) As always

advertisement should contain a brief description of our firm and the position, as well as a list of requirements.

Please e-mail the advertisements to Tess no later than Friday. Thanks.

READING TEST 1 2 3 4 5 6 7 8 9 10

GO ON TO THE NEXT PAGE

PART 7

Directions: In this part, you will be asked to read several texts, such as advertisements, articles or examples of business correspondence. Each text is followed by several questions. Select the best answer and mark the corresponding letter (A), (B), (C), or (D) on your answer sheet.

Questions 153-154 refer to the following notice.

Paul's Bar and Grill

We are celebrating our 10th anniversary and you're invited!

For the entire month of November, we have great specials on our food and drinks. Also, don't miss our Saturday night events, featuring performances from up-and-coming bands in today's music industry.

November 4 - Retro
(McMusic and Smart Waves)
November 11 - Acoustic Night
(The Pluckers and The Fireflies)
November 18 - Reggae Mania
(South Drifters)
November 25 - The Search for the Ultimate Rock Band
(Grand Prize: $2,000)

153. What is indicated about Paul's Bar and Grill?
(A) It has been operating for a decade.
(B) It features special menus on Saturdays.
(C) It offers complimentary beverages.
(D) It provides special exotic dishes.

154. When will the music contest be held?
(A) On November 4
(B) On November 11
(C) On November 18
(D) On November 25

GO ON TO THE NEXT PAGE

Questions 155-156 refer to the following advertisement.

Bay Shop

Finding the best gifts for your loved ones can sometimes be stressful and frustrating. But here at Bay Shop, we sell a wide array of gift items that will surely please the people dear to you. Our talented craftsmen make a variety of unique toys, handicrafts, and personal accessories. So if you are looking for presents for any occasion or tokens of appreciation, come and visit Bay Shop.

Our store is open every day from 9 A.M. to 7 P.M. You may also view our products online by visiting www.bayshop.com.

155. What most likely is Bay Shop?
(A) A handicraft importer
(B) A gift retailer
(C) A furniture distributor
(D) A fashion boutique

156. What is indicated about Bay Shop?
(A) It imports finished goods from nearby countries.
(B) Its customers can order items from a Web site.
(C) Its products are created by highly skilled workers.
(D) It gives gift certificates to clients registering online.

Questions 157-158 refer to the following article.

Allergy Reports Prompt Vaccine Recall

KUALA LUMPUR - The Health Department recalled 5,000 doses of tetanus vaccine after receiving several reports about its side effects on patients.

According to the department, 30 patients from around the capital suffered from rashes last week after receiving the shots at state hospitals, indicating a high rate of allergic reactions to the medicine. Health Secretary Rajah Hashmid immediately recalled the vaccines and ordered public hospitals to stop using them.

Manufactured by Indian pharmaceutical company Alhira, the tetanus vaccines were imported by the government last month along with other medicines. An investigation into the patients' cases is underway.

157. Why did Rajah Hashmid suspend use of the vaccines?
(A) They had passed an expiration date.
(B) They cause an adverse physical response.
(C) They were exposed to toxic materials.
(D) They were not approved by the Health Deparment.

158. What is mentioned about the shots?
(A) They were provided free of charge.
(B) They were only available at private hospitals.
(C) They were required for government workers.
(D) They were shipped from a foreign country.

GO ON TO THE NEXT PAGE

Questions 159-161 refer to the following letter.

The Kayak Resort

Kohala Coast, Hawaii

February 24

Dear Ms. Scott,

We regret that you did not enjoy your island excursion yesterday. However, we must clarify that we did not intend to cut your trip short. Your tour guides decided to skip some islands to allow more time for your parasailing activity, which you requested yesterday morning. We sincerely apologize for not discussing the matter with you immediately upon your return.

We have been informed that you are demanding a refund because of your unsatisfactory experience. Unfortunately, we are unable to provide a refund. Our policy states that fees for water recreation and sports activities are nonrefundable. To compensate you, we will give you two meal vouchers for any of the restaurants on the premises, which you may use during your stay with us.

Thank you for your understanding. We hope you will enjoy the rest of your holiday at the Kayak Resort.

Respectfully yours,

Luke Dunstan
Manager
The Kayak Resort

159. Why was the letter written?
(A) To make changes in a plan
(B) To schedule an island tour
(C) To apologize for an incident
(D) To introduce a new policy

160. What did Ms. Scott want to do?
(A) Recover her payment
(B) Transfer to another resort
(C) Try a different activity
(D) Confirm her flight

161. What is NOT suggested about the Kayak Resort?
(A) It operates more than one restaurant.
(B) It organized a tour for some guests.
(C) It maintains a strict refund policy.
(D) It overbooked a sports activity.

Questions 162-164 refer to the following advertisement.

Join the Team at Pan-Global Web!

Pan-Global Web Designs, based in Montreal, is searching for a full-time graphic artist. This job is for professional artists with at least two years of experience in a related field. Applicants must have graduated with a relevant degree, and be willing to move to Montreal by November 1. Those with strong French skills are also preferred.

Successful applicants will receive two weeks of training, along with a competitive salary package and a moving allowance. The position also includes medical benefits and quarterly incentives.

Those wishing to apply should send a résumé and cover letter to hrpanglobal@global.net. Applicants who meet our criteria will be contacted for an interview. The deadline for application is September 19. For further information, contact our human resources department at (503) 555-8899.

162. For whom is the advertisement most likely intended?
(A) Computer programmers
(B) Experienced graphic artists
(C) Web site owners
(D) Recruitment specialists

163. What requirement is necessary for the advertised position?
(A) Fluency in French
(B) Computer programming skills
(C) A degree in management
(D) Willingness to relocate

164. What is indicated about Pan-Global Web?
(A) It has international branches.
(B) It will sponsor a graphic arts workshop.
(C) It provides staff with medical insurance.
(D) It is moving its Montreal office.

GO ON TO THE NEXT PAGE

Questions 165-167 refer to the following e-mail.

From: Georgina Valencia <gina_valencia@aceconcrete.com>
To: Reagan Tan <r.tan@digconstruct.com>
Subject: Re: Xinjiang Cement Factory inquiry
Date: August 19

Dear Mr. Tan,

Thank you for your interest in purchasing our cement factory in Xinjiang. As one of Ace Concrete's largest cement factories, the plant has the capacity to produce 200,000 metric tons of cement annually and supply the needs of major construction firms such as yours.

We would be happy to show you our equipment, production line, and warehouse. If you want to stop by, we recommend that you make arrangements for Friday so that the factory's operations manager, Mr. Gerald Ong, will be available to give you a tour of the plant. Mr. Ong is currently setting up our new factory in Beijing, which will become the base of our operations over the next five years. He will be back in Xinjiang on Thursday.

Please let us know your decision before the end of the week. Feel free to contact us at 555-1478, and we would be happy to address any inquiries you may have.

We look forward to meeting you.

Sincerely,

Georgina Valencia

165. Why was the e-mail written?
(A) To arrange a factory tour
(B) To propose a merger
(C) To introduce an executive
(D) To evaluate an inspection

166. Why is Mr. Tan advised to visit on Friday?
(A) The factory is undergoing renovation.
(B) The operations manager will be available.
(C) The company needs time to prepare a presentation.
(D) The plant's selling price has yet to be finalized.

167. According to the e-mail, what will Mr.Tan NOT see during his visit?
(A) Machines
(B) Production line
(C) Warehouse
(D) Merchandise samples

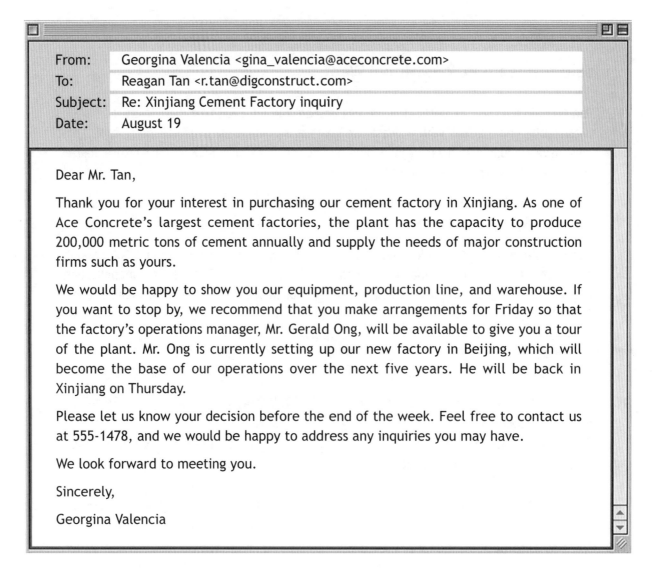

Questions 168-171 refer to the following letter.

Brosnan Lawyers Association

75 North Drive, Burbank, CA 9985

December 1

Dear colleagues,

Brosnan Lawyers Association (BLA) will hold a talk on corporate law on February 20 at the Lincoln Plenary Hall from 9 A.M. to 5 P.M. Experienced business attorneys will discuss key legal issues concerning companies. The talk is free-of-charge and is exclusive to BLA members only. The schedule is as follows:

Time	Topic	Speaker
9:00 A.M. - 10:30 A.M.	Corporate Policies	Francis Adams
10:30 A.M. - 12:00 P.M.	Financial Management	Jeffrey McMahon, Jr.
12:00 P.M. - 1:30 P.M.	BREAK	
1:30 P.M. - 3:00 P.M.	Mergers and Acquisitions	Philip Kaimo
3:00 P.M. - 5:00 P.M.	Intellectual Property Protection	Nathan Combs

Moreover, the association's newly elected officials will be introduced at a banquet to be held immediately following the talk. All members are requested to attend this celebration. To register for the talk and confirm your attendance to the banquet, please call the BLA office or e-mail events@bla.com by December 15.

Best regards,

Sarah Ludwig
Chairperson
Brosnan Lawyers Association

168. What does the letter mention about the speakers?
(A) They are partners in a law office.
(B) They work for large firms.
(C) They are accomplished legal professionals.
(D) They are university professors.

169. Who will deliver a lecture on company regulations?
(A) Jeffrey McMahon, Jr.
(B) Francis Adams
(C) Nathan Combs
(D) Philip Kaimo

170. What is suggested about the BLA?
(A) It has appointed new leaders.
(B) It is recruiting staff members.
(C) It is celebrating an anniversary.
(D) It has changed its regulations.

171. What information is NOT provided in the letter?
(A) An e-mail address
(B) A telephone number
(C) A seminar venue
(D) A cutoff date for registration

GO ON TO THE NEXT PAGE

Questions 172-176 refer to the following article.

Raul Vargas Reveals Retirement Plans

By Donny Chu

Despite his flourishing career in the English League, Stallions player Raul Vargas wants to become more than a sports star. At the Soccer Federation Awards on Saturday, the newly hailed Goalie of the Year revealed his plan to quit sports and pursue another profession.

"Lately, I have been thinking of giving up soccer," Vargas said during his acceptance speech. "Receiving this award is a sign that it's time for me to retire."

Such words were never expected to come from the Brazilian, who is the most treasured goalkeeper in the league. During *Stopwatch Magazine's* exclusive interview with the player, however, Vargas explained that he made the decision because he has responsibilities that have forced him to retire from soccer.

"I have reached the point where I have fully achieved my dreams as an athlete," Vargas said. "More importantly, I need to become more involved with my family's corporation, an obligation I have put aside since I began my career."

Being the sole heir of the Biobras Corporation, Vargas was originally groomed to lead the company. His parents sent him to Brasilia University to study industrial engineering, with the expectation that he would take up a master's degree in the United States later on. While preparing to lead the top biofuel company in Brazil, however, Vargas was making a name for himself as one of the best goalkeepers in college.

Because of his impressive talent, Vargas was offered a spot on the national team immediately after graduation. Thus, he set aside plans of obtaining a graduate degree and entering Biobras Corporation, choosing rather to accept the team's offer upon receiving the blessing of his parents.

Soccer fanatics witnessed how the career of the 29-year-old boomed. Apart from playing for the national team, Vargas joined English clubs East Hampton, Armorshire, and Hemel Finstead before he was signed by the Stallions.

"I have enjoyed putting on exciting matches with my teams. It's rewarding to bring joy to football fans," Vargas said.

However, Vargas has made the choice to take off his uniform and venture into the corporate world.

"Nothing is permanent in the sports industry. I have to establish a more stable career, and I hope this decision will allow me to do it. Nevertheless, soccer will always be my first love," Vargas said.

172. What is the main purpose of the article?
(A) To report about a soccer match
(B) To publicize a sports magazine
(C) To provide information about an athlete
(D) To introduce a new type of fuel

173. What is suggested about Mr. Vargas?
(A) He did not attend graduate school.
(B) He played soccer in high school.
(C) He is a young entrepreneur.
(D) He will transfer to a new team.

174. Why is Mr. Vargas retiring from soccer?
(A) He will continue his studies.
(B) He will play another sport.
(C) He wants to move to another location.
(D) He wants to enter the family business.

175. What is indicated about Biobras?
(A) It recently laid off some employees.
(B) It is involved in the fuel industry.
(C) It maintains a branch office in England.
(D) It sponsors a Brazilian soccer team.

176. What does Mr. Vargas mention about his current career?
(A) It is a well-paying job.
(B) It is not very predictable.
(C) It inspires him to play other sports.
(D) It does not develop his skills.

Questions 177-180 refer to the following advertisement.

MJA Cleaning Services

250 Grocer Drive, Salt Lake City, UT
www.mja.com

Imagine the relief of coming home to a spotless house after a busy day at work. Whether you have a studio apartment or a two-story house, MJA Cleaning Services can tidy it up for you. Spend your leisure hours enjoying the things that are important to you, and let us worry about your housework.

MJA has been serving the Salt Lake City area for the past 15 years and is well-known for its efficiency, professionalism, and speed. We offer weekly and biweekly cleaning, window washing, carpet cleaning, and floor stripping and waxing services. We also move furniture and clean up after parties. In addition, we use environmentally-friendly housekeeping materials and equipment.

Visit our Web site, check out our rates, and think about the money you will save by using our services. We supply professional-quality cleaning at a low cost.

As part of a special offer, we will give you a 50 percent discount on our carpet cleaning service for every biweekly cleaning. Contact us now at 555-2524, and we will set up a consultation.

177. What is implied about MJA services?
(A) It is affiliated with an environmental organization.
(B) It provides discounts for long-term customers.
(C) It offers round-the-clock assistance.
(D) It mainly does work in residential buildings.

178. What is NOT a service offered by MJA?
(A) Carpet cleaning
(B) Event cleanup
(C) Floor waxing
(D) Furniture cleaning

179. What does the advertisement suggest about the company?
(A) It opened very recently.
(B) It publishes rates online.
(C) It charges more than its competitors.
(D) It is looking to hire more staff.

180. What will be given to customers who have their house cleaned every two weeks?
(A) Gift certificates
(B) Housekeeping guidebooks
(C) A store coupon
(D) A discount on a service

GO ON TO THE NEXT PAGE

Questions 181-185 refer to the following e-mail and brochure.

To:	Pauline Sotto <psotto@pyrosbiz.com>
From:	Joey Clarete <joclare@comptav.org>
Date:	June 26
Subject:	Product Inquiry

I am one of the owners of CompTavern Internet Café, and we are set to open an additional branch in Rhode Island in September. *TechSavvy Magazine* recently came out with an excellent review of your newest merchandise, which was how I found out about your business.

We are currently looking to buy 32 web cameras for the desktop computers at our new branch. In addition, we are looking at the possibility of obtaining three color laser printers and a photocopier which has the capacity to produce a minimum of 60 pages per minute. Can you mail us a copy of your brochure describing all of your merchandise in detail? Please also include some information regarding your shipping. I hope to hear from you as soon as possible so that I can place an order.

Thank you.

Pyros Biz Summer Brochure

22 Cunningham Square, Providence, Rhode Island 02918

LASER PRINTER - Black and white printer ideal for small- to medium-size offices - Capable of double-sided printing	$289.99
PHOTOCOPIER - User-friendly LCD control panel - Capacity: 40 pages per minute	$576.16
FAX MACHINE - Transmits at 14,400 bits per second (bps) - Has an energy-efficient sleep mode function	$195.44
SCANNER - Fast precision scanning in black-and-white, 24-bit-color, and grayscale - Full-featured photo software solution	$118.37
WEB CAMERA - Superior image quality (two-megapixel sensor) - Comes with software and a sturdy stand	$59.50

SHIPPING POLICY

Please allow three to five business days for national delivery (within the United States). For foreign orders, a handling fee of $25 will be charged in addition to the regular shipping costs. Products can take two to five weeks to ship after an order is placed. Reduced shipping fees are available for both national and foreign bulk orders (20 pieces minimum). For more information, please call 555-8497 or log on to www.pyrosbiz.com.

181. How did Mr. Clarete learn about Pyros Biz products?
(A) Through a friend's recommendation
(B) Through an online advertisement
(C) Through a phone directory
(D) Through a published article

182. What is stated about CompTavern Internet Café?
(A) It will open a new branch.
(B) Its computers are outdated.
(C) It recently hired employees.
(D) Its number of customers has risen.

183. What items will Mr. Clarete probably order?
(A) Scanners
(B) Laser printers
(C) Web cameras
(D) Photocopiers

184. What is NOT mentioned as a characteristic of any Pyros Biz products?
(A) Stylish design
(B) User friendliness
(C) Energy efficiency
(D) Free software

185. What kind of shipping fees will Mr. Clarete probably be charged?
(A) Regular national fees
(B) Bulk national fees
(C) Regular foreign fees
(D) Bulk foreign fees

GO ON TO THE NEXT PAGE

Questions 186-190 refer to the following advertisement and e-mail.

NexusWire

Your Ultimate Link to the World

POSITIONS AVAILABLE:

To uphold our reputation as one of the most widely read news magazine in Europe, we are constantly seeking out talented staff writers to join our dynamic editorial team. At present, four full-time jobs are available at our main headquarters in Prague, where the selected candidates will start work on April 1. From time to time, they will also be assigned to cover events in Amsterdam, Copenhagen, Berlin, and other European cities.

Application forms are available for download on our Web site at www.nexuswire.com. Our section editors will personally review the applications, so please e-mail them directly with your form, references, and samples of your work.

SECTION	EDITOR	E-MAIL ADDRESS
Health and Lifestyle	Dwayne Perez	d.perez@nexuswire.com
Science and Technology	Roger Stanley	r.stanley@nexuswire.com
Travel and Leisure	Eleanor Hansen	e.hansen@nexuswire.com
Business and Finance	Claudia Young	c.young@nexuswire.com

The deadline for all applications is February 28. Qualified candidates will be invited for interviews which will take place at the Prague office on March 10.

To: c.young@nexuswire.com
From: jacob_v0918@zircmail.com
Date: February 18
Subject: Job Advertisement

Dear Ms. Young,

I am writing in response to *NexusWire's* posting for staff writers. Because of my knowledge and considerable experience in the field, I believe I am fully qualified for the position.

As a reporter for *The Liberic Business Daily* for two years, I was assigned to write a minimum of three articles per day. While writing full-time at the newspaper, I also did some freelance writing for several business journals. I obtained my university diploma from the Liberic School of Journalism and am fluent in English, Dutch, and German.

Attached to this e-mail are some of my published works, which I hope meet the standards of *NexusWire*. Thank you for your time and I look forward to your positive reply.

Respectfully,

Jacob Vaughn

186. What will most likely take place after February 28?
(A) A new magazine issue will be released.
(B) Applications for jobs will no longer be accepted.
(C) Candidates will be sent job application forms.
(D) Editorial staff will convene for a meeting.

187. Where will the successful applicants be based?
(A) In Copenhagen
(B) In Amsterdam
(C) In Prague
(D) In Berlin

188. Which qualification does Mr. Vaughn NOT mention?
(A) An internship at a media company
(B) Proficiency in foreign languages
(C) A degree from a journalism school
(D) Previous work as a business reporter

189. In the advertisement, the word "cover" in paragraph 1, line 4 is closest in meaning to
(A) conceal
(B) speak about
(C) protect
(D) report on

190. Which section of NexusWire is Mr. Vaughn most likely interested in?
(A) Travel and Leisure
(B) Health and Lifestyle
(C) Business and Finance
(D) Science and Technology

GO ON TO THE NEXT PAGE

Questions 191-195 refer to the following Web contact form and e-mail.

Xyther Software Unlimited

Please use the form below to contact us.

Name	Caleb Guillory
E-mail	cguillory@bwmail.com
Phone	555-6074
Subject	Software Problem
Message	I purchased a software program at your shop on September 3, but I've been having some problems using it. I was able to install it successfully on my desktop computer. However, every time I use the program for more than five minutes, the operating system automatically shuts down and then restarts. The same thing happened when I tried using the application a second time, and it has continued to happen since. I cannot seem to figure out what the problem is. I would be extremely grateful if you could help me with this issue before the 90-day warranty ends. Thank you, and I hope to hear from you soon.

To: cguillory@bwmail.com
From: custserv@xythersoftware.com
Date: September 28
Subject: Inquiry Form No. 95204 - Received September 27, 4:58 P.M.

Dear Mr. Guillory,

Thank you for your e-mail. We are so sorry for the troubles you have experienced in using our software. In the past three months, we have received inquiries from other customers who also had difficulties with their purchases, so we decided to conduct a series of tests. The results suggest that defective source codes caused the various programs to malfunction: Web Browser is unable to load pages completely; error messages appear upon the start-up of Database Organizer; certain files cannot be opened using Document Manager; and Image Editor shuts down computer systems after operating for about five minutes.

Rest assured, we have fixed the errors and would be more than happy to replace your software. Please do not forget to submit your official receipt when you return the item to our shop. And to make up for the trouble this incident has caused, we have attached a printable coupon that you can use on your next purchase.

Sincerely,

Customer Service Team
Xyther Software Unlimited

191. What did Mr. Guillory NOT include on the form?
(A) Contact information
(B) Purpose for writing
(C) Date of purchase
(D) Shipping address

192. Why was the e-mail written?
(A) To offer a solution to Mr. Guillory
(B) To request a warranty extension
(C) To conduct a customer survey
(D) To explain a reimbursement policy

193. What is indicated about Mr. Guillory?
(A) He will receive a full refund for the product.
(B) He has not yet received the software he purchased.
(C) He sent an inquiry on September 27.
(D) He does not agree with the research.

194. Which program did Mr. Guillory most likely use?
(A) Database Organizer
(B) Image Editor
(C) Document Manager
(D) Web Browser

195. What does Xyther Software Unlimited ask Mr. Guillory to do?
(A) Hand in a receipt
(B) Return an item by mail
(C) Reinstall a program
(D) Submit a payment

GO ON TO THE NEXT PAGE

Questions 196-200 refer to the following e-mail and announcement.

To: Parvati Malik <parvatim@fastmail.com>
From: Chandrika Rao <ChanRao@allmail.com>
Date: October 2
Subject: GPD Seminar

Dear Parvati,

I enjoyed talking with you at the Singapore convention last month. It was unfortunate that there wasn't enough time to speak about the several projects you are going to oversee in January. I completely understand your anxiety about working on all those projects, since I went through the same thing last year. I found that listening and talking to industry experts was very beneficial, which is why I strongly suggest that you participate in the three-day seminar my company is sponsoring next month. One of the speakers, Omar Pillai of Lakshman Developers, will go over the challenges of project management and provide corresponding solutions.

Attached are some seminar details. I would be happy to personally answer any questions you might have, so please contact me directly at (+9122) 555-1308.

Best regards,

Chandrika

9th GLOBAL PROPERTY AND REAL ESTATE SEMINAR

Satya Yuga Convention Center
November 7 to 9

Below are the presentations that were recently added to the seminar.
On October 31, the final timetable will be forwarded by e-mail to each participant who has signed up.

DATE/TIME	PRESENTATION	PRESENTER
November 6 10 A.M.	Investing in your First Property: For Beginners	Balram Jhadav Strategic Consultant VGS Consultancy
November 7 4 P.M.	Understanding Commercial Property Investment	Vineeta Das Corporate Finance Head Gandhari Property Incorporated
November 8 1 P.M.	Effective Building Project Management: Handling Various Projects All at Once	Omar Pillai Operations Director Lakshman Developers
November 9 9 A.M.	Moving Toward Sustainable Property Development	Menaka Sarin Chief Executive Officer Kaurava Enterprises

Registration has been extended to October 20.
For more information, please log on to www.gpdseminars.com.

196. What is the main purpose of the e-mail?
(A) To invite a speaker to a seminar
(B) To suggest participation in an event
(C) To request an opinion about a service
(D) To provide an update on a project

197. What is indicated about Ms. Malik?
(A) She has to recruit more staff for her department.
(B) She has been offered a higher position with a competitor.
(C) She is having difficulty finding major property investors.
(D) She will be managing multiple tasks at the same time.

198. What is suggested about the presentations described in the announcement?
(A) They will be held in different venues.
(B) They were recently added to the timetable.
(C) They are the only talks taking place at the seminar.
(D) They will be led by people from the same company.

199. Which date's presentation does Ms. Rao think will benefit Ms. Malik?
(A) November 6
(B) November 7
(C) November 8
(D) November 9

200. Who would most likely be interested in Mr. Jhadav's presentation?
(A) First-time property buyers
(B) Business consultants
(C) Recent college graduates
(D) Financial investors

This is the end of the test. You may review Part 5, 6, and 7 if you finish the test early.

解答 p.287 / 分數換算表 p.289 / 題目解析 p.369（解答本）

請翻到次頁「自我檢測表」檢視自己解答問題的方法與態度。

自我檢測表

TEST 08 順利的完成了嗎？

現在要開始透過以下的自我檢測表檢視自己在考試中的表現了嗎？

我的目標分數為：　　　　　　這次測試的成績為：

1. 70 分鐘內，我完全集中精神在測試內容上。

□是　□不是

如果回答不是，理由是什麼呢？

2. 70 分鐘內，連答案卷的劃記都完成了。

□是　□不是

如果回答不是，理由是什麼呢？

3. 70 分鐘內，100 題都解完了。

□是　□不是

如果回答不是，理由是什麼呢？

4. Part 5 和 Part 6 在 25 分鐘以內全都寫完了。

□是　□不是

如果回答不是，理由是什麼呢？

5. 寫 Part 7 的時候，沒有一題花超過五分鐘。

□是　□不是

如果回答不是，理由是什麼呢？

6. 請寫下你需要改善的地方以及給自己的忠告。

*回到本書第二頁，確認自己的目標分數並加強對於達成分數的意志。
對於要改善的部分一定要在下一次測試中實踐。這點是最重要的，也要這樣才能有進步。

TEST 09

Part 5

Part 6

Part 7

自我檢測表

等等！考前確認事項：

1. 關掉行動裝置電源了嗎？□ 是
2. 答案卷（Answer Sheet）、鉛筆、橡皮擦都準備好了嗎？□ 是
3. 手錶帶了嗎？□ 是

如果都準備齊全了，想想目標分數後即可開始作答。

考試結束時間為現在開始 70 分鐘後的______點______分。

Reading Test

In this section, you must demonstrate your ability to read and comprehend English. You will be given a variety of texts and asked to answer questions about these texts. This section is divided into three parts and will take 75 minutes to complete.

Do not mark the answers in your test book. Use the answer sheet that is separately provided.

PART 5

Directions: In each question, you will be asked to review a statement that is missing a word or phrase. Four answer choices will be provided for each question. Select the best answer and mark the corresponding letter (A), (B), (C), or (D) on the answer sheet.

101. The foreign delegates are expected to arrive at the hotel _______ noon on Friday at the latest.
(A) by (B) above
(C) within (D) of

102. Dr. Clark notified _______ patients that he would be out of town this week to attend a medical convention.
(A) its (B) his
(C) him (D) they

103. Mr. Barnett reserved his flight to Hanoi directly with the airline company because it was _______ than booking with a travel agent.
(A) simply (B) simpler
(C) simplest (D) simplicity

104. Because of his knowledge of foreign markets, Alex is a valuable _______ of the advertising and promotion department.
(A) resident
(B) applicant
(C) member
(D) tenant

105. According to his professor at Becker University, Arlen Thornton has earned adequate _______ to pursue a career in industrial engineering.
(A) quality (B) qualifications
(C) qualifying (D) qualified

106. The consumer survey conducted in the Eastern European region revealed a _______ decline in the residents' preference for online shopping.
(A) notes (B) notably
(C) noting (D) notable

107. Museum guests are not allowed to touch the sculptures on display, _______ are they permitted to take pictures of the art pieces.
(A) nor (B) so
(C) until (D) during

108. Once all the applications are received, Wei Foundation's scholarship committee _______ only 40 individuals to send to China for a year of study.
(A) to select (B) will select
(C) have selected (D) were selecting

109. Candidates who receive notifications to attend a second interview must ------- their intentions to proceed with the application process.
(A) confirmed
(B) confirm
(C) confirmation
(D) confirming

110. The workplace safety regulations ------- helped to prevent serious accidents from occurring at the construction site.
(A) define
(B) definitely
(C) definite
(D) definitions

111. The plumber conducted a thorough ------- of how much it would probably cost to replace the old water pipes in Ms. Kent's apartment.
(A) inspection
(B) inspects
(C) inspect
(D) inspecting

112. ------- to providing reliable electrical services to households and commercial establishments in Denver, Voltworks hires only highly skilled electricians.
(A) Consisted
(B) Regarded
(C) Reconstructed
(D) Committed

113. The new admissions standards that were implemented last year by Columna University made it ------- than before for graduating high school students to apply to the institution.
(A) easily
(B) easy
(C) ease
(D) easier

114. Many citizens across the state are having difficulty finding ------- these days due to the economic crisis.
(A) employable
(B) employing
(C) employed
(D) employment

115. The famous director found Rachel Burns to be sufficiently ------- to play almost any role, no matter how challenging.
(A) variable
(B) essential
(C) comprehensive
(D) versatile

116. The event organizer said that the annual organic products expo will be held ------- the Ivory Cultural Center next year.
(A) at (B) beneath
(C) about (D) through

117. The board gave Mr. Liebnitz a week to decide whether or not he would accept the ------- to the advertising department.
(A) vote (B) report
(C) transfer (D) advance

118. Upon ------- of the registration forms, scholarship applicants are advised to submit them to the registrar's office.
(A) computation
(B) completion
(C) declaration
(D) adaptation

119. Test results showed ------- some soaps and shampoos contain chemicals which may cause skin dryness and irritation.
(A) that (B) this
(C) whenever (D) what

GO ON TO THE NEXT PAGE

120. The new restaurant on Oak Grove Avenue is ------- by food critics for people who enjoy Mediterranean cuisine.
(A) recommended
(B) specialized
(C) delivered
(D) consumed

121. All passenger vessels are required by law to make ------- for people with physical disabilities.
(A) perceptions
(B) directions
(C) provisions
(D) restrictions

122. Mr. Hall visits the project site ------- to make sure that the renovation is going according to schedule.
(A) any (B) soon
(C) hardly (D) frequently

123. ------- returning a defective item to the store for replacement, please do not forget to bring the official receipt.
(A) Into
(B) When
(C) Whoever
(D) Following

124. For the past eight years, Vincent Silva has ------- supported organizations which protect endangered animals.
(A) nearly
(B) delicately
(C) convincingly
(D) consistently

125. The Cerea Hub is an online specialty shop ------- ceramic figurines crafted by people from around the world.
(A) offer (B) offering
(C) will offer (D) has offered

126. Dr. Munoz ------- experimental methods for obtaining energy from natural sources long before GDS Incorporated developed its own.
(A) is devising
(B) had devised
(C) was devised
(D) has devised

127. The job in the warehouse is best suited to someone who is physically strong as it will ------- involve lifting heavy objects.
(A) vividly
(B) mainly
(C) rarely
(D) summarily

128. The Orlando Bolts baseball team ------- a proposal to endorse the athletic shoes manufactured by Armor Basics.
(A) concentrated
(B) accepted
(C) originated
(D) assigned

129. Stage director Delfin Matthews ------- with Saguijo Theater Company's public relations team to promote the opening of his new play, *Nebuchadnezzar's Bane*.
(A) collaborated
(B) distributed
(C) drafted
(D) granted

130. Scientists believe that either volcanic activity or large meteor impacts ------- what led to the extinction of the dinosaurs.
(A) is
(B) has been
(C) are being
(D) are

131. Investors remain hopeful of a positive outcome despite only a ------- agreement being reached in the last round of negotiations between the two trading partners.
(A) vigilant
(B) tentative
(C) diligent
(D) reliant

132. The newly recruited junior data analysts at Adeco Technologies may begin working on actual projects ------- following the mandatory two-week training period.
(A) suddenly
(B) importantly
(C) immediately
(D) recurrently

133. Prior to the start of the leadership seminar, participants ------- to spend five minutes preparing a list of goals, which they later shared with the group.
(A) to be asked
(B) were asked
(C) would ask
(D) have been asking

134. The Silvanus Museum staff is organizing a retirement party in honor of its ------- director, Mr. Alvaro, who has served there for 25 years.
(A) definite
(B) total
(C) outgoing
(D) withdrawn

135. Staff members are required to obtain authorization from their supervisors before gaining access to ------- customer information in the firm's database.
(A) familiar (B) secluded
(C) confidential (D) formative

136. Esham Pharmaceuticals has adopted various preventive ------- to protect its employees from possible accidents in its laboratories.
(A) benefits
(B) strengths
(C) measures
(D) amounts

137. Instead of closing just the stations experiencing technical difficulties, the Transit Authority chose to shut down the subway system -------.
(A) differently
(B) altogether
(C) usefully
(D) halfway

138. At last month's conference, keynote speaker Dana Stewart identified the essential ------- that make a successful Web hosting business.
(A) varieties
(B) components
(C) exhibits
(D) lectures

139. ------- Mr. Ware departs for Belgium next week, he will present his cost-cutting proposal to the logistics department at the company-wide meeting this Friday.
(A) However
(B) Since
(C) Before
(D) Prior

140. ------- new employees found the weeklong orientation valuable and the assigned instructors both knowledgeable and professional.
(A) Most
(B) Any
(C) None
(D) Each

GO ON TO THE NEXT PAGE

PART 6

Directions: In this part, you will be asked to read an English text. Some sentences are incomplete. Select the word or phrase that correctly completes each sentence and mark the corresponding letter (A), (B), (C), or (D) on the answer sheet.

Questions 141-143 refer to the following article.

The Department of Culture has announced plans to ------- a cultural complex adjacent to

141. (A) demolish
(B) modernize
(C) construct
(D) repair

the Widmark Sports Center on Anders Avenue over the next 12 months. The structure, which will tentatively be named the Coleman Cultural Complex, will house a theater, a musical performance facility and a library. Funded by the city's local government office in conjunction with Coleman-Winters Transnational Corporation, the ------- is expected to be

142. (A) projected
(B) project
(C) projectile
(D) to project

completed by September of next year.

The huge theater will seat 2,000 persons, and several performances, including the Pembroke Orchestra and the opera La Bohème, are scheduled to take place at the complex. Preparations for the library are ------- and will soon be finalized. Updates on the

143. (A) in progress
(B) progress
(C) progressed
(D) progressively

date of the actual opening and schedule of events will be provided via press release in the future.

Questions 144-146 refer to the following letter.

Norman King
Unit 502, Maze Central
Albert Road, Bristol

Dear Mr. King,

You have made the right decision to lead a ------- lifestyle. We at Bud's Gym are happy to

144. (A) relaxed
(B) prosperous
(C) healthy
(D) green

assist you in achieving this goal. To get started, we will see you on Saturday for orientation. Please keep the enclosed membership card and present it at ------- reception

145. (A) our
(B) your
(C) his
(D) their

counter upon your arrival. A premium membership gives you unlimited access to gym facilities and fitness classes. The card is valid at all Bud's Gym branches across the country, allowing you to work out wherever you are. As you can see, membership with Bud's Gym is an ideal way to help ------- your fitness goals.

146. (A) fulfilling
(B) fulfill
(C) fulfillment
(D) has fulfilled

We look forward to seeing you on your first day at the gym.

Sincerely,

Alison Hanson
Manager
Bud's Gym

GO ON TO THE NEXT PAGE

Questions 147-149 refer to the following announcement.

SNA Summer Block Party

Southdale Neighborhood Association (SNA) invites all residents to a daylong block party on Marigold Street on the last Saturday of the month. This will be a great opportunity to ------- know your neighbors better and meet new people in the community. A solo

147. (A) stick to
(B) get to
(C) look up to
(D) turn to

performance from country musician Andrea McCain will start the event and will be followed by a dance number from the Elizabeth School of the Arts students. -------, SNA

148. (A) Nevertheless
(B) For instance
(C) Afterward
(D) However

chairperson Garry Moss will host games and other activities for adults and children. Tickets to the party cost $24 each and are ------- of dinner and drinks. Residents who

149. (A) inclusive
(B) included
(C) including
(D) inclusion

would like to attend may contact SNA secretary Lucy Lee at 555-3557 for ticket reservations and other inquiries.

Questions 150-152 refer to the following e-mail.

From: Daryl Craig <d.craig@fma.com>
To: Vernice Newmark <vn@firemail.com>
Subject: Auto Fair
Date: May 6

Dear Ms. Newmark,

Thank you for giving me an update on the final preparations for the Florida Motors Association's auto fair on Monday. I am ------- with the way you designed the booths for

150. (A) hesitant
(B) concerned
(C) anxious
(D) satisfied

the car companies. I think your method of arranging them alphabetically will make them more accessible to guests.

I would also like to inform you that the association's ------- are looking forward to the

151. (A) officials
(B) official
(C) officially
(D) offices

special presentations that will be given in the opening day's activities.

Because of the great work you have done, the association has decided to hire your company again for its silver anniversary. The celebration ------- in July. We will talk about

152. (A) will be held
(B) was held
(C) has been held
(D) could have been held

the details of this event after the fair. In the meantime, we hope that everything runs smoothly next week.

Thank you for your hard work and have a nice weekend.

Sincerely,

Daryl Craig
Vice President
Florida Motors Association

GO ON TO THE NEXT PAGE

PART 7

Directions: In this part, you will be asked to read several texts, such as advertisements, articles or examples of business correspondence. Each text is followed by several questions. Select the best answer and mark the corresponding letter (A), (B), (C), or (D) on your answer sheet.

Questions 153-154 refer to the following advertisement.

Felicity Salon

Where beauty is an art!

Open daily:

Weekdays	10 A.M. - 8 P.M.
Weekends	9 A.M. - 6 P.M.
National Holidays	11 A.M. - 5 P.M.

Basic Services Offered:

Haircut	
Ladies' precision cut (starts at*)	$30
Men's precision cut	$20
Blow-dry and style	$25
Permanent waves (starts at*) or straightening	$100
Semi-permanent color	$30
European hair coloring	$60

* Different rates apply depending on hair length

More information is available on our Web site:
www.felicitysalon.com

153. When does Felicity Salon close on Mondays?
(A) At 6 P.M.
(B) At 5 P.M.
(C) At 9 P.M.
(D) At 8 P.M.

154. What is indicated about the ladies' precision cut?
(A) Its price includes washing.
(B) It is currently on special promotion.
(C) Its rate varies with a client's hair length.
(D) It comes free with a coloring service.

GO ON TO THE NEXT PAGE

Questions 155-156 refer to the following article.

Children to Pose as Future Selves at Little Rock Party

Charleston, October 25 – In an effort to inspire children to start thinking about their future careers, the Little Rock Community Center will be holding a different kind of costume party at the end of the month.

With the theme of "My Future Self," children between the ages of seven and nine will come dressed in costumes that show what they want to be when they grow up. Each child will also be given a chance to speak in front of an audience about their chosen profession and what they hope to achieve in their field.

Catherine Knox, the director of the community center, believes that young children should already have an idea of what they want to do later in life. "They may not fully understand the demands of a career yet, but becoming aware of it at an early age may help them establish a clear path to follow as they study in school," says Ms. Knox.

The costume party will be held at the community center from 6 P.M. to 8 P.M. on October 30.

155. Why is the Little Rock Community Center hosting an event?

(A) To encourage children to consider possible occupations

(B) To mark the beginning of a school program

(C) To introduce a new method of teaching

(D) To celebrate the opening of a public facility

156. What is stated about the costume party?

(A) It will be held for an entire day.

(B) It is sponsored by an academic institution.

(C) It will give a chance for participants to show their talents.

(D) It is exclusively for a particular age group.

Questions 157-158 refer to the following article.

Mr. Enriquez Lobbies Child Health Care Bill

Regional State Representative Fernando Enriquez has proposed a law aimed at mandating health insurance for the state's youth population. "Our youth are the future of this nation. This bill will provide additional protection not only for our children, but the future prosperity of our country," Enriquez said in a press release. According to the Health Care for Young Bill, all children ages 18 and under will have free access to medical services in both private and public hospitals. Funding for the insurance will be derived from the Health Department and public assistance allowances of some legislators. The bill will undergo its first reading tomorrow in the nation's capital. If signed into law, the Healthcare for Young Bill will benefit more than two million children in the country.

157. What is suggested about Fernando Enriquez?
(A) He made a recent legislative proposal.
(B) He is a representative of a firm.
(C) He works in the medical industry.
(D) He is campaigning for a government position.

158. What is mentioned about the bill?
(A) It will assign more doctors to states.
(B) It will grant free medical checkups.
(C) It will promote disease prevention.
(D) It will privatize public hospitals.

GO ON TO THE NEXT PAGE

Questions 159-161 refer to the following notice.

NOTICE: Alison Grand to Visit Pageturners

Award-winning novelist, Alison Grand, will visit the Missoula branch of Pageturners on April 19 at 3 P.M. to promote her newest book, *A Laugh in the Dark*. She will read an excerpt from the novel which is part of her *Daughters of the Summer* series. Following the reading, Ms. Grand will answer questions from the audience. Copies of her book will be available for sale and Ms. Grand will be on hand to sign autographs at the conclusion of the event.

Ms. Grand has written more than 15 novels during her career, with many topping international bestsellers lists. Three of her works have been made into feature films, which have also experienced financial and critical success.

For information on other events scheduled at Pageturners, visit www.pageturners.com or check out the calendar posted at our service counter.

159. What is stated about Ms. Grand?
(A) She will be promoting her recent work.
(B) She recently performed in a movie.
(C) She is employed at a bookstore.
(D) She will visit several Pageturners branches.

160. What is NOT indicated about the upcoming event?
(A) It will be held in the afternoon.
(B) It will charge a small admission fee.
(C) It will include a question and answer period.
(D) It will be held at a retail outlet.

161. What is mentioned about some of Ms. Grand's books?
(A) They are unavailable at Pageturners.
(B) They were recently revised.
(C) They were developed into films.
(D) They will be given away at the event.

Questions 162-164 refer to the following letter.

High Pitch

Unit 901, Ellis Tower,
Brighton, Massachusetts

September 25

Dorothy Taylor
Sales Director
Soundbits

Dear Ms. Taylor,

Thank you for your interest in consigning your company's products with us. We understand you wish to supply us with violins and guitars. Unfortunately, we must respectfully decline as we have just signed contracts with three other manufacturers of stringed instruments.

However, we are interested in the possibility of selling your flutes, drum kits, and keyboards. We are impressed with the quality of your products, and we believe displaying them in our shops across the state would increase your brand's popularity in Massachusetts.

We hope to discuss the matter with you sometime this week. When you are available, please call me at 555-9632.

We eagerly await your response.

Truly yours,

Hubert Night
High Pitch, Massachusetts
Regional Manager

162. Why was the letter written?
(A) To end a contract
(B) To turn down a proposal
(C) To introduce a service
(D) To cancel an order

163. What is indicated about High Pitch?
(A) It imports musical instruments.
(B) It runs its own factory.
(C) It offers voice lessons.
(D) It operates multiple branches.

164. What is NOT a Soundbits product that High Pitch wants to sell in its store?
(A) Drums
(B) Keyboards
(C) Guitars
(D) Flutes

GO ON TO THE NEXT PAGE

Questions 165-167 refer to the following advertisement.

Career Specialist

(Jobs 1 out of 5) [next] [edit online profile] [home]

Application period: June 1 - October 30

PetroLine Corporation

Other Vacancies	**Credit Representative**
PR Specialists (3) Accountants (2) Finance Analysts (4) Marketing Assistants (2)	Duties ▪ Follow up on unpaid fuel deliveries ▪ Arrange payment terms for clients ▪ Participate in planning debt collection measures ▪ Document and report overdue debts that must be reported to the collection department Qualifications ▪ A bachelor's degree in accounting, finance, business management or equivalent. ▪ At least three years' work experience in a related industry ▪ Proficiency in basic computer applications ▪ Good command of English language, both oral and written Applicants may apply by clicking the button below or by sending their résumés and references to hr@petroline.com. Previous applicants need not apply. send résumé

165. What is suggested about PetroLine?
(A) It provides loans to clients.
(B) It delivers fuel to customers.
(C) It recently underwent expansion.
(D) It provides training to new staff.

166. What is NOT a requirement for the job?
(A) A college diploma
(B) A degree of experience
(C) A familiarity with computers
(D) A willingness to travel

167. According to the advertisement, what is NOT a position that needs to be filled?
(A) PR Specialist
(B) Account Manager
(C) Finance Analyst
(D) Credit Representative

Questions 168-172 refer to the following article.

Local Hospital to Have Better Facilities

AKRON, Ohio, August 14 – The Margaret Labonte Memorial Hospital will soon have improved facilities, as its board of directors finally approved a proposal to expand the 150-bed hospital in order to treat and accommodate more patients.

A groundbreaking ceremony and press conference will be held behind the main building of the hospital along Rickshaw Avenue on Wednesday, August 20, at 10 A.M.

Patricia Mellencamp, the hospital administrator, believes that the additional 30,000 square feet of space will bring more success and growth not only for their health professionals and staff but also to their medical programs. "Our hospital is known for its wide range of surgical treatments for various conditions. In addition, our team of well-respected doctors attracts patients who seek quality health care," says Ms. Mellencamp. "Patients will no longer need to go to other hospitals across or outside the state to seek medical treatment."

The project will provide the hospital eight new operating rooms with state-of-the-art medical equipment, 30 additional patient rooms, and an outpatient surgery waiting area. All these facilities will be housed in a new building designated as the Outpatient Surgery Center. The construction of the surgery center will start in September and is estimated to last a year and half. A new parking lot will also be completed within the same timeframe.

The Margaret Labonte Memorial Hospital was established 30 years ago and now has about 600 employees. It has been providing medical care to the residents of Akron and surrounding communities of Cuyahoga Falls, Tallmadge, Portage Lakes, and Hudson. The hospital is also affiliated with the Ohio Health Foundation, a non-profit organization dedicated to giving free medical health care to lowincome families several times a year.

168. What is suggested about the hospital?
(A) It concluded a construction project.
(B) It is transferring to another location.
(C) It is taking steps to improve its services.
(D) Its clinic plans to hire additional employees.

169. The word "conditions" in paragraph 3, line 7, is closest in meaning to
(A) terms (B) factors
(C) environments (D) ailments

170. What will happen on August 20?
(A) An event will take place in a nearby city.
(B) The beginning of a project will be celebrated.
(C) A series of medical training programs will begin.
(D) A new hospital building will be opened.

171. According to the article, what is the hospital known for?
(A) Advanced medical equipment
(B) Quality outpatient care
(C) Diverse health departments
(D) Treatments involving surgery

172. What is NOT being added to the hospital?
(A) Surgery rooms
(B) Parking spaces
(C) A pharmacy counter
(D) A waiting area

GO ON TO THE NEXT PAGE

Questions 173-176 refer to the following notice.

NOTICE TO ALL RESIDENTS

May 6

In an effort to conserve resources and ensure a steady supply of drinking water for residents, the Helena City Government will replace old water lines on Queensville Boulevard. The three-week project will start on Thursday, June 20. The outer lanes of the boulevard will be closed, as the excavation and replacement of water pipes will be done on both sides of the road.

In this regard, motorists regularly passing along Queensville are requested to take detours during this time. Signs to Canine Lane, Jostein Road, and Amerbliss Avenue will be put up on June 19. Those who still wish to take Queensville should expect heavy congestion from Mondays to Fridays between 8 A.M. and 5 P.M. Officers will be assigned to the area and the surrounding roadways to ensure smooth traffic flow.

Additional details about the project may be found by logging on to www.helenapublicworks.com.

Thank you for your cooperation.

Sincerely,

Carmen Boyle
Director of the Department of Transit
Helena City Government

173. What is the purpose of the notice?
(A) To request drainage system maintenance
(B) To announce an upcoming repair project
(C) To order road safety equipment
(D) To propose a construction plan

174. When is the project scheduled to begin?
(A) On a Monday
(B) On a Tuesday
(C) On a Thursday
(D) On a Friday

175. What is NOT an alternate route mentioned in the letter?
(A) Amerbliss Avenue
(B) Bellbay Avenue
(C) Jostein Road
(D) Canine Lane

176. What is indicated about Queensville Boulevard?
(A) It is connected to a major highway.
(B) It is often flooded.
(C) It will remain open to drivers.
(D) It needs new road signs.

Questions 177-180 refer to the following report.

BOARD MEETING SUMMARY REPORT:

Since the Rowers Foundation was established in 1960, we have accepted financial support for our scholarship programs. However, donations to the foundation have been diminishing over the past months due to economic constraints affecting our corporate benefactors. If this continues, the foundation will be incapable of going ahead with our scheduled projects for next year.

During the foundation's quarterly board meeting on Friday September 30, the chairperson proposed to temporarily stop accepting new scholars and funding overseas study programs. However, a majority of the board members disagreed with the proposal, saying it would not be the best solution to the problem. Thus, instead of limiting grants, the board has decided to seek aid from private individuals. The board plans to encourage executives and young professionals to sponsor a scholar's education by donating a portion of their monthly earnings. This campaign would be carried out in major business districts across the country. Apart from this, the board is considering accepting contributions and selling items on the Rowers Foundation Web site to generate additional funds.

Rowers will continue to solicit funding from corporate bodies, but is hopeful about the proposed funding methods. Public relations director Michelle Depuis says "We are counting on these solutions to generate enough money to bring the level of scholarships up to where it was previously."

177. What is mentioned about Rowers Foundation?
(A) It owns a university.
(B) It was founded in 1960.
(C) It has been raising funds through a store.
(D) It employs young executives.

178. What issue does the foundation face?
(A) It does not have sufficient funds.
(B) It has too many applicants.
(C) Its Web site is under repair.
(D) Its chairperson resigned.

179. How does the board plan to solve the problem?
(A) By seeking help from executives
(B) By decreasing scholarship grants
(C) By advertising programs online
(D) By reorganizing the board of directors

180. The phrase "carried out" in paragraph 2, line 7 is closest in meaning to
(A) moved away
(B) conducted
(C) held over
(D) illustrated

GO ON TO THE NEXT PAGE

Questions 181-185 refer to the following letter and e-mail.

Zoon Health and Fitness Club

Pamposh Deewani
Unit 507, Jadwali Apartments
Langu Road, Mumbai 400 001

November 4

Dear Ms. Deewani,

We hope that over the past 12 months you have found your membership at Zoon Health and Fitness Club to be a worthwhile investment. In the future, you can rest assured that we will continue with our commitment to providing excellent services to help our valued members stay fit and healthy.

Consequently, we are providing reduced rates to those who renew their memberships on or before December 31.

MEMBERSHIP TYPE	SPECIAL RATE
Student	$433.50
Individual	$493.00
Couple	$943.50
Corporate(seven or more)	$454.75/person

Enclosed you will find a membership renewal form. We strongly encourage you to renew now so that you are eligible for this limited-time offer to continue enjoying the advantages provided to Zoon members. You can send the completed form to our office either by fax or mail, or you can submit it at the front desk of our center.

If you have questions or concerns, please do not hesitate to contact us at +91-22-555-6801 or at custserv@zoonclub.com.

Sincerely yours,

Norman Misri
Membership Coordinator

To: <custserv@zoonclub.com>
From: Pamposh Deewani <pdeewani@ganjumail.com>
Date: January 28
Subject: Member ID 91211

To whom it may concern,

I called your office on January 21 to ask for a temporary suspension of my membership because I'm leaving for Copenhagen next week and won't be back until February 25. I was told then that my request would be processed in three business days, but it has already been a week and I still haven't heard back from anyone.

I have been a Zoon member for the past two years and have always been happy with your center. You have competent fitness instructors and state-of-the-art equipment and facilities. That was why I decided to renew my membership. If you check your records, you will see that I faxed the form to your office in December and transferred $493 through my bank. So, I would really appreciate it if you could attend to my concern as quickly as possible and notify me regarding the status of my request before my departure. Thank you.

Pamposh Deewani

181. Why was the letter written?
(A) To publicize new operating hours
(B) To announce special renewal rates
(C) To follow up on some unpaid bills
(D) To promote a new facility

182. What is indicated about Mr. Misri?
(A) His business license has expired.
(B) He is an athletic trainer.
(C) He lives in Jadwali Apartments.
(D) He works for a fitness center.

183. Which type of membership did Ms. Deewani request?
(A) Individual
(B) Corporate
(C) Student
(D) Couple

184. How did Ms. Deewani contact Zoon about her suspension request?
(A) By fax
(B) By mail
(C) By phone
(D) By e-mail

185. What is NOT stated about Ms. Deewani?
(A) She is going on an overseas trip.
(B) She submitted her renewal form in person.
(C) She has been satisfied with Zoon's services.
(D) She updated her membership before December 31.

GO ON TO THE NEXT PAGE

Questions 186-190 refer to the following e-mails.

To: Soledad Vasquez <manager@confianzacatering.com>
From: Javier Rivera <jay.rivera@virtuosoengineering.com>
Date: November 18
Subject: Annual Company Gala

Dear Ms. Vasquez,

We are interested in hiring Confianza Catering for our annual company gala. The event is set for December 21, from 6 P.M. to 10 P.M., in our building's conference room. All of Virtuoso Engineering's 45 employees will attend, plus 12 of our most important clients.

I have met with the other managers, and we all agreed that your Prudentia buffet package has the best selection of dishes. Could you give me a price quote for the number of attendees I have indicated above? Please also indicate the rental costs for tables, chairs, serving dishes, and utensils, as well as the fees for the wait staff.

Thank you, and I hope to hear from you soon.

Javier Rivera

To: Javier Rivera <jay.rivera@virtuosoengineering.com>
From: Soledad Vasquez <manager@confianzacatering.com>
Date: November 19
Subject: Re: Annual Company Gala

Dear Mr. Rivera,

We would be more than happy to once again be of service to Virtuoso Engineering. You have become one of our most valuable clients, and we thank you for recommending us to your affiliates. The number of our clients has increased in the past months due to your efforts.

Prudentia is one of our most popular buffet packages, but may I offer a recommendation? Our Veritas package might give you greater value for your money. The two have nearly the same food selections, but Veritas has a wider assortment of beverages, including coffee and tea, whereas you will be billed separately for those two if you order the Prudentia package.

To make your decision easier, I have attached the file you asked for, and another which provides all of the relevant details on the Veritas package. Once you have made your choice, you can contact me directly at 555-4218, and we will start making the necessary preparations.

Sincerely,

Soledad Vasquez
Manager
Confianza Catering

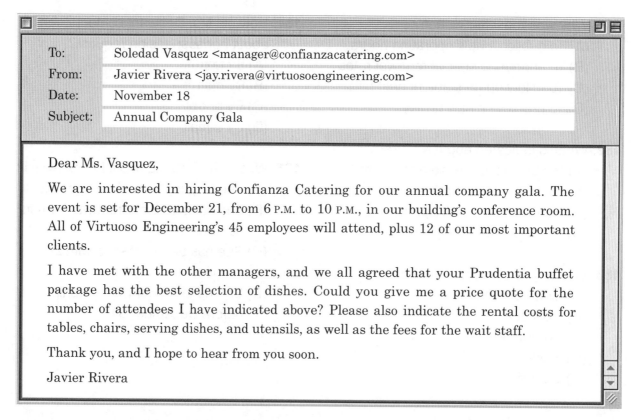

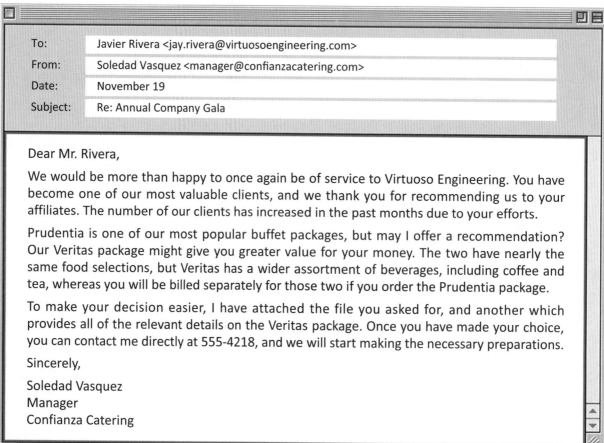

186. Why was the first e-mail written?
(A) To confirm attendance to a meeting
(B) To ask for details about a convention
(C) To inquire about hiring services
(D) To answer questions about order processing

187. What is suggested about Virtuoso Engineering?
(A) It has done business with Confianza Catering before.
(B) It underwent a management reorganization last month.
(C) It is negotiating a merger with one of its affiliate companies.
(D) It will host a banquet exclusively for its clients in December.

188. What does Ms. Vasquez indicate in the second e-mail?
(A) The buffet packages are discounted for a limited time.
(B) The customer base of Confianza Catering has grown.
(C) A whole week is needed to finalize the preparations.
(D) A deposit is required upon confirmation of a booking.

189. What does Ms. Vasquez recommend?
(A) Developing a dinner menu
(B) Choosing another package
(C) Moving the gala to a later date
(D) Reducing the number of guests

190. What did Ms. Vasquez send to Mr. Rivera?
(A) A revised schedule for a corporate gathering
(B) Price quotes for a catering service
(C) An updated list of buffet packages
(D) A product catalog for an establishment

GO ON TO THE NEXT PAGE

Questions 191-195 refer to the following advertisement and article.

GRAND AUTO JOURNAL

The First Fedfire Auto Racing Competition

Published quarterly by Aardvark Publishing, *Grand Auto Journal* is one of the country's most widely read car magazines. It offers comprehensive reviews of new and vintage automobiles as well as features on celebrities and their driving preferences. *Grand Auto Journal* is popular with car enthusiasts and those who enjoy motorbikes, recreational vehicles, or SUVs.

On its 10th anniversary, the magazine is organizing the First Fedfire Auto Racing Competition. It is open to both amateur and professional race car drivers.

CATEGORY	PRIZES
Adult (Professional)	$30,000
Adult (Amateur)	$20,000
Teens (Professional)	$25,000
Teens (Amateur)	$15,000

Interested parties can read the contest regulations in the latest issue of *Grand Auto Journal* or visit www.fedfirerace.com. You can download the registration form on the Web site and you must submit all the requirements before October 15. The one-day competition, which will be attended by some of the country's most esteemed sports celebrities, will be held at the Schoonmaker Field in Austin, Texas on November 17.

AUSTIN SENTINEL Volume X Issue 4

MOTORING NEWS

The First Fedfire Auto Racing Competition: A Success

AUSTIN – Over 5,000 people attended the First Fedfire Auto Racing Competition at the Schoonmaker Field on November 17. The event, organized by *Grand Auto Journal* in partnership with Raikonen Motors, is the first of its kind in the city, attracting numerous car enthusiasts from all over the country.

Hunter Harrington and Randy Wilson emerged as winners in the professional categories, for adults and teens respectively, beating 40 other participants in a competition that lasted for more than five hours. In the amateur categories, their counterparts were Louella Anderson and Dwight Morgan. City mayor Fred Gellar was the special guest at the awards ceremony that took place right after the competition. There he delivered a speech congratulating everyone involved in the day's events.

Eli Thomson, chief editor of *Grand Auto Journal*, thanked everyone who attended the event. "It fills me with satisfaction to know that we have turned our dream of organizing a community sports event into a reality," Thomson said. "It's unbelievable. We're already excited for next year!"

Along with cash prizes, winners were also given trophies and certificates, as well as free annual subscriptions to *Grand Auto Journal*. The auto racing competition was the culmination of the magazine's month-long celebration of its 10th anniversary.

191. According to the advertisement, when is the deadline to sign up for the competition?
(A) October 4
(B) November 10
(C) October 15
(D) November 17

192. Why are readers asked to visit a Web site?
(A) To view the tentative schedule for an upcoming automobile show
(B) To learn more about the details of a sporting event
(C) To participate in a discussion on an online forum
(D) To register for membership with an athletic organization

193. What is mentioned about Eli Thomson?
(A) He spoke on behalf of the mayor of Austin.
(B) He is responsible for overseeing a magazine.
(C) He was asked to write an article about the event.
(D) He was one of the participants at a competition.

194. What is NOT indicated about the contestants?
(A) Dwight Morgan was personally congratulated by Fred Gellar.
(B) Hunter Harrington raced as a professional adult.
(C) Louella Anderson placed first in the amateur adult category.
(D) Randy Wilson received a $25,000 cash prize.

195. What is suggested about the Fedfire Auto Racing Competition?
(A) It honored past winners during the awards ceremony.
(B) It will be broadcast on national television.
(C) It was a project of the local government.
(D) It is going to be held again in the coming year.

GO ON TO THE NEXT PAGE

Questions 196-200 refer to the following invitation and e-mail.

The Musen Academy of Motion Pictures
requests the pleasure of your company at the

23rd Liberaz Film Honors

to recognize remarkable accomplishments
in the film industry this year.

The black-tie affair will start at 6 P.M. on February 8
at the Fracasso Exhibition Facility.

PROGRAM

6:00	Introductory Speech	Violet Tyler - Director, The Musen Academy of Motion Pictures
6:20	Keynote Address	Joseph Roscoe - Liberaz Film Honors Hall of Fame Honoree
7:00	TROPHY PRESENTATION *Surviving Millicent,* Best Picture Zoren Graham, Best Director Carlo Sutter Best Actor	 *Surviving Millicent,* Best Script *The Alley,* Best Cinematography Lisette Hamilton, Best Actress
8:00	Closing Remarks	Penelope Daly - Board Member, Musen Academy of Motion Pictures

Please confirm your attendance by contacting Jacqueline Finney at jfinney@musen.org
or Kirby Velasco at kvelasco@musen.org on or before January 20.

To: Jacqueline Finney <jfinney@musen.org>
From: Kirby Velasco <kvelasco@musen.org>
Date: January 15
Subject: Mr. Laughlin

Jacqueline,

I got a call from acclaimed director Alexander Laughlin this morning. He agreed to deliver the keynote address at the Liberaz Film Honors ceremony in place of Joseph Roscoe, who is out of town until February 12 for the shooting of his new film. Mr. Laughlin only asks that we give him enough time to prepare his speech before he sends it to us for review. As co-organizer of the event, I took the liberty of telling him that it's OK and that we'll give him until January 22 to write his draft.

Anyway, most of the people we invited have already confirmed their attendance. If you'd like, I can write them a group e-mail to let them know about Mr. Laughlin being the new keynote speaker so there won't be any confusion on February 8.

Kirby

196. Who will be given a trophy for acting?
(A) Violet Tyler
(B) Lisette Hamilton
(C) Penelope Daly
(D) Jacqueline Finney

197. What is suggested about *Surviving Millicent*?
(A) It will be shown in theaters on February 8.
(B) It gained recognition from other prize-giving institutions.
(C) It will receive two awards from the Musen Academy of Motion Pictures.
(D) It has been scheduled for a special preview at the Fracasso Exhibition Facility.

198. What will Mr. Laughlin most likely do on February 8?
(A) Send a draft of his speech
(B) Deliver a talk
(C) Help organize the event
(D) Meet with Joseph Roscoe

199. What does Mr. Velasco say he can do?
(A) Help Mr. Laughlin edit his speech
(B) Notify attendees about a change in the program
(C) Follow up on the attendance of invited guests
(D) Give updates on the status of event preparations

200. What is NOT indicated about Mr. Laughlin in the e-mail?
(A) He is shooting a new movie.
(B) He was given a week to write his speech.
(C) He is well known in the film industry.
(D) He spoke to Kirby Velasco on January 15.

This is the end of the test. You may review Part 5, 6, and 7 if you finish the test early.

解答 p.288 / 分數換算表 p.289 / 題目解析 p.417（解答本）

▍請翻到次頁「自我檢測表」檢視自己解答問題的方法與態度。

自我檢測表

TEST 09 順利的完成了嗎？

現在要開始透過以下的自我檢測表檢視自己在考試中的表現了嗎？

我的目標分數為：　　　　　　　　這次測試的成績為：

1. 70 分鐘內，我完全集中精神在測試內容上。

   □是　□不是

   如果回答不是，理由是什麼呢？

2. 70 分鐘內，連答案卷的劃記都完成了。

   □是　□不是

   如果回答不是，理由是什麼呢？

3. 70 分鐘內，100 題都解完了。

   □是　□不是

   如果回答不是，理由是什麼呢？

4. Part 5 和 Part 6 在 25 分鐘以內全都寫完了。

   □是　□不是

   如果回答不是，理由是什麼呢？

5. 寫 Part 7 的時候，沒有一題花超過五分鐘。

   □是　□不是

   如果回答不是，理由是什麼呢？

6. 請寫下你需要改善的地方以及給自己的忠告。

*回到本書第二頁，確認自己的目標分數並加強對於達成分數的意志。
對於要改善的部分一定要在下一次測試中實踐。這點是最重要的，也要這樣才能有進步。

TEST 10

Part 5

Part 6

Part 7

自我檢測表

等等！考前確認事項：

1. 關掉行動裝置電源了嗎？□ 是
2. 答案卷（Answer Sheet）、鉛筆、橡皮擦都準備好了嗎？□ 是
3. 手錶帶了嗎？□ 是

如果都準備齊全了，想想目標分數後即可開始作答。

考試結束時間為現在開始 70 分鐘後的______點______分。

Reading Test

In this section, you must demonstrate your ability to read and comprehend English. You will be given a variety of texts and asked to answer questions about these texts. This section is divided into three parts and will take 75 minutes to complete.

Do not mark the answers in your test book. Use the answer sheet that is separately provided.

PART 5

Directions: In each question, you will be asked to review a statement that is missing a word or phrase. Four answer choices will be provided for each question. Select the best answer and mark the corresponding letter (A), (B), (C), or (D) on the answer sheet.

101. Glencore International would like to request ------- guests to present their invitation cards upon entering the ballroom.

(A) our (B) every
(C) ours (D) theirs

102. Please note that the application period for the credit manager position ------- tomorrow and conclude on September 15.

(A) will start (B) starting
(C) had started (D) started

103. Dukebox has been one of the most profitable recording companies in the music industry for ------- three decades.

(A) other (B) over
(C) throughout (D) much

104. Flight service ------- New York to Chicago will be unavailable until weather conditions improve.

(A) from (B) in
(C) at (D) between

105. Ms. Zaragoza was ------- notified of her reassignment to the Dublin office in a letter from the human resources director.

(A) officially (B) official
(C) officials (D) officiate

106. To receive online billing service, clients should ------- a request by e-mail including their name, e-mail address, and account number.

(A) submits (B) submitted
(C) submit (D) submitting

107. The main agenda of the board of directors' meeting was a ------- of the issues that would arise once the purchase of an affiliate pushed through.

(A) deliberate (B) deliberately
(C) deliberated (D) deliberation

108. A couple of trucks and three cranes are scheduled to arrive at the construction site no later than the ------- week.

(A) principal (B) random
(C) following (D) partial

109. Customers can inquire about the status of their orders by ------- calling our hotline or visiting one of the store branches.
(A) every
(B) either
(C) just as
(D) next

110. The accountant needs to finalize the expense report before noon tomorrow no matter ------- difficult the paperwork is.
(A) since
(B) how
(C) what
(D) now

111. Vielle Software releases free trial versions of its products ------- potential customers can try out the programs for a limited time.
(A) despite
(B) so that
(C) or
(D) though

112. Registration is required for all ------- of the Chamber of Commerce's workshop on marketing for small businesses.
(A) participants
(B) participation
(C) participated
(D) participate

113. The campaign sponsored by Green World Society is ------- focused on saving a huge area of land affected by rampant deforestation in Tanzania.
(A) satisfactorily
(B) promptly
(C) primarily
(D) successively

114. AirWheel ------- a Globetech International Certificate for its new line of industrial fans and will now start selling them in retail outlets.
(A) has attained
(B) attains
(C) is attained
(D) attaining

115. Only when the restaurant opened ------- the owner realize that she needed more kitchen help to complete the numerous cooking tasks.
(A) do
(B) is doing
(C) did
(D) has done

116. As this is a self-service laundry with coin-operated machines, all washing, drying and folding must be done on -------.
(A) yours
(B) your
(C) your own
(D) yourselves

117. As soon as he assumed his new position, sales director Carl Reynolds set an ------- target for the team for the next quarter.
(A) eligible
(B) affluent
(C) ambitious
(D) influential

118. Keeping clients happy by providing a variety of banking services in an efficient manner is the ------- of Midelson Savings Bank.
(A) condition
(B) structure
(C) priority
(D) range

GO ON TO THE NEXT PAGE

119. To confirm the _______ with the marketing director, please coordinate with his assistant, Ms. White, before Tuesday, June 6.
(A) interview
(B) interviewer
(C) interviewing
(D) interviewed

120. On April 3, the collections department will be _______ to a larger space on the third floor from its current office in the basement.
(A) declining
(B) transferring
(C) disappearing
(D) estimating

121. Health club members who are unable to pay their outstanding balance _______ the due date will be charged a late fee as penalty.
(A) by
(B) from
(C) inside
(D) toward

122. For further _______ precautions on installing the air conditioner, customers can refer to the product manual.
(A) safety
(B) most safely
(C) safes
(D) safeties

123. Parsons Financial Group _______ a new work schedule policy for contract workers in their regional branch offices.
(A) acted
(B) persuaded
(C) implemented
(D) informed

124. As explained in the company manual, employees may work overtime _______ their supervisor's written authorization.
(A) without (B) unless
(C) among (D) about

125. The staff member _______ current assignment is to arrange for applicant interviews is Joyce Moore of the personnel department.
(A) whoever (B) whose
(C) whom (D) who

126. All corporate giveaways made by Gorkis Creations may be _______ customized for an extra fee to fit the client's needs.
(A) cautiously
(B) enormously
(C) individually
(D) normally

127. On her daily morning show, Rachael Burns gives her viewers practical _______ on home decorating and maintenance.
(A) recommending
(B) recommendations
(C) recommended
(D) recommend

128. The _______ brochure includes additional information on some tiles and bricks that will be showcased at the construction fair.
(A) revision (B) revises
(C) revised (D) revise

129. Zaykov Enterprises is planning to hold another trade show next year given that the feedback from this year's participants was so _______.
(A) enthuse
(B) enthusiastic
(C) enthusiastically
(D) enthusiasm

130. Front row tickets to the final round of the Wilbur Tennis Championship are sold out as the event is fast -------.
(A) commenting
(B) admitting
(C) approaching
(D) happening

131. Jaydee Construction's management decided to transfer Cindy Lee to an ------- role because of her leadership experience.
(A) interested
(B) understood
(C) administrative
(D) unintended

132. Many tourists like to attend the annual cultural festival, which is usually held at the public park ------- the post office.
(A) upon (B) near
(C) between (D) toward

133. Most countries in Southeast Asia are undergoing gradual ------- from developing economies to industrialized nations.
(A) ignitions (B) transitions
(C) exchanges (D) corrections

134. In fulfillment of the Education Ministry's order, multimedia equipment will be ------- in public school classrooms nationwide.
(A) called back
(B) picked out
(C) set up
(D) counted on

135. Centuries ago, people in the mountain community developed effective techniques for farming on ------- slopes.
(A) steep
(B) concrete
(C) loaded
(D) temporary

136. In relation to the other projects currently being implemented, the proposal writing task recently given by the supervisor is of ------- importance.
(A) higher
(B) less highly
(C) highly
(D) most highly

137. Every six months, Filigre Insurance asks clients for their updated personal information and organizes its customer database -------.
(A) distinctly
(B) markedly
(C) accordingly
(D) exceptionally

138. The president has much ------- in his newly hired accountant, who has significant experience in the field.
(A) confidence
(B) confidently
(C) confide
(D) confident

139. Foreign nationals who would like to apply for work permits in the UAE must present substantial ------- that they are being hired by companies based in the country.
(A) evidence
(B) trust
(C) motivation
(D) perception

140. The Yarikh Art Gallery is known for its ------- collections of paintings and sculptures from the 17th century.
(A) various
(B) variety
(C) variously
(D) varies

GO ON TO THE NEXT PAGE

PART 6

Directions: In this part, you will be asked to read an English text. Some sentences are incomplete. Select the word or phrase that correctly completes each sentence and mark the corresponding letter (A), (B), (C), or (D) on the answer sheet.

Questions 141-143 refer to the following instruction.

To streamline the leave application and approval process, the management has made new guidelines for vacation leave requests. First, personnel who would like to take a day off must fill out the new forms supplied to their respective offices. The forms should be submitted to the human resources department at least two days before the date of -------.

141. (A) employment
(B) absence
(C) separation
(D) completion

Second, staff members who want to apply for long vacations should inform their superiors and the department at least two weeks in advance.

Since the department is currently busy recruiting new personnel for the company's satellite office, ------- will be assigned to receive leave forms until next month. In the

142. (A) someone
(B) everyone
(C) nobody
(D) anybody

meantime, all forms must be left in the receptacle near the department's entrance. A clerk ------- your office to confirm receipt of your form. You should receive a response to your

143. (A) has contacted
(B) was contacting
(C) is contacting
(D) will contact

request within a week.

Questions 144-146 refer to the following memo.

To: Sales Staff
From: Edward House, Solepad Assistant Manager
Subject: Silvercup Gift Certificate

To encourage everyone to sell more shoes, management has decided to reward staff members who meet their weekly quotas with gift certificates for Silvercup Mall. This new ------- program will be effective throughout the year. We have obtained the certificates

144. (A) incentive
(B) elaborate
(C) legislative
(D) economic

and the first sales team to be awarded will be announced tomorrow.

The certificates, which are worth $50, expire at the end of ------- year. In addition, they

145. (A) many
(B) both
(C) neither
(D) each

may be accumulated and used for larger purchases. Simply ------- the certificates at any

146. (A) copy
(B) prepare
(C) present
(D) exhibit

store in the Silvercup Mall. Any amount in excess of the certificates' total value, however, must be paid for by the holder.

READING TEST 1 2 3 4 5 6 7 8 9 10

GO ON TO THE NEXT PAGE

Questions 147-149 refer to the following letter.

April 14

Celeste Padilla, Admissions Director
Zuidema Business School
Calle La Guerta 96
Chuao, Caracas 1060A

Dear Ms. Padilla,

I would like to ------- Adela Ugarte's admission to your school's Master of Business

147. (A) postpone
(B) recommend
(C) evaluate
(D) disapprove

Administration program. I have worked closely with Ms. Ugarte and strongly believe that she deserves to be accepted to the Zuidema Business School.

Since Ms. Ugarte joined our firm as a financial analyst four years ago, she has always displayed a strong initiative and work ethic. Moreover, Ms. Ugarte functions well within a group setting but at the same time is capable of achieving results -------. She worked on

148. (A) cooperatively
(B) routinely
(C) exclusively
(D) independently

her own to form a definitive manual on forecast development, which eventually became a useful tool for our new employees.

I hope that my brief outline of Ms. Ugarte's skills will ------- all concerned that she

149. (A) benefit
(B) enable
(C) convince
(D) demonstrate

deserves to be admitted to Zuidema Business School's MBA program. If you would like to discuss her qualifications in more detail, please feel free to give me a call at 555-8321. Thank you for your time.

Yours truly,

Oswaldo Medina, Head, International Accounts
Frechilla Enterprises

Questions 150-152 refer to the following e-mail.

To: Elizabeth Marquez <emarquez@mayardbar.com>
From: Gladys Cross <melcross@pinnaclemedia.com>
Subject: Band Information
Date: December 10

Dear Beth,

I was wondering whether or not you received the package I mailed to your office earlier this week. It contains a profile and a CD of the band that I am suggesting you hire for the grand ------- of your restaurant next month.

150. (A) open
(B) opening
(C) openly
(D) opened

Velvet Jazz Band is a rising band in the local music industry. The group is composed of talented and ------- musicians. They can play jazz, rock, and other genres of music. In

151. (A) global
(B) selective
(C) versatile
(D) acceptable

addition, the group's vocalist comes from a pop group that topped the Asian charts three years ago.

I guarantee you that Velvet Jazz Band will ------- many customers to your restaurant and

152. (A) engage
(B) attract
(C) invite
(D) persuade

create a lasting impression of your establishment. Just let me know if you want to personally meet the members of the band so that I can schedule an appointment with them. Thanks!

Best regards,

Gladys

GO ON TO THE NEXT PAGE

PART 7

Directions: In this part, you will be asked to read several texts, such as advertisements, articles or examples of business correspondence. Each text is followed by several questions. Select the best answer and mark the corresponding letter (A), (B), (C), or (D) on your answer sheet.

Questions 153-154 refer to the following schedule.

Carpentry Association of Vermont

Presents woodworking courses, June 2 to July 6 at the Evergreen Community Center

Time	Course	Description	Instructor
Mon/Wed 9 A.M. to 12 P.M.	Woodworking 101	Recommended for beginners. Covers the basics of woodworking.	Jonathan Smith
Fri/Sat 1 to 4 P.M.	Simple Woodworking	Make objects such as picture frames, jewelry boxes, and pen holders.	Garrett Turner
Tue/Thu 3 to 6 P.M.	Great Wooden Things	Designed for home improvement enthusiasts with advanced skills.	Sean Langley
Tue/Fri 10 A.M. to 1 P.M.	Wood Imagination	Skills for those interested in using wood to make sculptures or fine art.	Frederick Burch

A certificate of completion will be given at the end of each course. Course materials will be provided. Sign up at www.woodcourses.org. Registration runs from May 10 to 25 only.

153. Who most likely will teach a class for artists?
(A) Garrett Turner
(B) Sean Langley
(C) Frederick Burch
(D) Jonathan Smith

154. What will happen after May 25?
(A) Registration for classes will be closed.
(B) An association will be accepting members.
(C) A Web site will be inaccessible.
(D) Course materials will be distributed.

GO ON TO THE NEXT PAGE

Questions 155-156 refer to the following advertisement.

Marigold Spa

▪ Theaterbelt ▪ Silvertown ▪ Bakerville ▪ Wesley

For 10 years now, Marigold Spa has been promoting personal well-being through natural methods of revitalization. To celebrate a decade of service, Marigold Spa is reducing prices by up to 30 percent on basic personal care treatments, including body massages, facials, and nail care for the entire month of June. In addition, Marigold Spa Club members will receive a free foot spa package when they visit any Marigold Spa branch this month. Celebrate with us and take advantage of this limited-time offer. For more information, log on to www.marigoldspa.com.

155. What is indicated about Marigold Spa?
(A) It is launching a new service.
(B) It is introducing a membership club.
(C) It is celebrating its anniversary.
(D) It is opening another branch.

156. What is NOT included in the discount promotion?
(A) Massages
(B) Spa packages
(C) Facials
(D) Manicure services

Questions 157-158 refer to the following notice.

Notice to All Marketing Staff Members

To provide everyone with an organized record of discussions about our projects, members will take turns in preparing minutes of every meeting and posting them on the Intranet. This should take place immediately after each team meeting or client appointment. In addition, everyone is expected to follow a uniform format when presenting information online.

Since we cannot access the Intranet right now due to ongoing network maintenance work, the format will be posted on the bulletin board later today. A schedule for taking minutes will be provided at our next meeting. If you have any questions, let me know.

From Justine Tuckfield
Marketing Department Head

157. What is the notice mainly about?
(A) Posting messages on the Intranet site
(B) Keeping online information secure
(C) Implementing a new office procedure
(D) Making schedule changes for monthly meetings

158. What does Ms. Tuckfield mention about the format?
(A) It will remain the same as before.
(B) It has been simplified.
(C) It was posted for staff yesterday.
(D) It is not yet accessible.

GO ON TO THE NEXT PAGE

Questions 159-161 refer to the following notice.

Kensington's Wants to Serve you Better!

Kensington's family restaurant is pleased to announce that we will be extending our hours of operation at all branches across the nation! This change will provide you with additional hours in the morning for breakfast service and extra time in the evening on weekends.

In line with this, Kensington's will also be introducing a new breakfast buffet on weekends including such favorites as omelets, pancakes, and waffles. The new offerings will be introduced starting this weekend on May 4.

Our new hours of operation are as follows:

Monday	7 A.M. to 10 P.M.
Tuesday	
Wednesday	
Thursday	
Friday	7 A.M. to 11:30 P.M.
Saturday *	8 A.M. to 11:30 P.M.
Sunday *	

*Breakfast buffet service is available from 9 A.M. through 12 P.M. Reservations are recommended. To book a table, please call (504) 555-6677.

For further information on our menu, locations, and promotions, visit www.kensingtons.co.ca.

159. Why was the notice written?
(A) To announce business hour changes
(B) To inform diners of menu items
(C) To promote a new restaurant
(D) To publicize a special discount offer

160. What is indicated about Kensington's family restaurant?
(A) It only has breakfast and lunch menus.
(B) It has numerous branches around the world.
(C) It offers a special dining option on weekends.
(D) It does not accept weekday reservations.

161. What is mentioned about the buffet?
(A) It is offered Monday through Friday.
(B) It is only available at a particular time.
(C) It requires advance bookings.
(D) It will no longer be provided on weekends.

Questions 162-164 refer to the following article.

School Aims to Meet Demand for Foreign Languages

by Vanna Tan

Proficiency in English and other foreign languages has become a major requirement for Chinese professionals with career aspirations. Given the increasing number of foreign companies operating in the country and fierce competition in the job market, people who speak many languages have a distinct advantage. This trend made linguist Kenny Mayer realize the need to establish a language school that would help citizens improve their performance.

"Since impressive language skills are essential in the corporate world, I decided to build a school for those who wish to enhance their abilities," Mayer said in an interview.

Mayer opened Fluency Masters Academy on Friday at the Collinsway Tower. All programs offered at the academy are tailored to students who are beginners and have never studied a foreign language. Among the courses currently available are English, Japanese, and French. Native speakers in each language will conduct lessons on weekday nights. Mayer says that the academy will allow professionals to learn a language without travelling abroad.

"If everything goes well during the year, I might consider offering Spanish and other European languages. But for now, the academy will continue to focus on its current three languages," Mayer said.

162. What is the article mainly about?
(A) A university activity
(B) The launch of a business
(C) Commonly used languages
(D) Communication techniques

163. What is NOT indicated about Fluency Masters?
(A) It was founded by a language expert.
(B) It offers classes on weekdays.
(C) It employs native English speakers.
(D) It is affiliated with a foreign company.

164. What does the article suggest?
(A) Ms. Tan speaks many languages.
(B) The school is in a business district.
(C) Ms. Tan interviewed Mr. Mayer.
(D) The academy will open on Friday.

GO ON TO THE NEXT PAGE

Questions 165-167 refer to the following letter.

FOREMOST EMPLOYMENT AGENCY

August 14

Dear Mr. Nehru,

I am sorry to inform you that your application for the position of senior technical director at Goldbear Technologies was turned down. The company was recently forced to reduce its managerial workforce due to the ongoing economic crisis. However, I plan to submit your application to another company in western India, Pioneer Plastics Manufacturing. This is a growing company in Maharashtra that is looking for someone with your specific qualifications. Please see the attachment for more details.

If you are interested in pursuing the application, I would urge you to phone Chynna Dara in our Indian branch at 555-1433 as soon as possible. She is familiar with Pioneer Plastics and has a good relationship with its human resources manager. In the meantime, I will go ahead and forward her your résumé and reference letters. I will also continue to scout for other opportunities, and let you know if I receive any news.

Good luck!

Sincerely,

Henry Tang
Director of Human Resources
Foremost Employment Agency

165. What is the main purpose of the letter?
(A) To apologize for a misunderstanding
(B) To terminate a manager's contract
(C) To discuss a client's application status
(D) To report on a company's economic crisis

166. What does Mr. Tang say he will do?
(A) Revise an application process
(B) Send some documentation
(C) Call another branch associate
(D) Forward information to Goldbear Technologies

167. Who most likely is Ms. Dara?
(A) An employment agent
(B) A technical director
(C) A factory inspector
(D) A business owner

Questions 168-172 refer to the following information.

If you're employed in the field of business, there is something you have likely experienced before: the feeling of helplessness and stress as deadlines pass and work piles up. For many, it seems like an endless battle. After all, there are only so many hours in a day. Thankfully, there is a way to make the most out of your time. Here are some tips from successful executives who have learned to manage their schedules and be more productive.

1. Plan ahead
Time management is less about managing time and more about managing activities. Assign "things to do" to specific times of the day, days of the week, months of the year, and so on. In addition, assign deadlines to each task or project, but set them at least two days ahead of the actual due dates so you will always be on time.

2. Prioritize tasks
If you have too much work, try to complete the most important tasks and projects early in the morning to avoid being overwhelmed with work later in the day. Too often throughout a day, other obligations and responsibilities creep in and distract you from your work.

3. Take notes
Keep a notebook handy to record something you have neglected to include in your schedule, or to write down ideas. Otherwise, it becomes increasingly difficult to stay focused on the tasks before you.

4. Put everything in its place
At home, in the car, and especially at work, minimize distractions by maintaining orderly surroundings. Keep frequently used items within reach, but store everything else in drawers and cabinets.

5. Reward yourself
Motivate yourself to finish tasks by rewarding major accomplishments. Depending on the nature of a completed task, your reward can be as simple as giving yourself a break to enjoy a leisurely activity.

168. What is the information mainly about?
(A) Becoming your own boss
(B) Being more productive
(C) Motivating coworkers
(D) Managing employees

169. Which method is NOT included in the information?
(A) Organizing personal belongings
(B) Keeping a notebook
(C) Turning off your phone
(D) Scheduling activities

170. What does the information suggest people with excessive workloads do?
(A) Outsource some of the workload
(B) Hire a professional assistant
(C) Go to the workplace early
(D) Rate the importance of tasks

171. The word "reach" in paragraph 5, line 2 is closest in meaning to
(A) proximity
(B) extension
(C) area
(D) category

172. According to the information, how can people motivate themselves?
(A) By scheduling their time carefully
(B) By giving themselves a reward
(C) By setting reasonable goals
(D) By writing down their successes

GO ON TO THE NEXT PAGE

Questions 173-176 refer to the following e-mail.

From:	Liza Singer <accounting@pencilstudios.com>
To:	Lisa Chang <lchang@pencilstudios.com>, Kevin Olsen <kolsen@pencilstudios.com>, William Kane <wkane@pencilstudios.com>
Date:	September 3
Subject:	Reimbursements

As we have discussed, all project leaders will be in charge of turning in monthly reimbursement requests to the accounting department beginning this month. To file a refund, fill out a reimbursement request form. Attach all original receipts for project expenses to the form and hand it in to Ms. Ricks. After that, she will forward the documents to Mr. Scott for evaluation and refund all valid expenses after three days.

Refunds may be claimed in cash or deposited into your payroll accounts. Please inform Ms. Ricks of the option you prefer.

In addition, please take note that expenses without official receipts will not be reimbursed. Therefore, you need to remind your team members to give you the receipts for all work-related expenditures.

Lastly, I request that you submit a summary of your team's expenses at least two weeks before the end of each quarter. This will hasten the process of preparing the company's quarterly income statement. If you have questions, send an e-mail to the accounting department.

Liza Singer

173. Who most likely is Ms. Singer?
(A) A company investor
(B) A member of accounting staff
(C) A public relations officer
(D) A company sales agent

174. According to the e-mail, what must be included with the request form?
(A) Account numbers
(B) An expense report
(C) Proof of payment
(D) A project outline

175. What most likely is Ms. Ricks responsible for?
(A) Organizing reimbursement documents
(B) Evaluating the results of projects
(C) Managing customer accounts
(D) Sending out billing statements

176. What is NOT indicated about the receipts?
(A) They should be sent to the accounting office.
(B) They serve as records of official expenses.
(C) They should be collected on a recurring basis.
(D) They are turned in at the end of every quarter.

Questions 177-180 refer to the following memo.

Merrick Foods, Incorporated

To: Factory personnel
From: Doug Leavesley, Chief Operations Officer
Re: Food Handling

The Consumer Safety Board (CSB) has issued a new set of policies for the proper handling of food. To conform to these new policies, we have revised some of our own internal regulations. Copies of the relevant sections have been posted in the employee lunchroom. The personnel department will issue a comprehensive document in a few weeks that includes our own changes.

Prior to ordering
Effective immediately, the purchasing control department must log on weekly to the CSB Web site at www.csb.gov to verify information provided about our farm sources' crop conditions and insect infestations. In addition, beginning in May, the company will no longer accept shipments of potatoes that are more than 30 days old.

Upon arrival
Unsorted potatoes must be washed and stored immediately. The temperature setting within storage containers can be no more than 40 degrees Fahrenheit. Following the initial inspection for blemishes, shipments whose rejected portions are more than 25 percent of the total gross weight must be returned in their entirety.

Processing stage
Potatoes must be washed a second time after slicing in order to reduce the vegetable's starch content. In addition, we will be applying a different chemical agent for color treatment that has already been approved by the CSB.

Lastly, all food handlers and machine operators are required to put on gloves, rubber aprons, and face masks. These items are to be deposited each day at the laundry department for sterilization.

Thank you for your cooperation in these matters.

177. What is the memo mainly about?
(A) Training for new employees
(B) Changes to a facility's practices
(C) Procedures for preparing a dish
(D) Advances in storage equipment

178. What is suggested about Merrick Foods?
(A) It is required to follow CSB guidelines.
(B) It is closing its factory in May.
(C) It uses outdated machinery.
(D) It had an issue related to food handling.

179. What is the purchasing control department required to do?
(A) Inspect for defects
(B) Limit their weekly budget
(C) Check a Web site regularly
(D) Count rejected items

180. What is mentioned in the memo?
(A) Shipments must be sterilized prior to delivery.
(B) Items must be sorted in the order they arrive.
(C) Chemicals must be refrigerated when not in use.
(D) Specific types of clothing must be worn.

GO ON TO THE NEXT PAGE

Questions 181-185 refer to the following e-mails.

To: Neil Grossman <neil.grossman@brooksconstruction.com>
From: Audrey Stanford <a.stanford@mckinleytiles.com>
Date: August 8
Subject: Order of Tiles

Dear Mr. Grossman,

This is concerning your recent order of floor tiles from our Web site. I am pleased to inform you that 600 pieces of Iklimler Ceramics (floral beige) and 400 pieces of Oakland Terrazzo (reddish brown) will be delivered to your office tomorrow at 8 A.M. Brian, my personal assistant, will supervise the delivery to make sure that the items are not mishandled. Please let him know if you encounter any problems.

With regard to your inquiry about customized tiles, I believe we have enough time to accommodate your order, but it would depend on the design and quantity. Could you give us a rough idea of what you're looking for by sending a draft of your design? Also, please specify the number of pieces you need so we can provide you with a price estimate. Then we will let you know when the order can be completed. Orders of 300 or more customized tiles usually take at least two weeks to manufacture. But in case you need the tiles sooner, we offer rush services for an additional fee of $150.

Please do not hesitate to contact me if you have any questions. You can call me at 555-9696. My extension number is 104.

Thank you.

Sincerely yours,

Audrey Stanford
Manager
McKinley Tiles Incorporated

To: Audrey Stanford <a.stanford@mckinleytiles.com>
From: Neil Grossman <neil.grossman@brooksconstruction.com>
Date: August 9
Subject: Re: Order of Tiles
Attachment: Tile Design

Dear Ms. Stanford,

I'd like to thank you for the timely delivery of the two orders of tiles. They arrived this morning in good condition. I really appreciate that you had Brian supervise the delivery. He was very kind and helpful.

I'm also grateful for your prompt response about the customized tiles. As I told you, they will not be for our clients but for our office. We're planning to renovate our customer service area, and we thought it would be a good idea to use tiles that better reflect our brand identity. I attached a copy of the design to this e-mail. The tentative schedule for the renovation project is in the third week of September. Do you think you can make 500 pieces by then?

By the way, as I mentioned in my previous e-mail, the company is organizing an event for the launch of our newly designed Web site, which will allow our customers to make online purchases. Since you are a trusted supplier, you might be interested in attending this activity. I will ask my secretary to send you a formal invitation once it's finalized.

Sincerely,

Neil Grossman
Supervisor
Brooks Construction Supplies

181. According to the first e-mail, why is Ms. Stanford sending her personal assistant?
(A) To install a set of floor tiles
(B) To collect payment for an order
(C) To ensure the safety of merchandise
(D) To take measurements of a room

182. In the first e-mail, the word "rough" in paragraph 2, line 3 is closest in meaning to
(A) coarse
(B) approximate
(C) difficult
(D) uneven

183. What is indicated about Brooks Construction Supplies?
(A) Its clients have recently given positive feedback about its services.
(B) It is providing customers with additional shopping options.
(C) It is extending its contract with McKinley Tiles Incorporated.
(D) Its sales of building materials increased in the previous quarter.

184. According to the second e-mail, what will happen next month?
(A) A merger agreement will be signed.
(B) An office space will be renovated.
(C) A company will transfer to a new location.
(D) A department will release the budget.

185. What is suggested about the items Mr. Grossman wants to order?
(A) They will require at least two weeks to be produced.
(B) They were delivered on schedule.
(C) They are being offered at a discounted price.
(D) They will be used in a new building.

READING TEST 1 2 3 4 5 6 7 8 9 10

GO ON TO THE NEXT PAGE

Questions 186-190 refer to the following e-mails.

To: All supervisors <supervisors@haydenboutique.com>
From: Julien Hirsch <julien.hirsch@haydenboutique.com>
Subject: Fashion Show
Attachment: One file
Date: February 15

Dear supervisors,

Over the past nine years, the Annual Hayden Couture Fashion Show has become one of the most highly anticipated events in the industry. Now in its 10th year, we plan to make it bigger and better. The event will not only showcase our latest collection of clothes but also introduce a selection of work from some of the country's young fashion designers. As supervisors, you will be responsible for receiving entries, so please make sure you are well informed about the details of the competition.

For this year, we will be accepting entries from university students for several categories in the show. Interested applicants are required to complete and submit a copy of the registration form attached with this e-mail. We have invited a panel of renowned fashion designers to screen the entries and serve as judges for each category. Once the final entries are chosen, applicants will be given time to execute their designs in time for the fashion show. Complete information about these categories is now available on our Web site.

CATEGORY	SCREENING COMMITTEE HEAD
Ready-to-Wear	Mr. Amir Salood
Specialty Hats	Ms. Marga Silverio
Athletic Wear	Mr. Vittorio Bellucci
Haute Couture	Ms. Shalani San Pedro

All entries should be submitted to the Hayden Boutique main office before March 20. We are still finalizing the arrangements for the venue, but if everything goes well, the show will be held on May 18 at Preminger Trade Center. That will give the short-listed applicants enough time to complete their designs. All inquiries should be sent directly to Ms. Vicki Bergamo at vicki.bergamo@haydenboutique.com. She is responsible for the organization of the entire event.

We look forward to your cooperation. Thank you.

Sincerely yours,

Julien Hirsch
Regional director
Hayden Boutique Incorporated

From: Vicki Bergamo <vicki.bergamo@haydenboutique.com>
To: Antoine Rohmer <antoine.rohmer@ohlala.fr>
Subject: Hayden Couture Fashion Show
Date: April 2

Dear Mr. Rohmer,

I'm pleased to inform you that your entry was selected to be part of the 10th Annual Hayden Couture Fashion Show. The panel of judges liked the stylishness of your swimwear design. It combines fashion and convenience while demonstrating your individuality as a designer. Congratulations!

As one of the finalists, you are required to attend the orientation on Friday, April 5, at the Hayden Boutique head office. You will be provided with the materials you need to complete your design, as well as detailed instructions about the fashion show in May. In addition to having your design presented at the event, your work will be included in our upcoming summer collection that will be launched in June.

If you have any questions, please call my assistant, Nicole, at 555-9009 local 125. I'm looking forward to seeing you on Friday.

Sincerely,

Vicki Bergamo
Operations manager
Hayden Boutique Incorporated

186. What does Julien Hirsch ask the supervisors to do?
(A) Organize individual store events
(B) Select applicants from a list of entries
(C) Attend a meeting with committee heads
(D) Become familiar with a contest's guidelines

187. What is NOT mentioned about the fashion show?
(A) It is celebrating its tenth anniversary.
(B) It is supplying production materials to participants.
(C) It is presenting an award to an esteemed artist.
(D) It is opening categories for young people.

188. What is indicated about Hayden Boutique?
(A) It has several branches outside the country.
(B) It designs clothes for renowned personalities.
(C) It is planning to launch some new merchandise.
(D) It is offering positions to new university graduates.

189. Who most likely screened Antoine Rohmer's entry?
(A) Vittorio Bellucci
(B) Marga Silverio
(C) Amir Salood
(D) Shalani San Pedro

190. What did Ms. Bergamo say will happen on Friday?
(A) Additional staff members will be hired.
(B) A new clothing store will open to the public.
(C) Some celebrities will be asked to participate in a fashion show.
(D) Some people will be given information about an event.

GO ON TO THE NEXT PAGE

Questions 191-195 refer to the following invitation and article.

Saggezza Historical Institute

cordially invites you

to the opening of a new exhibition

Alba Longa:

Demystifying the Legend

of the Ancient City

on Saturday, October 10

from 6 P.M. to 9 P.M.

Run date: October 11 to November 30

For further information, please read through the enclosed brochure.

Also please attend the special premiere of

the documentary film:

The Dionysius Chronicles

on October 23

at the Halicarnassus Auditorium

on the third floor of the Institute.

Audience members are welcome to stay

for a question and answer session with the director

after the screening.

The Dionysius Chronicles Wins ADF Prize

Amateur film director Giannina Balducci was awarded the coveted Amateur Documentary Filmmaker (ADF) prize for her movie *The Dionysius Chronicles*. The prize is presented annually to an amateur film director who shows promise and talent. Balducci's film explores historical sites and areas related to the ancient stories of Greek teacher and historian Dionysius. Balducci spent two years travelling and filming in various locations in the Mediterranean area and interviewed numerous history scholars and experts.

Balducci was born in Italy and expressed an interest in film since a young age. By the time she was 28, she had already filmed three documentaries. "I am so grateful for this honor and look forward to attending the movie's premiere on October 23. I hope others will also enjoy the film," said Balducci in a telephone interview.

A panel of six judges selected Balducci as best director among more than 300 entrants. Selection of the recipient was based on directorial technique, originality, editing, sound, and visual appeal. The winners receive a certificate along with a cash prize of $20,000. The ADF prize is awarded by the European Documentary Filmmakers Society. To learn more about this year's winner and past recipients of the ADF prize, visit www.adfprize.org.

191. What will most likely happen on November 30?
(A) An exhibition will conclude.
(B) A movie will be screened.
(C) A presentation ceremony will be held.
(D) An auditorium will be reopened.

192. Which information is NOT included in the invitation?
(A) The location of the event
(B) The date of an opening
(C) The cost of admission
(D) The name of a film

193. What is mentioned about Ms. Balducci?
(A) She is a member of a filmmakers' society.
(B) She has made several documentary films.
(C) She is an expert on Greek history.
(D) She has lived in Italy since she was born.

194. Why did Ms. Balducci win a prize?
(A) For acting in a film production
(B) For receiving high grades in film school
(C) For producing a series of documentaries
(D) For showing talent as a director

195. What will Ms. Balducci do on October 23?
(A) Give a talk at an exhibit opening
(B) Register to participate in a competition
(C) Attend an event at the Halicarnassus Auditorium
(D) Begin work on a new movie production

GO ON TO THE NEXT PAGE

Questions 196-200 refer to the following e-mails.

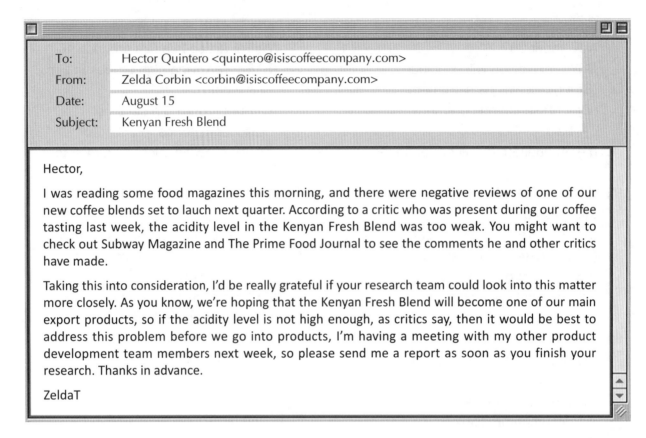

To:	Hector Quintero <quintero@isiscoffeecompany.com>
From:	Zelda Corbin <corbin@isiscoffeecompany.com>
Date:	August 15
Subject:	Kenyan Fresh Blend

Hector,

I was reading some food magazines this morning, and there were negative reviews of one of our new coffee blends set to lauch next quarter. According to a critic who was present during our coffee tasting last week, the acidity level in the Kenyan Fresh Blend was too weak. You might want to check out Subway Magazine and The Prime Food Journal to see the comments he and other critics have made.

Taking this into consideration, I'd be really grateful if your research team could look into this matter more closely. As you know, we're hoping that the Kenyan Fresh Blend will become one of our main export products, so if the acidity level is not high enough, as critics say, then it would be best to address this problem before we go into products, I'm having a meeting with my other product development team members next week, so please send me a report as soon as you finish your research. Thanks in advance.

ZeldaT

To:	Zelda Corbin <corbin@isiscoffeecompany.com>
From:	Hector Quintero <quintero@isiscoffeecompany.com>
Date:	August 22
Subject:	Re: Kenyan Fresh Blend
Attachment:	Two documents

Zelda,

My staff and I just finished the research you requested and our findings confirm what you mentioned in your last e-mail. As it turns out, the lab test conducted on the blend indicates that its acidity level is 5.0, which lacks that sharp, clean taste that coffee lovers look for. A report submitted by the staff who conducted the coffee tasting stated that most of the participants said the coffee was dull.

I have attached a copy of the lab test as well as the report on the coffee tasting held last week. Our research team recommends changing the blend. It is ready to produce several samples for your consideration, but will wait for your instructions. Please let me know if there is anything else you would like me to do to facilitate the development of this coffee as an export product.

I will be out of the office today to procure some coffee bean samples from a new supplier, so please call my mobile phone if there is anything you would like to discuss.

Hector

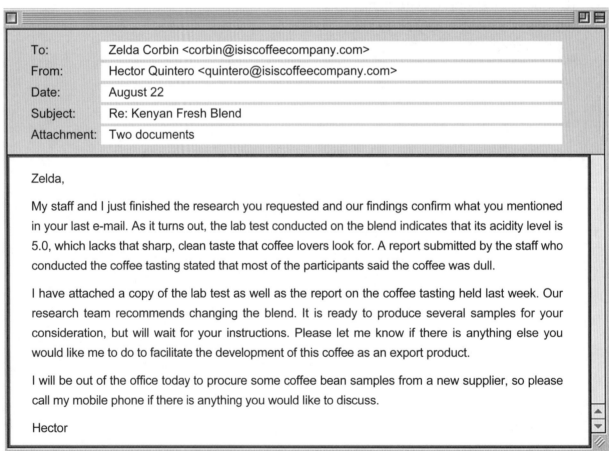

196. What is the purpose of the first e-mail?
(A) To ask a colleague to conduct a study
(B) To request a coworker to reschedule a meeting
(C) To cancel subscriptions to several food magazines
(D) To notify staff about a change in production schedules

197. What does Ms. Corbin most likely do?
(A) Writes critiques for a publication
(B) Leads a research team
(C) Manages a factory
(D) Develops new products

198. What is NOT indicated about the Isis Coffee Company?
(A) It purchases its merchandise from a supplier.
(B) Its Kenyan Fresh Blend is not yet on the market.
(C) It distributes its goods internationally.
(D) Its products were reviewed in two publications.

199. What does Mr. Quintero report about the Kenyan Fresh Blend?
(A) It was taken off the market temporarily.
(B) It is an expensive product.
(C) It has a very low acidity level.
(D) It has an unpleasant taste.

200. What does Mr. Quintero ask Ms. Corbin to do?
(A) Plan a marketing campaign
(B) Provide further instruction
(C) Arrange a meeting with critics
(D) Attend a magazine interview

This is the end of the test. You may review Part 5, 6, and 7 if you finish the test early.

解答 p.288 / 分數換算表 p.289 / 題目解析 p.465（解答本）

請翻到次頁「自我檢測表」檢視自己解答問題的方法與態度。

自我檢測表

TEST 10 順利的完成了嗎？

現在要開始透過以下的自我檢測表檢視自己在考試中的表現了嗎？

我的目標分數為：　　　　　　　這次測試的成績為：

1. 70 分鐘內，我完全集中精神在測試內容上。

   □是　□不是

   如果回答不是，理由是什麼呢？

2. 70 分鐘內，連答案卷的劃記都完成了。

   □是　□不是

   如果回答不是，理由是什麼呢？

3. 70 分鐘內，100 題都解完了。

   □是　□不是

   如果回答不是，理由是什麼呢？

4. Part 5 和 Part 6 在 25 分鐘以內全都寫完了。

   □是　□不是

   如果回答不是，理由是什麼呢？

5. 寫 Part 7 的時候，沒有一題花超過五分鐘。

   □是　□不是

   如果回答不是，理由是什麼呢？

6. 請寫下你需要改善的地方以及給自己的忠告。

*回到本書第二頁，確認自己的目標分數並加強對於達成分數的意志。
對於要改善的部分一定要在下一次測試中實踐。這點是最重要的，也要這樣才能有進步。

簡答
分數換算表
Anser Sheet

簡答 Answer Keys

TEST 01

101 (C)	102 (C)	103 (C)	104 (D)	105 (A)
106 (D)	107 (C)	108 (B)	109 (C)	110 (B)
111 (A)	112 (C)	113 (B)	114 (D)	115 (C)
116 (A)	117 (D)	118 (B)	119 (C)	120 (D)
121 (C)	122 (C)	123 (B)	124 (C)	125 (B)
126 (D)	127 (C)	128 (A)	129 (C)	130 (A)
131 (A)	132 (C)	133 (D)	134 (D)	135 (D)
136 (B)	137 (B)	138 (A)	139 (B)	140 (A)
141 (D)	142 (B)	143 (A)	144 (B)	145 (A)
146 (C)	147 (C)	148 (B)	149 (A)	150 (B)
151 (A)	152 (D)	153 (B)	154 (C)	155 (B)
156 (D)	157 (D)	158 (B)	159 (D)	160 (B)
161 (C)	162 (D)	163 (A)	164 (A)	165 (A)
166 (C)	167 (D)	168 (C)	169 (D)	170 (A)
171 (D)	172 (B)	173 (C)	174 (B)	175 (A)
176 (D)	177 (C)	178 (C)	179 (A)	180 (D)
181 (A)	182 (D)	183 (B)	184 (A)	185 (C)
186 (D)	187 (D)	188 (A)	189 (C)	190 (B)
191 (B)	192 (C)	193 (B)	194 (A)	195 (D)
196 (B)	197 (A)	198 (D)	199 (C)	200 (A)

TEST 02

101 (A)	102 (D)	103 (A)	104 (B)	105 (D)
106 (B)	107 (C)	108 (C)	109 (D)	110 (A)
111 (D)	112 (D)	113 (B)	114 (A)	115 (C)
116 (C)	117 (C)	118 (B)	119 (C)	120 (B)
121 (D)	122 (A)	123 (A)	124 (D)	125 (D)
126 (D)	127 (D)	128 (C)	129 (D)	130 (C)
131 (D)	132 (B)	133 (B)	134 (B)	135 (D)
136 (C)	137 (C)	138 (A)	139 (A)	140 (D)
141 (A)	142 (D)	143 (C)	144 (C)	145 (B)
146 (A)	147 (B)	148 (C)	149 (B)	150 (C)
151 (D)	152 (B)	153 (B)	154 (D)	155 (C)
156 (A)	157 (D)	158 (D)	159 (B)	160 (D)
161 (B)	162 (B)	163 (A)	164 (C)	165 (B)
166 (D)	167 (B)	168 (C)	169 (D)	170 (B)
171 (C)	172 (D)	173 (A)	174 (B)	175 (B)
176 (B)	177 (A)	178 (B)	179 (D)	180 (C)
181 (A)	182 (D)	183 (C)	184 (C)	185 (D)
186 (D)	187 (C)	188 (D)	189 (B)	190 (C)
191 (C)	192 (D)	193 (C)	194 (B)	195 (D)
196 (A)	197 (C)	198 (C)	199 (B)	200 (D)

TEST 03

101 (A)	102 (B)	103 (C)	104 (C)	105 (A)
106 (D)	107 (D)	108 (B)	109 (B)	110 (B)
111 (A)	112 (D)	113 (D)	114 (C)	115 (A)
116 (D)	117 (B)	118 (B)	119 (D)	120 (C)
121 (C)	122 (C)	123 (A)	124 (C)	125 (C)
126 (B)	127 (B)	128 (A)	129 (B)	130 (A)
131 (D)	132 (B)	133 (D)	134 (B)	135 (C)
136 (B)	137 (C)	138 (D)	139 (D)	140 (B)
141 (D)	142 (B)	143 (B)	144 (B)	145 (A)
146 (A)	147 (B)	148 (B)	149 (A)	150 (B)
151 (A)	152 (A)	153 (C)	154 (B)	155 (B)
156 (D)	157 (C)	158 (D)	159 (A)	160 (A)
161 (C)	162 (B)	163 (A)	164 (C)	165 (B)
166 (B)	167 (D)	168 (D)	169 (A)	170 (C)
171 (D)	172 (B)	173 (B)	174 (A)	175 (C)
176 (A)	177 (C)	178 (D)	179 (B)	180 (B)
181 (B)	182 (A)	183 (C)	184 (D)	185 (B)
186 (C)	187 (B)	188 (C)	189 (B)	190 (D)
191 (C)	192 (B)	193 (A)	194 (C)	195 (B)
196 (B)	197 (C)	198 (D)	199 (C)	200 (D)

TEST 04

101 (B)	102 (B)	103 (C)	104 (D)	105 (C)
106 (A)	107 (A)	108 (C)	109 (B)	110 (A)
111 (B)	112 (C)	113 (A)	114 (B)	115 (C)
116 (C)	117 (D)	118 (B)	119 (A)	120 (D)
121 (B)	122 (D)	123 (C)	124 (D)	125 (C)
126 (C)	127 (B)	128 (A)	129 (D)	130 (D)
131 (D)	132 (A)	133 (B)	134 (C)	135 (A)
136 (C)	137 (A)	138 (A)	139 (C)	140 (D)
141 (B)	142 (D)	143 (D)	144 (D)	145 (A)
146 (B)	147 (B)	148 (C)	149 (D)	150 (D)
151 (C)	152 (A)	153 (A)	154 (C)	155 (B)
156 (C)	157 (A)	158 (A)	159 (B)	160 (D)
161 (B)	162 (B)	163 (D)	164 (A)	165 (D)
166 (A)	167 (C)	168 (A)	169 (D)	170 (C)
171 (B)	172 (A)	173 (D)	174 (C)	175 (B)
176 (D)	177 (C)	178 (B)	179 (C)	180 (C)
181 (C)	182 (A)	183 (C)	184 (B)	185 (D)
186 (C)	187 (C)	188 (B)	189 (B)	190 (A)
191 (D)	192 (A)	193 (C)	194 (D)	195 (A)
196 (A)	197 (C)	198 (B)	199 (C)	200 (D)

TEST 05

101 (B)	102 (C)	103 (A)	104 (A)	105 (D)
106 (B)	107 (C)	108 (A)	109 (B)	110 (B)
111 (C)	112 (B)	113 (B)	114 (B)	115 (D)
116 (C)	117 (C)	118 (B)	119 (B)	120 (C)
121 (D)	122 (A)	123 (D)	124 (B)	125 (A)
126 (C)	127 (A)	128 (C)	129 (A)	130 (C)
131 (C)	132 (B)	133 (C)	134 (C)	135 (C)
136 (C)	137 (A)	138 (C)	139 (B)	140 (A)
141 (B)	142 (C)	143 (C)	144 (A)	145 (D)
146 (B)	147 (A)	148 (D)	149 (B)	150 (B)
151 (C)	152 (C)	153 (B)	154 (A)	155 (C)
156 (D)	157 (B)	158 (C)	159 (A)	160 (D)
161 (C)	162 (A)	163 (C)	164 (B)	165 (D)
166 (D)	167 (B)	168 (D)	169 (D)	170 (A)
171 (B)	172 (A)	173 (B)	174 (B)	175 (B)
176 (C)	177 (C)	178 (A)	179 (C)	180 (D)
181 (B)	182 (C)	183 (C)	184 (A)	185 (D)
186 (A)	187 (C)	188 (A)	189 (C)	190 (B)
191 (D)	192 (C)	193 (D)	194 (A)	195 (A)
196 (C)	197 (D)	198 (A)	199 (D)	200 (C)

TEST 06

101 (B)	102 (B)	103 (B)	104 (A)	105 (D)
106 (D)	107 (C)	108 (B)	109 (B)	110 (D)
111 (B)	112 (D)	113 (A)	114 (A)	115 (D)
116 (B)	117 (A)	118 (A)	119 (C)	120 (C)
121 (B)	122 (D)	123 (C)	124 (C)	125 (D)
126 (B)	127 (A)	128 (B)	129 (C)	130 (B)
131 (D)	132 (D)	133 (B)	134 (C)	135 (A)
136 (A)	137 (C)	138 (C)	139 (A)	140 (C)
141 (C)	142 (A)	143 (C)	144 (C)	145 (A)
146 (C)	147 (A)	148 (D)	149 (B)	150 (D)
151 (A)	152 (D)	153 (C)	154 (D)	155 (D)
156 (D)	157 (B)	158 (D)	159 (B)	160 (B)
161 (C)	162 (B)	163 (D)	164 (C)	165 (D)
166 (C)	167 (B)	168 (D)	169 (C)	170 (B)
171 (D)	172 (A)	173 (D)	174 (A)	175 (B)
176 (C)	177 (D)	178 (C)	179 (C)	180 (D)
181 (C)	182 (D)	183 (A)	184 (D)	185 (B)
186 (A)	187 (C)	188 (B)	189 (D)	190 (B)
191 (C)	192 (B)	193 (C)	194 (D)	195 (B)
196 (B)	197 (C)	198 (B)	199 (D)	200 (D)

TEST 07

101 (A)	102 (D)	103 (C)	104 (B)	105 (D)
106 (A)	107 (C)	108 (A)	109 (A)	110 (B)
111 (B)	112 (C)	113 (C)	114 (B)	115 (A)
116 (C)	117 (D)	118 (D)	119 (C)	120 (D)
121 (B)	122 (C)	123 (C)	124 (C)	125 (D)
126 (B)	127 (C)	128 (B)	129 (B)	130 (D)
131 (C)	132 (C)	133 (C)	134 (B)	135 (B)
136 (A)	137 (B)	138 (B)	139 (B)	140 (D)
141 (B)	142 (A)	143 (D)	144 (B)	145 (C)
146 (D)	147 (C)	148 (D)	149 (B)	150 (B)
151 (C)	152 (A)	153 (B)	154 (D)	155 (C)
156 (B)	157 (B)	158 (C)	159 (D)	160 (B)
161 (C)	162 (D)	163 (C)	164 (D)	165 (B)
166 (C)	167 (C)	168 (A)	169 (D)	170 (B)
171 (C)	172 (B)	173 (D)	174 (C)	175 (B)
176 (A)	177 (D)	178 (D)	179 (C)	180 (B)
181 (A)	182 (C)	183 (D)	184 (B)	185 (D)
186 (C)	187 (A)	188 (B)	189 (D)	190 (C)
191 (B)	192 (C)	193 (B)	194 (A)	195 (D)
196 (B)	197 (D)	198 (D)	199 (A)	200 (C)

TEST 08

101 (A)	102 (A)	103 (B)	104 (C)	105 (C)
106 (A)	107 (D)	108 (C)	109 (A)	110 (D)
111 (D)	112 (D)	113 (C)	114 (D)	115 (C)
116 (D)	117 (A)	118 (B)	119 (B)	120 (D)
121 (D)	122 (D)	123 (C)	124 (A)	125 (D)
126 (B)	127 (C)	128 (B)	129 (A)	130 (A)
131 (A)	132 (B)	133 (D)	134 (B)	135 (C)
136 (D)	137 (A)	138 (D)	139 (A)	140 (A)
141 (A)	142 (B)	143 (D)	144 (A)	145 (C)
146 (D)	147 (B)	148 (B)	149 (A)	150 (A)
151 (B)	152 (D)	153 (A)	154 (D)	155 (B)
156 (C)	157 (B)	158 (D)	159 (C)	160 (A)
161 (D)	162 (B)	163 (D)	164 (C)	165 (A)
166 (B)	167 (D)	168 (C)	169 (B)	170 (A)
171 (B)	172 (C)	173 (A)	174 (D)	175 (B)
176 (B)	177 (D)	178 (D)	179 (B)	180 (D)
181 (D)	182 (A)	183 (C)	184 (A)	185 (B)
186 (B)	187 (C)	188 (A)	189 (D)	190 (C)
191 (D)	192 (A)	193 (C)	194 (B)	195 (A)
196 (B)	197 (D)	198 (B)	199 (C)	200 (A)

TEST 09

101 (A)	102 (B)	103 (B)	104 (C)	105 (B)
106 (D)	107 (A)	108 (B)	109 (B)	110 (B)
111 (A)	112 (D)	113 (D)	114 (D)	115 (D)
116 (A)	117 (C)	118 (B)	119 (A)	120 (A)
121 (C)	122 (D)	123 (B)	124 (D)	125 (B)
126 (B)	127 (B)	128 (B)	129 (A)	130 (D)
131 (B)	132 (C)	133 (B)	134 (C)	135 (C)
136 (C)	137 (B)	138 (B)	139 (C)	140 (A)
141 (C)	142 (B)	143 (A)	144 (C)	145 (A)
146 (B)	147 (B)	148 (C)	149 (A)	150 (D)
151 (A)	152 (A)	153 (D)	154 (C)	155 (A)
156 (D)	157 (A)	158 (B)	159 (A)	160 (B)
161 (C)	162 (B)	163 (D)	164 (C)	165 (B)
166 (D)	167 (B)	168 (C)	169 (D)	170 (B)
171 (D)	172 (C)	173 (B)	174 (C)	175 (B)
176 (C)	177 (B)	178 (A)	179 (A)	180 (B)
181 (B)	182 (D)	183 (A)	184 (C)	185 (B)
186 (C)	187 (A)	188 (B)	189 (B)	190 (B)
191 (C)	192 (B)	193 (B)	194 (A)	195 (D)
196 (B)	197 (C)	198 (B)	199 (B)	200 (A)

TEST 10

101 (A)	102 (A)	103 (B)	104 (A)	105 (A)
106 (C)	107 (D)	108 (C)	109 (B)	110 (B)
111 (B)	112 (A)	113 (C)	114 (A)	115 (C)
116 (C)	117 (C)	118 (C)	119 (A)	120 (B)
121 (A)	122 (A)	123 (C)	124 (A)	125 (B)
126 (C)	127 (B)	128 (C)	129 (B)	130 (C)
131 (C)	132 (B)	133 (B)	134 (C)	135 (A)
136 (A)	137 (C)	138 (A)	139 (A)	140 (A)
141 (B)	142 (C)	143 (D)	144 (A)	145 (D)
146 (C)	147 (B)	148 (D)	149 (C)	150 (B)
151 (C)	152 (B)	153 (C)	154 (A)	155 (C)
156 (B)	157 (C)	158 (D)	159 (A)	160 (C)
161 (B)	162 (B)	163 (D)	164 (C)	165 (C)
166 (B)	167 (A)	168(B)	169(C)	170(D)
171 (A)	172(B)	173(B)	174(C)	175(A)
176 (D)	177(B)	178(A)	179(C)	180(D)
181 (C)	182(B)	183(B)	184(B)	185(A)
186 (D)	187(C)	188(C)	189(A)	190(D)
191 (A)	192(C)	193(B)	194(D)	195(C)
196 (A)	197(D)	198(A)	199(C)	200(B)

分數換算表

*可以透過下列分數換算表推算自己的多益閱讀分數。

答對題數	Reading	答對題數	Reading	答對題數	Reading
100	495	66	325	32	155
99	490	65	320	31	150
98	485	64	315	30	145
97	480	63	310	29	140
96	475	62	305	28	135
95	470	61	300	27	130
94	465	60	295	26	125
93	460	59	290	25	120
92	455	58	285	24	115
91	450	57	280	23	110
90	445	56	275	22	105
89	440	55	270	21	100
88	435	54	265	20	95
87	430	53	260	19	90
86	425	52	255	18	85
85	420	51	250	17	80
84	415	50	245	16	75
83	410	49	240	15	70
82	405	48	235	14	65
81	400	47	230	13	60
80	395	46	225	12	55
79	390	45	220	11	50
78	385	44	215	10	45
77	380	43	210	9	40
76	375	42	205	8	35
75	370	41	200	7	30
74	365	40	195	6	25
73	360	39	190	5	20
72	355	38	185	4	15
71	350	37	180	3	10
70	345	36	175	2	10
69	340	35	170	1	10
68	335	34	165		
67	330	33	160		

Answer Sheet

TEST **01**

READING (Part V~VII)									
NO.	ANSWER	NO.	ANSWER	NO.	ANSWER	NO.	ANSWER	NO.	ANSWER
	A B C D		A B C D		A B C D		A B C D		A B C D
101	Ⓐ Ⓑ Ⓒ Ⓓ	121	Ⓐ Ⓑ Ⓒ Ⓓ	141	Ⓐ Ⓑ Ⓒ Ⓓ	161	Ⓐ Ⓑ Ⓒ Ⓓ	181	Ⓐ Ⓑ Ⓒ Ⓓ
102	Ⓐ Ⓑ Ⓒ Ⓓ	122	Ⓐ Ⓑ Ⓒ Ⓓ	142	Ⓐ Ⓑ Ⓒ Ⓓ	162	Ⓐ Ⓑ Ⓒ Ⓓ	182	Ⓐ Ⓑ Ⓒ Ⓓ
103	Ⓐ Ⓑ Ⓒ Ⓓ	123	Ⓐ Ⓑ Ⓒ Ⓓ	143	Ⓐ Ⓑ Ⓒ Ⓓ	163	Ⓐ Ⓑ Ⓒ Ⓓ	183	Ⓐ Ⓑ Ⓒ Ⓓ
104	Ⓐ Ⓑ Ⓒ Ⓓ	124	Ⓐ Ⓑ Ⓒ Ⓓ	144	Ⓐ Ⓑ Ⓒ Ⓓ	164	Ⓐ Ⓑ Ⓒ Ⓓ	184	Ⓐ Ⓑ Ⓒ Ⓓ
105	Ⓐ Ⓑ Ⓒ Ⓓ	125	Ⓐ Ⓑ Ⓒ Ⓓ	145	Ⓐ Ⓑ Ⓒ Ⓓ	165	Ⓐ Ⓑ Ⓒ Ⓓ	185	Ⓐ Ⓑ Ⓒ Ⓓ
106	Ⓐ Ⓑ Ⓒ Ⓓ	126	Ⓐ Ⓑ Ⓒ Ⓓ	146	Ⓐ Ⓑ Ⓒ Ⓓ	166	Ⓐ Ⓑ Ⓒ Ⓓ	186	Ⓐ Ⓑ Ⓒ Ⓓ
107	Ⓐ Ⓑ Ⓒ Ⓓ	127	Ⓐ Ⓑ Ⓒ Ⓓ	147	Ⓐ Ⓑ Ⓒ Ⓓ	167	Ⓐ Ⓑ Ⓒ Ⓓ	187	Ⓐ Ⓑ Ⓒ Ⓓ
108	Ⓐ Ⓑ Ⓒ Ⓓ	128	Ⓐ Ⓑ Ⓒ Ⓓ	148	Ⓐ Ⓑ Ⓒ Ⓓ	168	Ⓐ Ⓑ Ⓒ Ⓓ	188	Ⓐ Ⓑ Ⓒ Ⓓ
109	Ⓐ Ⓑ Ⓒ Ⓓ	129	Ⓐ Ⓑ Ⓒ Ⓓ	149	Ⓐ Ⓑ Ⓒ Ⓓ	169	Ⓐ Ⓑ Ⓒ Ⓓ	189	Ⓐ Ⓑ Ⓒ Ⓓ
110	Ⓐ Ⓑ Ⓒ Ⓓ	130	Ⓐ Ⓑ Ⓒ Ⓓ	150	Ⓐ Ⓑ Ⓒ Ⓓ	170	Ⓐ Ⓑ Ⓒ Ⓓ	190	Ⓐ Ⓑ Ⓒ Ⓓ
111	Ⓐ Ⓑ Ⓒ Ⓓ	131	Ⓐ Ⓑ Ⓒ Ⓓ	151	Ⓐ Ⓑ Ⓒ Ⓓ	171	Ⓐ Ⓑ Ⓒ Ⓓ	191	Ⓐ Ⓑ Ⓒ Ⓓ
112	Ⓐ Ⓑ Ⓒ Ⓓ	132	Ⓐ Ⓑ Ⓒ Ⓓ	152	Ⓐ Ⓑ Ⓒ Ⓓ	172	Ⓐ Ⓑ Ⓒ Ⓓ	192	Ⓐ Ⓑ Ⓒ Ⓓ
113	Ⓐ Ⓑ Ⓒ Ⓓ	133	Ⓐ Ⓑ Ⓒ Ⓓ	153	Ⓐ Ⓑ Ⓒ Ⓓ	173	Ⓐ Ⓑ Ⓒ Ⓓ	193	Ⓐ Ⓑ Ⓒ Ⓓ
114	Ⓐ Ⓑ Ⓒ Ⓓ	134	Ⓐ Ⓑ Ⓒ Ⓓ	154	Ⓐ Ⓑ Ⓒ Ⓓ	174	Ⓐ Ⓑ Ⓒ Ⓓ	194	Ⓐ Ⓑ Ⓒ Ⓓ
115	Ⓐ Ⓑ Ⓒ Ⓓ	135	Ⓐ Ⓑ Ⓒ Ⓓ	155	Ⓐ Ⓑ Ⓒ Ⓓ	175	Ⓐ Ⓑ Ⓒ Ⓓ	195	Ⓐ Ⓑ Ⓒ Ⓓ
116	Ⓐ Ⓑ Ⓒ Ⓓ	136	Ⓐ Ⓑ Ⓒ Ⓓ	156	Ⓐ Ⓑ Ⓒ Ⓓ	176	Ⓐ Ⓑ Ⓒ Ⓓ	196	Ⓐ Ⓑ Ⓒ Ⓓ
117	Ⓐ Ⓑ Ⓒ Ⓓ	137	Ⓐ Ⓑ Ⓒ Ⓓ	157	Ⓐ Ⓑ Ⓒ Ⓓ	177	Ⓐ Ⓑ Ⓒ Ⓓ	197	Ⓐ Ⓑ Ⓒ Ⓓ
118	Ⓐ Ⓑ Ⓒ Ⓓ	138	Ⓐ Ⓑ Ⓒ Ⓓ	158	Ⓐ Ⓑ Ⓒ Ⓓ	178	Ⓐ Ⓑ Ⓒ Ⓓ	198	Ⓐ Ⓑ Ⓒ Ⓓ
119	Ⓐ Ⓑ Ⓒ Ⓓ	139	Ⓐ Ⓑ Ⓒ Ⓓ	159	Ⓐ Ⓑ Ⓒ Ⓓ	179	Ⓐ Ⓑ Ⓒ Ⓓ	199	Ⓐ Ⓑ Ⓒ Ⓓ
120	Ⓐ Ⓑ Ⓒ Ⓓ	140	Ⓐ Ⓑ Ⓒ Ⓓ	160	Ⓐ Ⓑ Ⓒ Ⓓ	180	Ⓐ Ⓑ Ⓒ Ⓓ	200	Ⓐ Ⓑ Ⓒ Ⓓ

算完TEST 01的分數後，在目標分數表記錄TEST 01的分數。
分數換算表在問題集第289頁，目標分數表則是在本書第二頁。

答對的題數：___ / 100

請沿線剪下

Answer Sheet

TEST **02**

READING (Part V~VII)									
NO.	ANSWER	NO.	ANSWER	NO.	ANSWER	NO.	ANSWER	NO.	ANSWER
	A B C D		A B C D		A B C D		A B C D		A B C D
101	Ⓐ Ⓑ Ⓒ Ⓓ	121	Ⓐ Ⓑ Ⓒ Ⓓ	141	Ⓐ Ⓑ Ⓒ Ⓓ	161	Ⓐ Ⓑ Ⓒ Ⓓ	181	Ⓐ Ⓑ Ⓒ Ⓓ
102	Ⓐ Ⓑ Ⓒ Ⓓ	122	Ⓐ Ⓑ Ⓒ Ⓓ	142	Ⓐ Ⓑ Ⓒ Ⓓ	162	Ⓐ Ⓑ Ⓒ Ⓓ	182	Ⓐ Ⓑ Ⓒ Ⓓ
103	Ⓐ Ⓑ Ⓒ Ⓓ	123	Ⓐ Ⓑ Ⓒ Ⓓ	143	Ⓐ Ⓑ Ⓒ Ⓓ	163	Ⓐ Ⓑ Ⓒ Ⓓ	183	Ⓐ Ⓑ Ⓒ Ⓓ
104	Ⓐ Ⓑ Ⓒ Ⓓ	124	Ⓐ Ⓑ Ⓒ Ⓓ	144	Ⓐ Ⓑ Ⓒ Ⓓ	164	Ⓐ Ⓑ Ⓒ Ⓓ	184	Ⓐ Ⓑ Ⓒ Ⓓ
105	Ⓐ Ⓑ Ⓒ Ⓓ	125	Ⓐ Ⓑ Ⓒ Ⓓ	145	Ⓐ Ⓑ Ⓒ Ⓓ	165	Ⓐ Ⓑ Ⓒ Ⓓ	185	Ⓐ Ⓑ Ⓒ Ⓓ
106	Ⓐ Ⓑ Ⓒ Ⓓ	126	Ⓐ Ⓑ Ⓒ Ⓓ	146	Ⓐ Ⓑ Ⓒ Ⓓ	166	Ⓐ Ⓑ Ⓒ Ⓓ	186	Ⓐ Ⓑ Ⓒ Ⓓ
107	Ⓐ Ⓑ Ⓒ Ⓓ	127	Ⓐ Ⓑ Ⓒ Ⓓ	147	Ⓐ Ⓑ Ⓒ Ⓓ	167	Ⓐ Ⓑ Ⓒ Ⓓ	187	Ⓐ Ⓑ Ⓒ Ⓓ
108	Ⓐ Ⓑ Ⓒ Ⓓ	128	Ⓐ Ⓑ Ⓒ Ⓓ	148	Ⓐ Ⓑ Ⓒ Ⓓ	168	Ⓐ Ⓑ Ⓒ Ⓓ	188	Ⓐ Ⓑ Ⓒ Ⓓ
109	Ⓐ Ⓑ Ⓒ Ⓓ	129	Ⓐ Ⓑ Ⓒ Ⓓ	149	Ⓐ Ⓑ Ⓒ Ⓓ	169	Ⓐ Ⓑ Ⓒ Ⓓ	189	Ⓐ Ⓑ Ⓒ Ⓓ
110	Ⓐ Ⓑ Ⓒ Ⓓ	130	Ⓐ Ⓑ Ⓒ Ⓓ	150	Ⓐ Ⓑ Ⓒ Ⓓ	170	Ⓐ Ⓑ Ⓒ Ⓓ	190	Ⓐ Ⓑ Ⓒ Ⓓ
111	Ⓐ Ⓑ Ⓒ Ⓓ	131	Ⓐ Ⓑ Ⓒ Ⓓ	151	Ⓐ Ⓑ Ⓒ Ⓓ	171	Ⓐ Ⓑ Ⓒ Ⓓ	191	Ⓐ Ⓑ Ⓒ Ⓓ
112	Ⓐ Ⓑ Ⓒ Ⓓ	132	Ⓐ Ⓑ Ⓒ Ⓓ	152	Ⓐ Ⓑ Ⓒ Ⓓ	172	Ⓐ Ⓑ Ⓒ Ⓓ	192	Ⓐ Ⓑ Ⓒ Ⓓ
113	Ⓐ Ⓑ Ⓒ Ⓓ	133	Ⓐ Ⓑ Ⓒ Ⓓ	153	Ⓐ Ⓑ Ⓒ Ⓓ	173	Ⓐ Ⓑ Ⓒ Ⓓ	193	Ⓐ Ⓑ Ⓒ Ⓓ
114	Ⓐ Ⓑ Ⓒ Ⓓ	134	Ⓐ Ⓑ Ⓒ Ⓓ	154	Ⓐ Ⓑ Ⓒ Ⓓ	174	Ⓐ Ⓑ Ⓒ Ⓓ	194	Ⓐ Ⓑ Ⓒ Ⓓ
115	Ⓐ Ⓑ Ⓒ Ⓓ	135	Ⓐ Ⓑ Ⓒ Ⓓ	155	Ⓐ Ⓑ Ⓒ Ⓓ	175	Ⓐ Ⓑ Ⓒ Ⓓ	195	Ⓐ Ⓑ Ⓒ Ⓓ
116	Ⓐ Ⓑ Ⓒ Ⓓ	136	Ⓐ Ⓑ Ⓒ Ⓓ	156	Ⓐ Ⓑ Ⓒ Ⓓ	176	Ⓐ Ⓑ Ⓒ Ⓓ	196	Ⓐ Ⓑ Ⓒ Ⓓ
117	Ⓐ Ⓑ Ⓒ Ⓓ	137	Ⓐ Ⓑ Ⓒ Ⓓ	157	Ⓐ Ⓑ Ⓒ Ⓓ	177	Ⓐ Ⓑ Ⓒ Ⓓ	197	Ⓐ Ⓑ Ⓒ Ⓓ
118	Ⓐ Ⓑ Ⓒ Ⓓ	138	Ⓐ Ⓑ Ⓒ Ⓓ	158	Ⓐ Ⓑ Ⓒ Ⓓ	178	Ⓐ Ⓑ Ⓒ Ⓓ	198	Ⓐ Ⓑ Ⓒ Ⓓ
119	Ⓐ Ⓑ Ⓒ Ⓓ	139	Ⓐ Ⓑ Ⓒ Ⓓ	159	Ⓐ Ⓑ Ⓒ Ⓓ	179	Ⓐ Ⓑ Ⓒ Ⓓ	199	Ⓐ Ⓑ Ⓒ Ⓓ
120	Ⓐ Ⓑ Ⓒ Ⓓ	140	Ⓐ Ⓑ Ⓒ Ⓓ	160	Ⓐ Ⓑ Ⓒ Ⓓ	180	Ⓐ Ⓑ Ⓒ Ⓓ	200	Ⓐ Ⓑ Ⓒ Ⓓ

算完TEST 02的分數後，在目標分數表記錄TEST 02的分數。
分數換算表在問題集第289頁，目標分數表則是在本書第二頁。

答對的題數：___ / 100

請沿線剪下

Answer Sheet

TEST 03

READING (Part V~VII)

NO.	ANSWER				NO.	ANSWER				NO.	ANSWER				NO.	ANSWER				NO.	ANSWER			
	A	B	C	D		A	B	C	D		A	B	C	D		A	B	C	D		A	B	C	D
101	Ⓐ	Ⓑ	Ⓒ	Ⓓ	121	Ⓐ	Ⓑ	Ⓒ	Ⓓ	141	Ⓐ	Ⓑ	Ⓒ	Ⓓ	161	Ⓐ	Ⓑ	Ⓒ	Ⓓ	181	Ⓐ	Ⓑ	Ⓒ	Ⓓ
102	Ⓐ	Ⓑ	Ⓒ	Ⓓ	122	Ⓐ	Ⓑ	Ⓒ	Ⓓ	142	Ⓐ	Ⓑ	Ⓒ	Ⓓ	162	Ⓐ	Ⓑ	Ⓒ	Ⓓ	182	Ⓐ	Ⓑ	Ⓒ	Ⓓ
103	Ⓐ	Ⓑ	Ⓒ	Ⓓ	123	Ⓐ	Ⓑ	Ⓒ	Ⓓ	143	Ⓐ	Ⓑ	Ⓒ	Ⓓ	163	Ⓐ	Ⓑ	Ⓒ	Ⓓ	183	Ⓐ	Ⓑ	Ⓒ	Ⓓ
104	Ⓐ	Ⓑ	Ⓒ	Ⓓ	124	Ⓐ	Ⓑ	Ⓒ	Ⓓ	144	Ⓐ	Ⓑ	Ⓒ	Ⓓ	164	Ⓐ	Ⓑ	Ⓒ	Ⓓ	184	Ⓐ	Ⓑ	Ⓒ	Ⓓ
105	Ⓐ	Ⓑ	Ⓒ	Ⓓ	125	Ⓐ	Ⓑ	Ⓒ	Ⓓ	145	Ⓐ	Ⓑ	Ⓒ	Ⓓ	165	Ⓐ	Ⓑ	Ⓒ	Ⓓ	185	Ⓐ	Ⓑ	Ⓒ	Ⓓ
106	Ⓐ	Ⓑ	Ⓒ	Ⓓ	126	Ⓐ	Ⓑ	Ⓒ	Ⓓ	146	Ⓐ	Ⓑ	Ⓒ	Ⓓ	166	Ⓐ	Ⓑ	Ⓒ	Ⓓ	186	Ⓐ	Ⓑ	Ⓒ	Ⓓ
107	Ⓐ	Ⓑ	Ⓒ	Ⓓ	127	Ⓐ	Ⓑ	Ⓒ	Ⓓ	147	Ⓐ	Ⓑ	Ⓒ	Ⓓ	167	Ⓐ	Ⓑ	Ⓒ	Ⓓ	187	Ⓐ	Ⓑ	Ⓒ	Ⓓ
108	Ⓐ	Ⓑ	Ⓒ	Ⓓ	128	Ⓐ	Ⓑ	Ⓒ	Ⓓ	148	Ⓐ	Ⓑ	Ⓒ	Ⓓ	168	Ⓐ	Ⓑ	Ⓒ	Ⓓ	188	Ⓐ	Ⓑ	Ⓒ	Ⓓ
109	Ⓐ	Ⓑ	Ⓒ	Ⓓ	129	Ⓐ	Ⓑ	Ⓒ	Ⓓ	149	Ⓐ	Ⓑ	Ⓒ	Ⓓ	169	Ⓐ	Ⓑ	Ⓒ	Ⓓ	189	Ⓐ	Ⓑ	Ⓒ	Ⓓ
110	Ⓐ	Ⓑ	Ⓒ	Ⓓ	130	Ⓐ	Ⓑ	Ⓒ	Ⓓ	150	Ⓐ	Ⓑ	Ⓒ	Ⓓ	170	Ⓐ	Ⓑ	Ⓒ	Ⓓ	190	Ⓐ	Ⓑ	Ⓒ	Ⓓ
111	Ⓐ	Ⓑ	Ⓒ	Ⓓ	131	Ⓐ	Ⓑ	Ⓒ	Ⓓ	151	Ⓐ	Ⓑ	Ⓒ	Ⓓ	171	Ⓐ	Ⓑ	Ⓒ	Ⓓ	191	Ⓐ	Ⓑ	Ⓒ	Ⓓ
112	Ⓐ	Ⓑ	Ⓒ	Ⓓ	132	Ⓐ	Ⓑ	Ⓒ	Ⓓ	152	Ⓐ	Ⓑ	Ⓒ	Ⓓ	172	Ⓐ	Ⓑ	Ⓒ	Ⓓ	192	Ⓐ	Ⓑ	Ⓒ	Ⓓ
113	Ⓐ	Ⓑ	Ⓒ	Ⓓ	133	Ⓐ	Ⓑ	Ⓒ	Ⓓ	153	Ⓐ	Ⓑ	Ⓒ	Ⓓ	173	Ⓐ	Ⓑ	Ⓒ	Ⓓ	193	Ⓐ	Ⓑ	Ⓒ	Ⓓ
114	Ⓐ	Ⓑ	Ⓒ	Ⓓ	134	Ⓐ	Ⓑ	Ⓒ	Ⓓ	154	Ⓐ	Ⓑ	Ⓒ	Ⓓ	174	Ⓐ	Ⓑ	Ⓒ	Ⓓ	194	Ⓐ	Ⓑ	Ⓒ	Ⓓ
115	Ⓐ	Ⓑ	Ⓒ	Ⓓ	135	Ⓐ	Ⓑ	Ⓒ	Ⓓ	155	Ⓐ	Ⓑ	Ⓒ	Ⓓ	175	Ⓐ	Ⓑ	Ⓒ	Ⓓ	195	Ⓐ	Ⓑ	Ⓒ	Ⓓ
116	Ⓐ	Ⓑ	Ⓒ	Ⓓ	136	Ⓐ	Ⓑ	Ⓒ	Ⓓ	156	Ⓐ	Ⓑ	Ⓒ	Ⓓ	176	Ⓐ	Ⓑ	Ⓒ	Ⓓ	196	Ⓐ	Ⓑ	Ⓒ	Ⓓ
117	Ⓐ	Ⓑ	Ⓒ	Ⓓ	137	Ⓐ	Ⓑ	Ⓒ	Ⓓ	157	Ⓐ	Ⓑ	Ⓒ	Ⓓ	177	Ⓐ	Ⓑ	Ⓒ	Ⓓ	197	Ⓐ	Ⓑ	Ⓒ	Ⓓ
118	Ⓐ	Ⓑ	Ⓒ	Ⓓ	138	Ⓐ	Ⓑ	Ⓒ	Ⓓ	158	Ⓐ	Ⓑ	Ⓒ	Ⓓ	178	Ⓐ	Ⓑ	Ⓒ	Ⓓ	198	Ⓐ	Ⓑ	Ⓒ	Ⓓ
119	Ⓐ	Ⓑ	Ⓒ	Ⓓ	139	Ⓐ	Ⓑ	Ⓒ	Ⓓ	159	Ⓐ	Ⓑ	Ⓒ	Ⓓ	179	Ⓐ	Ⓑ	Ⓒ	Ⓓ	199	Ⓐ	Ⓑ	Ⓒ	Ⓓ
120	Ⓐ	Ⓑ	Ⓒ	Ⓓ	140	Ⓐ	Ⓑ	Ⓒ	Ⓓ	160	Ⓐ	Ⓑ	Ⓒ	Ⓓ	180	Ⓐ	Ⓑ	Ⓒ	Ⓓ	200	Ⓐ	Ⓑ	Ⓒ	Ⓓ

算完TEST 03的分數後，在目標分數表記錄TEST 03的分數。
分數換算表在問題集第289頁，目標分數表則是在本書第二頁。

答對的題數： ____ / 100

請沿線剪下

Answer Sheet

TEST 04

READING (Part V~VII)

NO.	ANSWER				NO.	ANSWER				NO.	ANSWER				NO.	ANSWER				NO.	ANSWER			
	A	B	C	D		A	B	C	D		A	B	C	D		A	B	C	D		A	B	C	D
101	Ⓐ	Ⓑ	Ⓒ	Ⓓ	121	Ⓐ	Ⓑ	Ⓒ	Ⓓ	141	Ⓐ	Ⓑ	Ⓒ	Ⓓ	161	Ⓐ	Ⓑ	Ⓒ	Ⓓ	181	Ⓐ	Ⓑ	Ⓒ	Ⓓ
102	Ⓐ	Ⓑ	Ⓒ	Ⓓ	122	Ⓐ	Ⓑ	Ⓒ	Ⓓ	142	Ⓐ	Ⓑ	Ⓒ	Ⓓ	162	Ⓐ	Ⓑ	Ⓒ	Ⓓ	182	Ⓐ	Ⓑ	Ⓒ	Ⓓ
103	Ⓐ	Ⓑ	Ⓒ	Ⓓ	123	Ⓐ	Ⓑ	Ⓒ	Ⓓ	143	Ⓐ	Ⓑ	Ⓒ	Ⓓ	163	Ⓐ	Ⓑ	Ⓒ	Ⓓ	183	Ⓐ	Ⓑ	Ⓒ	Ⓓ
104	Ⓐ	Ⓑ	Ⓒ	Ⓓ	124	Ⓐ	Ⓑ	Ⓒ	Ⓓ	144	Ⓐ	Ⓑ	Ⓒ	Ⓓ	164	Ⓐ	Ⓑ	Ⓒ	Ⓓ	184	Ⓐ	Ⓑ	Ⓒ	Ⓓ
105	Ⓐ	Ⓑ	Ⓒ	Ⓓ	125	Ⓐ	Ⓑ	Ⓒ	Ⓓ	145	Ⓐ	Ⓑ	Ⓒ	Ⓓ	165	Ⓐ	Ⓑ	Ⓒ	Ⓓ	185	Ⓐ	Ⓑ	Ⓒ	Ⓓ
106	Ⓐ	Ⓑ	Ⓒ	Ⓓ	126	Ⓐ	Ⓑ	Ⓒ	Ⓓ	146	Ⓐ	Ⓑ	Ⓒ	Ⓓ	166	Ⓐ	Ⓑ	Ⓒ	Ⓓ	186	Ⓐ	Ⓑ	Ⓒ	Ⓓ
107	Ⓐ	Ⓑ	Ⓒ	Ⓓ	127	Ⓐ	Ⓑ	Ⓒ	Ⓓ	147	Ⓐ	Ⓑ	Ⓒ	Ⓓ	167	Ⓐ	Ⓑ	Ⓒ	Ⓓ	187	Ⓐ	Ⓑ	Ⓒ	Ⓓ
108	Ⓐ	Ⓑ	Ⓒ	Ⓓ	128	Ⓐ	Ⓑ	Ⓒ	Ⓓ	148	Ⓐ	Ⓑ	Ⓒ	Ⓓ	168	Ⓐ	Ⓑ	Ⓒ	Ⓓ	188	Ⓐ	Ⓑ	Ⓒ	Ⓓ
109	Ⓐ	Ⓑ	Ⓒ	Ⓓ	129	Ⓐ	Ⓑ	Ⓒ	Ⓓ	149	Ⓐ	Ⓑ	Ⓒ	Ⓓ	169	Ⓐ	Ⓑ	Ⓒ	Ⓓ	189	Ⓐ	Ⓑ	Ⓒ	Ⓓ
110	Ⓐ	Ⓑ	Ⓒ	Ⓓ	130	Ⓐ	Ⓑ	Ⓒ	Ⓓ	150	Ⓐ	Ⓑ	Ⓒ	Ⓓ	170	Ⓐ	Ⓑ	Ⓒ	Ⓓ	190	Ⓐ	Ⓑ	Ⓒ	Ⓓ
111	Ⓐ	Ⓑ	Ⓒ	Ⓓ	131	Ⓐ	Ⓑ	Ⓒ	Ⓓ	151	Ⓐ	Ⓑ	Ⓒ	Ⓓ	171	Ⓐ	Ⓑ	Ⓒ	Ⓓ	191	Ⓐ	Ⓑ	Ⓒ	Ⓓ
112	Ⓐ	Ⓑ	Ⓒ	Ⓓ	132	Ⓐ	Ⓑ	Ⓒ	Ⓓ	152	Ⓐ	Ⓑ	Ⓒ	Ⓓ	172	Ⓐ	Ⓑ	Ⓒ	Ⓓ	192	Ⓐ	Ⓑ	Ⓒ	Ⓓ
113	Ⓐ	Ⓑ	Ⓒ	Ⓓ	133	Ⓐ	Ⓑ	Ⓒ	Ⓓ	153	Ⓐ	Ⓑ	Ⓒ	Ⓓ	173	Ⓐ	Ⓑ	Ⓒ	Ⓓ	193	Ⓐ	Ⓑ	Ⓒ	Ⓓ
114	Ⓐ	Ⓑ	Ⓒ	Ⓓ	134	Ⓐ	Ⓑ	Ⓒ	Ⓓ	154	Ⓐ	Ⓑ	Ⓒ	Ⓓ	174	Ⓐ	Ⓑ	Ⓒ	Ⓓ	194	Ⓐ	Ⓑ	Ⓒ	Ⓓ
115	Ⓐ	Ⓑ	Ⓒ	Ⓓ	135	Ⓐ	Ⓑ	Ⓒ	Ⓓ	155	Ⓐ	Ⓑ	Ⓒ	Ⓓ	175	Ⓐ	Ⓑ	Ⓒ	Ⓓ	195	Ⓐ	Ⓑ	Ⓒ	Ⓓ
116	Ⓐ	Ⓑ	Ⓒ	Ⓓ	136	Ⓐ	Ⓑ	Ⓒ	Ⓓ	156	Ⓐ	Ⓑ	Ⓒ	Ⓓ	176	Ⓐ	Ⓑ	Ⓒ	Ⓓ	196	Ⓐ	Ⓑ	Ⓒ	Ⓓ
117	Ⓐ	Ⓑ	Ⓒ	Ⓓ	137	Ⓐ	Ⓑ	Ⓒ	Ⓓ	157	Ⓐ	Ⓑ	Ⓒ	Ⓓ	177	Ⓐ	Ⓑ	Ⓒ	Ⓓ	197	Ⓐ	Ⓑ	Ⓒ	Ⓓ
118	Ⓐ	Ⓑ	Ⓒ	Ⓓ	138	Ⓐ	Ⓑ	Ⓒ	Ⓓ	158	Ⓐ	Ⓑ	Ⓒ	Ⓓ	178	Ⓐ	Ⓑ	Ⓒ	Ⓓ	198	Ⓐ	Ⓑ	Ⓒ	Ⓓ
119	Ⓐ	Ⓑ	Ⓒ	Ⓓ	139	Ⓐ	Ⓑ	Ⓒ	Ⓓ	159	Ⓐ	Ⓑ	Ⓒ	Ⓓ	179	Ⓐ	Ⓑ	Ⓒ	Ⓓ	199	Ⓐ	Ⓑ	Ⓒ	Ⓓ
120	Ⓐ	Ⓑ	Ⓒ	Ⓓ	140	Ⓐ	Ⓑ	Ⓒ	Ⓓ	160	Ⓐ	Ⓑ	Ⓒ	Ⓓ	180	Ⓐ	Ⓑ	Ⓒ	Ⓓ	200	Ⓐ	Ⓑ	Ⓒ	Ⓓ

算完TEST 04的分數後，在目標分數表記錄TEST 04的分數。
分數換算表在問題集第289頁，目標分數表則是在本書第二頁。

答對的題數： ____ / 100

請沿線剪下

Answer Sheet

TEST 05

READING (Part V~VII)																								
NO.	ANSWER				NO.	ANSWER				NO.	ANSWER				NO.	ANSWER				NO.	ANSWER			
	A	B	C	D		A	B	C	D		A	B	C	D		A	B	C	D		A	B	C	D
101	Ⓐ	Ⓑ	Ⓒ	Ⓓ	121	Ⓐ	Ⓑ	Ⓒ	Ⓓ	141	Ⓐ	Ⓑ	Ⓒ	Ⓓ	161	Ⓐ	Ⓑ	Ⓒ	Ⓓ	181	Ⓐ	Ⓑ	Ⓒ	Ⓓ
102	Ⓐ	Ⓑ	Ⓒ	Ⓓ	122	Ⓐ	Ⓑ	Ⓒ	Ⓓ	142	Ⓐ	Ⓑ	Ⓒ	Ⓓ	162	Ⓐ	Ⓑ	Ⓒ	Ⓓ	182	Ⓐ	Ⓑ	Ⓒ	Ⓓ
103	Ⓐ	Ⓑ	Ⓒ	Ⓓ	123	Ⓐ	Ⓑ	Ⓒ	Ⓓ	143	Ⓐ	Ⓑ	Ⓒ	Ⓓ	163	Ⓐ	Ⓑ	Ⓒ	Ⓓ	183	Ⓐ	Ⓑ	Ⓒ	Ⓓ
104	Ⓐ	Ⓑ	Ⓒ	Ⓓ	124	Ⓐ	Ⓑ	Ⓒ	Ⓓ	144	Ⓐ	Ⓑ	Ⓒ	Ⓓ	164	Ⓐ	Ⓑ	Ⓒ	Ⓓ	184	Ⓐ	Ⓑ	Ⓒ	Ⓓ
105	Ⓐ	Ⓑ	Ⓒ	Ⓓ	125	Ⓐ	Ⓑ	Ⓒ	Ⓓ	145	Ⓐ	Ⓑ	Ⓒ	Ⓓ	165	Ⓐ	Ⓑ	Ⓒ	Ⓓ	185	Ⓐ	Ⓑ	Ⓒ	Ⓓ
106	Ⓐ	Ⓑ	Ⓒ	Ⓓ	126	Ⓐ	Ⓑ	Ⓒ	Ⓓ	146	Ⓐ	Ⓑ	Ⓒ	Ⓓ	166	Ⓐ	Ⓑ	Ⓒ	Ⓓ	186	Ⓐ	Ⓑ	Ⓒ	Ⓓ
107	Ⓐ	Ⓑ	Ⓒ	Ⓓ	127	Ⓐ	Ⓑ	Ⓒ	Ⓓ	147	Ⓐ	Ⓑ	Ⓒ	Ⓓ	167	Ⓐ	Ⓑ	Ⓒ	Ⓓ	187	Ⓐ	Ⓑ	Ⓒ	Ⓓ
108	Ⓐ	Ⓑ	Ⓒ	Ⓓ	128	Ⓐ	Ⓑ	Ⓒ	Ⓓ	148	Ⓐ	Ⓑ	Ⓒ	Ⓓ	168	Ⓐ	Ⓑ	Ⓒ	Ⓓ	188	Ⓐ	Ⓑ	Ⓒ	Ⓓ
109	Ⓐ	Ⓑ	Ⓒ	Ⓓ	129	Ⓐ	Ⓑ	Ⓒ	Ⓓ	149	Ⓐ	Ⓑ	Ⓒ	Ⓓ	169	Ⓐ	Ⓑ	Ⓒ	Ⓓ	189	Ⓐ	Ⓑ	Ⓒ	Ⓓ
110	Ⓐ	Ⓑ	Ⓒ	Ⓓ	130	Ⓐ	Ⓑ	Ⓒ	Ⓓ	150	Ⓐ	Ⓑ	Ⓒ	Ⓓ	170	Ⓐ	Ⓑ	Ⓒ	Ⓓ	190	Ⓐ	Ⓑ	Ⓒ	Ⓓ
111	Ⓐ	Ⓑ	Ⓒ	Ⓓ	131	Ⓐ	Ⓑ	Ⓒ	Ⓓ	151	Ⓐ	Ⓑ	Ⓒ	Ⓓ	171	Ⓐ	Ⓑ	Ⓒ	Ⓓ	191	Ⓐ	Ⓑ	Ⓒ	Ⓓ
112	Ⓐ	Ⓑ	Ⓒ	Ⓓ	132	Ⓐ	Ⓑ	Ⓒ	Ⓓ	152	Ⓐ	Ⓑ	Ⓒ	Ⓓ	172	Ⓐ	Ⓑ	Ⓒ	Ⓓ	192	Ⓐ	Ⓑ	Ⓒ	Ⓓ
113	Ⓐ	Ⓑ	Ⓒ	Ⓓ	133	Ⓐ	Ⓑ	Ⓒ	Ⓓ	153	Ⓐ	Ⓑ	Ⓒ	Ⓓ	173	Ⓐ	Ⓑ	Ⓒ	Ⓓ	193	Ⓐ	Ⓑ	Ⓒ	Ⓓ
114	Ⓐ	Ⓑ	Ⓒ	Ⓓ	134	Ⓐ	Ⓑ	Ⓒ	Ⓓ	154	Ⓐ	Ⓑ	Ⓒ	Ⓓ	174	Ⓐ	Ⓑ	Ⓒ	Ⓓ	194	Ⓐ	Ⓑ	Ⓒ	Ⓓ
115	Ⓐ	Ⓑ	Ⓒ	Ⓓ	135	Ⓐ	Ⓑ	Ⓒ	Ⓓ	155	Ⓐ	Ⓑ	Ⓒ	Ⓓ	175	Ⓐ	Ⓑ	Ⓒ	Ⓓ	195	Ⓐ	Ⓑ	Ⓒ	Ⓓ
116	Ⓐ	Ⓑ	Ⓒ	Ⓓ	136	Ⓐ	Ⓑ	Ⓒ	Ⓓ	156	Ⓐ	Ⓑ	Ⓒ	Ⓓ	176	Ⓐ	Ⓑ	Ⓒ	Ⓓ	196	Ⓐ	Ⓑ	Ⓒ	Ⓓ
117	Ⓐ	Ⓑ	Ⓒ	Ⓓ	137	Ⓐ	Ⓑ	Ⓒ	Ⓓ	157	Ⓐ	Ⓑ	Ⓒ	Ⓓ	177	Ⓐ	Ⓑ	Ⓒ	Ⓓ	197	Ⓐ	Ⓑ	Ⓒ	Ⓓ
118	Ⓐ	Ⓑ	Ⓒ	Ⓓ	138	Ⓐ	Ⓑ	Ⓒ	Ⓓ	158	Ⓐ	Ⓑ	Ⓒ	Ⓓ	178	Ⓐ	Ⓑ	Ⓒ	Ⓓ	198	Ⓐ	Ⓑ	Ⓒ	Ⓓ
119	Ⓐ	Ⓑ	Ⓒ	Ⓓ	139	Ⓐ	Ⓑ	Ⓒ	Ⓓ	159	Ⓐ	Ⓑ	Ⓒ	Ⓓ	179	Ⓐ	Ⓑ	Ⓒ	Ⓓ	199	Ⓐ	Ⓑ	Ⓒ	Ⓓ
120	Ⓐ	Ⓑ	Ⓒ	Ⓓ	140	Ⓐ	Ⓑ	Ⓒ	Ⓓ	160	Ⓐ	Ⓑ	Ⓒ	Ⓓ	180	Ⓐ	Ⓑ	Ⓒ	Ⓓ	200	Ⓐ	Ⓑ	Ⓒ	Ⓓ

算完TEST 05的分數後，在目標分數表記錄TEST 05的分數。
分數換算表在問題集第289頁，目標分數表則是在本書第二頁。

答對的題數： ____ / 100

請沿線剪下

Answer Sheet

TEST 06

READING (Part V~VII)																								
NO.	ANSWER				NO.	ANSWER				NO.	ANSWER				NO.	ANSWER				NO.	ANSWER			
	A	B	C	D		A	B	C	D		A	B	C	D		A	B	C	D		A	B	C	D
101	Ⓐ	Ⓑ	Ⓒ	Ⓓ	121	Ⓐ	Ⓑ	Ⓒ	Ⓓ	141	Ⓐ	Ⓑ	Ⓒ	Ⓓ	161	Ⓐ	Ⓑ	Ⓒ	Ⓓ	181	Ⓐ	Ⓑ	Ⓒ	Ⓓ
102	Ⓐ	Ⓑ	Ⓒ	Ⓓ	122	Ⓐ	Ⓑ	Ⓒ	Ⓓ	142	Ⓐ	Ⓑ	Ⓒ	Ⓓ	162	Ⓐ	Ⓑ	Ⓒ	Ⓓ	182	Ⓐ	Ⓑ	Ⓒ	Ⓓ
103	Ⓐ	Ⓑ	Ⓒ	Ⓓ	123	Ⓐ	Ⓑ	Ⓒ	Ⓓ	143	Ⓐ	Ⓑ	Ⓒ	Ⓓ	163	Ⓐ	Ⓑ	Ⓒ	Ⓓ	183	Ⓐ	Ⓑ	Ⓒ	Ⓓ
104	Ⓐ	Ⓑ	Ⓒ	Ⓓ	124	Ⓐ	Ⓑ	Ⓒ	Ⓓ	144	Ⓐ	Ⓑ	Ⓒ	Ⓓ	164	Ⓐ	Ⓑ	Ⓒ	Ⓓ	184	Ⓐ	Ⓑ	Ⓒ	Ⓓ
105	Ⓐ	Ⓑ	Ⓒ	Ⓓ	125	Ⓐ	Ⓑ	Ⓒ	Ⓓ	145	Ⓐ	Ⓑ	Ⓒ	Ⓓ	165	Ⓐ	Ⓑ	Ⓒ	Ⓓ	185	Ⓐ	Ⓑ	Ⓒ	Ⓓ
106	Ⓐ	Ⓑ	Ⓒ	Ⓓ	126	Ⓐ	Ⓑ	Ⓒ	Ⓓ	146	Ⓐ	Ⓑ	Ⓒ	Ⓓ	166	Ⓐ	Ⓑ	Ⓒ	Ⓓ	186	Ⓐ	Ⓑ	Ⓒ	Ⓓ
107	Ⓐ	Ⓑ	Ⓒ	Ⓓ	127	Ⓐ	Ⓑ	Ⓒ	Ⓓ	147	Ⓐ	Ⓑ	Ⓒ	Ⓓ	167	Ⓐ	Ⓑ	Ⓒ	Ⓓ	187	Ⓐ	Ⓑ	Ⓒ	Ⓓ
108	Ⓐ	Ⓑ	Ⓒ	Ⓓ	128	Ⓐ	Ⓑ	Ⓒ	Ⓓ	148	Ⓐ	Ⓑ	Ⓒ	Ⓓ	168	Ⓐ	Ⓑ	Ⓒ	Ⓓ	188	Ⓐ	Ⓑ	Ⓒ	Ⓓ
109	Ⓐ	Ⓑ	Ⓒ	Ⓓ	129	Ⓐ	Ⓑ	Ⓒ	Ⓓ	149	Ⓐ	Ⓑ	Ⓒ	Ⓓ	169	Ⓐ	Ⓑ	Ⓒ	Ⓓ	189	Ⓐ	Ⓑ	Ⓒ	Ⓓ
110	Ⓐ	Ⓑ	Ⓒ	Ⓓ	130	Ⓐ	Ⓑ	Ⓒ	Ⓓ	150	Ⓐ	Ⓑ	Ⓒ	Ⓓ	170	Ⓐ	Ⓑ	Ⓒ	Ⓓ	190	Ⓐ	Ⓑ	Ⓒ	Ⓓ
111	Ⓐ	Ⓑ	Ⓒ	Ⓓ	131	Ⓐ	Ⓑ	Ⓒ	Ⓓ	151	Ⓐ	Ⓑ	Ⓒ	Ⓓ	171	Ⓐ	Ⓑ	Ⓒ	Ⓓ	191	Ⓐ	Ⓑ	Ⓒ	Ⓓ
112	Ⓐ	Ⓑ	Ⓒ	Ⓓ	132	Ⓐ	Ⓑ	Ⓒ	Ⓓ	152	Ⓐ	Ⓑ	Ⓒ	Ⓓ	172	Ⓐ	Ⓑ	Ⓒ	Ⓓ	192	Ⓐ	Ⓑ	Ⓒ	Ⓓ
113	Ⓐ	Ⓑ	Ⓒ	Ⓓ	133	Ⓐ	Ⓑ	Ⓒ	Ⓓ	153	Ⓐ	Ⓑ	Ⓒ	Ⓓ	173	Ⓐ	Ⓑ	Ⓒ	Ⓓ	193	Ⓐ	Ⓑ	Ⓒ	Ⓓ
114	Ⓐ	Ⓑ	Ⓒ	Ⓓ	134	Ⓐ	Ⓑ	Ⓒ	Ⓓ	154	Ⓐ	Ⓑ	Ⓒ	Ⓓ	174	Ⓐ	Ⓑ	Ⓒ	Ⓓ	194	Ⓐ	Ⓑ	Ⓒ	Ⓓ
115	Ⓐ	Ⓑ	Ⓒ	Ⓓ	135	Ⓐ	Ⓑ	Ⓒ	Ⓓ	155	Ⓐ	Ⓑ	Ⓒ	Ⓓ	175	Ⓐ	Ⓑ	Ⓒ	Ⓓ	195	Ⓐ	Ⓑ	Ⓒ	Ⓓ
116	Ⓐ	Ⓑ	Ⓒ	Ⓓ	136	Ⓐ	Ⓑ	Ⓒ	Ⓓ	156	Ⓐ	Ⓑ	Ⓒ	Ⓓ	176	Ⓐ	Ⓑ	Ⓒ	Ⓓ	196	Ⓐ	Ⓑ	Ⓒ	Ⓓ
117	Ⓐ	Ⓑ	Ⓒ	Ⓓ	137	Ⓐ	Ⓑ	Ⓒ	Ⓓ	157	Ⓐ	Ⓑ	Ⓒ	Ⓓ	177	Ⓐ	Ⓑ	Ⓒ	Ⓓ	197	Ⓐ	Ⓑ	Ⓒ	Ⓓ
118	Ⓐ	Ⓑ	Ⓒ	Ⓓ	138	Ⓐ	Ⓑ	Ⓒ	Ⓓ	158	Ⓐ	Ⓑ	Ⓒ	Ⓓ	178	Ⓐ	Ⓑ	Ⓒ	Ⓓ	198	Ⓐ	Ⓑ	Ⓒ	Ⓓ
119	Ⓐ	Ⓑ	Ⓒ	Ⓓ	139	Ⓐ	Ⓑ	Ⓒ	Ⓓ	159	Ⓐ	Ⓑ	Ⓒ	Ⓓ	179	Ⓐ	Ⓑ	Ⓒ	Ⓓ	199	Ⓐ	Ⓑ	Ⓒ	Ⓓ
120	Ⓐ	Ⓑ	Ⓒ	Ⓓ	140	Ⓐ	Ⓑ	Ⓒ	Ⓓ	160	Ⓐ	Ⓑ	Ⓒ	Ⓓ	180	Ⓐ	Ⓑ	Ⓒ	Ⓓ	200	Ⓐ	Ⓑ	Ⓒ	Ⓓ

算完TEST 06的分數後，在目標分數表記錄TEST 06的分數。
分數換算表在問題集第289頁，目標分數表則是在本書第二頁。

答對的題數： ____ / 100

請沿線剪下

Answer Sheet

TEST **07**

READING (Part V~VII)									
NO.	ANSWER A B C D	NO.	ANSWER A B C D	NO.	ANSWER A B C D	NO.	ANSWER A B C D	NO.	ANSWER A B C D
101	Ⓐ Ⓑ Ⓒ Ⓓ	121	Ⓐ Ⓑ Ⓒ Ⓓ	141	Ⓐ Ⓑ Ⓒ Ⓓ	161	Ⓐ Ⓑ Ⓒ Ⓓ	181	Ⓐ Ⓑ Ⓒ Ⓓ
102	Ⓐ Ⓑ Ⓒ Ⓓ	122	Ⓐ Ⓑ Ⓒ Ⓓ	142	Ⓐ Ⓑ Ⓒ Ⓓ	162	Ⓐ Ⓑ Ⓒ Ⓓ	182	Ⓐ Ⓑ Ⓒ Ⓓ
103	Ⓐ Ⓑ Ⓒ Ⓓ	123	Ⓐ Ⓑ Ⓒ Ⓓ	143	Ⓐ Ⓑ Ⓒ Ⓓ	163	Ⓐ Ⓑ Ⓒ Ⓓ	183	Ⓐ Ⓑ Ⓒ Ⓓ
104	Ⓐ Ⓑ Ⓒ Ⓓ	124	Ⓐ Ⓑ Ⓒ Ⓓ	144	Ⓐ Ⓑ Ⓒ Ⓓ	164	Ⓐ Ⓑ Ⓒ Ⓓ	184	Ⓐ Ⓑ Ⓒ Ⓓ
105	Ⓐ Ⓑ Ⓒ Ⓓ	125	Ⓐ Ⓑ Ⓒ Ⓓ	145	Ⓐ Ⓑ Ⓒ Ⓓ	165	Ⓐ Ⓑ Ⓒ Ⓓ	185	Ⓐ Ⓑ Ⓒ Ⓓ
106	Ⓐ Ⓑ Ⓒ Ⓓ	126	Ⓐ Ⓑ Ⓒ Ⓓ	146	Ⓐ Ⓑ Ⓒ Ⓓ	166	Ⓐ Ⓑ Ⓒ Ⓓ	186	Ⓐ Ⓑ Ⓒ Ⓓ
107	Ⓐ Ⓑ Ⓒ Ⓓ	127	Ⓐ Ⓑ Ⓒ Ⓓ	147	Ⓐ Ⓑ Ⓒ Ⓓ	167	Ⓐ Ⓑ Ⓒ Ⓓ	187	Ⓐ Ⓑ Ⓒ Ⓓ
108	Ⓐ Ⓑ Ⓒ Ⓓ	128	Ⓐ Ⓑ Ⓒ Ⓓ	148	Ⓐ Ⓑ Ⓒ Ⓓ	168	Ⓐ Ⓑ Ⓒ Ⓓ	188	Ⓐ Ⓑ Ⓒ Ⓓ
109	Ⓐ Ⓑ Ⓒ Ⓓ	129	Ⓐ Ⓑ Ⓒ Ⓓ	149	Ⓐ Ⓑ Ⓒ Ⓓ	169	Ⓐ Ⓑ Ⓒ Ⓓ	189	Ⓐ Ⓑ Ⓒ Ⓓ
110	Ⓐ Ⓑ Ⓒ Ⓓ	130	Ⓐ Ⓑ Ⓒ Ⓓ	150	Ⓐ Ⓑ Ⓒ Ⓓ	170	Ⓐ Ⓑ Ⓒ Ⓓ	190	Ⓐ Ⓑ Ⓒ Ⓓ
111	Ⓐ Ⓑ Ⓒ Ⓓ	131	Ⓐ Ⓑ Ⓒ Ⓓ	151	Ⓐ Ⓑ Ⓒ Ⓓ	171	Ⓐ Ⓑ Ⓒ Ⓓ	191	Ⓐ Ⓑ Ⓒ Ⓓ
112	Ⓐ Ⓑ Ⓒ Ⓓ	132	Ⓐ Ⓑ Ⓒ Ⓓ	152	Ⓐ Ⓑ Ⓒ Ⓓ	172	Ⓐ Ⓑ Ⓒ Ⓓ	192	Ⓐ Ⓑ Ⓒ Ⓓ
113	Ⓐ Ⓑ Ⓒ Ⓓ	133	Ⓐ Ⓑ Ⓒ Ⓓ	153	Ⓐ Ⓑ Ⓒ Ⓓ	173	Ⓐ Ⓑ Ⓒ Ⓓ	193	Ⓐ Ⓑ Ⓒ Ⓓ
114	Ⓐ Ⓑ Ⓒ Ⓓ	134	Ⓐ Ⓑ Ⓒ Ⓓ	154	Ⓐ Ⓑ Ⓒ Ⓓ	174	Ⓐ Ⓑ Ⓒ Ⓓ	194	Ⓐ Ⓑ Ⓒ Ⓓ
115	Ⓐ Ⓑ Ⓒ Ⓓ	135	Ⓐ Ⓑ Ⓒ Ⓓ	155	Ⓐ Ⓑ Ⓒ Ⓓ	175	Ⓐ Ⓑ Ⓒ Ⓓ	195	Ⓐ Ⓑ Ⓒ Ⓓ
116	Ⓐ Ⓑ Ⓒ Ⓓ	136	Ⓐ Ⓑ Ⓒ Ⓓ	156	Ⓐ Ⓑ Ⓒ Ⓓ	176	Ⓐ Ⓑ Ⓒ Ⓓ	196	Ⓐ Ⓑ Ⓒ Ⓓ
117	Ⓐ Ⓑ Ⓒ Ⓓ	137	Ⓐ Ⓑ Ⓒ Ⓓ	157	Ⓐ Ⓑ Ⓒ Ⓓ	177	Ⓐ Ⓑ Ⓒ Ⓓ	197	Ⓐ Ⓑ Ⓒ Ⓓ
118	Ⓐ Ⓑ Ⓒ Ⓓ	138	Ⓐ Ⓑ Ⓒ Ⓓ	158	Ⓐ Ⓑ Ⓒ Ⓓ	178	Ⓐ Ⓑ Ⓒ Ⓓ	198	Ⓐ Ⓑ Ⓒ Ⓓ
119	Ⓐ Ⓑ Ⓒ Ⓓ	139	Ⓐ Ⓑ Ⓒ Ⓓ	159	Ⓐ Ⓑ Ⓒ Ⓓ	179	Ⓐ Ⓑ Ⓒ Ⓓ	199	Ⓐ Ⓑ Ⓒ Ⓓ
120	Ⓐ Ⓑ Ⓒ Ⓓ	140	Ⓐ Ⓑ Ⓒ Ⓓ	160	Ⓐ Ⓑ Ⓒ Ⓓ	180	Ⓐ Ⓑ Ⓒ Ⓓ	200	Ⓐ Ⓑ Ⓒ Ⓓ

算完TEST 07的分數後，在目標分數表記錄TEST 07的分數。
分數換算表在問題集第289頁，目標分數表則是在本書第二頁。

答對的題數：____ / 100

請沿線剪下

Answer Sheet

TEST **08**

READING (Part V~VII)									
NO.	ANSWER A B C D	NO.	ANSWER A B C D	NO.	ANSWER A B C D	NO.	ANSWER A B C D	NO.	ANSWER A B C D
101	Ⓐ Ⓑ Ⓒ Ⓓ	121	Ⓐ Ⓑ Ⓒ Ⓓ	141	Ⓐ Ⓑ Ⓒ Ⓓ	161	Ⓐ Ⓑ Ⓒ Ⓓ	181	Ⓐ Ⓑ Ⓒ Ⓓ
102	Ⓐ Ⓑ Ⓒ Ⓓ	122	Ⓐ Ⓑ Ⓒ Ⓓ	142	Ⓐ Ⓑ Ⓒ Ⓓ	162	Ⓐ Ⓑ Ⓒ Ⓓ	182	Ⓐ Ⓑ Ⓒ Ⓓ
103	Ⓐ Ⓑ Ⓒ Ⓓ	123	Ⓐ Ⓑ Ⓒ Ⓓ	143	Ⓐ Ⓑ Ⓒ Ⓓ	163	Ⓐ Ⓑ Ⓒ Ⓓ	183	Ⓐ Ⓑ Ⓒ Ⓓ
104	Ⓐ Ⓑ Ⓒ Ⓓ	124	Ⓐ Ⓑ Ⓒ Ⓓ	144	Ⓐ Ⓑ Ⓒ Ⓓ	164	Ⓐ Ⓑ Ⓒ Ⓓ	184	Ⓐ Ⓑ Ⓒ Ⓓ
105	Ⓐ Ⓑ Ⓒ Ⓓ	125	Ⓐ Ⓑ Ⓒ Ⓓ	145	Ⓐ Ⓑ Ⓒ Ⓓ	165	Ⓐ Ⓑ Ⓒ Ⓓ	185	Ⓐ Ⓑ Ⓒ Ⓓ
106	Ⓐ Ⓑ Ⓒ Ⓓ	126	Ⓐ Ⓑ Ⓒ Ⓓ	146	Ⓐ Ⓑ Ⓒ Ⓓ	166	Ⓐ Ⓑ Ⓒ Ⓓ	186	Ⓐ Ⓑ Ⓒ Ⓓ
107	Ⓐ Ⓑ Ⓒ Ⓓ	127	Ⓐ Ⓑ Ⓒ Ⓓ	147	Ⓐ Ⓑ Ⓒ Ⓓ	167	Ⓐ Ⓑ Ⓒ Ⓓ	187	Ⓐ Ⓑ Ⓒ Ⓓ
108	Ⓐ Ⓑ Ⓒ Ⓓ	128	Ⓐ Ⓑ Ⓒ Ⓓ	148	Ⓐ Ⓑ Ⓒ Ⓓ	168	Ⓐ Ⓑ Ⓒ Ⓓ	188	Ⓐ Ⓑ Ⓒ Ⓓ
109	Ⓐ Ⓑ Ⓒ Ⓓ	129	Ⓐ Ⓑ Ⓒ Ⓓ	149	Ⓐ Ⓑ Ⓒ Ⓓ	169	Ⓐ Ⓑ Ⓒ Ⓓ	189	Ⓐ Ⓑ Ⓒ Ⓓ
110	Ⓐ Ⓑ Ⓒ Ⓓ	130	Ⓐ Ⓑ Ⓒ Ⓓ	150	Ⓐ Ⓑ Ⓒ Ⓓ	170	Ⓐ Ⓑ Ⓒ Ⓓ	190	Ⓐ Ⓑ Ⓒ Ⓓ
111	Ⓐ Ⓑ Ⓒ Ⓓ	131	Ⓐ Ⓑ Ⓒ Ⓓ	151	Ⓐ Ⓑ Ⓒ Ⓓ	171	Ⓐ Ⓑ Ⓒ Ⓓ	191	Ⓐ Ⓑ Ⓒ Ⓓ
112	Ⓐ Ⓑ Ⓒ Ⓓ	132	Ⓐ Ⓑ Ⓒ Ⓓ	152	Ⓐ Ⓑ Ⓒ Ⓓ	172	Ⓐ Ⓑ Ⓒ Ⓓ	192	Ⓐ Ⓑ Ⓒ Ⓓ
113	Ⓐ Ⓑ Ⓒ Ⓓ	133	Ⓐ Ⓑ Ⓒ Ⓓ	153	Ⓐ Ⓑ Ⓒ Ⓓ	173	Ⓐ Ⓑ Ⓒ Ⓓ	193	Ⓐ Ⓑ Ⓒ Ⓓ
114	Ⓐ Ⓑ Ⓒ Ⓓ	134	Ⓐ Ⓑ Ⓒ Ⓓ	154	Ⓐ Ⓑ Ⓒ Ⓓ	174	Ⓐ Ⓑ Ⓒ Ⓓ	194	Ⓐ Ⓑ Ⓒ Ⓓ
115	Ⓐ Ⓑ Ⓒ Ⓓ	135	Ⓐ Ⓑ Ⓒ Ⓓ	155	Ⓐ Ⓑ Ⓒ Ⓓ	175	Ⓐ Ⓑ Ⓒ Ⓓ	195	Ⓐ Ⓑ Ⓒ Ⓓ
116	Ⓐ Ⓑ Ⓒ Ⓓ	136	Ⓐ Ⓑ Ⓒ Ⓓ	156	Ⓐ Ⓑ Ⓒ Ⓓ	176	Ⓐ Ⓑ Ⓒ Ⓓ	196	Ⓐ Ⓑ Ⓒ Ⓓ
117	Ⓐ Ⓑ Ⓒ Ⓓ	137	Ⓐ Ⓑ Ⓒ Ⓓ	157	Ⓐ Ⓑ Ⓒ Ⓓ	177	Ⓐ Ⓑ Ⓒ Ⓓ	197	Ⓐ Ⓑ Ⓒ Ⓓ
118	Ⓐ Ⓑ Ⓒ Ⓓ	138	Ⓐ Ⓑ Ⓒ Ⓓ	158	Ⓐ Ⓑ Ⓒ Ⓓ	178	Ⓐ Ⓑ Ⓒ Ⓓ	198	Ⓐ Ⓑ Ⓒ Ⓓ
119	Ⓐ Ⓑ Ⓒ Ⓓ	139	Ⓐ Ⓑ Ⓒ Ⓓ	159	Ⓐ Ⓑ Ⓒ Ⓓ	179	Ⓐ Ⓑ Ⓒ Ⓓ	199	Ⓐ Ⓑ Ⓒ Ⓓ
120	Ⓐ Ⓑ Ⓒ Ⓓ	140	Ⓐ Ⓑ Ⓒ Ⓓ	160	Ⓐ Ⓑ Ⓒ Ⓓ	180	Ⓐ Ⓑ Ⓒ Ⓓ	200	Ⓐ Ⓑ Ⓒ Ⓓ

算完TEST 08的分數後，在目標分數表記錄TEST 08的分數。
分數換算表在問題集第289頁，目標分數表則是在本書第二頁。

答對的題數：____ / 100

Answer Sheet

TEST **09**

READING (Part V~VII)																								
NO.	ANSWER				NO.	ANSWER				NO.	ANSWER				NO.	ANSWER				NO.	ANSWER			
	A	B	C	D		A	B	C	D		A	B	C	D		A	B	C	D		A	B	C	D
101	Ⓐ	Ⓑ	Ⓒ	Ⓓ	121	Ⓐ	Ⓑ	Ⓒ	Ⓓ	141	Ⓐ	Ⓑ	Ⓒ	Ⓓ	161	Ⓐ	Ⓑ	Ⓒ	Ⓓ	181	Ⓐ	Ⓑ	Ⓒ	Ⓓ
102	Ⓐ	Ⓑ	Ⓒ	Ⓓ	122	Ⓐ	Ⓑ	Ⓒ	Ⓓ	142	Ⓐ	Ⓑ	Ⓒ	Ⓓ	162	Ⓐ	Ⓑ	Ⓒ	Ⓓ	182	Ⓐ	Ⓑ	Ⓒ	Ⓓ
103	Ⓐ	Ⓑ	Ⓒ	Ⓓ	123	Ⓐ	Ⓑ	Ⓒ	Ⓓ	143	Ⓐ	Ⓑ	Ⓒ	Ⓓ	163	Ⓐ	Ⓑ	Ⓒ	Ⓓ	183	Ⓐ	Ⓑ	Ⓒ	Ⓓ
104	Ⓐ	Ⓑ	Ⓒ	Ⓓ	124	Ⓐ	Ⓑ	Ⓒ	Ⓓ	144	Ⓐ	Ⓑ	Ⓒ	Ⓓ	164	Ⓐ	Ⓑ	Ⓒ	Ⓓ	184	Ⓐ	Ⓑ	Ⓒ	Ⓓ
105	Ⓐ	Ⓑ	Ⓒ	Ⓓ	125	Ⓐ	Ⓑ	Ⓒ	Ⓓ	145	Ⓐ	Ⓑ	Ⓒ	Ⓓ	165	Ⓐ	Ⓑ	Ⓒ	Ⓓ	185	Ⓐ	Ⓑ	Ⓒ	Ⓓ
106	Ⓐ	Ⓑ	Ⓒ	Ⓓ	126	Ⓐ	Ⓑ	Ⓒ	Ⓓ	146	Ⓐ	Ⓑ	Ⓒ	Ⓓ	166	Ⓐ	Ⓑ	Ⓒ	Ⓓ	186	Ⓐ	Ⓑ	Ⓒ	Ⓓ
107	Ⓐ	Ⓑ	Ⓒ	Ⓓ	127	Ⓐ	Ⓑ	Ⓒ	Ⓓ	147	Ⓐ	Ⓑ	Ⓒ	Ⓓ	167	Ⓐ	Ⓑ	Ⓒ	Ⓓ	187	Ⓐ	Ⓑ	Ⓒ	Ⓓ
108	Ⓐ	Ⓑ	Ⓒ	Ⓓ	128	Ⓐ	Ⓑ	Ⓒ	Ⓓ	148	Ⓐ	Ⓑ	Ⓒ	Ⓓ	168	Ⓐ	Ⓑ	Ⓒ	Ⓓ	188	Ⓐ	Ⓑ	Ⓒ	Ⓓ
109	Ⓐ	Ⓑ	Ⓒ	Ⓓ	129	Ⓐ	Ⓑ	Ⓒ	Ⓓ	149	Ⓐ	Ⓑ	Ⓒ	Ⓓ	169	Ⓐ	Ⓑ	Ⓒ	Ⓓ	189	Ⓐ	Ⓑ	Ⓒ	Ⓓ
110	Ⓐ	Ⓑ	Ⓒ	Ⓓ	130	Ⓐ	Ⓑ	Ⓒ	Ⓓ	150	Ⓐ	Ⓑ	Ⓒ	Ⓓ	170	Ⓐ	Ⓑ	Ⓒ	Ⓓ	190	Ⓐ	Ⓑ	Ⓒ	Ⓓ
111	Ⓐ	Ⓑ	Ⓒ	Ⓓ	131	Ⓐ	Ⓑ	Ⓒ	Ⓓ	151	Ⓐ	Ⓑ	Ⓒ	Ⓓ	171	Ⓐ	Ⓑ	Ⓒ	Ⓓ	191	Ⓐ	Ⓑ	Ⓒ	Ⓓ
112	Ⓐ	Ⓑ	Ⓒ	Ⓓ	132	Ⓐ	Ⓑ	Ⓒ	Ⓓ	152	Ⓐ	Ⓑ	Ⓒ	Ⓓ	172	Ⓐ	Ⓑ	Ⓒ	Ⓓ	192	Ⓐ	Ⓑ	Ⓒ	Ⓓ
113	Ⓐ	Ⓑ	Ⓒ	Ⓓ	133	Ⓐ	Ⓑ	Ⓒ	Ⓓ	153	Ⓐ	Ⓑ	Ⓒ	Ⓓ	173	Ⓐ	Ⓑ	Ⓒ	Ⓓ	193	Ⓐ	Ⓑ	Ⓒ	Ⓓ
114	Ⓐ	Ⓑ	Ⓒ	Ⓓ	134	Ⓐ	Ⓑ	Ⓒ	Ⓓ	154	Ⓐ	Ⓑ	Ⓒ	Ⓓ	174	Ⓐ	Ⓑ	Ⓒ	Ⓓ	194	Ⓐ	Ⓑ	Ⓒ	Ⓓ
115	Ⓐ	Ⓑ	Ⓒ	Ⓓ	135	Ⓐ	Ⓑ	Ⓒ	Ⓓ	155	Ⓐ	Ⓑ	Ⓒ	Ⓓ	175	Ⓐ	Ⓑ	Ⓒ	Ⓓ	195	Ⓐ	Ⓑ	Ⓒ	Ⓓ
116	Ⓐ	Ⓑ	Ⓒ	Ⓓ	136	Ⓐ	Ⓑ	Ⓒ	Ⓓ	156	Ⓐ	Ⓑ	Ⓒ	Ⓓ	176	Ⓐ	Ⓑ	Ⓒ	Ⓓ	196	Ⓐ	Ⓑ	Ⓒ	Ⓓ
117	Ⓐ	Ⓑ	Ⓒ	Ⓓ	137	Ⓐ	Ⓑ	Ⓒ	Ⓓ	157	Ⓐ	Ⓑ	Ⓒ	Ⓓ	177	Ⓐ	Ⓑ	Ⓒ	Ⓓ	197	Ⓐ	Ⓑ	Ⓒ	Ⓓ
118	Ⓐ	Ⓑ	Ⓒ	Ⓓ	138	Ⓐ	Ⓑ	Ⓒ	Ⓓ	158	Ⓐ	Ⓑ	Ⓒ	Ⓓ	178	Ⓐ	Ⓑ	Ⓒ	Ⓓ	198	Ⓐ	Ⓑ	Ⓒ	Ⓓ
119	Ⓐ	Ⓑ	Ⓒ	Ⓓ	139	Ⓐ	Ⓑ	Ⓒ	Ⓓ	159	Ⓐ	Ⓑ	Ⓒ	Ⓓ	179	Ⓐ	Ⓑ	Ⓒ	Ⓓ	199	Ⓐ	Ⓑ	Ⓒ	Ⓓ
120	Ⓐ	Ⓑ	Ⓒ	Ⓓ	140	Ⓐ	Ⓑ	Ⓒ	Ⓓ	160	Ⓐ	Ⓑ	Ⓒ	Ⓓ	180	Ⓐ	Ⓑ	Ⓒ	Ⓓ	200	Ⓐ	Ⓑ	Ⓒ	Ⓓ

算完TEST 09的分數後，在目標分數表記錄TEST 09的分數。
分數換算表在問題集第289頁，目標分數表則是在本書第二頁。

答對的題數： ___ / 100

請沿線剪下

Answer Sheet

TEST **10**

READING (Part V~VII)																								
NO.	ANSWER				NO.	ANSWER				NO.	ANSWER				NO.	ANSWER				NO.	ANSWER			
	A	B	C	D		A	B	C	D		A	B	C	D		A	B	C	D		A	B	C	D
101	Ⓐ	Ⓑ	Ⓒ	Ⓓ	121	Ⓐ	Ⓑ	Ⓒ	Ⓓ	141	Ⓐ	Ⓑ	Ⓒ	Ⓓ	161	Ⓐ	Ⓑ	Ⓒ	Ⓓ	181	Ⓐ	Ⓑ	Ⓒ	Ⓓ
102	Ⓐ	Ⓑ	Ⓒ	Ⓓ	122	Ⓐ	Ⓑ	Ⓒ	Ⓓ	142	Ⓐ	Ⓑ	Ⓒ	Ⓓ	162	Ⓐ	Ⓑ	Ⓒ	Ⓓ	182	Ⓐ	Ⓑ	Ⓒ	Ⓓ
103	Ⓐ	Ⓑ	Ⓒ	Ⓓ	123	Ⓐ	Ⓑ	Ⓒ	Ⓓ	143	Ⓐ	Ⓑ	Ⓒ	Ⓓ	163	Ⓐ	Ⓑ	Ⓒ	Ⓓ	183	Ⓐ	Ⓑ	Ⓒ	Ⓓ
104	Ⓐ	Ⓑ	Ⓒ	Ⓓ	124	Ⓐ	Ⓑ	Ⓒ	Ⓓ	144	Ⓐ	Ⓑ	Ⓒ	Ⓓ	164	Ⓐ	Ⓑ	Ⓒ	Ⓓ	184	Ⓐ	Ⓑ	Ⓒ	Ⓓ
105	Ⓐ	Ⓑ	Ⓒ	Ⓓ	125	Ⓐ	Ⓑ	Ⓒ	Ⓓ	145	Ⓐ	Ⓑ	Ⓒ	Ⓓ	165	Ⓐ	Ⓑ	Ⓒ	Ⓓ	185	Ⓐ	Ⓑ	Ⓒ	Ⓓ
106	Ⓐ	Ⓑ	Ⓒ	Ⓓ	126	Ⓐ	Ⓑ	Ⓒ	Ⓓ	146	Ⓐ	Ⓑ	Ⓒ	Ⓓ	166	Ⓐ	Ⓑ	Ⓒ	Ⓓ	186	Ⓐ	Ⓑ	Ⓒ	Ⓓ
107	Ⓐ	Ⓑ	Ⓒ	Ⓓ	127	Ⓐ	Ⓑ	Ⓒ	Ⓓ	147	Ⓐ	Ⓑ	Ⓒ	Ⓓ	167	Ⓐ	Ⓑ	Ⓒ	Ⓓ	187	Ⓐ	Ⓑ	Ⓒ	Ⓓ
108	Ⓐ	Ⓑ	Ⓒ	Ⓓ	128	Ⓐ	Ⓑ	Ⓒ	Ⓓ	148	Ⓐ	Ⓑ	Ⓒ	Ⓓ	168	Ⓐ	Ⓑ	Ⓒ	Ⓓ	188	Ⓐ	Ⓑ	Ⓒ	Ⓓ
109	Ⓐ	Ⓑ	Ⓒ	Ⓓ	129	Ⓐ	Ⓑ	Ⓒ	Ⓓ	149	Ⓐ	Ⓑ	Ⓒ	Ⓓ	169	Ⓐ	Ⓑ	Ⓒ	Ⓓ	189	Ⓐ	Ⓑ	Ⓒ	Ⓓ
110	Ⓐ	Ⓑ	Ⓒ	Ⓓ	130	Ⓐ	Ⓑ	Ⓒ	Ⓓ	150	Ⓐ	Ⓑ	Ⓒ	Ⓓ	170	Ⓐ	Ⓑ	Ⓒ	Ⓓ	190	Ⓐ	Ⓑ	Ⓒ	Ⓓ
111	Ⓐ	Ⓑ	Ⓒ	Ⓓ	131	Ⓐ	Ⓑ	Ⓒ	Ⓓ	151	Ⓐ	Ⓑ	Ⓒ	Ⓓ	171	Ⓐ	Ⓑ	Ⓒ	Ⓓ	191	Ⓐ	Ⓑ	Ⓒ	Ⓓ
112	Ⓐ	Ⓑ	Ⓒ	Ⓓ	132	Ⓐ	Ⓑ	Ⓒ	Ⓓ	152	Ⓐ	Ⓑ	Ⓒ	Ⓓ	172	Ⓐ	Ⓑ	Ⓒ	Ⓓ	192	Ⓐ	Ⓑ	Ⓒ	Ⓓ
113	Ⓐ	Ⓑ	Ⓒ	Ⓓ	133	Ⓐ	Ⓑ	Ⓒ	Ⓓ	153	Ⓐ	Ⓑ	Ⓒ	Ⓓ	173	Ⓐ	Ⓑ	Ⓒ	Ⓓ	193	Ⓐ	Ⓑ	Ⓒ	Ⓓ
114	Ⓐ	Ⓑ	Ⓒ	Ⓓ	134	Ⓐ	Ⓑ	Ⓒ	Ⓓ	154	Ⓐ	Ⓑ	Ⓒ	Ⓓ	174	Ⓐ	Ⓑ	Ⓒ	Ⓓ	194	Ⓐ	Ⓑ	Ⓒ	Ⓓ
115	Ⓐ	Ⓑ	Ⓒ	Ⓓ	135	Ⓐ	Ⓑ	Ⓒ	Ⓓ	155	Ⓐ	Ⓑ	Ⓒ	Ⓓ	175	Ⓐ	Ⓑ	Ⓒ	Ⓓ	195	Ⓐ	Ⓑ	Ⓒ	Ⓓ
116	Ⓐ	Ⓑ	Ⓒ	Ⓓ	136	Ⓐ	Ⓑ	Ⓒ	Ⓓ	156	Ⓐ	Ⓑ	Ⓒ	Ⓓ	176	Ⓐ	Ⓑ	Ⓒ	Ⓓ	196	Ⓐ	Ⓑ	Ⓒ	Ⓓ
117	Ⓐ	Ⓑ	Ⓒ	Ⓓ	137	Ⓐ	Ⓑ	Ⓒ	Ⓓ	157	Ⓐ	Ⓑ	Ⓒ	Ⓓ	177	Ⓐ	Ⓑ	Ⓒ	Ⓓ	197	Ⓐ	Ⓑ	Ⓒ	Ⓓ
118	Ⓐ	Ⓑ	Ⓒ	Ⓓ	138	Ⓐ	Ⓑ	Ⓒ	Ⓓ	158	Ⓐ	Ⓑ	Ⓒ	Ⓓ	178	Ⓐ	Ⓑ	Ⓒ	Ⓓ	198	Ⓐ	Ⓑ	Ⓒ	Ⓓ
119	Ⓐ	Ⓑ	Ⓒ	Ⓓ	139	Ⓐ	Ⓑ	Ⓒ	Ⓓ	159	Ⓐ	Ⓑ	Ⓒ	Ⓓ	179	Ⓐ	Ⓑ	Ⓒ	Ⓓ	199	Ⓐ	Ⓑ	Ⓒ	Ⓓ
120	Ⓐ	Ⓑ	Ⓒ	Ⓓ	140	Ⓐ	Ⓑ	Ⓒ	Ⓓ	160	Ⓐ	Ⓑ	Ⓒ	Ⓓ	180	Ⓐ	Ⓑ	Ⓒ	Ⓓ	200	Ⓐ	Ⓑ	Ⓒ	Ⓓ

算完TEST 10的分數後，在目標分數表記錄TEST 10的分數。
分數換算表在問題集第289頁，目標分數表則是在本書第二頁。

答對的題數： ___ / 100

我的答錯題目筆記

Test ______ 題號：______

問　題	
我選擇的答案和選擇該答案的理由	
正確答案	
主要單字和文法	
疑問或提醒	

Test ______ 題號：______

問　題	
我選擇的答案和選擇該答案的理由	
正確答案	
主要單字和文法	
疑問或提醒	

*請將本頁表格剪下，複印後使用。

請沿線剪下

我的答錯題目筆記

Test ______ 題號：______

問　　題	
我選擇的答案和 選擇該答案的理由	
正確答案	
主要單字和文法	
疑問或提醒	

Test ______ 題號：______

問　　題	
我選擇的答案和 選擇該答案的理由	
正確答案	
主要單字和文法	
疑問或提醒	

*請將本頁表格剪下，複印後使用。

請沿線剪下

我的答錯題目筆記

Test ______ 題號：______

問　題	
我選擇的答案和 選擇該答案的理由	
正確答案	
主要單字和文法	
疑問或提醒	

Test ______ 題號：______

問　題	
我選擇的答案和 選擇該答案的理由	
正確答案	
主要單字和文法	
疑問或提醒	

*請將本頁表格剪下，複印後使用。

我的答錯題目筆記

Test ______ 題號：______

問　題	
我選擇的答案和選擇該答案的理由	
正確答案	
主要單字和文法	
疑問或提醒	

Test ______ 題號：______

問　題	
我選擇的答案和選擇該答案的理由	
正確答案	
主要單字和文法	
疑問或提醒	

*請將本頁表格剪下，複印後使用。